THERESA

THERESA

THE CHRONICLE OF
A WOMAN'S LIFE

BY
ARTHUR SCHNITZLER

Translated by
WILLIAM A. DRAKE

SIMON AND SCHUSTER PUBLISHERS

NEW YORK   MCMXXVIII

❧

Second Printing before Publication

I

THERESA was just sixteen years old, that spring, when Lieutenant Hubert Fabiani was retired on his pension and left Vienna, his last post, to settle down in Salzburg—not, like most of his companions, in Graz. When they sat down to breakfast and looked out of the windows of the house which they had rented, and saw across the roofs as far as the Bavarian mountains beyond, the lieutenant never failed to remind his wife and children how fortunate it was that he had been enabled to leave the smoke and dust of the great city while still a hale and hearty man, scarce sixty years of age, and retire to enjoy the delights of Nature, which he had longed for since his youth. He loved to take little walks with Theresa, and sometimes also with her brother Karl, who was three years older than his sister. Their mother remained at home, reading novels—always reading novels—just as she had done in Komorn, where they had first lived, and afterwards in Lemberg, and before that, in Vienna. She took no interest in her home, but, just as in the other cities, she soon surrounded herself with a group of women, the wives or widows of officers and officials, who would stop in for coffee two or three times each week and bring her all the gossip of the little town.

1

On these occasions, if he chanced to be at home, the Lieutenant would invariably retire to his room. And afterwards, at the evening meal, he did not fail to deliver himself of various malicious remarks concerning his wife's guests. His wife would respond with vague allusions to certain social diversions in which her husband had formerly indulged. Thereupon, it frequently happened that the Lieutenant would rise and leave the house, without saying a word. Late at night, the hollow sound of his footsteps could be heard reverberating through the hall as he slowly mounted the stairs.

When he had gone, his wife would caution her children against the disappointments of life, from which no one is exempt; and in particular, she would declaim against the martyr's lot which falls to women. She took her examples from the books which she had just read, and her narrative was frequently so badly confused that one was inclined to suspect that she had mingled the contents of several novels together. Sometimes, in jest, Theresa could not forbear to give voice to that suspicion. Then her mother would reprove her loudly and, turning to her son, she would caress his hair and stroke his cheeks, as if to reward him for his patient and credulous attention. But she did not observe how he would glance at his disgraced sister and slyly wink his eye at her. Then, presently, Theresa would return to her embroidery or, sitting down at the upright piano, which was always out of tune, continue her practice. She had begun to study piano in Lemberg and had continued in Vienna, under the guidance of a cheap instructress.

The walks with her father suddenly ceased, even before the beginning of autumn. For some time past, Theresa had observed that her father continued his walks only in order not to contradict his former inclinations. Whereas, formerly, he had greeted each new aspect of Nature with cries of delight, forcing his children to join in his pleasure, he now walked silently, without a word, intent upon arriving at the destination which he had set. Only when he had returned and faced his wife did he exhibit a certain belated excitement, and then he would endeavour to stimulate some enthusiasm within himself by recalling the various incidents of the trip. But even that soon ceased, and the tourist costume which the Lieutenant had worn since his retirement was definitely put aside and replaced by a dark business suit.

One morning, however, Fabiani appeared at the breakfast table in his uniform, and with such a stern and forbidding expression on his face that even his wife forbore to permit herself any comments upon this sudden change. Several days later, a shipment of books arrived from Vienna, and soon thereafter, another shipment was received from Leipzig, and a local second-hand dealer also sent a package. Thenceforth, the retired officer passed many hours at his desk, acquainting no one with the nature of his work, until, one evening, with elaborate mysteriousness, he summoned Theresa to his room and read her what

he had written. For four successive evenings he read to
her, in the brusque tones of a commanding officer, from
his carefully written, almost calligraphically inscribed manuscript, which proved to be a treatise on comparative
strategy, dealing with the most important battles of the
modern era. Theresa had great difficulty in simulating
attention, for it was impossible for her to follow with
understanding this dull and fatiguing discourse. Still, of
late, her father had aroused her more and more to sympathy and pity, so she successfully resisted the insistence
of her sleepy, heavy eyelids, and even attempted to express an active interest in the subject which had absorbed
him. When the reading was ended, she kissed her father,
as if she were grateful for the honour which he had con-
ferred upon her.

At the conclusion of the reading, the Lieutenant carefully carried his manuscript to the Post Office. Thenceforward, from that day, he passed his time in various restaurants and cafés, in the company of certain recent acquaintances. These were, for the most part, men like himself; that is, elderly retired persons, pensioned officers,
former lawyers, and even a superannuated actor, who had
become too old for the theatre of the town and now gave
elocution lessons, when he was fortunate enough to find a
pupil. The erstwhile so reserved Lieutenant bloomed forth
as a talkative, in fact somewhat obstreperous fellow, who
chattered of social and political opinions which came rather
strangely from the lips of a former officer. But since he

always ended by giving in, as if the whole discussion had only been in jest, no one interfered with him—not even an important police official, who sometimes took part in the discussions.

II

O<small>N</small> Christmas Eve, a well-wrapped package, inscribed to the Lieutenant, lay beneath the Christmas tree, along with the other modest gifts with which the members of the family remembered one another. Inside was the manuscript, accompanied by a rejection slip from the publisher of the military periodical to which the author had sent it. Fabiani was furious. The date of the postmark informed him that it had been received several days before, and he at once accused his wife of having withheld it and placed it among the Christmas gifts with the intention of taunting and ridiculing him. He hurled the cigar case which she had given him at her feet and strode out of the house, slamming the door behind him. Afterwards, it was learned that he had passed the night in a disreputable house near Saint Peter's Cemetery, in the company of one of those wretched women who sell the service of their bodies to boys and old men. After this, he remained shut up in his study for a few days, to reappear suddenly, in the splendour of his parade dress uniform, while his wife was entertaining her guests at coffee. He surprised every one by his amiability and wit; and he might have left the impression of a consummate man of the world, had he not annoyed some of the ladies in the dark vestibule.

In the days that followed, the Lieutenant spent most of his time away from home, but on his brief appearances there, he was always genial and inoffensive. Then, when at last the calm of relief had settled upon the little household, he astonished his family by asking them suddenly, one evening, how they would fancy the idea of leaving this tiresome town and returning to the capital. He also hinted at some marvelous change impending in their condition of life. Theresa's heart began to beat so excitedly at the prospect that she realized, all at once, how very much she had really been longing to return to the city where they had lived for three years. It was true that she had been able to enjoy none of the pleasures which the city offers to the rich, but she had had such wonderful times just wandering aimlessly through the streets, trying to get lost— a delicious happening which had actually occurred on two or three occasions, and each time had given her an exquisite spasm of terror. Her eyes were still glistening with these memories as she caught her brother's disapproving glance. He had greeted her with just such an expression a few days before, when she had entered his room as he was busy with his mathematics problems, in company with his schoolmate, Alfred Nuellheim. She realized that he always looked at her disapprovingly, whenever she was full of joy. He was doing so now. Her heart was crushed. It was only a few years ago that they were boy and girl together, and then they were boon companions, laughing and playing and happy all day long. What had occurred to change all this?

Even Mother, who, to be sure, was never very much of a companion, had not formerly looked so perpetually displeased. Unconsciously, Theresa glanced at her mother, and the anger which she saw in her parent's face frightened her. She seemed never to have forgiven her husband for having been pensioned off before his time. She gazed at him as he raised his voice and declared that their days of plenty were not far distant, and her eyes were full of hate—as though she were recalling her youth, on her father's estate in Slavonio, when she rode through the primitive forest of their park, mounted on her fiery pony.

Suddenly the father looked at his watch, arose, and excusing himself, left the house at once, on the plea of an important engagement.

He did not return home that night. At the café, he made incomprehensible speeches against the Minister of War and against the Emperor; and from there he was taken to the guard-room, and thence, after a medical examination, to an insane asylum. Subsequently, it developed that he had previously written a letter to the office of the Minister, applying for reinstatement, with advancement to a generalship. Thereupon, an order was received from Vienna to have him watched, but without arousing his suspicion; and his lamentable performance in the café that evening was all that was further necessary to justify his detention and commitment to an institution.

III

His wife visited him on eight successive days. After
a few weeks, Theresa received permission to see him. In
a large garden surrounded by high walls, down an avenue
of tall chestnut trees, garbed in a shabby officer's coat,
with a military cap on his head, an old man with a short,
thick white beard came forward on the arm of an attendant
whose pale face matched his filthy yellow uniform.
"Father!" Theresa cried, stricken by a deep emotion, yet
happy that at last she might see him once again. He passed
on, apparently without having recognized her, mumbling
some unintelligible words.

Theresa remained where she stood, disconcerted, unable
to grasp this painful situation. Then she observed that the
orderly was trying to explain something to her father. At
first, the latter merely shook his head; then, he turned
round and ran back to his daughter. As if she were still
a little girl, he caught her up in his arms and held her in
the air, staring at her. Then, suddenly, he released her,
and began to weep bitterly. Presently, he covered his face
with his hands, as if overcome with shame, and hastened
off toward the dull gray building that was faintly visible
through the trees. The orderly followed slowly.

Theresa's mother had watched the entire proceedings with complete indifference. When Theresa returned to her side, she arose languidly, as if all the while she had merely been sitting there, waiting for her daughter.

The two left the park and emerged upon the broad highway, glittering and white in the blinding sun. Before them was the city, nestled in the side of the mountain and surmounted by the fortress of Hohensalzburg. It was only a fifteen minutes' walk to Salzburg, yet it seemed to Theresa that they would never reach their destination. The hills lifted themselves out of the hot mist of noon. A van went by noisily, the driver sleeping on the box. From a farm-house across the fields, a dog barked mournfully at the silent world.

"Father!" Theresa whimpered.

Her mother glanced at her angrily.

"What do you want? It is his own fault!"

They walked in silence along the sunny road toward the city.

At table, that evening, Karl remarked:

"Alfred Nuellheim tells me that such sicknesses often last many years. Eight, ten, twelve . . ."

Theresa opened her eyes wide in horror. Karl compressed his lips and looked away from her at the wall.

IV

SINCE autumn, Theresa had been attending the next to the last grade at the Lyceum. There she had soon been made to realize that diligence and attention were not in themselves enough. Her supervisor distrusted her. Although she was no more lax in her religious studies than her fellow students, and although she attended all the religious exercises which were obligatory, just like every one else, she was suspected of being lacking in piety. Her teacher once encountered her in the company of young Nuellheim, whom she had met by chance one evening on the street; and this the instructress turned to account as an opportune moment to deliver herself of various acrid comments upon certain customs of the big cities which were, as it would appear, gaining a foothold in the provinces. The look which she gave Theresa was hardly to be misunderstood. Theresa felt all the more wronged, since no such commotion was ever aroused by the behaviour of some of her schoolmates, who were, if the gossip were true, guilty of much more flagrant offenses.

Young Nuellheim, however, came to the Fabiani house more frequently than his studies with Karl would seem to have required. In fact, he even came on several occasions

11

when Karl was not at home. At such times, he would sit near Theresa, admiring the cunning of her hands as they embroidered colourful flowers on a background of dull lilac canvas. Or he would listen as she somehow managed to get through one of Chopin's nocturnes on her out-of-tune piano. Once, remembering some earlier remark, he asked her if she still intended to become a teacher. She did not know exactly what to answer. One thing, at least, was certain. She did not propose to live much longer in these rooms and in this town. Soon—as soon as possible, in fact—she would find herself some kind of work, and preferably, that would be in some other city.

The situation at home was becoming worse and worse, as even Alfred could perceive. Theresa had ceased to speak, and had lapsed into an attitude of impassive retrospection. Her mother still received her friends, just as before—there were some strange men among them now,—and they frequently remained far into the night. This, in itself, did not greatly disturb Theresa, but it widened the breach between herself and her mother. Her brother not only carefully avoided his mother, but he likewise kept away from Theresa. At meals, no more than the absolutely necessary words were spoken. And sometimes it seemed to Theresa as though, in some incomprehensible manner, she were being held responsible for the downfall of the household. Somehow, although she could not grasp the cause or meaning of this sentiment, the fault was upon her head.

V

THERESA was almost afraid to contemplate paying another visit to the asylum; but, curiously enough, it turned out very well, except for one disturbing incident. That incident, however, completely obliterated all the hopes which had of late arisen in her heart with regard to her father's condition. At first, her father had conversed with her in his old, gay manner; and then he had taken her about, showing her the extensive grounds of the institution, as though she were some distinguished visitor. He seemed perfectly rational. But when she took leave of him, he mentioned casually that, when she came the next time, he would receive her in his General's uniform, in anticipation of his approaching appointment.

The next day, she related the incidents of her visit to Alfred Nuellheim, who immediately asked to be allowed to accompany her on her next trip. It was his ambition, as Theresa knew, to study medicine and become a nerve specialist and psychiatrist. So, a few days later, they met, as if for a secret assignation, outside the boundaries of the town, and proceeded together to the asylum, where the former Lieutenant greeted Alfred as though he had been expecting him all the while. This time, he spoke of his

13

youth, of the various garrisons which he had known, and of the Croatian estate where he had met his wife. He spoke of her as if she no longer existed, and he seemed to have completely forgotten his son.

Alfred was introduced to the officiating physician, who treated him with considerable deference; in fact, almost as though they were already colleagues. On their long walk home, Theresa was profoundly agitated at the thought of Alfred, walking beside her and talking with pleasant excitement of the episodes of their visit, but with no sorrow at all—just as if it were all merely a somewhat momentous occasion in his new career. He did not notice the tears streaming down her cheeks.

VI

It was likewise at about this time that Theresa became conscious of a new attitude in the manner in which her schoolmates conducted themselves toward her. She became aware that they were whispering among themselves. Conversations suddenly ceased when she approached, and her teacher never spoke to her or questioned her any more at all. Never, nowadays, did she have a companion on the way home. Only in Clara Traunfurt's eyes did Theresa observe a sign of pity. It was this girl who, at last, took her aside and told her of the rumour that the company which gathered at her mother's house was not quite proper, and that the police had summoned Frau Fabiani to court and had warned her. Then, for the first time, it occurred to Theresa that, in fact, there had been no gatherings at the house in the past two or three weeks.

That evening, after Clara's explanations, she noticed that Karl did not speak a single word to his mother during the entire meal. Then she realized that, for at least a week, she had not seen him address her even once. When Karl had left the room and her mother followed shortly, she breathed more easily. She remained seated at the table, bathed in the rays of the descending spring sun. She sat there for a long time, gazing before her with fixed eyes, as if she were troubled by a nightmare.

That same night, she was awakened by a noise in the drawing room. She heard the front door being carefully opened and as carefully closed, and then she heard steps on the stairs. She arose from bed and looked out of the window. A few minutes later, the door below was opened, and she saw a man in uniform, his face hidden by the raised collar of his coat, accompanied by a woman, veiled and wrapped in a cloak, step out and quickly disappear round the corner.

Theresa determined to demand of her mother some explanation of these strange proceedings. But when an opportunity presented itself, her courage failed her. She felt, more now than ever before, how unapproachable her mother had become. They had become practically strangers. Lately, it seemed as if that aging, flighty woman wished to make herself appear a personage of mystery. She had cultivated a queer, shuffling gait, and upset things noisily, for no good reason, mumbling incoherent phrases; and no sooner had she finished her meal, than she left the table and locked herself for hours at a time in her room, where she remained writing with a scratching pen on long sheets of paper.

At first, Theresa suspected that she was preparing her defense against the police; but then she recollected that her mother had frequently declared her intention of compiling her memoirs. As it happened, however—Frau Fabiani mentioned it at table, very casually, as though it were a matter of common knowledge—she was writing a novel. Theresa glanced at her brother with involuntary surprise. But he was gazing beyond her at the Sonnenkringel.

VII

Early in July, Karl Fabiani and Alfred Nuellheim
stood for their final examinations. Alfred received the highest marks in his class, whereas Karl received merely a
passing grade. Some days later, he set out on a walking
trip, after having bidden his mother and sister farewell,
hastily and coldly, quite as though he intended to return
home that same evening. Alfred, who, according to their
earlier plans, was to have accompanied him on this journey,
seized upon a slight illness of his mother as a pretext to remain temporarily in the city. He came almost daily to the
Fabiani household, at first, presumably to fetch books, and
at other times to inquire for news of Karl. It so happened
that these afternoon visits were followed, on fine summer
evenings, by promenades with Theresa—promenades that
were gradually extended into longer and more intimate
walks.

One evening, as they were seated on a bench in the
neighbourhood of Monchsburg, he again spoke of his intention of entering the University of Vienna in the fall,
to study medicine. This, as well as most of the things
which he told her, was not news to Theresa. In fact, when
he confessed that he had foregone the pleasures of his

18

vacation trip only to be enabled to pass these last few months in her company, she was not in the least surprised. She remained quite untouched, unmoved, and was even a little exasperated; it seemed to her almost as if this young creature, this shy boy, was presuming to present her with a promissory note which she had no desire to pay.

Two officers went by. One of them Theresa knew by sight, as she did almost all the men in the regiment stationed there. The other, however, was a stranger. He was a clean-shaven, dark-haired, slim young person, and—a peculiarity which attracted her attention—he carried his hat in his hand.

His eyes passed lightly over Theresa; and, as Nuellheim and the other officer greeted one another, he likewise greeted the pair; but, being bareheaded, contented himself with repeated nods of the head, at the same time fixing a vivacious, almost laughing glance upon Theresa. Nevertheless, he did not glance back to look at her, as she half expected he would, but turned a bend in the Allee and disappeared with his friend. After this interruption, Theresa and Alfred were unable to reëstablish the cordial tenor of their former conversation. They sat for a short interval in silence; then they arose, and walked slowly homeward in the twilight.

VIII

Karl was expected back around the beginning of August; but instead, a letter arrived, announcing his decision not to return to Salzburg at all, and expressing the wish that his monthly allowance should be forwarded to Vienna, where, through the aid of an advertisement, he had already secured a position as tutor to a young student. A casual inquiry as to his father's present condition and greetings to both his mother and his sister closed his letter, in which there was to be found not the remotest suggestion of regret at this apparently permanent separation. The content and tone of the letter made little impression upon the mother; but to Theresa, despite the coolness which had gradually arisen between herself and her brother, there persisted, to her own astonishment, a certain sense of injury, of having been forsaken. Her inveterate annoyance with Alfred deepened. He was not man enough to help her overcome this depressing loneliness, and his shyness began to irritate her and to appear somewhat ridiculous in her eyes. Once, while they were walking outside the city, he attempted to take her arm, and pressed it ever so gently; but she tore herself away from him with alarming violence, and for the remainder of the walk, and even while he was taking leave of her before her door, she continued to maintain a cold and unbending attitude toward him.

One day, Frau Fabiani accused her daughter of gross neglect of her duties to her mother, of paying absolutely no attention to her, and of seeming to have time for no one else but Alfred Nuellheim. In that very hour, Theresa accompanied her mother on a walk through the city; and during their promenade, she had occasion to note that two women, who had formerly frequented the Fabiani household, passed her mother without greeting her.

A few days later, a similar excursion led them to the outskirts of the city. On the far side of the stone boundary wall, an elderly gentleman with a gray mustache came toward them and was apparently about to walk by; but, instead, he suddenly turned and stopped, remarking, in a tone that sounded somewhat self-conscious, "Frau Fabiani, if I am not mistaken!" Frau Fabiani addressed him as "Count," and presented her daughter. He inquired as to the health of the former Lieutenant, and, quite unasked, told of his two sons, who, since the recent death of his wife, were being brought up in a French academy.

When he had taken his leave, Frau Fabiani remarked: "Count Benkheim, the former District Commissioner! Didn't you recognize him?" Theresa involuntarily looked back. She observed his extreme leanness, the elegant though somewhat too light suit which he wore, and the youthful, quick, and intentionally soft step with which he went away, somewhat more hastily than he had come forward.

IX

SOME days after this encounter, Theresa was at home, awaiting Alfred Nuellheim. He had promised to bring her some books and take her for a walk. As a matter of fact, the prospect itself bored her somewhat; she would have much preferred to go out alone, even though, of late, strange men had accosted her, and a few had even dared to follow her. At this time of the year, the city was usually overrun with strangers.

Ever since her childhood, Theresa had felt a strong curiosity and attraction toward everything that bore the marks of elegance and refinement. At the age of twelve, while in Lemberg, she had been smitten by the charms of a handsome dashing young Archduke, who was then serving in her father's regiment in the capacity of Lieutenant. How often she regretted that Alfred, whose parents were well-to-do and who had a good figure and fine features, never seemed to observe the changes in styles; that his clothes were persistently small-townish.

Entering the room, Frau Fabiani expressed surprise at finding that, on such an exquisite day, Theresa should have chosen to remain indoors. Quite casually, she began talking of Count Benkheim, whom she said she had met accidentally again that day. The Count was greatly interested in everything pertaining to the science of war. He intended, one day, to stop in and examine Father's library, with a view to purchasing it, should the books prove interesting to him.

"That is not true!" said Theresa, and without another word, left the room.

She took her hat and coat, ran down the stairs, and met Alfred at the door.

"At last!" she cried.

He apologized profusely—he had been unavoidably detained at home. It was already growing dark.

"What is wrong?" asked Alfred. "Why are you so hot and excited?"

"It is nothing," she replied.

At that moment, a novel thought occurred to her. Did not Alfred think it would be delightful to dine this evening in one of those big hotel gardens? He and she, alone, among all those strange people? He reddened. How happy he would have been to comply with her desire! But, alas! today it was quite impossible. He had very little money with him—certainly, not enough to cover the expense of dinner for two at a fashionable hotel. She looked at him and smiled.

He blushed an even deeper red, and she was a little touched.

"Another time!" he begged, shyly.

She merely nodded her assent.

They resumed their walk through the streets, and were soon outside the city. Then they directed their steps along their favourite path through the fields. The evening air was stifling. Over them stretched a starless sky. The city receded further and further into the background, as they wandered on through the fields of wheat. Alfred held Theresa's hand lightly in his own. He asked about Karl. She shrugged her shoulders.

"Oh, he seldom writes!" she replied.

"I have not had a word from him since he went away," said Alfred.

Soon again the topic of conversation was his impending journey to Vienna. Theresa was silent. Her eyes looked beyond him. Would she at least write to him? She grew impatient.

"What shall I write to you? Nothing ever happens here. One day is just like another."

"Yes, but even now, one day is like the other," he answered, "and yet, we have so much to tell one another! Still, I shall be perfectly contented, even happy, with merely a word of greeting from you."

Emerging from the undulating fields, they entered the street. The forts of Nonnberg and the tall poplars were clearly outlined against the wall of darkness.

Suddenly, in a much milder spirit, Theresa asked if he thought he would be homesick.

"Only for you!" he replied, gravely.

This was the first time that Alfred, in speaking to her,

had employed the more familiar *"Du,"* and she was grateful.

"I can't understand why you and your mother continue to live in Salzburg. You have nothing to keep you here."

"Nor anything to attract us elsewhere!"

"It might even be possible to place your father in another asylum, in the vicinity of Vienna."

"No, no!" she objected, vehemently.

"But you had intended—that is, you spoke of a profession, of taking a position!"

"Do not anticipate! I still have another year of school, before I can take my normal examinations!" She shook her head decidedly. In some strange manner, she seemed rooted to the spot. Her agitation subsiding, she added:

"But you will doubtless come back for the Christmas holidays, if only for the sake of your family."

"But we are a long way from Christmas, Theresa!"

"You won't even have time to think of me, with your studies and all! You will meet new people—women and girls!" She smiled to herself, fully aware that, where he was concerned, she felt no jealousy—that, in fact, she was quite devoid of any emotion.

"In less than six years, I shall be a doctor!" The words shot out abruptly. "Will you wait for me that long?"

She gazed at him. At first, her mind did not grasp the situation. Then, a slight smile played upon her lips. She was touched. It seemed to her that she was so much older than he! In that very instant, she realized that all this was sheer childishness, and that nothing more would ever come of it. She took his hand and stroked it gently.

Later, in the darkness, in the secluded vestibule of her home, as she was bidding him good-night, she closed her eyes and returned his kiss almost passionately.

X

Every evening, they would wander outside the city,
through the seldom frequented paths in the fields, talking
without end of a future in which Theresa could not believe.

At home, during the day, she embroidered a little, studied
her French, practiced the piano, or read for short intervals;
but for the greater part of the time, she sat almost without
a thought, gazing idly out of the window.

In spite of the impatience with which she daily awaited
Alfred's coming, she would not be in his company more
than a quarter of an hour when she was overcome by an
inexpressible boredom. Then, when he spoke once again,
in the course of their walk, of his impending departure,
she would realize, with a little shock, how eagerly she was
awaiting that day.

He was aware that she felt no painful revulsion at the
thought of his absence, and he told her as much. She was
exasperated, and answered evasively.

Their first quarrel ensued.

They continued on their way homeward in silence, and
parted without a kiss. Afterwards, for a long time, she sat
on her bed in the darkness, staring out of the open window
into the hot, black night. Her heart was heavy.

27

There, not far distant, under this selfsame heaven, was the bleak building in which her poor, insane father was slowly perishing. Who knew how long—how long!—he might have to wait for the end! In the next room, her mother, also wakeful, was writing without pause. She, too, seemed to have fallen under a spell. They had become more and more estranged as the days had multiplied.

No girl friend sought Theresa's company. Even Clara no longer came. Alfred meant nothing to her—less than nothing, for he did not understand her. He was noble, he was clean—and Theresa knew instinctively that she herself possessed neither of these virtues; furthermore, that she had no desire to cultivate them. Inwardly, she held them in contempt. Why could he not have been a little more imperative in his attentions? Yet, all the while, she knew that any untoward advances upon his part would have been instantly repulsed.

Thoughts of other young people entered her mind; people she knew but slightly, and some possibly only from having seen them several times, but for whom, as she admitted to herself, she was sensible of a more keen attraction, a warmer feeling of kinship, than she had ever experienced in Alfred's company. And so she realized that even a quick exchange of glances on the street between two certain persons of opposite sexes, might constitute a stronger bond than hours of close companionship between two others.

With a delicious little shiver, she recalled that lovely

summer day, near Monchsberg, when a young officer, hat
in hand, had walked by. His eyes had met hers and glowed;
then he had gone on, without so much as a glance behind
him. She felt certain that in that moment, he knew more,
much more, about her than Alfred, who believed himself
engaged to her; Alfred, who had kissed her so many times,
and who clung to her with all the fervour of his soul. She
felt that all this was not as it should be. But the fault, if
fault there was, was not hers.

XI

THE next day brought a letter from Alfred. He had
not slept at all the night before. Would she please forgive
him, if he had hurt her yesterday? For him, the slightest
cloud upon her brow was sufficient to darken the brightest
day. Through four long pages, he continued in this vein.
She smiled, somewhat softened, and pressed the letter
mechanically to her lips. Then, half purposely and half
accidentally, she allowed the letter to fall on her sewing
table. She was exceedingly glad that she did not have to
answer it. After all, they would meet this evening at their
accustomed trysting place.

About mid-day, her mother entered her room, smiling
sweetly.

"Count Benkheim is here for the second time"—it quite
escaped her that she had failed to mention a former visit—
"so as to give Father's library a more thorough and careful examination. He is ready to pay a very tidy sum to
secure it. The Count expressed a sincere interest in the
condition of Father's health,—and, by the way, he also
asked about you, Theresa."

As Theresa remained seated and continued her embroider-
ing in complete silence, her lips pressed tightly together,
her mother drew nearer and whispered:

"Come, we owe him thanks! Yes, you, too! It would be tactless not to greet him. I demand it of you!"

Theresa arose and, with her mother, went into the next room, where the Count was in the act of turning the leaves of a large illustrated octavo volume that was lying on the table. He came forward immediately and expressed his happiness at being permitted to see Theresa once again.

In the course of the polite and entirely unconstrained conversation which ensued, he desired to know if the ladies cared to make use of his carriage when paying their visits to the former Lieutenant. Also, he suggested that they might use it for a little excursion to Hellbrun, or to go wherever they wished. He would be delighted to place the carriage at their disposal. He became somewhat more reticent, when he discovered only opposition and unfriendliness in Theresa's manner.

Soon he took his leave, with the promise to come back after his return from a short business trip, which he could no longer postpone. And then, he promised, he would settle the business transactions concerning the purchase of the library. As a parting token of esteem, he kissed the hands of both mother and daughter.

The door closed after him. There was a heavy silence. Theresa was about to leave the room, without speaking. Her mother's voice retained her.

"You certainly might have been a little more cordial!"

Theresa turned, but remained at the door.

"Indeed, I was too cordial!"

And she again turned to depart. At this, her mother, although entirely unprovoked, began to heap abuse on Theresa's head, using many harsh words to describe her displeasure at her daughter's impolite, yes, impudent behaviour. It almost seemed that she was now giving vent to a resentment which she had allowed to rankle within her for days and weeks.

Surely, the Count was as fine a gentleman as that young Nuellheim, with whom her daughter chose to be seen promenading the streets of the city and its environs at all times of the day and night! Was it not a hundred times more decent to display a certain degree of acquiescence toward a settled, well-established gentleman of refinement, rather than to throw herself away on a student who was, after all, merely playing his own little game with her?

As Frau Fabiani grew more and more unsparing in her choice of words, her daughter could no longer doubt the truth of certain suspicions which for some time past she had entertained. Without shame, her mother now spoke of what she expected of her; what in fact, she felt herself entitled to require of her daughter.

"Do you imagine for one moment that things can go on as they are? We are starving, Theresa! Are you so madly in love that you are unaware of this? And the Count would support you—all of us—even Father. No one need know of it, not even young Nuellheim!"

In her anxiety, she came closer and closer to her daugh-

ter. Theresa could feel her breath upon her cheek. Shrink-
ing away, she rushed to the door. Her mother called after
her:

"Don't go away! Dinner is ready!"

"I don't want any dinner! Aren't we starving, anyhow?"
Theresa cried, almost hysterical with excitement and scorn,
as she rushed from the house.

It was dinner time, and the streets were almost deserted.
Should she go to Alfred, who lived with his parents? Oh,
he was not man enough to take up her cause, to defend her
against peril and shame. And yet her mother was deluded
by the belief that he was her lover! It was really amusing!
Well, then, where to? Had she possessed sufficient money,
she would have simply gone straightway to the depot and
taken a train, bound no matter where, though preferably
straight to Vienna. There were opportunities in plenty there
to support oneself and to live decently, even though one had
not been graduated from the Normal School. For example,
the sixteen-year-old sister of one of her schoolmates had
recently gone to Vienna to accept a position as nurse-maid
in the home of an attorney. She was evidently getting on
famously. One had only to manage such things. Had not
this long been her plan? Without more ado, she bought a
Viennese newspaper and, finding a shaded bench in the gardens, seated herself and began perusing the advertisements.
She found a few offers that seemed to suit her purpose.
Some one was looking for a governess for a five-year-old

girl; another desired one for two boys; and a third, a suitable companion to take care of a somewhat backward little girl. In one house, a slight knowledge of French was re-required; in another, skill in needlecraft was desired; in still another, the rudiments of a musical education. She could satisfy all of these requirements. Thank God, she was not completely lost! At the very first opportunity, she would pack up her belongings and depart.

Possibly, matters might be so arranged that she and Alfred could travel to Vienna together. She smiled to herself. She would not tell him anything before, but simply board the same train, the same compartment—wouldn't that be jolly?

Then, she found herself reflecting that, after all, she would prefer to travel alone, or with anybody else but Alfred. She would not mind undertaking the trip with some one wholly unknown to her; say, that elegant stranger who had stared her so shamefully out of countenance as she was crossing the Salzbach Bridge, only a short time ago. He must have been either Italian or French. She carelessly turned the pages of her paper and read of the display of fireworks at the Prater, of a train wreck, of an accident which had occurred in the mountains, when suddenly she was held by the following headline: "Attempt to Murder Lover."

The story was that of an unmarried mother, who had shot and severely wounded her faithless lover. Maria Meitner— that was the poor creature's name. Yes, such things were likely to happen to any one. But no, not to her! Never to those who were clever. One must not take a lover nor have a child. One must never lose one's head. Above all, one must never trust a man!

XII

THERESA walked home slowly, much quieter in spirit now. In her heart, she no longer felt any anger against her mother. The meagre meal had been kept warm. Her mother silently placed it before her. Then she reached for the paper which Theresa had dropped on the table. She searched for the most recent installment of a romance which she was following, and read with almost feverish excitement.

After eating, Theresa picked up her embroidery and seated herself near the window. She thought of poor Fräulein Maria Meitner, who was probably in prison by now. Did she have parents? Had she been shunned? Deep down in her heart, had she loved some other man more than she did her lover? And why did she have a child? There were many women who enjoyed life, yet suffered no such unfortunate consequences.

All sorts of things came to her mind; forbidden things, which she had learned within the last two or three years, through the confidences of her schoolmates. The subjects of several indecent conversations, as she was wont to term such talk, were again animated in her mind. Suddenly, a distaste arose within her for all the things touching sex. She remembered how, only a few years ago, while she was still a mere child, she and two of her little friends had solemnly pledged their word to one another to enter a convent. Now, at this moment, she again experienced that same yearning. Only, this time it was different, more sober, and tinged with unrest and fear, as if there could be no peace or security against the hazards which existence in this world entailed, save behind the walls of a cloister.

The heat of the day was graduallly abating, and the evening sun cast shadows across the house fronts—long shadows, which reached almost as high as the fourth floor. Her fear and sadness disappeared. She found herself more happy than she had ever been before at the prospect of seeing Alfred.

As was their custom, they met on the outskirts of the city.

Alfred's eyes glowed mildly. Theresa noted the almost noble candour of his face.

She felt a queer pang at her heart, and became ill at ease at the thought of how much more she knew or surmised of the facts of life than he. At the same time, she felt so unworthy of him! He came from a cleaner, finer atmosphere than she. He resembled his father in figure and carriage. She frequently saw Doctor Nuellheim on the street, and he had invariably passed by her without the slightest sign of recognition. Alfred's mother, and his sisters, too, likewise knew her by sight. Could it be that they suspected anything? Recently, when she had encountered them by accident, they had turned sharply round and had stared at her strangely. Alfred's sisters were nineteen and twenty respectively. No doubt, they both would soon be married. The family was well-to-do, and respected in the community. How easy it was for them! How completely absent from their thoughts was the most remote possibility that Doctor Nuellheim, physician to the city's best families, might ever be placed in an asylum for the insane!

Alfred, perceiving that Theresa's mind was elsewhere, asked to know if anything was amiss. She merely shook her head, and pressed his hand fervently.

The days were growing shorter, and twilight came early. Alfred and Theresa were seated on a bench, in the midst of the greensward. The horizon stretched out before them, broken by the blue hills in the distance. Vague sounds came up from the city. The long, droning whistle of a locomotive could be heard. Now and again, carriages rolled by in the road, and the shadows of pedestrians flitted past in the dying light.

Alfred and Theresa were pressed in each other's arms. Theresa's heart was filled with tenderness. Later, when she remembered this first love, it was always this evening that the recollection evoked in her memory—she and he, sitting on a bench between the fields and the plains, with the night spreading itself over the hills and far-stretching horizon. Faint whistling sounds came to their ears. It was the croaking of the frogs in a lake, somewhere beyond the darkness.

XIII

SOMETIMES they spoke of the future.

Then, Alfred would call Theresa his dearest, his bride. She must wait for him! In six years' time, at the very most, he would have received his doctor's degree; and then, she would become his wife. And, as if she were now mysteriously protected, she was no longer obliged to suffer harsh words from her mother, but was treated almost lovingly by her.

One morning, Frau Fabiani came to Theresa's bed and, with gleaming eyes, handed her a newspaper. There, on the page reserved for fiction and general features, was the beginning of a romance, entitled: "The Magnate's Curse," by Julie Fabiani-Halmos. Frau Fabiani seated herself on the edge of the bed, while Theresa read. The story began precisely as did hundreds of others. Every sentence was familiar to Theresa, as if she had read it many times before. When she had finished, she nodded silently to her mother, with pretended amazement.

Frau Fabiani took the paper and proceeded to read the entire installment again aloud, her voice filled with emotion and importance. When she had finished, she said:

"The novel will run serially for three months. I have

already received half of the money—almost as much as half a year's pension for a Lieutenant."

That evening, when Theresa met Alfred, she was greatly surprised to find him more carefully, yes, almost elegantly dressed. He might easily have been mistaken for one of the better class of travellers who frequented the city at this time of the year. Alfred was pleased to note the satisfaction in Theresa's eyes, and, with mock formality, begged the honour of her company, that night, at dinner in the Hotel Europe.

She accepted with delight.

Soon, they were sitting in the brightly-lighted, park-like garden, before a tastefully laid table, looking for all the world like a fashionable couple on their wedding trip.

The waiter received Alfred's order with some condescension. But they were served an excellent meal. By the unusual vigour of her appetite, Theresa was made conscious of the fact that her hunger had not actually been appeased this long while. The mild, sweet wine was quite delicious. At first, she was shy and constrained, hardly daring to lift her eyes from her plate. Then, gradually, she was liberated from her embarrassment, and glanced mischievously at those about her. On all sides, she saw eyes turned in her direction. Not only young and older men, but also women, as well seemed to look at her with pleasure and surprise.

Alfred became expansive, talking all manner of gallant nonsense, as he had never done before. Theresa laughed, from time to time, in a shrill and unnatural staccato. Alfred, apparently suffering from a poverty of amusing ideas, was asking in a whisper, for the third or fourth time, whether she fancied that they were being taken for an eloping pair of lovers, or perhaps for a young married couple, just returned from their honeymoon in France. At that moment, several officers passed by, and among them Theresa immediately recognized an officer with dark hair and yellow lapels as the person who had disturbed her thoughts more than once that week.

The officer knew her at once—she was sure of it—though he had the delicacy to turn his eyes away. He seated himself, not, as she had hoped, at a nearby table, but at one some distance from theirs. Alfred's good humour was suddenly gone. The gleam in Theresa's eyes had not escaped him. With the intuition of a jealous lover, he was aware that something of deep portent had just occurred.

As he was refilling her glass, she guiltily pressed his hand; then, realizing the clumsiness of her gesture, said quickly:

"Shall we go?"

There was an awkward silence.

"Mother will be anxious about me," she added, although certainly she had no need to be deterred in her pleasure by such a fear. "What did you tell them at home, Alfred?"

He blushed.

"You know that my parents are away," he replied.

"Oh, yes!" she said.

Now she understood why he had been so bold today.

How clumsily he arose, after paying the check! Instead of allowing her to precede him, as was customary, he passed in front of her; and then she perceived how much he resembled a schoolboy in his Sunday clothes. She, on the other hand, clad in a simple blue and white foulard dress, walked between the tables toward the exit like a young lady accustomed to dining in a big hotel every evening. After all, her mother was a Baroness, who had been raised in a castle and had ridden on a fiery pony! For the first time in her life, Theresa was proud of that.

They walked silently through the empty streets. Alfred pressed Theresa's arm in his own.

"What would you say," he remarked, in a frivolous tone that did not suit him at all, "what would you say if we were to go now to a coffee house?"

She refused. It was too late. Oh, yes, he was indeed a schoolboy! He might have suggested something better than a farewell hour in a coffee house! For example, why had he not hailed that cabby there, asleep at his post, so that he might ride her out into the beautiful, mild, summer night? How closely she would have nestled in his arms; how ardently she would have kissed him; how much she would have loved him, if he had! But she could not expect such clever ideas to be born in his stolid brain!

A short time afterwards, they were standing before Theresa's door. The street was quite dark. Alfred drew Theresa to him more passionately than he had ever done before. She gave him her lips eagerly and, with eyes tightly closed, she knew how noble and pure was his love.

As she ascended the stairs, she was filled with yearning and sadness. She unlocked the apartment door very softly, so as not to disturb her mother; and, after she had gone to bed, she remained awake far into the night, reflecting that, after all, the evening had not been entirely unsuccessful.

XIV

WHILE at table with her mother, the following day, Theresa received a beautiful bouquet of white roses, brought to her in a narrow cut-glass vase. Her first thought was of the officer; her second, of Alfred.

The card read:

"Count Benkheim begs that the sweet little Fräulein Theresa will be good enough to accept this modest offering."

Frau Fabiani gazed steadily before her, as though the entire matter were of no consequence at all. Theresa placed the vase on the sideboard and, forgetting to return to the table, picked up a book and sat down near the window in a rocking chair.

Her mother continued her meal alone. Then, not uttering a word, she left the room, her feet dragging after her.

On the way to the station, the rendezvous arranged for the evening—she and Alfred daily chose a different place—Theresa encountered the officer. He greeted her with elaborate politeness, never betraying, by the slightest revelatory smile, their mutual secret. Her nod thanked him. She quickened her pace until she was almost running. She was relieved that Alfred, whom she found waiting, failed to observe her excitement. He seemed moody and confused.

They strolled along the dusty, monotonous road towards Maria Plain. Some effort was made at conversation, though each painstakingly avoided all reference to the preceding night. As a storm threatened, they were soon forced to re-trace their steps. They parted earlier than usual.

For all their sadness, the ensuing evenings were still delightful. The moment of separation approached. Alfred was to leave for Vienna during the first week in September, to meet his father.

Theresa's heart was grieved. When Alfred discussed his impending departure, she vowed eternal faithfulness and promised to persuade her mother to move to Vienna as soon as such a change might be practicable. She told him that, for the moment, her mother would hear nothing of it. But things might alter, during the winter.

In all this, she knew that there was not a morsel of truth. Theresa was more determined than ever to leave home, but she would do so alone. In her scheme, Alfred played no part. And this was by no means her primary deception of him.

Several days after the meeting at the station, she again saw the young officer, who was preceding her on the Dom-platz as she was leaving the church which she occasionally frequented at this hour, though not through piety so much as in the desire of securing peaceful communion with her-self.

As though it were the most natural thing in the world, he stopped and greeted her. She knew only his Christian name, Max. He apologized for at last seizing the opportunity to meet her personally. The regiment to which he was attached was leaving for three weeks of manoeuvres, during which time he sincerely hoped that Fräulein Theresa . . .

Why, of course he knew her name! Fräulein Theresa Fabiani was not an unknown person in Salzburg! Besides, was not a novel by her mother at that very time running in the "Tageblatt"? He hoped that Fräulein Theresa would think of him while he was away, as she might of a friend— a quietly adoring, patiently aspiring friend.

He took her hand, kissed it, and was instantly gone.

She turned round to ascertain if any one had witnessed the encounter. The sun-flooded Domplatz was almost deserted. Only a few women remained on the other side. She knew them by sight. Whom does one not know in a small town? Alfred, all the same, would probably never learn from them that an officer had addressed her and kissed her hand.

He heard nothing. Nor did he know of Count Benkheim's visits to the house, or of the roses he had sent her, or of the second bouquet which had come that morning. He was in ignorance of her mother's changed attitude. She was consistently friendly and gentle, as though confident that she could calmly await further developments.

Theresa quietly permitted many purchases to be made for her—nothing costly; only necessities like underwear, several pairs of shoes, and English material for a street frock.

She also observed that the quality of the food served at home was improved. All this, surely, could not be coming from the money which her mother had received from the sale of the novel! Well, it was all equally inconsequential to her. It would not be long now. She was determined to leave home and, long before the Lieutenant returned, she would be far away.

Of all these facts, as well as problems, Alfred was happily ignorant. He still called her his dearest bride, and talked as though it were absolutely a foregone conclusion that, within six years, when he should become a doctor, he would lead Theresa to the altar.

When they sat on that same bench in the fields, as so often happened, and she listened to his protestation of love, she would sometimes respond. In those moments, she almost believed all that he told her, and part of what she herself replied.

XV

O<small>NE</small> morning, after an evening that had been like
so many others, a letter came from him. Only a few words.
He wrote that, by the time she read these lines, he would
already be on the train that was to take him to Vienna.
He had not had the courage to tell her yesterday. Would
she please try to understand and forgive him? He loved her
inexpressibly, eternally!

She let the page slip from her hand. She was most unhappy, but she did not weep. It was all over. She knew that
it was all over—and for ever. It was more uncanny than
tragic that she should be aware of this, and he should not.
Her mother came back from town. She had been shopping
at the market.

"Imagine whom I saw this morning," she asked, glee-
fully, "rushing with bag and baggage toward the depot?
Why, who but your Céladon! Yes, now he is gone. Didn't
you bid him God-speed?" She was much inclined to use
trite, old fashioned, bookish phrases in her ordinary speech.

Her mother's relief at this turn of affairs was only too
manifest. At last, the sole obstacle to the successful culmination of her plans had been eliminated!

Meanwhile, Theresa's thoughts centered upon the prospect of immediate departure. She would leave today; she would follow him at once.

"I will borrow the few gulden I need for the trip. Perhaps Clara . . ."

She left the house, and was soon standing beneath the windows of her friend's home. Her courage forsook her; she did not dare to mount the steps. The shutters were closed. Perhaps the Braunfurts were still in the country! No, for there was Clara, coming out of the entrance. Pretty and well dressed, as usual, seemingly pure and innocent. She greeted Theresa effusively, then began almost at once on the themes that she loved best. Without actually expressing anything off-colour, she constantly toyed with double meanings. After casually mentioning her regret at the infrequency of these meetings, she presently alluded to the Nuellheim family in a tone the significance of which was unmistakable. It left Theresa in no doubt whatever as to her friend's attitude regarding her relation with Alfred.

Theresa was not offended, but, completely conscious of her innocence, she endeavoured to enlighten Clara. Whereupon that young lady replied, contemptuously:

"How can any one be so stupid!"

An acquaintance approached, and Clara took her departure with conspicuous haste.

XVI

TOWARD evening, at the hour when Theresa was accustomed to meet Alfred, she attempted to write to him. She was surprised to find it so difficult, and contented herself with only a few lines. She was more unhappy than he, had no thoughts but of him, and hoped that God would arrange all things for the best.

She mailed the letter, knowing it to be stupid and insincere.

Returning home immediately, she found it difficult to keep her mind occupied. She picked up her embroidery, tried to read, practiced piano scales and exercises—to no avail. Finally, nervous and bored, she glanced at the paper that contained her mother's novel.

What a trite tale it was, and how pompous its language! It described the romance of a noble family. The father, according to the repetitious descriptions, was a hard and stern, though generous magnate; his wife, a sweet-natured, ailing creature; their son, a gambler, duelist, and seducer; their daughter, a blond person of angelic purity, a veritable fairy princess. A dark family secret was being unearthed. An ancient, worn-out, loyal servant knew that somewhere in the park a treasure was buried; that it had in fact remained there since the Turkish invasion. There was much talk about piety and virtue. No person in the world would have attributed to the author a desire to force an old Count on her own daughter.

Alfred's letters came almost daily. His father, he informed her, had awaited him at the station, and rented a room for him in the Alservorstadt. Together, they had visited the museums and theatres. The paternal attitude indicated an inkling of knowledge of their affair. While dining in a restaurant one evening, he had remarked that all young people cherish a host of impractical ideas which must of necessity be discarded. He, in his youth, had been obsessed by similar ideas, but had naturally overcome them. Before all else, Alfred must now think only of his studies, his career, and the serious business of life.

Theresa felt that Alfred might have spared her these details. Was he already trying to escape his responsibilities? She had demanded nothing of him. He could do as he liked. It was harder than ever to answer him now. Almost apologetically, she complained of the dearth of material for letter-writing in so small a town. Everything was pursuing its accustomed course.

She could not tell him of what was actually occurring— nothing about Count Benkheim's last visit, for example. He had been very entertaining, without making his real intentions too manifest. He spoke of his travels in the Orient. As a young man, he had been attached to the embassy in Persia; and at present, he was planning a trip round the world. With this last remark, he had gazed at her, intently and significantly. She pretended not to grasp his innuendos. Yes, a world tour would have been very much to her liking—but preferably, with some one other than the Count.

He likewise spoke of her father, not without sympathy and respect. He was certain that the shock to his pride, attendant upon his dismissal, had been the sole cause of his misfortune.

Theresa, in contrition over her neglect—it was now three weeks since she had given a thought to her poor, insane father—visited the asylum the next day. She found him seemingly in full possession of his faculties. He devoted particular attention to his dress. Not since the old days had she seen him so carefully and fastidiously garbed. But, alas! he did not recognize his daughter, and addressed her as though she were an utter stranger.

In a letter to Alfred, she alluded to the compassion and filial piety which she felt for the old man, but was incapable of revealing her true feelings in this matter, any more than in the expressions of tenderness and yearning which she addressed to her absent beloved. What could she do? It was impossible to tell him the truth—that she sought pitifully to bring his features to mind, that she could not remember the tone of his voice, and that hours went by in which she never even gave him a thought.

She thought more often of another, of whom she had no

right to think at all. One evening, Count Benkheim made his appearance, just as she was struggling desperately with a letter to Alfred. He hoped that he was not disturbing her. She, relieved for the moment of the labour of writing, came forward in a more friendly manner than usual. He, misunderstanding this amiability, drew nearer and spoke to her in a manner which he had not dared to employ before.

Without circumlocution, as though some previous conversation had given him license to assume this attitude, he began:

"Well, what does the little Fräulein think of a trip round the world? After all, we need not go to India or Africa."

He took her hands and spoke of a delightful spot, situated on an Italian lake, where he had sojourned many years ago. It was such a beautiful little villa, surrounded by a glorious park! Marble steps led directly to the lake. As late as November, the weather was warm enough for bathing. In the next villa, he continued, there lived three young ladies. At noon, all three used to step from their terrace into the water, first dropping their cloaks, under which they wore absolutely nothing. Yes, they swam in the lake, entirely naked.

He drew still closer to Theresa, and became so importunate that she was seized with fear and disgust. In her efforts to elude his too robust tenderness, she sprang up, striking the table with such violence that the lamp upon it vacillated perilously.

The door opened, and there, in the flood of light that crossed the threshold, stood her mother, as though she had just returned home. Her hat was set at an angle on her unkempt hair, and she was covered by an old-fashioned black mantilla with a beaded fringe.

She greeted the Count, begging him to remain seated, and took no notice of her daughter's confusion nor of the sounds which the swaying table had made only a moment before.

A banal conversation ensued, and when the Count addressed a question directly to Theresa, nothing remained but to make a harmless reply, which she did without much effort.

When the Count took his leave, he had every reason to believe himself forgiven. He could not know that he had only strengthened Theresa in her determination instantly to complete her plans for departure.

In answer to advertisements in the newspapers, she wrote to Graz, Klagenfurt, Brunn, and Vienna, requesting in her letters that the replies be sent *poste restante*. She received none, however, except from several employment bureaus at Vienna and Graz, and each of these demanded a deposit.

She was considering the advisability of leaving at once and trusting to luck for the rest when, to her own astonishment, the situation at home suddenly became much more comfortable. Her mother behaved quite amiably. The household seemed to lack nothing for its complete comfort. And from Count Benkheim, she received a note of apology, written in a pleasantly humorous, almost touching style. At his next visit, the Count's behaviour was quite perfect, as though he were a guest in the house of a refined family of his social equals.

Nevertheless, Theresa answered a few more advertisements of people who desired either a nurse or a governess. But on the whole, she was no longer as eager to make her escape as she had been before.

What it really was that held her in Salzburg, she would not admit even to herself.

XVII

ONE rainy evening, as Theresa was standing at the entrance of the postoffice, reading a reply to one of her letters, she heard some one say:

"Good evening, Fräulein."

She recognized the voice at once. A delicious little shiver raced through her body, and although she did not utter a syllable, her entire being seemed to exclaim: At last! She turned slowly and, with a smile, greeted the Lieutenant as though she had long awaited him. Somewhat later, she realized that it might have been better if she had not smiled so happily.

"Well, here I am," said the Lieutenant, grasping Theresa's hand and kissing it repeatedly. "I am in town one hour, and the first earthly creature I meet is Fräulein Theresa! Well, if that isn't fate! . . ."

He continued to hold her hand tightly in his own.

"Are the manoeuvres over so soon?" asked Theresa. "That surely was quick work!"

"I was gone an eternity," said the Lieutenant. "Is it possible that you didn't notice it? Twenty-one days and twenty-one nights—every night full of dreams of you. Yes, and the days, too. Shall I tell you something?"

"I am not curious."

"But I am—quite! and for that reason, I should like to know what may be in that letter which has to be taken from the postoffice so secretly!"

She was still holding the letter in her hands, but now she crushed it and hid it in the pocket of her raincoat, meanwhile looking amiably at the Lieutenant.

"This does not seem to be quite the place for a chat," said the officer. "Will not Fräulein Theresa take pity on a poor, dripping Lieutenant, and share her shelter with him?"

Without further ado, he took her umbrella and held it over them both. He slipped his arm under hers and, as they walked out into the pouring rain, he began to recount his experiences—of camping out in the open three thousand metres above sea-level, of a storm on a Dolomite peak, of capturing an enemy patrol—it goes without saying that he was invariably victorious.

Meanwhile, they continued on their promenade through the empty, ill-lit streets, until they reached a narrow street and came to a pause before an old house. There the Lieutenant suggested, quite casually, that she come in with him and have a cup of tea with rum. He was concerned lest the dampness make her ill.

Theresa returned to earth suddenly. For what did he take her? Was he stark mad? And as he placed his arm about her, as though to draw her with him, she glanced sharply at him, to determine, once and for all, whether he were making sport of her.

He released her and assured her that he was well aware—in fact, had immediately observed—that she was a creature quite apart from ordinary considerations, and unlike the other women whom he had known. Since first meeting her, he had not thought of another woman, much less looked at one. And, though the gesture might put him in danger of appearing ridiculous, he would stand here before his door, every evening, at seven o'clock sharp. Yes, he would wait here until at last she came, if he had to stand there every evening for ten years. He swore it on his honour, by all that he held sacred. And whenever he might chance to pass her on the street, he would greet her politely, but never presume to address her until she herself gave him permission. He would stand right here by the door. In any case, she must remember the house number—seventy-seven. Every evening, at seven! He had nothing else to do. His comrades—well, they were good enough fellows, but who the devil cared about them? He had no women friends—had not had any for a long time, he added, as he caught Theresa's doubting smile. If she was not there promptly at seven, he would simply remain in his room on the second floor. He lived alone. His landlady was an old woman, and quite deaf. He would sit in his cozy room, drink his tea, eat buttered rolls, smoke cigarettes and—hope for the next evening.

"Well, go on hoping, then, until Judgment Day," Theresa cried, as she turned and rushed away, without even extending her hand.

The next evening, at exactly seven, she slipped by his

door. There he stood, smoking a cigarette, cap in hand, just as he had been that first time she met him. The yellow lapels of his uniform shone brightly, as though in all this world there was no lovelier colour. His eyes, his entire face, lit up.

Did he whisper her name? She hardly knew. At all events, she nodded smilingly and walked up to him in the doorway. Nestled closely in his arm, they mounted the stone stairs until they reached a dark brown wooden door that was slightly ajar. It closed mysteriously and silently after they had entered.

XVIII

THEY kept their happiness secret. No one knew that, every evening, Theresa crept up the dimly lit stairs to the Lieutenant's apartment. No one saw her as a few hours later, she slipped out of the house. And had any one seen her, he never would have recognized Theresa in that heavily veiled figure.

Frau Fabiani had been commissioned by a famous illustrated periodical in Germany to write a novel. She imparted the news to Theresa with a great display of pride and conceit. Thenceforward, she remained behind locked doors, writing incessantly all through the day and half through the night. The household duties devolved entirely on Theresa. Though again reduced to very moderate circumstances, at this period mother and daughter laid less stress than ever on material comforts.

Meanwhile, Alfred's letters came daily. They were overflowing with tenderness and passion. For that matter, Theresa replied with more tenderness and passion than she had ever been capable of summoning before. She was not conscious of her falsehood, for she loved Alfred no less than before—nay, it sometimes seemed to her that she loved him more than when he had been very close to her. The letters that passed between them, and the sentiments that they expressed, had nothing whatever to do with the experiences that Theresa was undergoing at the same time. She was conscious of no feeling of guilt toward either of her lovers.

Theresa by no means allowed her days to pass idly. She had not forgotten her plans for the future. She pursued her French and English studies, and practiced at the piano regularly.

Max often presented her with theatre tickets. Usually, she would go with her mother, who did not trouble herself to inquire as to how she came by the tickets. On those evenings, Max generally sat in one of the first rows. True to his promise, he pretended not to notice Theresa and her mother, who had seats further back. Occasionally, he smiled through half-closed lids, and she knew that this smile signified a remembrance of the preceeding night, or a fond hope for the ensuing evening.

While, for Theresa, these visits to the theatre were a welcome distraction, for her mother, they were a source of constant excitement. She saw, in the dramas, reflections of her own experience or the experience of those about her. She discovered allusions that the author, completely unknown to her or perhaps dead, had permitted to creep into his work, or which the local management had caused to be inserted out of consideration for the famous woman novelist. At such moments, she glanced meaningfully at Theresa, who never seemed aware of these strange occurrences.

Count Benkheim had ceased to visit the Fabiani house-

hold. Theresa hardly noticed it. She was reminded of him
again only when she chanced to notice him sitting in a box
with a lady whom she had seen in a French farce a few days
before. She remembered that she had not been attracted to
her by any exceptional ability as an actress, but by the ex-
travagance of her gowns.

XIX

O<small>NE</small> evening, soon after she had come into Max's apartment and was still occupied in removing her veil, there was a knock at the door. To her astonishment, Max, without surprise or question, called out: "Come in!" A tall, blond young man entered, accompanied by a young lady. Theresa remembered her as an actress in an operetta which she had recently seen.

"Oh, what a surprise!" exclaimed Max.

Theresa was not for a moment deceived. It was quite apparent that this surprise had been carefully planned.

The newcomer—likewise a Lieutenant—proved himself a very amiable and polite entertainer. The actress, contrary to Theresa's expectations, was reticent, and spoke only in monosyllables. She had evidently been cautioned on Theresa's account. She addressed her escort as "Herr Ober-leutnant," using the more formal "Sie." Besides, she found occasion to mention the fact that her elder sister was married to a lawyer, and that her mother, the widow of a high official, intended moving from Vienna to Salzburg around Christmas time.

The conversation was then directed toward the theatre. When the company's various opinions and criticisms of histrionic art were exhausted, the general trend of the talk turned toward the love affairs of the directors, and especially that of one Count Benkheim with a very worldly lady.

The evening was brought to a close with a bottle of wine in a neighbouring restaurant. Here the conversation developed in a somewhat more entertaining, but, to Theresa, still unexciting fashion.

A few officers, seated at another table, greeted their comrades politely, and thereafter took no further notice of them.

Theresa excused herself at a rather early hour, but insisted that Max should remain with the others. She walked homeward, oppressed by sadness and feeling slightly ashamed at this turn of affairs.

The next meeting in Max's apartment was somewhat more lively. He had prepared cold cuts, cake, and wine.

It did not surprise Theresa to observe that Max and the actress were on more intimate terms than they had wished to betray. Although the latter still maintained a certain reserve, she spoke again of her mother, who would not be able to come at Christmas, but would fetch her daughter on Palm Sunday.

Later, in a coffee house, the comedian of the theatre, who was sitting on the other side of the room, winked humorously and called over to her: "Servus, Sintscherl." She thanked him curtly, and remarked: "The impudent thing! What does he imagine, anyway?"

Once, during an undisturbed hour, Theresa begged Max

to refrain from arranging these "foursomes," as she really felt more at ease when alone with him.

He smiled, as though flattered; then, suddenly, he turned on her and chided her rather severely for her snobbishness. She cried a little, and the evening was sad and tiresome. At heart, Theresa was really happy when, a few days later, Max's friend and his fair companion again knocked at the door. And during their subsequent gatherings in the restaurants, and even in larger parties, Theresa was, if not the happiest, at least the gayest of the company.

XX

THE winter, though it came late, was ushered in with heavy snowstorms. The entire city was hidden beneath a soft, white mantle. The sudden thought of Alfred's possible coming disturbed the peaceful calm of Theresa's existence.

The snowfall ceased. Beautiful, sunny, wintry days followed. Theresa and Max went on sleighing parties in Berchtesgaden and Königsee. At first, they went alone; later, they were joined by officers and friends, almost all of whom were attached to the theatre. At the inns, Max frequently permitted his friends to exceed the bounds of good taste, and to take liberties with Theresa. He showed no displeasure or jealousy. Theresa spent Christmas Eve and night with Max at one of the hotels. As she was returning home, she could not overcome a slight anxiety as to her mother's attitude regarding her absence. The latter met her with a special delivery letter. Frau Fabiani said not a word. She merely looked at her daughter reproachfully.

Theresa felt a strange guilt when she observed, by the date on the envelope, that the letter had arrived the day before. She recognized Alfred's handwriting and, without opening the letter, was aware of its contents. The element of surprise was therefore lacking as she read.

Alfred wrote that he was deeply ashamed of having wasted his affections on her, and that he hoped sincerely that she would be happy with the Lieutenant. He had unfortunately, been unable to awaken in her such delightful sentiments.

The quiet tone in which the letter was written at first shamed Theresa. After a short period of contrition, she sighed with relief. She need no longer place any restrictions upon herself. From that time on, she was seen everywhere with her lover, even at the theatre. She also permitted—and this was a thing to which formerly she had emphatically objected—the offering of small gifts. Among others, there was a medallion and chain which she wore constantly about her neck, a half-dozen handkerchiefs, and a pair of mules, made of red leather and trimmed with swan's-down; the exact duplicate of a pair which the Lieutenant's actress friend had recently worn in a play.

It was shortly after the beginning of the New Year that Theresa met Clara in front of the Lieutenant's house. Her friend was just returning from a sleighing trip. Almost immediately, Clara began to berate Theresa—not on account of her manner of existence, but because of her indiscretion.

"Surely, it doesn't do you any good to have everybody talking about you," she said. "Now, take me, for instance. I am having my fourth affair, and no one has the slightest suspicion of it! Were you to spread the story, no one would believe you." Laughingly, she promised to visit Theresa soon and tell her all about her adventures. She confessed that she herself felt a veritable craving to do so.

Theresa watched her friend depart with somewhat mixed emotions. Uppermost in her mind was the desire to be alone. Confidences always seemed to induce this reaction in her.

Alfred's letter, though apparently a farewell note, was not the last. He maintained a complete silence for several weeks; then, suddenly, he began to send letters in an entirely different vein. They were filled with reproaches. He used words which brought blushes to Theresa's cheeks. She had never dreamed that a person like Alfred could ever bring himself to put such words on paper.

She was determined to burn unread any other letters which might come. Yet, when a few days passed without mail from him, she was seized with a strange unrest that was not quieted until a letter had arrived, although she herself had offered him no response. After a dozen such, Alfred's letters abruptly ceased. In one of the rare missives from her brother, he mentioned having met Alfred in the city. He had found him looking very well, in good spirits, and elegantly clothed. On this last remark he laid especial stress.

Thereafter, Alfred's angry letters seemed like so many ridiculous lies to Theresa. She threw a number of them in the stove and watched them as they were slowly reduced to ashes.

Some time elapsed before Clara redeemed her promise. She entered Theresa's room one day, late in February. The snow was beginning to melt and the first spring breezes were wafted in through the open window.

Instead of relating the chronicle of her adventures, as she had promised to do, she imparted the news of her engagement to an engineer. All that talk of a few weeks ago had been utter nonsense, she explained. She had been moved to it by exasperation over her fiancé's reticence. She felt that she could count on Theresa never to breathe a word to a soul of what she had said. Then she expatiated on her sweetheart and the prospect of her future peace and happiness in the little mountain village where her husband-to-be was directing the construction of a railroad.

She remained less than a quarter of an hour, embraced Theresa rather brusquely, and neglected to invite her to the wedding.

XXI

O<small>N</small> these deceptive early spring days, Theresa felt
depressed, although not actually pained, at realizing that
her affection for Max was spending itself. Day by day, she
became increasingly aware of the utter emptiness and hope-
lessness of her existence.

It had been months since she had last visited the asylum
where her father was confined. She now unwillingly placed
the blame for this neglect upon a chance remark made by
the assistant physician, that "her father did not derive any
benefit from these visits, and that she herself merely carried away painful impressions that would torment her for
the rest of her life."

But, one day, a letter from the institution arrived. As
frequently occurs in such maladies, the old Lieutenant was
surprisingly improved, and had expressed a desire to see
his daughter. Theresa discovered in these words more significance than they were really intended to convey. She was
already prepared to hear her father's voice uplifted in advice and comforting sympathy.

And so she wandered, one dreary day, down the main
road toward the asylum. The snow was melting, and had
filled the road with dirty little pools. Theresa was depressed.

As she entered the little cell-like compartment, she saw her father sitting at a table covered with books and maps, just as he had loved to sit in former days. He looked up, and his eyes seemed filled with intelligence and the joy of living. But as soon as he perceived her presence (it was never clear to her whether he had recognized her or not) his features became distorted and his fingers contracted over a book as though he were about to hurl it at her. The attendant seized his hands. At the same moment, the doctor entered and took in the situation at a glance.

"This is your daughter," he said. "You wanted to see her. Now that she is here, you probably have something to say to her.—Calm yourself!" he added, as he noticed with what difficulty the attendant was restraining the raving man.

The old Lieutenant, freeing his right hand, pointed commandingly to the door. As Theresa made no move to obey his gesture, his eyes so forbiddingly darkened with rage that the doctor himself grasped her and almost thrust her from the room. The door was locked immediately afterwards.

"Strange," said the doctor, as they stood in the corridor. "Even we physicians are frequently deceived. When I spoke to him this morning of your intended visit, he seemed overjoyed. He should not have been given the maps and books."

As she hesitated at the door, he pressed her hand with a warmth that was not customary with him, and remarked:

"Perhaps the Fräulein will try again in a few days. I

will speak to him, and personally see to it that the dangerous books are removed. Reading seems to induce all sorts of memories. Just drop me a line, Fräulein, to let me know when you are coming, and I will wait for you at the door."

He looked at her strangely, and pressed her hand still more firmly. She was convinced that it was not the visit to her father that most interested him. She nodded. But she knew that this was her last visit.

She returned slowly to the city.

"He knows everything," she told herself. "That is why he ordered me out. What is to become of me now?"

Suddenly, like a ray of light, the idea came to her that when Max received his discharge he might enter his uncle's factory, of which he had recently spoken. Then he could marry her. Yes, he must do so! One of his comrades had but shortly before left the service to marry a woman of questionable character, whereas she had been "a respectable, decent girl," before Max had seduced her. At this phrase, she for the first time became conscious of what had transpired. Was she not the daughter of an officer? Though in poor circumstances, she belonged to a good family. Her mother had noble blood in her veins. Max owed it to her to make her his wife!

At their next meeting, without awaiting the right moment, she ventured on little innuendos. Either he would not or did not understand. She laughed and kissed away his ill-humour. When, later, she made her demands more clear, they provoked a quarrel. Though she had no real tenderness for him, she was still in love; and, accordingly, she abandoned her attempts as suddenly as she had begun them, allowing matters to go on as usual.

Spring was coming. The theatrical season was at an end. Max was often detained and unable to receive Theresa. He even occasionally spent a day or two out of town. These circumstances would never have struck Theresa as unusual, were it not for the fact that, one evening in a restaurant, the name of a very popular actress was mentioned, and she intercepted a knowing wink directed towards Max by one of his comrades. Max seemed annoyed at this betrayal.

Theresa became suspicious and, at their next visit to the theatre, it did not escape her notice that the young lady in question, while taking her bow, glanced and nodded to Max, who was sitting in the first row. Under one pretext or another, Theresa allowed her mother to go home alone, while she waited for the Lieutenant. He was very much upset at this, and declined her offer to go with him to his apartment. He had made other arrangements for the night; he had promised to meet some friends.

His anger, however, suddenly evaporated, and in the next moment he became very pleasant, asked if he might escort her home, took her arm, and actually led her to her door. He cursed his inopportune promise, and simulated annoyance at his deprivation so well that Theresa's fears were allayed.

As Theresa opened the door to her room, to her amazement she beheld her mother, kneeling before Theresa's own dresser and rummaging through the lower drawer. Theresa's entrance frightened her mother, who stammered:

"I only wanted to set your things in order. You never seem to have the time!"

"You are setting my things in order, in the middle of the night! You don't say so!"

"Now, don't excite yourself so, child. I really meant no harm!" Still confused, she added: "Look for yourself, and you will see that nothing is missing."

She left, and Theresa immediately knelt before the open drawer. After Theresa had burned the majority of Alfred's letters, she had received several more at various times. These were in similar vein, yet a little more sentimental, like the gradual vanishing of a storm on the horizon. Several were missing, and some of the hastily scribbled notes that Max had occasionally written to her were not there.

What could her mother want with them? Did she have ideas of practicing extortion? Was it merely curiosity? Or did she feel the need of warming her aged heart with the love adventures of others?

She knew, in any case, that she could not longer live under the same roof with her mother. Why, she wondered, had she so quickly abandoned her plans of persuading Max to marry her? She decided to pursue this matter to a conclusion upon the following day. This decision, which must necessarily conduce to a clearer understanding between

them, calmed her so much that she sank into a deep sleep.
The rest so strengthened her that, the next day, she could
appear amiable toward her mother and avoid all allusion
to the happenings of the preceding night.

It may have been the beautiful March day that held
the suggestion of spring within it, or the fact that the
morrow was Palm Sunday and that the whole theatrical
company would disband the day following; whatever the
reason, she actually looked forward with pleasant expectation to her appointment with Max.

Max had not yet come home when, at an early hour, she
entered his room. A strange thought flitted through her
mind, as though induced by the occurrence of the night
before: she thought of examining her lover's bureau drawers. To ward off temptation, she picked up a book lying
on the table. Max was accustomed to reading whatever
chanced to fall into his hands: novels, occasionally plays,
invariably in well-worn copies, since they had already
passed through many hands before they came to his. She
glanced through this and that book, without paying particular attention to the contents. As she carelessly pushed
one aside, she found the typewritten manuscript of the new
play which she had witnessed only a few days before. It
seemed almost as though it had been purposely hidden
there. She turned the pages of the copy, and noticed that
the name "Beate" was underlined throughout with a red
pencil. Beate? Was that not the name of the heroine in the
play? The part was played by the woman whom she sus-

pected of intimate relations with Max! Beate—why, of
course! The connection was clear.

After this discovery, she felt justified in making a further
search. This she did, with such complete disregard of consequences that, when Max entered, he found her before his
bureau drawers. The letters, veils, and suspicious under-
things of lace which she had strewn about her on the floor,
spared him the trouble of lying.

He rushed at her. She freed herself, screaming: "Cad!"
Without awaiting a reply, any excuses, or attempted justi-
fications, she rushed to the door.

He caught her by the shoulders.

"What a child you are!" he said.

She stared at him, wide-eyed.

"She isn't here any more!"

She continued to stare dazedly at him, and he added:
"Upon my word of honour!"

At last she understood, laughed harshly, and left. He
hurried after her, and, on the dark stairs, grasped her by
the arm.

"Be so good as to let me go!" she demanded, through
tightly clenched teeth.

"I shall do nothing of the kind!" he replied. "You are a
little fool. Now, listen to me. I couldn't help it. She ran
after me. You can ask her, if you wish. I am certainly glad
she is gone. I had every intention of telling you the whole
story today—honestly!"

He held her close to him. She was weeping. Again and

again, he repeated: "Child!" With one arm, he still held her fast, while with the other, he caressed her hair, cheeks, and arms.

"Anyway," he said, "you forgot your hat upstairs. For heaven's sake, calm yourself! Let me explain! Then you will still be at liberty to do whatever you choose."

She followed him to his room. He drew her upon his knee, and swore that she was the only one he had ever loved, and that "such a thing" should never happen again.

She did not believe a word he said. Yet, she remained. The instant she came home, she locked herself in her room.

Tired and disgusted, she packed her belongings, left a frigid little note for her mother, and boarded the noon train for Vienna.

XXIII

THERESA's first night in Vienna was spent in a very mediocre hotel near the railway station. The next morning, according to the schedule which she had planned for herself, she made her way through the town.

The day was warm and spring-like. Violets were being sold on the streets. Though women were wearing their new spring clothes, Theresa felt quite at ease in her simple and becoming winter costume. She was happy to have left Salzburg—to be alone at last.

She made a list of the names and addresses of those who required nursemaids or governesses, and wandered about the entire day, with only a pause for lunch at noon. Some found her too young; others would not consider her without recommendations; again, she did not feel sympathetically inclined towards those who might have engaged her. As evening was coming on and she was thoroughly exhausted, she decided to accept a position in a family with two children aged respectively three and seven years.

In comparison with what she was to experience in this house, her life at home, even at its worst, was glorious.

The family was in poor circumstances. The children were always hungry, and brought noise, but no happiness, into the little circle. The parents were mean and discouraged.

Theresa had to supplement the meagre meals they gave her out of her own money. Soon, her little earnings were exhausted, and after a few weeks, unable to tolerate her employers any longer, she left. In her next position, as governess to a widow's two children, she was treated as a servant. A third engagement displeased her because of the uncleanliness which she found in the house. In still another place, the importunities of the male member of the household soon drove her away.

She changed her position many more times, not without a feeling that she herself was partly to blame for her misfortunes. She was impatient and haughty, and totally indifferent to the children entrusted to her care.

These were indeed bad times. Theresa had not a moment for introspection, though occasionally, when lying in her narrow bed against a cold wall, or awakened by the crying of one of her charges, or disturbed by the morning noises of servants, or possibly when she was in the park with the children and thus had an unexpected moment of leisure, then the utter poverty and dreariness of her situation would overcome her with sudden poignancy.

She was usually too weary to take advantage of the few free afternoons allotted to her. Once, she took a walk with a nursemaid of the neighbourhood. This person told of the innumerable and successfully evaded attempts made upon her by the fathers and sons of the families in which she had worked.

On this particular Sunday afternoon in the Prater, this nurse permitted the most offensive kind of addresses from all sorts of young men, and her answers were quite as unrestrained. Theresa was overcome with disgust. She managed to slip away unobserved, and returned home alone.

XXIV

Dᴜʀɪɴɢ this time, news from Salzburg was very
scant. Theresa's sudden departure had made it impossible
for her to leave an address, and the first answer she received to her letters, after months of waiting, was as hastily written as her own parting note had been. In the beginning of her letter, Frau Fabiani's tone was that of a
person who had been slighted, but toward the end, it
changed completely, as if mother and daughter had parted
on the most friendly terms.

In spite of the fact that Theresa's letters were written
discreetly and with utmost reticence, a sympathetic soul
would have been able to read her misery between the lines.
Her mother seemed to notice nothing of the kind, and even
went so far as to write her of her pleasure in Theresa's
happiness—though that, which might otherwise have been
construed as sarcasm, was in reality nothing more than
lack of understanding. Often names were mentioned in
these letters that were unknown or wholly uninteresting to
Theresa. Of Theresa's father, Frau Fabiani only said that
his condition was unimproved; of her brother, not a word,
until one day came a card in which she reproached Theresa
for her neglect, and expressed the wish that she should

look up her brother. It was weeks since Frau Fabiani had heard from him, and she had waited for him in vain during the vacation period.

The address in her hands, Theresa visited her brother late one summer afternoon. She found him in a poor but neatly kept room, the window of which offered no better view than a bare wall with great cracks in it, through which one caught a glimpse of neighbouring fire-escapes.

Karl took it for granted that Theresa had arrived in Vienna a very short time ago, and thought it very wise that she had chosen to become independent. He expressed pity over his father's unimproved condition, which might continue for years. He never even mentioned his mother. He told her further that he was teaching the two sons of a clinical professor four times a week, and was receiving a substantial remuneration. This might, at some future date, prove advantageous to him.

He spoke heatedly of the injustices perpetrated by the University, such as the favoritism shown toward professors' sons by the scholarship committees. He was particularly incensed against the Jews, who were absolutely over-running the University, making life there unbearable.

After a little while, he excused himself, saying that he had an appointment in a coffee-house, where a few of his companions of similar tastes held their club meetings; he, being the secretary, would naturally have to be present.

He escorted Theresa down the stairs and left her with a hasty and casual farewell.

"Let me hear from you soon again," was all he said.

She looked after him as he walked quickly away. His clothes were neat, though carelessly worn; he seemed to have grown older; in fact, his appearance had altered so much that she felt a complete stranger to him.

Theresa had expected more of this visit. She made her way homeward, more dejected and lonely than she had ever been before.

XXV

For some weeks now, Theresa had had charge of the five-year-old son of a travelling man. She rarely saw the father, who was a soured, embittered little man, while his wife treated Theresa with a casual friendliness. The boy, a pretty, blond child, soon endeared himself to her. She hoped sincerely that she might find a certain degree of permanency in this house.

Arriving home, one Sunday evening, a little earlier than usual, she found her charge already in bed. From a neighbouring room came whispered voices. After a while, the mistress stepped out of the room, clad only in a dressing gown. She was confused and irritated. She requested Theresa to buy some cold cuts at a nearby store. When Theresa returned, the mistress, carefully dressed, was seated on the baby's bed, showing the child a picture book. She addressed Theresa gaily, appeared quite at ease, and talked about many matters pertaining to the household. The next day, she seized some trifling pretext to discharge her.

Again Theresa was homeless. For the first time, she thought of returning to Salzburg; but alas! she did not have enough money for the fare. She betook herself, as she always did in the interims between positions, to the suburban home of the widow Kausick. Here she slept in a dingy little room with Frau Kausick and her two children. The house reeked of petroleum and rancid fat. At three o'clock in the morning, the noises in the courtyard, of creaking wagon wheels, neighing horses, and loud, raucous male voices would awaken her out of her sleep. She thought of the hours of quiet, gradual awakening that she had been accustomed to at home, and was seized with panic at the depths of her descent. For the first time, she weighed the possibilities of taking advantage of her youth and beauty, as so many others were doing, and selling her body.

The other possibility, of being loved and happy again, had not entered her mind since her first great disappointment. The advances, within the last few months, of employers, clerks, and the like, had not been sufficiently alluring to betray her into another adventure.

And so her poor, tired, and disappointed soul hoped to find in prostitution the cleanest and most decent form of love. She decided to give herself another week. If, within that time, she still had no position, then nothing would be left—or so it seemed to her, in this dreary morning hour—but to walk the streets.

XXVI

THE widow Kausick earned her meagre livelihood as a servant. Though often ill-humoured, she was withal a good-hearted person. She was wont to arise at five o'clock in the morning. A little later, the children began to disturb the dreary unrest which ushered in the day in this poor household. Then Theresa was forced out of bed.

She drank her coffee out of a cracked white cup. After breakfast, she escorted Frau Kausick's children, a boy of nine and a girl of eight, to school. The children were very much attached to Theresa.

An hour's walk through Stadtpark, blooming with early summer flowers, seemed somewhat to lift her spirits.

She entered an employment bureau, where she was treated with little friendliness, in consequence of her inability to remain in one position for any length of time. Despite this, she was given several addresses.

The first attempts were unsuccessful.

About midday, when her hopes were at low ebb, she mounted the stairs of a beautiful apartment house in the Ringstrasse, where a governess was needed for two girls, one thirteen and the other eleven years old.

The lady of the house, a pretty woman, although somewhat too heavily rouged, was about to leave the house, and therefore was at first inclined to be a little impatient at this delay. Nevertheless, she permitted Theresa to enter, and demanded her references. Theresa, following a sudden impulse, replied that she had none to offer, since this was the first time she had applied for employment.

The lady was a little hesitant, but, after talking to her for a short time, she found her appealing, and was particularly impressed by the fact that Theresa's father was an officer. Finally, she decided that it would be better if Theresa could come again on the morrow, when the girls were home from school. In the corridor, Theresa read the following sign, inscribed in gold lettering on a black background: "Dr. Gustav Eppich, Attorney at Law. Criminal Cases."

The next day, at one o'clock, Theresa entered the salon, where she found the lady of the house, in the company of her daughters. The friendly manner in which the two well-bred children greeted her led Theresa to suppose that their mother had influenced them favourably in her behalf. Soon afterwards, the head of the family came in. He remarked, in a lightly reproachful tone, that his wife's summons had obliged him to leave his office earlier than was his habit. He, too, seemed impressed with Theresa, especially since she came of an officer's family. This circumstance had not failed to have its effect upon both the heads of the house.

In answer to a question, Theresa replied that her father

had died a few years before, through grief at having been pensioned off prematurely. Over the features of the entire Eppich family there played an expression of sympathy. Although the salary offered was less than she had expected, Theresa could hardly restrain her joy when informed that she was to report for duty on the following day.

At Frau Kausick's house she found a letter from her mother, informing her of her father's death. She had to repress a little shiver, almost a sentiment of guilt, before she became conscious of her grief.

Following the impulses of her sorrow, she made her way to her brother's house. He had not yet heard of their loss, and, when told, did not take it much to heart. He paced the room in silence, then stood still in front of Theresa, who was seated on the bed, since both chairs were littered with books. Suddenly he bent forward and kissed her on the brow, as though he were fulfilling a duty.

"Did you hear anything else from home?" he asked.

Theresa told him the little she knew; among other things, that their mother had sold all the furniture, and was now living in a furnished room.

"Sold the furniture!" exclaimed Karl, with a wry smile. "She might have consulted us first."

Then, seeing the look of amazement in Theresa's face, he added:

"After all, we are part owners, and justly entitled to our share!"

"Quite right," said Theresa. "She mentioned something

about that in her letter. We are to receive a certain percentage in a short time."

"A certain . . . hmm! I shall have to look into this matter more carefully!"

He began to pace up and down again and, with a quick glance at Theresa remarked:

"Poor father gave up at last!"

Theresa did not know what to reply to this. Feeling very much more ill at ease than she was willing to admit to herself, she took leave of her brother, without telling him of her new position. Karl made no move to restrain her.

On her way home, she entered a church and spent some time there without praying, thinking piously of the departed one. He appeared in her mind's eye as he was when she was a child, when she had loved him dearly. She recalled the boisterous gaiety with which he used to step into the room, lift her from the floor where she had been playing, press her close to him, and fondle her. To this image was added the image of her mother as she was then— bright, young, almost beaming. This was mere illusion, for, in reality, she had never seen her thus.

Again she felt a shudder pass through her. How could two people change so completely within such a short time? It seemed to her as if they were both dead and long since buried, and that there was absolutely nothing in common between the late insane Lieutenant and the mean, weirdly aging authoress in Salzburg.

XXVII

THE next day, Theresa took up her new duties. At their first dinner together, they made a polite effort to help Theresa to overcome her confusion. The son of the house was also present. His name was George. They pronounced it in the French manner. He was enrolled in the University as a law student.

A schedule for Theresa was arranged. Both girls attended school and were escorted there and back by Theresa. She helped them with their home-work. Frau Eppich was particularly anxious that the girls should take their daily walk. The attitude of both parents continued to be friendly, though Theresa could not long remain in ignorance of the complete indifference with which they regarded her.

They made it easy for her to join in the conversation at table. Often political subjects were discussed. Dr. Eppich held very liberal ideas, which no one but his son dared oppose. George accused his father of being entirely too idealistic. Dr. Eppich heard this with evident pleasure; in fact, he was obviously flattered by the rebuke.

As for Fräu Eppich, there were days in which she showed not the slightest interest in her daughters or in any household matters. Then, without warning, she would appear at an unexpected moment and give scrupulous orders for the most insignificant details.

George found many more excuses to take him to his sisters' room than was absolutely necessary. His glances, at times shy, then again bold, betrayed to Theresa his desire to be near her. Perhaps he had hopes, but Theresa was very cold and reticent, and pretended to notice nothing.

The elder of the two girls was inclined to attach herself to Theresa. Sometimes she almost yielded to an impulse to confide in her; but whenever this occurred, she purposely became more reserved and distant during the following days. The younger one was of an even-tempered, still very childish disposition. Both daughters clung affectionately to their mother, although Theresa noticed that the latter was abstracted and often impatient in her responses.

Theresa had very little leisure. True, she had every alternate Sunday free, but she scarcely knew how to take advantage of these hours of liberty. She walked much, without deriving any pleasure from that recreation, and visited the theatre on exceedingly infrequent occasions.

Theresa had no complaints to make toward the family, as far as their behaviour to herself was concerned, though she was aware of a growing unrest, almost a feeling of uncertainty, which she could not account for, except by the strange change in the Eppich family's attitude and spirit toward each other. Unwittingly, she seemed drawn into this inexplicable conflict.

There was not a soul in whom she could—or, for that

matter, wished to—confide. Only a French governess who did not strike Theresa as being so very young, though she was not yet thirty, was somewhat more sympathetic to her. Theresa had seized the opportunity of her acquaintance with this woman to practice French conversation.

Sylvia was amusing. She told Theresa little stories of her past—she was not altogether discreet—and tried to encourage Theresa to similar confidences. Being of a very reticent nature, Theresa related no more than she would have told an utter stranger, though it was clearly apparent all the while that Sylvia was not in the least convinced of her innocence.

Theresa wondered at times how it was possible that her heart—indeed, her very senses—scarcely remembered the delight she had experienced in the Lieutenant's arms. She no longer suffered over his betrayal. Yet she was certain that she could never again repose her trust in a man, and she was glad of it. She flattered herself that she enjoyed a good reputation; and Fräu Eppich, whenever the occasion arose, boasted to her friends of Theresa's antecedents.

XXVIII

Spring had come. Early one afternoon, during the Easter holidays, Theresa was at the Stefansplatz, awaiting a governess employed by friends of the Eppich family—a good-hearted, somewhat faded creature, for whom Theresa felt more pity than friendliness. The Fräulein was late. Theresa amused herself by watching the passersby. They all seemed free of worries on this lovely, mild holiday, and all bent toward some happy goal. There was no dearth of lovers. Theresa, without envy, found it ridiculous that instead of a lover, she should be waiting for an old governess with whom she had nothing more in common than a similarity of profession. She was slightly irritated at the prospect of the tiresome afternoon which she would have to spend in her company.

Since it was a half-hour past the appointed time, she decided to proceed alone. Once more, through a feeling of conscientiousness, she looked round on all sides to see if the Fräulein might be coming; then, almost hastily, she left the place and mingled with the stream of walkers. She was glad to be free and alone, happy in the uncertainty of what the next hour would bring forth.

It happened that she was shoved along with the crowd

towards the Prater, and soon found herself in the Hauptal-lee. The earth smelled of the spring, though the trees that lined both sides of the Allee were still in their winter bareness.

The driveway was alive with cabs and carriages. People were returning from the races at Freudeau. Like many others, Theresa stood on the curb for a while. Many glances rested on her, and many men turned to look at her again. One in particular was a young officer who resembled Max, though he appeared to her much more elegant than her seducer. She knew now that she had simply thrown herself away then, and she was determined to be more wise in the future.

She walked along the crowded Allee until she came to the bandstand, where music was played for the general public and not merely for the guests in the overflowing restaurant gardens. Thousands passed by, paused, pressed forward. Theresa was happy. She enjoyed the way the different instruments took up the theme—the quiet start, the sudden swelling of the drums, the tinkling tones of the bells—all this delighted her. The tramp of horses, the whistle of locomotives, the chatter and laughter of the throng—everything seemed to join in this spring festival concert.

Her dark, unpretentious clothes and habitually grave mien were not conducive to advances. Only when she stood for a while near the fence of the restaurant garden did a young man press close to her. She made a repelling gesture with her hand, and he quickly disappeared, before she was even able to discern his features.

As she walked under the still leafless trees, away from the noise and the music, she recalled his touch, which had doubtless been premeditated, with little or no resentment. Quickly, almost like a person in flight, she went on. Gradually the crowds began to disperse, and Theresa decided to rest on the first unoccupied bench which she could find.

A young man walked past her. His appearance had struck her from afar—a lean, haggard figure, dressed in a ridiculously bright suit, well-pressed, but ill-fitting. Both hands were in his pockets, and he danced along rather than walked. Between two fingers, he dangled a soft brown hat.

He looked at Theresa with a childish, timid glance. Without being too audacious, he nodded and smiled in a friendly manner, so that Theresa, in spite of herself, returned his smile. He took a few steps forward, then suddenly turned, walked toward her, and seated himself beside her. She attempted to rise, but he had already begun to talk, entirely oblivious of her gesture. He spoke of the delightful spring weather, the races which he had just attended, the fall of a jockey, and joked about an ostentatiously dressed couple who chanced to be passing by at that moment. Finally, he asked Theresa if she had noticed the carriage of the Erzherzogin Josefa and that of the Baron Springer go by? Was it not nice to listen to music from a distance? It came to one as though from another world.

Theresa, confused by this sudden flow of words, answered

laconically, yet not unamiably. Then she rose and hastily bowed. But he, too, rose, walked beside her, and continued his chatter.

He tried to guess who she might be. A Viennese? No, never! She smiled. Perhaps a German, since she was so educated! Ah, she was an Italian! Yes, most certainly! The dark hair and glowing, ardent eyes! That's it —an Italian!

Almost frightened, she looked up at him. He laughed. Well, of course, her parents—her grandparents, at least— must have come from the south. She herself was a Viennese. That one could guess from her accent even though she talked very little and, at that, "Hochdeutsch." Was she an actress, a singer, a prima donna, or a noblewoman? Surely a noblewoman, condescending to watch at close range the doings of the people. Goodness knows, she might even be a princess or a duchess! A duchess, of course!

He would not be deprived of that idea; he even pretended to be in earnest about it. Everything seemed to point to it. The unpretentious clothing, the bearing, the walk, the glance! He allowed her to precede him a few paces, the better to admire her bearing and walk.

"Your Highness," he said, suddenly, as they were nearing the bandstand, "I would deem it a great honour to invite Your Highness to supper, but, truth to tell—poverty is no shame and wealth no misfortune!—my fortunes are unfortunately low; about a gulden in all. That would not provide a very handsome meal. So Her Highness would have to pay for her own supper!"

She asked him, laughingly, if he were quite insane?

"Never less so!" he answered, seriously.

She quickened her steps. It was getting late. She had better be on her way home. Well, surely she would permit him at least to escort her to the court equipage that was waiting for her somewhere nearby. At the Schweitzerhaus or the Preussischen Museum? Or perhaps near the Viaduct?

In the meantime, they had arrived at a little lane. Behind green hedges, in a modest restaurant, some people were enjoying the music that floated from a distant café, while regaling themselves with cheese, salami, and beer. And soon, to Theresa's astonishment, she found herself seated with her escort at a rather rickety table covered with a red-flowered cloth. Both ate heartily of whatever the frock-coated, over-heated waiter placed before them.

Theresa's escort talked to him as though he were an old friend, and put all sorts of jesting questions to him.

"Oh, Herr Swoboda, how is your grandfather? Still a fortune-teller? And your daughter? Still the legless wonder?"

Then he surpassed himself in comic excuses for having dared to bring a princess to such an impossible place. Of course, here her incognito was far less likely to be discovered. Afterwards, he called her attention to the various people round them. That man in the dark coat, with his stiff hat brought low over his forehead—surely he was a defrauder, fleeing from justice! He had something to say of each individual—of the two soldiers who drank beer out of the same glasses as their sweethearts; the man with the protruding eyes, with his fat wife and four children; and the ancient, smooth-shaven gentleman who sat under the lantern and talked to himself. At last, with well simulated fright, he discovered, in a remote corner of the garden, a man wearing a black suit and high hat, who he insisted was a private detective, come to watch over the princess.

These trivialities were not in the least droll, and Theresa was fully aware of this. But after all these depressing months of conventional respectability in which no one had ever uttered a harmless joke in her presence, a tremendous yearning for fun and laughter was taking possession of Theresa. Sitting beside this man whom she had known for less than an hour, she felt free and happy. Her excitement heightened by two glasses of wine, she relinquished the restraint in which she had thus far held herself, and laughed merrily.

In her mind, she was trying to determine what manner of man her escort might be; whether a painter, or perhaps an actor. Well, what matter, after all? He was young and unrepressed. Surely, it was jollier today than when she had accompanied Alfred to the elegant Hotelgarten!

He had been in the Tyrol, in Italy, in Spain, and in Malta. Had she not yet guessed that he was a peddler, who travelled through the world with a pack on his back? He had arrived only yesterday, and was ready to start again tomorrow. But, of course, if he might hope to see Her Highness again, he would willingly sacrifice a few days— and nights, even, he added, casually.

They each paid their own check, then left the garden. The stranger took Theresa's arm and would not release it. The festivities were gradually drawing to an end. They made their way between booths, shooting galleries, restaurants, and games of chance, toward the exit. A barker who spoke in the Bohemian dialect tried to inveigle them to patronize the magic cabinet, promising them many surprises. To the evident enjoyment of the crowd, Theresa's escort entered into a conversation with the barker, imitating his dialect to perfection.

This displeased Theresa. She freed her arm, and started to leave; but there he was again beside her. He stood by the wagonstand and pretended to be disconsolate at not finding the court carriage there.

"Now the joke is ended," said Theresa, "and I think it best we bid each other farewell!"

"Well, if the joke is over," he said, with unexpected seriousness, "then it is only proper for me to present myself with due formality—Kasimir Tobisch!—Formerly," he added, ironically, "von Tobisch." "But," he explained, "there is no sense in insisting upon the title, when one is nothing more than a poor wretch. And now Her Highness might guess what my profession is."

"A painter," she answered, without much thought. He nodded quickly. That was right. He was a painter, and a musician, upon occasion. Would she not visit his studio, some time? As she made no reply, he began talking again of his travels. He had been a musician and a painter, not only in Italy, but also in Paris, Madrid, and England. He played nearly all instruments, from the flute to the kettle-drums. Ah, what a city, Madrid—mysterious and romantic! But Rome surpassed them all! The catacombs, for instance—a thousand skeletons and deaths' heads deep underground: it was eerie walking round down there. If one got lost in that maze, there was absolutely no hope. It had happened once to a friend of his, but he was saved. And the Colosseum—a giant circle, in which a hundred thousand people could be seated. Now it is in ruins, and the moon shines over it. Only at night, of course!

They were nearing the house in which Theresa lived. She begged him to leave her, and, upon his insistence, gave him her name and address. She also promised to meet him two weeks later, at an appointed hour and place. She noticed that he followed her at a distance and watched her from the corner until she disappeared in the doorway. Suspicion? It might just as well be infatuation.

XXIX

During the next fourteen days, she received three letters from him. The first was formal and gallant; the second, a bit more sprightly. He called Theresa "Princess" and "Your Highness," and inscribed himself Kasimir, the great drummer, flutist, and journeyman. The third letter, however, held a touch of tenderness, and, as though carelessly, he signed his initials, "C. v. T."

They met each other as pre-arranged on the Praterstern. The rain was pouring down. Kasimir came without an umbrella, cloaked in the romantic folds of a travelling coat. He had tickets for the afternoon performance at the Karlstheater. Oh, he hadn't paid for them! He knew the director well, and some of the actors. He met them occasionally in restaurants and at studio parties. Well, one should not take that word, "party," too literally. Still, they had some jolly times together, although things were never as lively as similar gatherings which he had attended in Paris; at least they were not as abandoned. There they held artists' balls at which the models danced entirely nude or, what was even worse, covered with transparent veils.

Thus he entertained her on the way to the theatre. They sat in the second row of the third gallery. The production, an operetta, was neither better nor worse than many others which Theresa had seen in Salzburg. The play was quite amusing, and Kasimir's whispered comments on it made her laugh and blush in turn. When the darkened hall emboldened him to become too familiar, she had forbidden his caresses.

He changed immediately, remaining decent and quiet in his seat until the end of the play. He did not even answer her questions, although that was only another manner of clowning.

It was light and still raining when they stepped out into the street. They entered a nearby coffee house and sat on a window-seat. Theresa gazed absently at the illustrated papers, while Kasimir interested himself in a game of billiards, gave the players advice, and even tried a few strokes without much luck. He blamed this on the faulty cue.

Theresa found it strange that he should pay so little attention to her. When finally he did return it was already time to leave. He helped her into her jacket, threw his own coat about his shoulders, opened and held the umbrella over her, but did not attempt to take her arm.

He was reticent, almost melancholy; and she pitied him. As they passed a well-lit restaurant, his features assumed such a hungry look, that Theresa was almost impelled to invite him to supper. Yet, she feared to offend him; and perhaps she was still more afraid that he might accept.

They walked along silently. While taking leave of each

other on a street corner, he declared suddenly, with some passion, that he could not possibly wait fourteen days before seeing her again. She shrugged her shoulders. It could not be helped. He insisted. She was a slave. Why should they not see each other for an hour, some day this week? Of course she was not a slave, she replied, but she held a position which entailed certain duties.

Duties! Toward whom? Strange people, who took advantage of her? That was no better than actual slavery. No, under no conditions would he wait fourteen days! Surely they would not refuse her an occasional evening off during the week! Although she remained outwardly firm, she thought that he was right.

The next evening he sent her a little note, saying that he had something of importance to talk over with her, and would wait for her on the corner. The lady of the house was present, and saw Theresa blush. There was no answer, Theresa informed the messenger. She did not hear from Kasimir again until the day of their rendezvous.

XXX

THERESA waited at the entrance to the Stadtpark. Opposite her, in a café on the Ringstrasse, the guests sat in the open and sunned themselves. A pale child offered violets for sale. Theresa took a small bouquet. A passerby whispered something in her ear; an insulting invitation, couched in shameless words. She did not dare turn round. She blushed a deep red, and not entirely from anger. Was she not mad to live like a slave, like a nun? How everybody gazed at her! Some turned to look again. One handsome, elegant man walked by her several times, evidently wondering how long she would remain alone. Perhaps it was just as well that Kasimir did not come. A poor devil and a fool, to boot—and why, of all men, he? She could take her choice of men!

There he was, now, in his light summer suit, not of the latest cut, yet rather becoming; his soft hat in his hand, as usual, and the other hand in his pocket. His stride was free and easy. He kissed her hand. They wandered through the park, arm in arm, stood near the lake, and watched the children feed the swans. Kasimir told her of an experience on a lake in a park in Paris, where he had wandered about happily all the evening, and then had passed the night in the shadow of a beautifully fashioned rock.

104

"Surely not alone," said she. He placed his hand over his heart. "I can't remember any more. A thing of the past!"

Theresa wanted to hear no more of Paris, Rome, or any other foreign city. If he yearned so much for them, why did he not go back?

He pressed her arm firmly against his own, and invited her to have tea with him on the terrace of the Kursalon. They seated themselves at a small table, and Theresa was suddenly overcome with a ridiculous fear that some one might see her there with Kasimir and inform her employers.

As these thoughts passed through her mind, she involuntarily bowed her head; and Kasimir, who sat very formally, with legs crossed, smoking a cigarette, confronted her with precisely what was going on within her mind. She shook her head slowly, on the verge of tears.

"Poor child!" said Kasimir; and, with determination, he added: "all that will be remedied!"

He called the waiter and paid him, allowing the money to clink a little ridiculously on the marble top of the table. Then they descended the wide stairs into the park. He told her how much he had yearned for her. Only when working could he find any peace. He spoke of a fantastic landscape which he was painting, a sort of "tropical Utopia," and of others that he carried in his imagination, pictures of home.

Of home?

Yes, strange as it might seem, he, too, had a home. And he talked of the little German-Bohemian city in which he was born; of his mother, the widow of a notary, who still lived there; of the flower beds in the front garden where he had played as a child.

In turn, Theresa described her family. Her father had shot himself through offended pride; her mother wrote for the newspapers under an assumed name; her brother was a University student. And she herself—yes, why not admit it?—had been engaged to an officer whose parents had refused to consent to his marriage with a poor girl—but she would rather not speak of that; the memory of it was too sad. Kasimir did not press her.

They promenaded through streets that were unfamiliar to Theresa. She thought of her childish dreams—of losing herself in strange paths and, suddenly, when least expected, returning home.

"Well, here we are!" said Kasimir simply.

She looked up. They stood before an apartment house, exactly similar to a hundred others. He took her arm and together they entered the house, walked up the stairs, past doors with brass plates and others with calling cards tacked on them, past hall windows in back of which shadows flitted to and fro, and at last reached the top floor. Kasimir opened the door with a key that screeched in the lock. In the large foyer stood a laundry bag. The walls were almost bare. On one wall hung a large calendar. Through still another door, they entered the studio.

The tremendous window was three quarters covered with a dark green curtain, so that on one side it was day, and on the other side, almost night. In the darkness stood a big easel. On it rested a picture, hidden by a dirty cloth. On an old wardrobe were some books. A paint-smeared palette lay on a long box beside a blue velvet cloak. On the floor were several half-filled gloomy looking bottles. The room reeked of turpentine, leather shoes, and a sweet-scented perfume.

Kasimir threw his hat boldly in a corner, came up to Theresa, took her head in both his hands, looked into her eyes, put his arm around her, and drew her upon his knee as he sank into the armchair. She screamed a little, for it seemed to her that one leg of the armchair was about to give way. He reassured her; then he began to kiss her, almost deliberately. His moustache smelled of pomade, exactly like a barber shop where she had once gone to fetch her father. His lips were moist and cool.

XXXI

In order to see Kasimir more often than once in two weeks, Theresa had to resort to various excuses. Once she said that she was going to a theatre with a girl friend; another time, there was a meeting with her brother which could not be postponed. Since she performed her duties as governess conscientiously, these trifling irregularities were passed over rather lightly.

Kasimir's friend, with whom he shared the studio, according to his story, had returned unexpectedly from a trip, which made it impossible for them to continue there. So the lovers, to remain undisturbed, were forced to take a room in a third-rate hotel, for which the rent was paid by Theresa when Kasimir's funds ran low. She did not mind this. In fact, it gave her a certain satisfaction. Of course, his constant financial troubles were responsible for his frequent ill-humour; once, without evident reason, he spoke to her very harshly. But when she, unaccustomed to this tone, silently left his side, quickly dressed herself, and was about to leave, he threw himself on his knees before her and begged her forgiveness—a grace which she knew she was only too ready to accord him.

During the first days of July, the attorney's family was

to move to Ischl, there to spend the summer months. Theresa wished to change her position, so as to remain near Kasimir. He himself advised her against this, and promised to visit her. He might even be venturesome enough to rent a room at a nearby farmhouse, so that they might soon be together again.

On the last Sunday before the family were to move, Theresa and Kasimir took a little excursion into the Wienerwald. Late that afternoon, they sat in a restaurant garden situated on a lawn, surrounded on all sides by swaying trees. Around the tables, people were drinking, singing, and laughing. Children were running to and fro. In the house, by an open window, a fat man in his shirt sleeves was playing a harmonica.

Today, Kasimir had money, and he deprived neither himself nor Theresa of anything. Near them sat a young married couple with two children. Kasimir began a conversation with the parents. He praised the exquisite view of the Danube, drank their health, and poured the "Weinerl" to his taste. He talked of all the delicious outlandish wines he had drunk during his travels; of Veltliner, Sankta Maura, Lacrimae Christi, and of the Xeres de la Frontera. He related stories of intoxications which he had witnessed. Then, to the amusement of the company, he imitated the contortions of a drunkard, and finally sang a comic song, to the accompaniment of the harmonica. Everybody applauded, and Kasimir bowed his thanks.

Theresa felt herself growing more and more melancholy. If she were to disappear, would he even notice it? And if she were suddenly to go out of his life, would he miss her, think about her? Frightened by her sudden insight into reality, she wondered if it would not have been better to have told him on the way of certain fears which she believed she had reason to feel, and which would also be of importance to him. Now she could not bring herself to impart such news. And why should she? Tomorrow might prove her apprehensions premature.

The sun had long since gone down. The forest stood in darkness. Night was falling gently. Several students, in red caps, marched by. Theresa looked involuntarily to see if her brother might be among them. But he did not belong to a "Colour." That, too, had been a lie, like much else that she had told Kasimir. What would Karl say, should her anxieties prove well founded? Ah, what did he care? He cared as little as the others. She did not have to account to anyone except herself.

It was almost dark when she and Kasimir made their way homeward. His arm around her, they walked down the path along the woods. They ran down an incline and she almost fell, whereupon they laughed like children. He pressed her closer, and she was happy again. All too soon they reached the valley. They wandered through the streets at a brisk pace and rode to the city in a crowded car.

Theresa was again uneasy, but Kasimir was apparently in his element among the mob of tired women, laughing children, and excited men. He joined in the stupid banter exchanged between the passengers, played the gallant, and told a fat man that he must at once relinquish his seat to the charming young lady who had just entered. He passed his cigarettes round to everyone.

Theresa was happy when the trip was over. It was not far to her house. At the door, they arranged a rendezvous for the end of the following week.

Kasimir seemed suddenly to be in haste. He did not even turn round to look after her.

XXXII

T HERESA could scarcely wait until the next meeting. During that interval, she wrote him two loving letters, but received no reply. On Saturday night, an undefinable fear trembled within her, which changed to instant delight as she saw him coming toward her, as young and jaunty as ever.

Why had he not answered her letters? What did she mean by "answered"? He had received no letters. She must have forgotten that he had moved. Moved? Of course! He had told her so. His friend had gone to Munich, and they had had to give up the studio. He was living temporarily in a small room, which was good enough for his purposes.

They had not walked far before they arrived at an old house in a narrow, unlit street, in the centre of the city. They climbed a narrow stairway to the fourth floor. Kasimir opened the apartment door. The hall was in total darkness, save for a small ray of light that gleamed through the keyhole of the kitchen door. The place smelled of gasoline.

They entered the room. Through the window, the outlines of chimneys on the houses opposite were dimly visible. The roof was so close that one could almost reach it with an extended hand. When Theresa looked out over the roofs and chimneys, she could see a large stretch of the street below. A clear view, and a quiet, central location. Perhaps he would take a lease for a year.

"Can one paint here?" asked Theresa.

"Oh, small pictures," he remarked, casually.

Kasimir had not yet lighted the candle, and in the clear moonlight that filled the room, the wardrobe, the narrow bed pushed against the window, and particularly the porcelain oven, looked cozy enough.

Kasimir laid emphasis upon the fact that they were now in one of the oldest houses in Vienna—a former palace. Part of the furniture had once belonged to a Count. Theresa wanted to look into the wardrobe, but Kasimir would not permit it. He had not been able to straighten things out yet, having only moved in that same morning. What, only this morning, yet he had not received her letters at the studio? That was strange, she thought; but she said nothing.

He had a little confession to make to her. He had been obliged to help his friend out of a difficulty, and he had not left himself enough money to provide supper. She handed him her purse, and he rushed out.

She sighed deeply, alone there, in the dark room. Why did he always lie, as though it were a matter of shame to be only a poor devil—and yet he was sometimes almost proud of it. All his lies seemed to turn upon his poverty. She would beg him to confide his troubles to her. Conditions were such that neither he nor she ought to have any secrets from one another. Today she would tell him that she expected a baby.

Kasimir was gone a long time. The thought flashed through her mind that he might never come back. Again she felt an impulse to open the wardrobe; but, unnoticed by her, he had surreptitiously abstracted the key. A small trunk stood under the bed. She pulled it out. It was unlocked. There was nothing in it except a few pieces of well patched underclothing and a frayed necktie. She closed the lid and shoved the trunk back in place. She was deeply moved. Kasimir's poverty cut her to the quick more deeply even than her own misery ever had. She felt more strangely bound to him than ever before, almost as though fate had destined them for one another. Each could help the other to bear his burdens.

As he entered with a little package and a bottle of wine, she threw her arms tempestuously about his neck. He condescendingly indulged her caresses. Whether it was only the wine that made her soul light and unloosed her tongue, or whether it was this sentiment of kinship which she had never experienced before, she did not know; but suddenly nestling in his arms, she confessed what had been locked in her bosom these many days. He was positive that she was mistaken. They would wait for a time, and then see. He said many things that would have hurt her, had she understood or cared to hear them aright.

When they descended the stairs, everything was as if she

had never divulged anything. It was long past midnight
when they bid each other goodnight at Theresa's door.
Again he was in great haste. Everything was arranged;
she knew his address, and he knew hers. Perhaps in a
few weeks they would be together again on the green, under
the starry heavens.

XXXIII

The fashionable Villa Ischl was situated in a large garden. From the balcony, one could see the bathers and cure-seekers walking up and down the esplanade. The men of the house being still in the city, the spirit of the Eppich household seemed freer; both girls were happier than Theresa had ever seen them. Frau Eppich was more friendly and kind to her than she had ever been in the city.

There were many visitors. An elegant, bald-headed young man, who had frequently dined with the Eppichs in the city, came almost daily. In the evening, he sat with Frau Eppich in the garden. Theresa took long walks with the girls. Occasionally, they were joined by younger and older friends, with their governesses, and now and again by boys and young men. Sometimes they went rowing, and, at home, there were usually harmless parlour games, in which even Theresa took part.

The older girl had become sincerely attached to Theresa, and made her her confidante. They often walked arm in arm apart from the others, and she would confide to her many of her innocent little affairs of the heart.

The beautiful countryside, the summer air, the walks out in the open—all greatly contributed to Theresa's wellbeing; and since she received a short letter from Kasimir about every other day, her spirit was free from care.

Then, abruptly, the letters ceased. Theresa became terribly excited. Her condition, which was now unmistakable, and which, at times, even delighted her, overwhelmed her suddenly with its seriousness. She sent Kasimir a special delivery letter, in which she spoke unrestrainedly of her anxiety. No word came from him; but, instead, a letter from her mother. Could not Theresa manage to visit her, now that she was only a few hours away? Theresa mentioned the invitation quite casually to Frau Eppich; and, as though they had just been waiting for such an excuse, an immediate visit to Salzburg was arranged.

The next day, Theresa started on her trip, in the company of the Eppichs and of a family acquaintance, with her son and daughter; and in addition, the elegant bald young man. At the station, Theresa left the others and hurried to her mother, who had moved to an airy corner room in a house near their old home. Frau Fabiani received her daughter in a quiet, yet affectionate manner. The strange, uncanny creature of a few years ago had entirely disappeared, and instead, there appeared an old woman.

She was pleased to hear that Theresa was happy. She herself, fortunately, had nothing to complain of. She earned a little more than was necessary for her needs, and as far as being alone was concerned, her work was benefited thereby. She wanted to know all about Theresa's present and former positions. Theresa was somewhat touched by this display of interest. But during dinner, which was ordered from a nearby restaurant, the conversation lapsed and Theresa became uncomfortable. She felt as if she were the guest of some strange, distracted old woman.

While her mother took her afternoon nap, Theresa gazed out of the window into the street. She could see the distant bridge and could almost hear the rushing of the water. She thought of the people with whom she had come to Salzburg; at that very moment, they were probably dining at the hotel. She thought of Max, of Alfred, and finally, of that strangest of strangers, Kasimir, whose child she was carrying, and who had not answered her last letters. Were he even less a stranger, he could not help her. With or without his love, she was alone.

Without disturbing her mother, she slipped quietly away, and wandered through city streets that were deserted on this hot, summer afternoon. At first, she felt inclined to visit those places which held memories for her; but these memories had lost their glamour.

Almost mechanically, she walked to the hotel where her travelling companions were stopping; they, however, had gone on a little excursion. Theresa sat in the cool lobby and glanced through the illustrated periodicals. Her eye happening to fall upon the writing room, she thought of once more sending a letter to Kasimir. She wrote to him in words of the warmest tenderness, intended to awaken anew within him the memories of the delights which they had enjoyed in common. She painted for him an alluring picture of the possibility of a meeting at night in the garden of the villa, and purposely refrained from all mention of that which was now so gravely troubling her.

She felt a certain relief when she had finished the letter. There remained nothing for her to do but return to her mother's room. Frau Fabiani was already at her work. Theresa took a book from the shelf, the nearest one at hand. It happened to be a detective story, which held her fascinated until far into the evening.

At last, her mother put aside her work and invited Theresa to walk with her. Silently, the two women strolled in the cool evening air, along the river bank; and later turned in at a modest, seldom-frequented restaurant. Frau Fabiani was treated as an habitué, and, to Theresa's surprise, drank three glasses of beer.

For the night, Theresa had to make herself as comfortable as she could on the couch. She awoke much cramped. Although there was still plenty of time before she would be required to meet the others at the station, she soon took leave of her mother, who was sleeping in a curtained alcove. She was much relieved when she found herself outside.

The morning was clear and bright. Theresa sat in the Mirabel gardens, amid the colours and odours of thousands of flowers. Two young girls, former schoolmates, passed by. They did not recognize her at first, but soon turned round and greeted her. Then they questioned one another. Theresa told them that she was a companion in a

refined Viennese home, and had just come in to visit her
mother. She wanted to know all the news of the city. But
since she did not dare to ask about Max or Alfred, she
heard only small-town gossip, which did not interest her.
Though of the same age as her two former schoolmates,
she felt years older than they. She had nothing more in
common with them or with this city, and she was glad
when, an hour later, the little company assembled at the
station, ready to leave.

XXXIV

THE next day, at Villa Ischl, Theresa waited feverishly for news from Kasimir. It was in vain. Her agitated
condition was beginning to be noticed. It was clear to her
that something would have to be done. At least, she must
talk to some one. In whom should she confide? She felt
nearest to the fifteen-year-old Bertha, who fell in love with
a different man every day. At night, before going to bed,
she would cry out her heart on Theresa's bosom. This child
seemed closer to her than any one, at that moment; she
would understand and comfort her. But soon she saw the
stupidity of the idea, and so remained silent.

Among the governesses and companions whom she had
met during the summer, there was not one toward whom she
felt inclined in friendship. They, too, may have had their
own personal experiences; yet, she feared ridicule, indiscretion and betrayal. Naturally, she knew that there were ways
and means to help her out of difficulty. She knew also that
this could not be accomplished without danger. One might
be sent to jail, become ill, or even die. She recalled a
half-forgotten story of a similar nature that had ended
tragically.

She gave herself a respite of eight days more in which

to await news from Kasimir. During this time, the distractions of country life kept her comparatively calm. When the eight days had elapsed, she pleaded for a leave of three days. She had some very important matters to discuss with her brother regarding the inheritance left them by their father. The leave was granted without question.

XXXV

THERESA arrived in Vienna at noon. She went directly to Kasimir's rooming house, and ran quickly up the stairs. An old woman opened the door. Herr Kasimir Tobisch did not live here; in fact, no one of that name had ever lived here. A few weeks ago, a man had rented the room and paid a small deposit, but he had disappeared the very next day, without leaving any clue of his present whereabouts.

Theresa was downcast and ashamed. Through the superintendent, she learned that a few letters addressed to Kasimir Tobisch had been received at that house, but that only one had been called for. Theresa saw her own handwriting staring her in the face. She begged to be allowed to take the letters. The superintendent refused to give them to her. Theresa blushed to the roots of her hair, and withdrew.

She then proceeded to the studio in which Kasimir had formerly lived. Here the name of Kasimir Tobisch was entirely unknown. Perhaps the two artists occupying the room at present might know something about him. Theresa hurried upstairs. An elderly person in a paint-besmeared smock opened the door. He knew nothing of a man named Kasimir Tobisch. The former tenant had been a Rumanian, who had left without paying his rent. Theresa stammered thanks for the information. In the artist's eyes there glowed something akin to pity. She felt his glance follow her as she descended the stairs.

Now she stood forlorn in the street. In spite of everything, she could not believe that Kasimir had left Vienna. Fortunately, she was not obliged to return immediately. She could walk the streets a few days, until she found him. Though inwardly aware of the futility and ridiculousness of her efforts, she nevertheless walked for hours, hither and thither, back and forth, until, at last, hunger and fatigue drove her into a restaurant. She sat alone in the unprepossessing room, this being much later than the usual dinner hour. While waiting for the meal to be served, she sat feverishly counting the tables, over and over again, from those in the daylight near the window to those placed in the darkest niches of the room. The restaurant in which she now sat was the dining-room of a second-rate hotel. She decided to engage quarters there.

In her room, she washed away the dust of her journey. Evening was still far distant. She looked out of her fourth floor window into the dusty street. The inimical, monotonous noises of the city reached her even there. If Kasimir were to pass, would she have time to rush down the stairs and reach him? Would she be able to recognize him at all from such a distance? The faces all seemed to fade into nothingness. Perhaps he was passing at this very moment, and she did not know it! She leaned out of the window until she became dizzy. She drew back and seated herself at the table. The noises of the street receded.

Her loneliness, her complete detachment, and the consciousness that, at this moment, no one knew of her whereabouts, gave her, for a time, a strange feeling of calm, almost of well-being. Why had she been so restless during these past days and weeks, as though she were actually threatened by some palpable danger? What had she to fear? To whom did she owe an accounting? To her mother? Or to her brother? They certainly had never troubled themselves about her. To her employers, who paid her for her services and would, whenever it pleased them, dismiss her like a stranger? What did these people matter to her?

When last in Salzburg, she had learned from her mother that her inheritance was somewhat larger than she had imagined. With that, she could surely manage for a few months, and therefore would not be a burden to any one. Perhaps, after all, it was best for all concerned that she had not met and would have nothing more to do with Kasimir. Who knows? He might even have been capable of extorting those few gulden from her that were to tide her over her difficult period.

Why had she come to Vienna? What did she want of him? Ah, why question? She knew only too well. She wanted him—his kisses, his caresses. And then again, after a short time of peace, she became despondent. It was for his sake that she had come to Vienna—hoping, yearning, yet filled with anxiety lest she find him not. Now she knew

without a doubt that he was gone. He had simply fled, so
as to avoid all responsibilities and all unpleasantness.

Was that not stupid of him? Did he not realize that she
would never have made any demands upon him? Why
had she not told him? He had no duties toward her. She
had not been an innocent, inexperienced girl when she gave
herself to him. And she always knew that he was a poor
wretch. She would never have required anything of him.
And the child? Well, that was her affair—hers, alone!

The room had grown quite dark. Outside, the city was
covered by a dismal light. What now? Should she go out
into the street? Wander aimlessly about? And then the
night, and morning! She could not possibly meet him
accidentally, even if he were still in the city. She had nothing more to do here. Almost with a feeling of relief, she
determined to return to Ischl at once. She paid her bill,
ran down the stairs, and took a cab to the station. When
at last she had settled herself in a compartment, she instantly fell into a deep sleep, from which she did not
awaken until the train was within fifteen minutes of her
destination.

XXXVI

THERESA was treated with great consideration by the Eppich household. Even the guests were polite to her, almost as though she were a poorer yet entirely worthy member of the family. A young, unprepossessing lawyer, quite myopic and of a delicate, sickly appearance, paid her marked attention. He spoke to her of his sad youth, his studies, and his experiences as a teacher. She felt that he was somewhat overrating her; yes, mistaking her for a person entirely remote from what she actually was.

She, upon her part, told him many things—about her parents, her brother, and about Alfred, her first love; all in the slightly casual and often untruthful manner to which she had lately become accustomed. She was completely silent about Max, and related her adventure with Kasimir as though it had been most harmless—just a few friendly walks.

On the last day of his stay, while in the woods, the two lagged behind the rest of the company. With a very clumsy gesture, the young lawyer attempted to embrace her. She pushed him back vehemently; then, forgave him, and gave him permission to write to her. She never heard from him again.

127

Toward the end of August, young Herr Eppich arrived. His sisters, who did not get on very well with him, were nevertheless happy to see him, and all their girl friends promptly fell in love with him. According to the current style, he had shaved his moustache, and every one found that he resembled a certain famous actor and matinee idol.

At first, he was very reticent with Theresa. One day, on the stairs, he jestingly refused to allow her to pass, and she did not resist him as strongly as she had intended to. When she had entered her room, she locked the door after her. She looked out of the window and saw the young gentleman step out into the garden, a cigarette between his lips, without so much as a backward glance.

Dr. Eppich had come for two days. Something unpleasant seemed to have happened between his wife and himself. Every one noticed it. He left without making his farewells. The younger daughter cried much during the next few days. It was quite apparent to Theresa that this twelve-year-old knew more about the matters then going on, and felt them more deeply, than any of the others.

One night, Theresa started up in fright. She had heard a noise at her door. The thought came to her that George was trying to gain entrance to her room. Instead of fear, she felt a pleasurable excitement; and when all remained still after that, she was frankly disappointed. That which had flashed through her mind many times since that day on the stairs, was becoming a sort of plan during the sleepless night. She felt that in George she might assure her child of a father. Of course, it was high time for her to look for one. But as if the young man had divined her intentions, he kept aloof and distant. Theresa was at first surprised at his reticence, but during the course of the next few days, she discovered that he was carrying on an intrigue with a young woman who frequented the house.

She was by no means jealous. Her anger with herself soon changed to shame. She felt deserted. And more and more, she was conscious of the distressing nature of her condition and the danger of her situation. Above all, the thought of meeting her brother filled her with an almost ridiculous panic. At the same time, she was certain that most of the women she knew, and in particular, those of her profession, had gone through similar experiences and had known how to procure help for themselves. One could not ask outright, but surely, one might turn the conversation in such a manner as to learn something useful.

Among the nursemaids and governesses of her acquaintance, there were only two with whom she occasionally conversed in a lighter vein, without, however, touching upon any really delicate themes. One was a thin, pale, faded, and seemingly sweet person, who chattered, not only of the family in which she was employed, but of every one she knew, in the most acrimonious manner. She was addressed as Fräulein, though it was known that she was either a widow or a divorcée.

The other was a brunette, not yet thirty, and a girl of

exceptionally pleasant qualities. Many amours were attributed to her, though not one had ever been proven against her. This was the person, Theresa thought, best able to advise her. While walking with her one drizzly afternoon in the middle of September, their charges some little distance ahead of them, she began, in a rather clumsy fashion, to talk of the many children in the Bank Director's house where Fräulein Rosa was employed. But since she hesitated to put a direct question to her, she learned nothing that she did not already know . . . namely, that there were obliging women, and also doctors, to whom one might resort in such emergencies, and that the attendant dangers were not at all too great.

This superficial information had the effect of calming Theresa. The light, careless manner in which the other treated the entire subject, convinced her that that which had appeared obnoxious and dangerous was in reality not so difficult, if it were not indeed to be regarded merely as a matter of routine. It was an accident that occurred in the lives of many women, and left no further traces. For her, too, it should mean nothing more serious than that.

XXXVII

Autumn had come, and the family moved back to the city. Theresa scanned the papers, not for advertisements of positions, but for other information which might prove more useful to her in her present exigency. One afternoon, she entered an old house in the central part of the city, mounted the tortuous stairs, and, a few minutes later, sat opposite a pleasant, middle-aged lady, who was bathed in the pink light that penetrated through the curtains.

The comfortable room, furnished in the usual style, did not in any way divulge the secret of the lady's profession. Theresa, with no timidity, yet with some care, managed to put forth her troubles. The pleasant lady mentioned that, scarcely half an hour before, a young Baroness had come to her for an appointment—the second this year. She told further of her fashionable "clientèle," that she had recruited even from the nobility. She jested mildly of the light-headedness of young girls; then without transition, spoke of a very wealthy manufacturer who had recently come in with an actress. This man was tiring of his sweetheart, and she thought she could arrange a meeting for Theresa.

Theresa took leave with the promise to think the matter

over and come again on the following day. As she stepped
out of the door, she saw a man standing there. He was
dressed in a black overcoat with a shabby black velvet
collar, and carried a brief-case. Her heart throbbed painfully. She saw herself arrested, accused, and thrown into
prison. And only when she had lost herself in the crowd
below did she really become calmer.

This first experience did not discourage her. The very
next evening, she visited a woman who had likewise advertised in the paper, but would not give her address except
through mail. On the third floor of a new house was a
sign on which was printed in gold letters: "Gottfried
Ruhsam." A neatly dressed maid ushered Theresa into an
almost elegant salon. While waiting, she looked at a photo-
graph album, in which she recognized the familiar faces
of many famous personages of the stage.

At last, a man entered, greeted her hastily, and then disappeared through another door. A little later he came back
in the company of a slim, no longer young lady, dressed
in a comfortable, though well-fitting house-dress. Again
the man disappeared, after murmuring a quiet "pardon!"
Theresa intercepted the affectionate glance with which Frau
Ruhsam followed him to the door. "My husband," she
said; and, almost by way of apology, she added: "He is
nearly always on the road." Then:

"Well, how can I be of service to you, my dear child?"
Theresa expressed herself even more carefully than she had

the day before. The woman understood her at once, and asked when she proposed to take up her abode in her house. Theresa answered that such a thought had not entered her mind. The lady stiffened a little, and declared that she seldom agreed to any such arrangement as that which Theresa wished, but she would make an exception in this case, and take all the risks and responsibilities upon herself. She mentioned, however, a price which was out of the question for Theresa.

At that, Frau Ruhsam warned her not to commit any stupidities. She spoke of a man who had married a young girl, even though he knew she had had a child by another man. She cautioned Theresa to beware of the women who advertised in the papers. Only recently, two of them had been arrested.

Theresa was red and confused. She wandered through the streets in the warm, autumn rain as though in a dream. By pure chance, she found herself presently before the house in which she and Kasimir had last been together. Following a sudden impulse, she asked the superintendent if Herr Tobisch had called for the other letters. To her utter astonishment, she discovered that he had, and that only the day before. A new hope sprung up within her.

In a nearby coffee-house, she wrote Kasimir a letter that held no reproaches, but only passionate assurances of her unalterable love. She would ask him no questions; she realized that there were secrets in an artist's life. She was in excellent health, and wanted much to see him again, no matter where, if only for a quarter of an hour. She left the letter with the janitor. That night she slept well, and awoke with a hazy, happy feeling, as though something uncommonly agreeable had happened to her the day before.

XXXVIII

For a time, Theresa attempted nothing at all. Sometimes, in the evening, after her day's duties were done, a certain calm would come over her. She would wake at night and think. Everything seemed unreal. Her present condition, her entire life, all seemed strange to her. The figures of her father, her mother, Alfred, Max, Kasimir passed through her mind like phantoms. And the most unreal, impossible thing of all was that, almost without her being aware of it, something alive was developing within her, her mother's grandchild—a creature destined to fate, to youth and age, to fortune and misfortune, to love, sickness, and death, like every one else—just as herself. And since she did not understand it, she simply could not believe it possible, as though, after all, in spite of everything, she must be mistaken.

A too abrupt, well-meant, but not to be misunderstood remark made by the servant, brought her to her senses with a start. People were beginning to suspect how matters stood with her. At the thought, her heart almost stood still with fear. She realized again the seriousness of her position. Once again she attempted what she had twice before tried in vain. This time, the woman whom she went to see im-

mediately inspired her with confidence. She spoke sensibly
and kindly to her, stressing the illegality of her profession,
of which she was not in ignorance. The laws were stupid,
and had no consideration for one's social position. She
closed her discourse philosophically with the remark that
it were best on all accounts for people not to be born at
all. The charges were not exorbitant, and it was arranged
that Theresa should present herself for the operation in
two days.

Theresa felt a great sense of release. The peaceful seren-
ity in which she passed the next day made the fictitious-
ness of her calm in the past few weeks all the more clear
in her mind. Her condition seemed perfectly natural, and
not at all serious. All thought of the disagreeableness and
the dangers which she had feared now left her mind. She
was serene.

Yet, as she mounted the stairs, on the appointed day, her
calm suddenly left her. She rang the bell quickly, so as
not to be tempted to flee down the stairs again. But the
maid informed Theresa that her employer was out on a
case, and would not be back for several days. Theresa
breathed freely again. It seemed to her that a painful duty
had not merely been postponed, but actually accomplished.

On the first floor, two women stood talking. When
Theresa passed, they ceased their conversation, looked at
each other queerly, and smiled knowingly. A cab stood
below in front of the door. The cab driver greeted her so
politely that she felt certain he was enjoying a private jest

at her expense. On the way home, she felt that she was being followed. Of course, she knew that all was purely imaginary. She no longer felt conspicuous because the cab driver bowed politely, and even the two women on the stairs did not frighten her. Nevertheless, she knew that she could not make that trip again, nor venture her luck with another such obliging woman.

It occurred to her to go back to Salzburg and confess everything to her mother. She surely would understand and know of some means to help her daughter. Even worse predicaments than this occurred in her romances; and they ended happily, for all that. And in the Salzburg house, many suspicious things had happened. Had she not seen officers and veiled women slip out mysteriously in the dead of the night? And had not her mother attempted to foist her on the old Count? But even so, how could her mother be of any use? She gave up the idea.

Then she thought of going away, anywhere, until after the child was born. She could place it in the care of a young, childless couple; give it to them, or simply leave it on somebody's doorstep and flee. Finally, she wondered, should she not look up Alfred, confide in him, and plead for his counsel? Such ideas and many others passed through her mind, but she discarded them all as futile. These thoughts came to her not only at night, when she was alone, but even at the dinner table and when she was out walking with the girls. Yes, even when she was helping them with their lessons. She was so accustomed to performing her duties mechanically and spiritlessly that no one seemed to notice what was going on within her.

Meanwhile, the woman to whom she had last appealed for help and advice must surely have returned from her case. Theresa reflected that she could do nothing more sensible than go once again to this woman. She made an appointment for the next day by letter. She did not mention her name, but recalled herself to the lady's mind by mentioning their former conversation.

A few hours before the time set for the visit, there came a letter from Kasimir. He had been, so he wrote her, at home with his mother; he was greatly surprised that he had received no communication from Theresa while she was at Ischl. It was only a moment ago that he had discovered her letter in the janitor's lodge of the house "where once we were so blissfully happy." Those were his words. Theresa became faint as she perused them. He must see her again, he concluded, even though his life depended on it.

She realized very well that he was lying. She felt certain that he had never been away; that he had most assuredly received all of her letters, and not merely the last one, as he claimed. Even his lies, she reflected, were part of him; the very part, indeed, that made him so adorable and attractive. And at that moment she experienced such a deep love for him that she desired nothing more than to hold him for ever, to bind him to herself for all eternity. And this was possible, so she reflected, primarily because there still was plenty of time; still many weeks must intervene before she would have to inform him of her condition. What she had already told him some time ago, he had no doubt already forgotten. However, if he still remembered it and she herself kept silent about it, he would gladly infer, then, that she had been mistaken. Nothing mattered but to be with him, to lie again in his beloved arms.

They met near the entrance of the Stadtpark, as they had done many a time before, in those lovely days of long ago. It was a cold, miserable autumn evening, and Kasimir was already awaiting her when she appeared. He seemed to her to have become somewhat more slender. He wore a rather short, bright-coloured raincoat, with the collar upturned; a coat that seemed much too thin for protection against the raw weather. He greeted her as though they had last seen each other but a few days ago. Why in the world, he asked, had she not written to him? She assured him timidly, in reply, that she had written; and, what was more, that the letters had been called for and delivered.

"What, called for?" he cried out, in surprise. "In all probability, they fell into the hands of an impostor. It's positively dreadful. Just wait until I get back. I'll make it hot for the janitor!"

She asked him why he had not sent her word at Ischl that he had left to pay a visit to his mother.

"Yes, you're right in asking that. But if you had any idea of the conditions at home! My mother's brother committed suicide."

As he said this, he pointed shyly to the black band surrounding his soft, gray hat.

"But I would rather not tell you now all the things I learned while at home. Some other time, dearest, I'll let you know everything."—In such wise did he express himself.—"Now, everything is all right again. I even have hopes of obtaining a permanent position on the staff of an illustrated newspaper, and in addition, an art dealer has undertaken to sell a few of my pictures."

In the dining-room which she recognized so well, and which she noticed had not become any more pleasant since her last visit, he became more tender than he had ever been, and happy, too, just as in the days when she had first known him. He questioned her about her summer vacation, and jestingly demanded to be informed if she had also remained faithful to him. In reply, she stared dumbly at him, quite failing to comprehend his question, as though certain plans, which she had afterwards discarded, had never really existed for her. She told him of her walks, her trip to Salzburg, and the demands of her work which, she complained, exhausted her.

Kasimir shook his head disapprovingly at this last comment.

"It's beastly," he asserted, with vigour, "to have to exist in such a state of slavery. But it won't last much longer, you may rest assured! In any case, you must leave your position with the Eppich family and try to support yourself by giving lessons. I'll soon have a fixed income;

then, we can occupy an apartment together. And really, after all is said and done, why should we not, as a matter of fact, get married? Wouldn't it really be the most sensible thing to do—why, in a certain sense, even the most practical thing to do?"

Notwithstanding the warnings of her better judgment, she could not forbear to accord him again her complete confidence. To be sure, timid doubts tried to assert themselves in her mind; but she crushed them, before they could take possession of her. Nevertheless, she was careful not to betray anything of her condition to Kasimir. The right moment for confession, so she thought, had not yet arrived. "Who knows," she mused herself, "how long it will be before the confession will be received by him as welcome and joyful news?"

XXXIX

THREE days later, on a Sunday afternoon, they met again. For the first time since their acquaintance began, he brought her some flowers, and what aroused her to even greater excitement, he offered a small sum of money—in payment, as he expressed it, "of a part of his debt." She refused to think of receiving it, but he insisted with so much vigour that she at last consented to take the money out of his first month's salary. He readily agreed to this proposal, and pocketed the money once more.

"And now," he proceeded, "I must beg your forgiveness for mentioning a matter of which I have never spoken to you before, but which I can no longer conceal."

This preamble seemed ominous to her; but how quickly and gladly did she pardon him, when all that he had to confess was that he had this time spoken to his mother about her.

"And why not? In a short time, you two women will know each other and love each other well!"

Tears arose in Theresa's eyes. Now she, too, refused to conceal any secrets from him. He listened to her confession calmly, earnestly, and with obvious emotion.

"I had a suspicion that things were so; and all in all,

it is a sign that we were meant for each other and that we must live together for ever. It's a genuine sign of fate. But," he continued, "I consider it my duty to warn you against acting in too much haste. In the meantime, you had better not give up your position with the Eppich family. One can't notice it on you at all. You mustn't leave the place before the New Year, in any case. It is two months until then, and goodness knows what might not take place in the meanwhile, especially as my affairs are apparently beginning to change for the better."

She left his arms calmed and almost joyful.

"I'll let you hear from me," he assured her, "in two or three days, at the very most."

Yet she had to wait a whole week for the promised information; and when it came, it proved to be a terrible disappointment, for Kasimir wrote that he was compelled to leave for home very suddenly on some business in connection with the settlement of his late uncle's estate. She wrote to him at once, in care of the address which he left her. She wrote a second and even a third time, but received no answer. At last, she decided to do something that she had not done before; namely, to fill out a return address envelope. Three days later, she received it back in person from the letter-carrier. It was marked: "Addressee Unknown."

Her shock was not so keen as she had anticipated, for she was in reality prepared, deep down in her soul, for precisely such an eventuality. But now she also knew that there could be no other way out for her, however the af·

fair might turn, but the way which she had determined upon long ago. Nevertheless, she postponed from day to day putting her decision into execution; her anxiety mounted. Bad dreams troubled her sleep. And to cap this, it chanced that again, just at this time, there appeared articles in the newspapers about a suit against a physician for a crime against "budding life." Theresa became fully convinced that she would assuredly die, if she permitted the fearful operation to be performed upon her. But, as soon as she had decided to do nothing definite and let matters run their natural course, there came upon her a strange feeling of restfulness, at once blissful and incomprehensible.

XL

ONCE, as she was walking with her wards through the central section of the city, she led them, partly by accident, partly with conscious intent, into the Cathedral of Saint Stephan. Since that memorable summer day when she had received the news of her father's death, she had not been inside a church. They halted in front of a side altar, which stood in almost total darkness. The younger girl, who was inclined to piety, knelt down and seemed to pray. The elder allowed her glance to wander at random. Her whole attitude bespoke her boredom.

Theresa felt her heart rise again with new courage. She had never been religious, in the true sense of the word. As a child and as a young girl, she had always taken part in the prescribed religious exercises, with zeal, but without genuine emotion. Today for the first time, a strong inner need caused her to bow her head. She folded her hands prayfully, but her lips were firmly closed. When she left, she did so with the firm intention of returning again, soon and often. And, in fact, thenceforward she seized every opportunity, either when alone or with the girls, though it might be but for a few minutes, to enter any church that she happened to encountered on her path, to say a short prayer. Soon that failed to satisfy her, and on the first Sunday in December, she asked permission of Frau Eppich, who manifested no surprise at the request, to take the morning off to go to early mass. There, whether on account of early morning fatigue or because of a lack of real piety, of which she accused herself—there, in the crowd, she remained unmoved, despite the rich music of the organ and the sacred unction of the ceremonies; and when she left the church and stepped out into the cold, frosty morning air, she felt more downcast than ever.

She now recited her prayers every evening at home, with an intensity even greater than any that she had ever displayed in the days of her childhood. And just as in those days prayer had come easily to her and she had begged the grace of heaven upon her parents, her teachers, her girl friends, and even her dolls, so now she prayed for divine mercy and forgiveness, not alone for herself, but also for her mother, whom she recognized as a lost and erring soul; for the child, whose first stirrings she now felt within her; and even for Kasimir, who, whatever else he might be, had sired this child, and who would perhaps one day find his way back to it—and perhaps also to her. And once she even offered up a prayer for her father's everlasting bliss, and then dropped bitter but healing tears upon her pillow.

A few days before Christmas, Frau Eppich called Theresa into her room and informed her that she was sorry that they could not longer keep her in the house. "I was really hoping that you would voluntarily take your leave at the right time," she said, "but since, for some incomprehensible reason, you seem to fail to realize your situation, I must insist, if only on account of the girls, that you leave today, or at the very latest, tomorrow."

"To-morrow," replied Theresa, almost in a whisper.

Frau Eppich nodded assent.

"Everybody in the house is already prepared for your departure. I have told them," Frau Eppich explained, "that your mother in Salzburg is ill."

Softly, and as if mechanically, Theresa replied:

"In any case, I thank you for your kindness, my gracious lady!"

She went immediately to her room and started to pack her belongings.

The leave-taking took place quickly and without any special excitement. Dr. Eppich expressed the hope that her mother might soon be well again; the girls believed, or pretended to believe, that Theresa would soon return; but in the mocking face of young Master George, she clearly read the thought: What a clever dog I am!

XLI

SHE spent another night with Frau Kausick. But before the next morning had come, she realized that she could not prolong her sojourn among so much wretchedness and squalor. She considered her situation. Since her entire portion of her father's estate had been paid to her, she hoped, with some economy, to make it last possibly a year. Above all else, she had to find a suitable refuge for her approaching confinement. "But after that?" she asked herself. "What then, when all this will no longer concern myself alone?" Thought and breath failed her, as though she now for the first time realized with complete clearness what the future held in store for her. And suddenly she thought of Frau Ruhsam as the only person from whom she might receive sympathetic understanding, not only of her physical condition, but of her spiritual situation as well.

The friendly aspect of Frau Ruhsam, as evoked in her memory, aroused her to new hope. She went to seek her at once, without confessing to herself that any expectation drew her thither, other than of merely finding a haven for the period of her confinement.

Frau Ruhsam did not appear the least surprised at seeing Theresa again. As the latter approached the subject of her mission by asking timid and clumsy questions, Frau Ruhsam exhibited some impatience and, thinking that Theresa lacked the courage to state the actual issue, sought to come to her assistance by volunteering the information that she could recommend a physician who might perform the small operation at her home.

"Of course, the costs—" said Frau Ruhsam; but Theresa cut her short. She explained that she had not come on that account; that she no longer contemplated such measures. "Oh, I see!" observed Frau Ruhsam. "Then it is to arrange for lodgings. That would be"—she paused and eyed Theresa critically—"until about the middle or the end of May." As it happened, she had a few calls for just about that time, but she would see what could be done.

Though Theresa had not thought of it before, the offer attracted her. Here she would find rest, friendliness, and perhaps kindness—everything she longed for. She inquired as to the terms. At the rate quoted, a stay of three weeks would have consumed Theresa's whole fortune.

"It's really not too high," declared Frau Ruhsam. "Perhaps you will come sometime with your husband, and your husband will then see that for himself. I don't think you'll find anything better, and I promise absolute discretion. As regards the police notification, even that I can manage to arrange."

Theresa replied that she would talk the matter over with her husband, and left.

She decided to remain with Frau Kausick for the time being, at any rate. Soon she even became adapted to the humble circumstances which she found in the Kausick establishment. Frau Kausick was away all day. Theresa thus spent most of her time with the children, and she enjoyed helping them with their lessons and playing with them, thus keeping her tutorial talents in practice, so to speak. In addition, she felt safe here from any possibility of discovery, precisely as if she were in a strange city. And gradually, she adapted herself to the people among whom she now moved, not alone in her physical manner of living, but also in her language, even to the point of speaking in their dialect. From day to day, she spent less care upon her clothes; and the rapidly changing form of her body encouraged in her a carelessness which further operated to shut her out at the same time from her former world.

In order to dispel the monotony which frequently seized her, she subscribed to a circulating library in the suburbs, and quickly devoured many carelessly chosen books during the numerous hours which she spent alone in her wretched chamber, always fascinated by, and often deeply engrossed in the spectacle of a fantastic and trivial world. There were also a few casual conversations, held mostly on the stairs, with the humble families of the neighbourhood. And if ever anybody made a remark about Theresa's condition, it happened casually, goodnaturedly, jestingly, for no one in this circle found anything unusual in Theresa's pregnancy, or even particularly noticed it.

But there were moments, especially in the early morning, while she still lay in bed, when, awakening from her stupor, she would see her whole existence as an unintelligible and unworthy thing. But no sooner did she become aware of her corpulency, as she usually did after her first involuntary movement, than she felt as though there rushed forth from the new life that was developing within her, a stream of sweet exhaustion, which seeped through all her limbs from some hidden source—a stream in which her whole being, given over fearlessly and humbly to a natural fate, magically dissolved.

She was singularly free from all the ailments which confinement usually brings to women; on the contrary, she experienced a condition of increased wellbeing. Only a certain physical lassitude increased from day to day; and it frequently happened that when, in the morning, she sat on the bed, combing her hair, she would remain for minutes with the comb in her hair as though petrified, and she would stare at the strange face which looked back at her from the wooden framed mirror which hung on the otherwise bare wall in front of her—a pale, mealy, almost bloated face, with half-open, somewhat livid lips, and large, amazed, vacuous eyes. Then, suddenly recovering from her blankness, she would shake her head, comb her hair, sing softly to herself, rise with some difficulty, and approach the mirror, so that, for a moment, her image would disappear in the vapour of her breath. When it reappeared, a queer expression of sorrow would seem to suffuse it—

an expression which Theresa had not noticed before.

On a clear day in February, when she had just read a chapter in a novel in which the activities of a large city at night were temptingly described, the desire awoke in her to go again and see something equally happy and brilliant; and it seemed to her that nothing could be easier than to satisfy this longing. All that was necessary was to conceal her face behind a veil; with her figure, she felt certain that no one would recognize her.

Late in the afternoon, she left the house. At first, she felt a perceptible heaviness in her limbs, which, however, disappeared as though by magic as soon as Theresa arrived on a principal thoroughfare whose long and well-illuminated parallels seemed but to hint of still brighter and more beautiful regions. She rode on the street-car to the opera, allowed herself to be pushed forward by the crowds, stopped here and there in front of window displays, and was both excited and overjoyed at all the light, the noise, and the crowds.

She attended to a few minor, long-needed purchases; and it gave her a queer feeling to be spoken to, for the first time in her life, as "gnädige Frau." When she left the store, a great feeling of lassitude overcame her. She hastened home, and went to bed at once.

Frau Kausick asked her casually what plans she had made for the near future.

"You cannot possibly remain here," said she, "and I

think it high time that you looked about for a suitable place."

Frau Kausick mentioned the Foundling Hospital. Theresa shuddered at the thought. On the following morning, she went out to look for a room.

XLII

THE undertaking proved to be more difficult than she had anticipated. Every room had its own drawbacks, which were not at first apparent. It thus happened that Theresa had to change her residence three times in several weeks. Then, at last, she found a room on the fourth floor of a rooming house. It was kept by an old woman, was very clean and neat—and, by luck, was not above a room where children could be heard crying and screaming, or a drunken couple quarreling at every hour. The landlady seemed, from her appearance and speech, to belong to the better class. At home, she wore a faded, though well-made dress of pink satin, and while house-cleaning, which she herself attended to, she wore long gloves, which showed signs of frequent mending. During the first few days, she spoke only briefly to Theresa as she prepared her humble lunch, and seemed not to desire to enter into a more protracted conversation. In the afternoon, she usually left the house not to return until late at night.

Hence, Theresa was much alone; and when alone, she loved to take advantage of her privilege to use the so-called parlour. With its bright curtains and the oil paintings on the wall, the parlour seemed more pleasant than Theresa's bare room. After many changes of lodgings which she had made in the last few weeks, she felt so tired and heavy that she could hardly bring herself to go out of the house.

She stopped reading books, but still continued to read the newspapers, which she devoured from the first to the last word, in a thoroughly mechanical manner, without really knowing in the end what the news of the day really was. Then she attempted to recall to her memory the various people who had been of significance in her life. But she seldom succeeded in concentrating her attention on any definite person, even for a short time. All the images disappeared at once, and they all floated about, vague and remote, like figures fancied in a dream. She fared no better even when she thought about herself. Once again she contemplated herself objectively. She felt lost; she could not comprehend her being or her fate—that the bloated body upon which she gazed, the hands which lay clasped upon her knees, really belonged to her; that her father had died in an insane asylum; that she had been the sweetheart of a Lieutenant, that in some Moravian or Bohemian village, or God knows where, somewhere out in the world, lived a man whose child she was bearing. All this seemed as unreal to her as the child itself—the child which, these many weeks, had given unmistakable signs of its existence, and whose heart she could feel beating in unison with her own.

It seemed to her as if some time in the past, she had loved this still unborn child. She hardly knew when, and whether it had been for an hour or for many days. Now she experienced none of this love. Neither did she feel surprise or regret that things stood with her as they did.

A mother . . . she knew that she was destined to become one, that she was actually a mother already; but it really concerned her not at all. She asked herself: would it have been different, if she had fulfilled the duties of her sex in a more fitting way than that fated to her; for example, if she were legally bound to the father of the child, or if, as a wife, she awaited the hour of birth in a well-ordered home. But all this was so far beyond her comprehension she could not even visualize it as a happy state.

Now and then, she was visited by another fancy. Since she felt no mother love stirring within her—no longing for, and hardly any knowledge of the child—perhaps, after all, it might be a delusion, a monstrous mistake. She had once read or heard of cases which bore all the resemblances of pregnancy, but yet were not. Was it possible, since her soul knew nothing and desired to know nothing of the child, that that which she had experienced physically in the past months was nothing else than repentance, bad conscience, fear—emotions which she denied to herself, and which betrayed their presence in this manner? The strangest thing, however, was that she did not long for her term of pregnancy to end; on the contrary she felt a certain diffidence about having to return to the world which she had left. Would she ever again be able to adapt herself to the normal routine of life; ever again be able to talk with intelligent people, and follow a regular routine of business. Could she ever again be a woman among women? She was now far removed from any willing or doing; and she had no other connection with the world than the bit of blue sky which she could see as she leaned back in the corner of the sofa. Thus, Theresa's mind willingly lost itself in idle speculations, as though she perceived that, as soon as she returned to practicality, only sorrow and pain would await her.

What appeared at times as somewhat strange to Theresa, was the circumstance that Frau Nebling seemed to notice absolutely nothing of her condition. At any rate, she did not take the slightest interest in it. At noon, the two women would sit together; in the afternoons, Frau Nebling always left the house, not to return before a late hour. At times, the consciousness of her solitude completely overwhelmed Theresa, like a sudden shock. Once she decided to invite Sylvia to come to see her and wrote her a short note. But when the latter called to see her on the following Sunday, Theresa instructed Frau Nebling to inform her that she had again moved away, she did not know where.

One day, as she was looking out of the window, she saw her brother rounding the corner. She quickly retreated into the room and feared for a few minutes that he had seen her and had gone into the house to ask for her. But immediately she felt annoyed at this silly apprehension because, as she said to herself, there was no man in the world to whom she was less responsible than to him. Furthermore, she felt quite secure from detection.

Frau Nebling had not even hinted that Theresa's further stay would be uncomfortable or painful to her. She did not lack money, for the time being. "And if it becomes necessary," thought Theresa, "I can have a doctor called who will be sworn to secrecy. It is unthinkable that Frau Nebling would turn me out of the house with a child on only a day's notice. Whatever happens, I shall manage to set things in order here, without having to hurry."

During these days, she toyed at times with the idea of writing to Alfred. She knew, however, that she would not do so; but this was a picture which she loved to embroider. She would imagine him calling on her, deeply moved by her plight—very deeply moved. She dreamed on—he still loved her, and surely he would also love her child; he had made her his wife; he was a country doctor, and they lived in a beautiful region; she bore him two children, no, three. And was he not really the father of this first child whom she was expecting? That fellow, Kasimir Tobisch—did he really exist? Had he not always seemed somewhat like a ghost? He might have been Satan himself!

Alfred was her friend—her only friend. Yes, he was her lover, even though he knew nothing about it. And his appearance took on a new and wonderful transformation in the recollection of her heart. His soft, much too soft features were ennobled, so that he almost appeared to her in the image of a saint. His voice seemed to her, through the distances of time, to be low and sweet; and when, in her retrospective thoughts, she saw him tenderly embracing her in that wide, dark field at home, she felt as though she were soaring with him above the earth, heaven-bent.

XLIII

On a night in April, ten days earlier than she had anticipated, Theresa was surprised by the pangs of childbirth. She leaped out of bed and knocked on Frau Nebling's door. The landlady was not yet home. She thought of running downstairs, or at least of calling to the porter's wife from the landing. But she stopped before she reached the door: the pains had already abated. She turned back into her room and got into bed. A few minutes later, the pains began to manifest themselves again.

"Is there still time to get to a hospital?" she asked herself. "Shall I call a carriage from the window? Could I not manage to go there on foot? It is not far from here."

She rose again, opened her bureau, and began to remove pieces of clothing and linen. Then, exhausted, she dropped her hands and sat down again. A short while later, she paced up and down the room in renewed, ever more harrowing pain. Then she returned to her bed, lay down, and moaned and sobbed. Could she be heard? She wanted people to hear her.

"Why should they not hear me? Is what is happening to me shameful? Nobody in the house knows who I am. My name itself means little. But why did I give them the right one? Why did I stay in Vienna, anyhow? Couldn't I have hidden away in the country? Is it really possible? Am I actually bearing a child? I, Theresa Fabiani, the daughter of a Lieutenant and of a noble lady—am I bearing a child? Will it really be true that I have borne an illegitimate child?"

Frau Nebling suddenly appeared at the open door, her eyes wide with fright. She had heard Theresa's cries below on the stairs.

"What, have I cried? Oh, it was nothing. It can't be anything yet. At the very earliest, there will still be ten days. I was only startled at awakening from a bad dream."

Frau Nebling left, reassured. Theresa heard the moving of furniture and the hushed voices in the next room, which she had become accustomed to hear every evening. A window was opened, then closed again. She began to fall asleep. Then, suddenly, the pain returned. She fought it down again with great effort, clenching a handkerchief between her teeth and stretching her arms on the pillow.

"Am I mad?" she asked herself. "What am I doing? What do I want? Oh, if only I could die! Perhaps I am dying! Then everything will be all right. What shall I do with my child? What will my brother say about it?"

All the modesty of her girlhood days awakened again within her. It seemed inexplicable to her, like the evil deception of a nightmare—such a thing as happens only to others, or such as one might read about in the newspapers and in novels. But that such a thing should actually be in the process of being fulfilled upon her was incredible.

"Perhaps there is still time to make an end of it all!" she thought. Then, suddenly, she cried out: "Help! Help!"

Again she jumped out of bed and dragged herself through the hall to the door of Frau Nebling's room. She listened a moment, then knocked. There was no sound. Then she recovered her self-possession.

"What do I want of Frau Nebling? I don't need her. I don't need anybody. I want to be alone, just as I have been for so long a time. I like it better that way."

She lay quietly in her bed, until the pains suddenly overwhelmed her with such mighty force that she could not even cry out.

"Now," she thought, "now it is too late to call for any help. No, no! Help! No! I want to die! It is best that I should die—I, and the child, and the whole world with us!"

XLIV

Relief had come at last. An exhaustion, deep as death, yet filling her with joy, took possession of Theresa as she lay on the bed. The candle on the table had been burning the whole night. "When did I light it?" She could not recall. And there was the child. There it lay, with its half-open, blinking eyes and a wrinkled, ugly, senile face.

He is probably dead. Surely it is dead. And if it is not yet dead, it will surely die in the next moment. "That is exactly what ought to happen, for the mother who bore you must also die!"

She lacked the strength to turn her head. Her lids kept closing in spite of her efforts to stay awake, and she breathed short, deep sighs.

Suddenly it seemed to her that the child's features had moved; its arms and feet moved also, and its mouth was pursed as though it were about to cry. She heard a soft, complaining voice. Theresa was amazed. Now that the child gave evidence of life, its presence became strangely ominous; yes, even threatening.

"My child!" she thought. "And this child is an independent being, existing for itself alone! It has breath, sight, and a wee, small voice; a very tiny bright little voice, which comes from a new, live soul! And it is my child! But I do not love it. Why do I not love it, since it is my child? Perhaps it is merely because I am so tired; too tired to love anything on earth."

And it seemed then to her that she would never recover from her utter weariness.

"Why should you want to come into the world?" she asked, in the depths of her heart, of the gently whimpering, wrinkled creature, as she stretched out her right arm toward it and tried to draw it close to her. "What will you do in the world, without father, or mother? And what shall I do with you? It is well that you are soon to die. I will tell everybody that you never really lived at all. Who will care? Were you not already dead? Did I not consult three or four women, so that you might not be born? What shall I do with you now? Can I travel about the world with you? I must worry about other people's children. I would have to give you away, just the same. I could not keep you. I already killed you, three or four times, before you were born. What shall I do with a dead child, my whole life long? Dead children belong in the grave!

"I cannot throw you out of the window, or into the river, or in the canal. God preserve me from that! I will only look at you severely, so that you may know that you are dead. The instant you know that you are dead, you will fall asleep and pass into eternal life. It won't be long, and I shall soon follow you. Oh, look at all the blood!

Frau Nebling, Frau Nebling! Oh, why am I calling her? They will find me soon enough. Come, my babe! Come, my little Kasimir! You don't want to be a bad man, like your father, do you? Come! You will lie comfortably here. I will cover you well, so that nothing, nothing, will hurt you. Here, under the pillow, it is good to sleep, good to die. Another pillow, so that you may be warmer. Good-bye, my child! One of us will never awaken—or both of us, perhaps—never again! I mean it for your good, my sweet little child. I am not the right mother for you. I do not deserve you. You must not live. I am here for other children; I have no time for you. Good-night! good-night! . . ."

Theresa awoke as from a horrible dream. She wanted to weep, but could not achieve tears.

"What has really happened? Where is the child? Did they take it away from me? Is it dead? Was it buried? What have I done with my child?"

Then she perceived the pillows piled high beside her. She pushed them away, and beheld the child. It lay there; it opened its lips; its nostrils distended; it moved its fingers; it sneezed. Theresa breathed deeply; she felt herself smiling, and knew that she had tears in her eyes. She drew the baby close to her, took him in her arms, and pressed him to her breast. He snuggled against her and drank.

Theresa groaned. She looked round. It was an awakening like none that she had ever known. The early morning light filtered into the room. The bristling noises of the day penetrated to her. The world was awake.

"My child, my child!" sobbed Theresa. "It lives, lives, lives! But who will nurse it, when I am dead? For I want to die! I must die!"

But her longing for death was tinged with a singular sentiment of bliss. The child would drink her life out of her soul. He would suck her life into his, drop by drop, and her own lips would become hard and dry.

She stretched out her arm for the cup of tea which had been standing on the night table since the previous evening. But she feared to disturb the child, and hesitated an instant. The child, however, as though understanding, stopped suckling, thus enabling Theresa to grasp the cup. In fact, she had strength enough to sit somewhat more erect, and to bring the cup to her lips. With her other arm, she continued to hold the child; to hold it tightly. And to her memory came the picture of that distant hour in a wretched little hotel room when she had been loved by a strange man, and had received this child.

That hour, and this one; that night, and this morning; that frenzy, and this perfect clarity of mind—was it possible that they had any connection whatever? She drew the boy closer to herself, and knew that he belonged to her alone.

When Frau Nebling entered the room, she showed not the slightest trace of astonishment at what had happened.

Without losing time or asking questions, she attended, with the skill of a midwife, to everything which the occasion required. It was now apparent that she had anticipated every possible need. A physician appeared—an elderly, cheerful man, dressed in the fashion of a past generation. He sat down at Theresa's bed, examined her, gave orders and advice, and, on leaving, pinched her cheek in a fatherly, somewhat hesitant manner.

On this and on the ensuing day, Theresa received as much attention as could be bestowed, during the time immediately after a confinement, on a blissful young wife in her well-ordered home.

XLV

Frau nebling seemed a person transformed since the birth of the child. She who was formerly so silent, now chatted with Theresa as if she were an old friend. Without having to ask questions, Theresa learned much of her life. Among other things she ascertained that she was engaged by a light opera company to play the part of an elderly lady, but that, during the few weeks past, she had not been required. She had been thrice a mother; her children were alive, but living abroad. She failed to inform Theresa whether or not she was married, or about the common parentage of children, just as Theresa failed to mention the paternity of her own child and the circumstances of her sorrowful experience.

Much as they discussed motherhood and the happiness of being a mother, they had little to tell each other about the happiness and the pangs of love, as though these things had not the remotest connection with the pangs and the joys of motherhood.

The doctor came to see Theresa several times after this, but rather to pay her friendly visits, than because of any real need of his attentions. It turned out that he was the house physician at the theatre, and was a good friend of

Frau Nebling. Occasionally he told, with a certain dry humour, several anecdotes out of his experience; and some of these held a double meaning, which Theresa did not at all resent.

There was another frequent visitor—a young woman who lived in the same house: the childless wife of an ill-paid clerk, who was away all day at his employment. She would sit on the edge of Theresa's bed, and stare with moist eyes at the week-old child as the mother held him to her breast.

After a week, Theresa began to realize that she must soon make her plans for the future. As it developed, Frau Nebling's activities had anticipated her even on this point. One day, a chubby little country woman arrived, and offered to undertake the care of the child in her own home, for a relatively small monthly payment. She had brought along her own eight-year-old girl, whose red cheeks inspired confidence, even if she did squint a little.

She explained that she had often taken care of children. The last one had just left her house, the parents having married and taken the little one with them. She mentioned this with a friendly smile, as though it might be taken as a portent of felicity for Theresa. A few days later, Theresa, holding her youngster in her arms, sat beside Frau Nebling in a one-horse cart, which took them to the railway station. Soon after they left the house, a pedestrian at a street corner crossed in front of the wagon and chanced to glance up at its occupants.

Only the instant before, Theresa had taken the precaution of leaning back under the half-open cover. But a gleam in the pedestrian's eye assured her that he had seen and recognized her, just as she had him.

It was Alfred, and it touched Theresa deeply that he should see her in such circumstances, after so long a period of separation. It happened, by mere chance, much to Theresa's delight, that, just a second before, Frau Nebling had taken the child for a moment out of Theresa's arms into her own.

"That was the man!" said Theresa, as though to herself, with a happy smile.

Frau Nebling looked out of the wagon, to the rear, and faced Theresa again.

"The young man with the gray hat?" she asked.

Theresa nodded.

"He is still standing there," said Frau Nebling significantly.

And only now it dawned upon Theresa that, after her cry of recognition, Frau Nebling had undoubtedly taken the young man with the gray hat to be the father of the child. Theresa did not trouble to inform her of her error. It curiously pleased her to be so misunderstood, and she remained silently smiling until they had reached the station.

XLVI

AFTER a ride of hardly two hours in the crawling train, they reached their destination. The woman, Frau Leutner, awaited them at the station. They walked through the village, past comfortable little villas, most of which were still unoccupied, until they reached a narrow side lane which led up a steep incline to a not unattractive house, surrounded by blossoming fruit trees. Despite the low elevation, the situation afforded a considerable view of the whole neighbourhood. The village, a humble summer resort, lay at their feet; the railway tracks disappeared in the distance. The main thoroughfare was soon lost among the forest-clad hills. Behind the farmhouse lay a meadow, reaching to a stone wall whose upper edge was overgrown with bushes. In a clean, low-raftered room, the farmer's wife served her guests with milk, bread, and butter, and began at once to busy herself about Theresa's child, all the while explaining in great detail how she would nourish and attend it.

Then, while Frau Nebling remained with the child, she showed Theresa about the house. She took her to see the garden, the chicken coop, and the barn. The farmer himself, a tall fellow with drooping whiskers, came home from the fields. His body bent forward in walking. He said little, observed the child with glassy eyes, nodded a few times, shook Theresa's hand, and left.

Agnes, the eight-year-old child, returned from school and seemed pleased at finding that there was a baby in the house again. She took him in her arms; her whole behaviour indicated that she already perfectly understood how to deal with babies. In the meantime, Frau Nebling reclined on her raincoat beneath an oak tree, which stood in majestic isolation a little to the side of the house, and on whose massive trunk was suspended a picture of the Virgin Mary, framed in wood, protected by a glass pane, and surrounded by a faded wreath.

Time flew by. Only when the moment of leave-taking approached, did Theresa begin to realize that she must part with her child, and that, despite her many worries, an exceptional and beautiful epoch in her life was ending. On the way home, she spoke not a word to Frau Nebling. When she finally reached the house where everything reminded her of her boy, she felt as though she were returning from his funeral.

She awoke in a bad mood the next morning. Nothing would have pleased her more than to revisit Ensbach. A sudden rainstorm prevented this. The day after, it rained and stormed again. Not until the fourth day could she be with her child again.

It was a mild spring day. They sat out in the open under the pale blue sky, whose hue reflected in the eyes of her child.

Frau Leutner discussed in detail all sorts of domestic and farm matters, and narrated her many experiences during the years which she had devoted to the care of children.

This time, her husband joined them and remained a little longer, though still, for the most part, as silent as ever. Agnes appeared for dinner, paid little attention to the child, and soon afterwards ran off.

Theresa departed, more reassured and less sad than on the former occasion.

She remarked to Frau Nebling that same evening, that it was high time she began looking for work. Again Frau Nebling had anticipated her, and instantly supplied her with a number of addresses. Before the next day had run its course, Theresa had interviewed several ladies, and before evening had her choice of three positions. She chose one where she would have only a seven-year-old girl to supervise. The father was a rich merchant, the mother a good-natured, somewhat phlegmatic woman. The child was docile and pretty.

Theresa felt quite happy in her new surroundings. She had made arrangements to have a day off every other Sunday, and one afternoon every other week. Until late in the summer, her employers interposed no difficulties in the matter, but on a certain beautiful morning in July, the mistress, for some reason or other, asked Theresa to dispense this time with her day off, and instead to select any day during the following week that might be agreeable to her. Theresa, however, had been looking forward with eagerness to seeing her child. Contrary to her usual attitude, she insisted with unnecessary vehemence on her rights, which were finally granted. But this occasioned her discharge, and she had to leave the house after the customary notice.

XLVII

SHE soon found another position in the house of a doctor, as governess of two girls and a boy. The two girls, aged respectively ten and eight years, attended school, and in addition, received instruction at home in French and piano. The six-year-old boy was entrusted entirely to the care of Theresa. It was a model household. There she found everything conducive to comfort, without superfluous luxuries; the marital relationship was ideal, and all the children were docile and well bred. And despite the invariably strenuous day's work from which the doctor returned, there was never a word of impatience or unkindness, never a trace of sullenness, or even an occasional quarrel such as she had been accustomed to witness in so many other families.

Toward the middle of August, she was enabled to spend three entire days with her child. Unfortunately, two of these days were rainy ones. There were times when, sitting in the stuffy room with the farmer's family, a feeling of boredom and emptiness overpowered her. When she clearly realized this, she would rush, as though driven by a twinge of guilt, to the side of her child, who lay quietly sleeping in his crib. In the dim light of this rainy day, his tiny

round face appeared to her unusually pale, small, and
strange. With some fear, she would breathe on the eye-lids
of the child, who at first would make a face as if about to
cry, but, recognizing the well-remembered features of his
mother looking down at him, began to smile instead. Theresa, overjoyed, would then take the child in her arms, fondle it, and weep with happiness. The farmer's wife, apparently moved, prophesied a happy future for her, and especially a good father for the boy. But Theresa shook
her head at this. She declared that she had no intention
or desire to share her darling with any one. He belonged
to her, and would continue to be hers alone.

The parting was particularly difficult after these three
days. When Theresa arrived at Semmering, where Frau
Regan was vacationing with the children, she could not
conceal her melancholy from the mother and children.
In her gentle and friendly manner, without asking a single
question, Frau Regan expressed the hope that the fresh
mountain air would soon strengthen her. Impulsively,
Theresa kissed her hand with emotion, but at the same
moment decided not to betray her secret. As a matter of
fact, she recovered much more quickly than she had anticipated. Her colour improved, as did her disposition.
Strolls and mountain walks were the order of the day.
The easy-going familiarity of the summer resort made it
possible for her occasionally to meet certain young and
elderly gentlemen who refused to respect her wishes for
solitude. She resisted all attempts at intimacy. When, dur-

ing the first days of September, the family returned to town, she did not regret it, but was on the contrary happy to be so near her child again.

The few hours at Ensbach, each week or fortnight, were hours of purest joy. And that feeling of emptiness and monotony, which had overtaken her that rainy summer day, never returned, not even during the dreariest days of autumn. In anticipation, she somewhat feared the winter trips, but soon found her apprehensions on this score unwarranted.

When the farm was snow-covered, nothing was more delightful than to hold her child in her arms and, from the well-heated room, gaze through the windows at the prospect of a white landscape dotted with sleepy cottages and, in the distance, the tiny railway station, from which the dark tracks converged in the distance.

Then came beautiful, spring-heralding days, when she fled the smoky city and found not only spaciousness and release, but also the pleasant companionship of the farm. Her boy on her lap, she would sit on a bench in front of the house and bathe herself in the glorious sunshine.

When spring returned, Theresa fancied that she perceived a portentous connection between the development of her child and the rebirth of Nature. The day when the first cherry blossoms appeared was likewise the day on which her boy ran toward her a few steps without assistance. The day on which the rosebushes of the white villa "Good Rest" in the Bahnhofstrasse were liberated from

their straw coverings, was the very one in which Franz
cut his second eye-tooth. On one of the gladdest days in
April—for this had been an unusually long winter—on
her way to the farmhouse, she surveyed the landscape, with
its forests, gardens, and hills, clad in its early green dress.
Then she caught sight of her little boy, held tightly by the
farmer's wife, standing at the window and clapping his
little hands as he watched his mother approach across the
meadow with a small package in her hand—for she always
brought something along for him. And on a certain day
in June, when she picked the first ripe cherries, the boy
had, for the first time, spoken a few connected words.

XLVIII

THREE years followed—years so similar in their passage, that later, in Theresa's memory, one spring always merged into the other, one summer into its counterpart, and so with autumn, and winter. And this, despite the fact—or perhaps because of the fact—that she led a sort of double existence: the one as governess to the Regan family, the other as the mother of a small boy, who was staying in the country under the care of peasants.

Even on the way to Ensbach, when she went to spend an occasional day there, everything that she left behind her in the city, disappeared; the Regan couple and their children disappeared; the house disappeared, and even the room which she occupied. The whole city was enveloped in a gray mist of unfamiliarity, of which the reality slowly dawned on her only when she left the train, and sometimes not until she had actually entered the house.

But when she sat at table with the Regan family, or played with the children, or took walks with them, or when, her duties completed, she stretched her weary body on the bed, then reappeared the familiar Ensbach landscape, brilliant in the summer sunshine, or covered with the white frost of winter; the house on the hill, with a green or white blanket; the oak tree with the flower-decked image of the Virgin Mary; the rustic couple on the bench before the house or in the low living-room beside the stove. Always it seemed an incredible, fairy-like world. And always, like a marvel, when slowly climbing the sloping road to the Leutner farm, she saw everything as she had left it days or weeks before; and she could see her boy, the same and yet always a different creature, in her arms or on her lap. And it happened sometimes, when she closed her eyes for a short time and then opened them again, that somehow a different lad lay in her arms than him whom she had imagined with her eyes shut.

But things were not always so pleasant as her hopes had pictured them. There were times when Herr Leutner was sullen for long periods. Even the farmer's wife too, usually good-tempered and much inclined to gossip, was sometimes altogether different, unfriendly, and positively combative. On such occasions, when Theresa ventured the slightest criticism, she would make vicious remarks, complaining about the trouble which the boy gave her and the insufficient thanks and appreciation which Theresa gave her for her efforts.

Even after continued increase of payment, much resentment remained. Once they had forgotten to let Theresa know that her child had a rather mild illness. Or items would be added to her account for medicines which could not be properly accounted for. Again and again, Theresa thought she detected, by one sign or another, proofs that

Frau Leutner by no means cared for the child as much as she professed. On other occasions, jealous feelings aroused, not only between Theresa and the farmer's wife, but between Theresa and young Agnes. Then Theresa would complain that Frau Leutner and her daughter spoiled the child by too great attention, as though they wished to alienate its affections from her. And, sometimes, bad weather was not exactly conducive to happy thoughts and harmonious feelings. It was enough to drive a person mad, this sitting with wet feet in the cold or over-heated room, which reeked of cheap tobacco smoke, and which was certainly detrimental to the child's lungs.

Theresa several times decided not to ride out to Ensbach, and would let one or two free Sundays pass without seeing her child. At other times, she believed that she could hardly contain her longing, which was so greatly impregnated with fear that her nights were troubled with baleful dreams.

On the whole, however, everything ran smoothly. Theresa often thought herself infinitely happier than many a mother who had her children always with her and could not therefore fully appreciate her happiness. As for her, the meetings with her child, at least in anticipation, always afforded her the thrill of a holiday.

She was, moreover, quite happy in the Regan house. The doctor, not quite devoid of pride in his work, always remained pleasant, despite the strenuous nature of his profession. Frau Regan continued, moreover, to be a very exacting, though always fair and never moody housewife. The girls were lively, yet diligent and obedient, and greatly attached to their governess. The boy had a quiet nature and a distinct inclination to music, so that already in his eighth year he could, on musical evenings, render the piano accompaniment for Haydn and Mozart quartettes. Theresa often played duets with him, and received, on such evenings, her humble share of the applause. In the atmosphere of activity, order, and respectability which surrounded her here, she was concerned more than ever before with her own instruction, and found time somewhat to further her own musical and linguistic studies.

In this well-ordered existence, there were small occurences which interrupted the habitual routine of the day.

Whenever Frau Fabiani came to Vienna, on occasional business with publishers and editors, the Regan family would graciously insist on having the governess' mother to dinner. On these occasions, Frau Fabiani displayed a faultless, even actually dignified behaviour. She would take the opportunity to mention her son, a student of medicine, who, despite his extreme youth, had already begun to play an important rôle in the University, and had recently made a speech at the students' meeting that provoked comment.

After one of these maternal visitations, Theresa met her brother, whom she had not seen in several months, in the city. They discussed their mother, to whose last novel, now appearing serially in a Viennese newspaper, Karl referred with derision and contempt. Theresa felt singularly hurt. Brother and sister bade each other a cold farewell. At the next corner, Theresa turned to regard her brother, and noticed how little to his advantage he had changed in the lapse of only a few years. True, he dressed more carefully than before. But the drooping posture of his head, his somewhat too long, poorly shorn hair, which brushed against his coat collar, and his hopping gait, gave to his whole bearing an ignoble, hesitant, and degraded atmosphere which repelled her.

At first, she had several times felt the obligation of visiting Frau Nebling. One evening, she attended an operetta, for which the actress had presented her with a complimentary ticket. Frau Nebling sang in a shrill, strange voice, and played the part of an elderly, overdressed vampire. She acted in such fashion that Theresa almost blushed for her, and shuddered at the thought that one of her sons might return from abroad and see his own mother in such an indecent costume, painted with scarlet rouge, and prancing about the stage with lecherous looks and demeanour, to the derision even of her fellow actors.

Once, on the street, she fancied that she saw Kasimir Tobisch approaching her. But she was mistaken, for there was hardly any similarity between the father of her child and the gentleman who brushed past her. And when such mistakes occured to her two or three times thereafter in quick succession, and she always experienced the same painful excitement, she realized that she actually feared to meet Kasimir Tobisch. She did not wish him, of all persons, to hear anything more of her life, and especially, of the existence of the child. But she was even more thrilled when she thought that she recognized, in some passerby, Alfred, whom she would have liked to see again. Though she knew that he lived in the same city, no fortunate accident ever brought them together.

Even the summer weeks with the Regan family, though spent at a different mountain resort each year, became miraculously merged in her mind into a single summer vacation.

Later, she could not differentiate, in her memory, the many young and old men who, at the country resorts, had tried to flirt with her. That none really succeeded in the attempt was not so much due to her own resistance, or carefulness, or indifference—for in contrast with many precedent and subsequent periods of her life, her senses in these years seemed atrophied—as to the lack of freedom necessitated by her work, which constantly prevented any budding relationship from ripening into intimacy.

It would occasionally happen that she became quite envious of more successful women when, on mild summer evenings, she observed ladies who, after the governesses had retired with the children to their rooms, could promenade up and down the brilliantly illumined square near the hotel, walk as long as they liked and with whomever they willed; or even disappear in the dark. She saw—this, of course, was nothing new to her—women, matrons, and young girls ex-

change significant glances with men and carry on flirta-
tions; she well knew to what such beginnings generally led.

Frau Regan, though still a pretty, quite attractive, and
desirable lady, was one of the few who seemed almost entirely untouched by the prevailing atmosphere. This afforded Theresa some comfort, and she felt protected and
guarded in her presence.

Nothing suggested an impending change. Dr. Regan and
his wife still continued to treat her with friendliness, and
even affection. A kind of friendship had developed between
her and the girls, especially the elder. Her duet playing
with the gifted boy had become a pleasant habit. Suddenly,
one morning in June, just before they were to leave for the
country, Frau Regan called her to her room and told her,
with some uneasiness, though in a firm and businesslike
manner, that they had decided to employ a French governess, and that consequently they must let her go, though,
of course, they should do so with the greatest regret. She
explained that there was no hurry about her departure.
They would give her weeks, or months even, to find another
suitable position. For the immediate future, Theresa could
decide, according to her own wishes, whether she cared to
accompany the Regan family to the Dolomites, or whether,
under the circumstances, she would prefer to have the entire
summer vacation at her disposal.

Theresa stood pale, stricken to the heart; but she declared at once, without betraying any of the emotions which
she felt at this abrupt dismissal, that she would not take ad-

vantage of Frau Regan's offer, but would, if possible, leave the house even before the expiration of the usual two weeks' notice.

It appeared strange to her that her unhappiness did not long continue. Indeed, in that same hour, she experienced a certain pleasure, almost a decided joy, at the prospect of a change. She quickly confessed to herself that she had by no means been as happy in this house as she had many times tried to convince herself that she was. And on the following day, when she spoke of her dismissal to Fräulein Steinbauer, the governess in a family that was friendly with the Regans, the governess—an old, embittered creature— quickly convinced Theresa that she had simply been exploited in the Regan house, and was now thrown out into the streets—a destiny repeatedly experienced by all of her kind. The constant kindness of Frau Regan now appeared to her as a mixture of weakness and deception. The self-satisfied and self-sufficing character of the beloved doctor had always been hateful to her, she now realized. The boy, though truly a highly talented musician, was mentally backward; and the girls, although one could not deny their industry, were nevertheless mediocre. The younger was already somewhat spoiled, while the older one was not without guile. She felt that Frau Regan had long ago informed the girls about the change that was to be made. Falseness and hypocrisy existed everywhere.

She left the house with bitterness in her heart, and swore never to enter it again.

XLIX

THERESA spent the next few weeks in Ensbach, with her child. The country life calmed her. Indeed, at first, it made her so happy that she conceived the idea of looking for pupils among the summer residents, so as possibly to establish herself there, rather than among the city people, whose children she educated only to be dismissed in the end.

She met a number of the townsfolk with whom she would occasionally chat; they sympathized with her and her boy. Some time before, she had made the acquaintance of a cousin of Frau Leutner, one Sebastian Stiozuer, a man still in his prime, who had lately become widowed. He was not at all bad-looking, was well built, in comfortable circumstances, and was seeking a second wife to care for his home.

It happened, not exactly by chance, that he often called on the Leutners, and on these visits he amused Theresa with his naïve and humorous ways. He would also occupy himself, in a touchingly clumsy fashion, with her boy. His growing inclination for her was manifest.

Frau Leutner did not fail to convey clear hints, and there were times when Theresa seriously considered a possible alliance with him. But the longer he visited her, and the more plainly he conveyed his sentiments, especially on one occasion when, walking together, he had drawn her to him with unexpected brutal strength—the more consciously did she feel that there could never be a lasting affection between them. This she showed so plainly that he instantly withdrew his suit.

But when, following her refusal, boredom seized her, she at first accused herself because the companionship of her boy did not utterly engross her. Then she would tell herself that, despite her love for her boy, she was simply incapable of enduring inactivity any longer; that, furthermore, she had no right to lead an idle life on the farm, without working, and without giving thought to the matter of earning a living.

L

AND SO, summer was still far from ended when she again took a position, this time with a family that at first struck Theresa as being quite fashionable. She was to act as teacher or companion to a fourteen-year-old girl. Several days after accepting the post, she accompanied this family on a trip to a small health resort in Styria, where they took lodgings in a hotel that was far from immaculate. The husband, a prominent public official, remained behind in Vienna.

The Baroness was polite enough to Theresa, but never addressed a single superfluous word to her. The people who lived at the resort were, for the most part old, gouty, and rheumatic. A thin, poorly dressed man of about sixty, who, much to Theresa's bewilderment, bore the name of a famous old family of Hungarian nobles, would sometimes, after dinner, hobble over to their table, leaning on his cane, and converse with them in his native language. Otherwise, they associated with nobody. In addition, the meals were so insufficient and poor that Theresa was reminded of the bitterest days of her youth.

At times, when she was alone with the young Baroness, Theresa would attempt to provoke some sort of conversa-

188

tion with her, by making jesting remarks about the people whom they met on their walks and in the park. But the girl was apparently unable to appreciate any harmless jest, much less understand it; and all that Theresa could get in response was a belated, if not entirely stupid, reply.

They travelled back to Vienna during the most distressing heat of the summer. The meals at home did not prove to be by any means more interesting, even though the husband now shared them. When, for the first time, Theresa had the opportunity to go to Ensbach, she breathed deeply, as though she had just escaped from a prison. From a distance, the house of the Baroness, in which she was now condemned to live, appeared even worse than ever—positively weird. She could hardly understand how she had managed to endure it for so long a time. She put off leaving from week to week, however, perhaps through sheer indifference, or perhaps because she was impressed by the unction of a noble name. But at last, when, at Christmas time, they presented her with a ridiculously small present of money, her patience came to an end, and she gave notice of her intention to find another post.

LI

But now, evil days overtook her. It almost seemed as though fate had decreed that she should witness at close range all the annoyances and ugliness of bourgeois family life. Or was it merely that she had become more observant than before? Three times in succession, she came in contact with unsuccessful marriages. First, it was a young couple, who, without regard for their two children of, six and eight years, and without the slightest regard for Theresa, said such frightful things to each other over their meals that Theresa believed she would die of shame.

At the first quarrel which she witnessed, she simply left the table. When, a few days later, she attempted to do the same thing, the husband called her back, demanding that she should remain, in order that he might have a witness to the cursing to which his wife subjected him. The next time, it was the wife who demanded the same service of Theresa. Both often entertained company at home, on which occasions, they acted the part of a happy couple before the guests. At times, though—and this was a thing quite incomprehensible to Theresa—the couple seemed to understand one another quite perfectly; and just as Theresa had been an unwilling witness of their mutual execrations, so at times she was forced to witness scenes of tenderness, which moved her even more painfully and disagreeably than the more frequent quarrels.

Her next position was in a well-managed, amply provided house, where the occupation of the husband, who was seldom at home, even at nights, remained a mystery to her. She liked the place fairly well, at the beginning. The seven-year-old girl who was entrusted to her care was pretty, confiding, and clever. The mother on some days hardly left her room, while on others, she remained away from home from early morning until late at night, and seemed, in a way that was totally incomprehensible to Theresa, to be absolutely indifferent and unconcerned about her child. But she treated Theresa with friendliness. This cordiality continued to grow, and gradually took on a form which at first filled Theresa with suspicion, then with disgust, and finally with fear. Like an escaping prisoner, she left the house, one morning, following a night during which she had been compelled to keep her door securely locked. She wrote to the master of the house from the station, where she was taking the train to Ensbach for a few days' stay, explaining that a sudden indisposition of her mother had compelled her to leave unexpectedly.

Her next position, as governess of two bright boys of seven and eight, was made untenable by the behaviour of the master. She pretended at first not to understand his significant glances and seemingly accidental contacts with her body, especially since the relationship between the man and his young and still pretty wife seemed to be entirely harmonious. Soon, however, Theresa could no longer ignore the intentions of this man, who in other respects did not displease her. She was obliged to confess that she could not, or would not, long be able to resist his advances. Then, one evening, when his wife and children were in an adjoining room, he made a deliberate attempt to overpower her—an attempt which inspired Theresa with more fright than resistance, but once more necessitated her sudden departure.

LII

NEXT, she accepted what at first appeared to be an excellent position. The employment agent who procured it for her looked upon it as such an unusual opportunity that he expected to receive a special compensation for securing it. The head of the household, Emil Greitler, a bank director, and a man over fifty, was gracious and respectable, and almost diplomatically reserved in his deportment. His wife, an unattractive and faded lady, clung to him with unreciprocated love, and looked up to him with admiration. They had four children. Theresa had nothing to do with the two oldest boys, one of whom studied law and the other, banking. The thirteen-year-old girl and the youngest child, a boy of nine, attended the public schools and in addition, had so many private instructors that Theresa's duty was limited to accompanying the children on their way to and from their lessons and taking them for walks.

Theresa desired to be on terms of greater intimacy with the young girl. But, like her father, whom she also closely resembled in features, she was unapproachable, and responded coldly to Theresa's sympathetic advances. This, at first, annoyed Theresa. She changed her tactics, and was even more severe with the girl than she really cared to be. At last, there developed between them an attitude of complete indifference, which was broken on but rare occasions, either because of a silly and ludicrous fit of temper on the part of Margaret, or of some stubborn decision on the part of Theresa. These episodes would direct their attention again to their former, almost forgotten, half unconscious battle. The nine-year-old Siegfried was a happy child, unusually clever for his age, whom Theresa often had to scold for his talkativeness, but whose droll notions and quaint turns of speech moved to laughter all who heard him. This position left Theresa plenty of leisure, but her employers did not like her to leave the house for any great length of time. Although her services were required only rarely, they wished her to be available at all times. Although there were often small or large parties at the house, Theresa was never invited to join them.

Towards the end of Carnival, in 1902, a large ball was planned. Frau Greitler, who was somewhat ill, depended much on Theresa for assistance in her preparations for this event. Consequently, she could hardly fail to invite her to participate in the festivities. After the music had begun, Theresa was invited to dance by a young man with a small blond moustache. The young masters of the family, the law student and the bank clerk, as well as other guests, also danced with her; but the blond young man came again and again, and chaffed with her in an animated and somewhat familiar manner.

A Lieutenant of Dragoons poured her out a glass of

champagne at the buffet, and drank to her health. A dark, curly-headed fellow, with a light wound on his forehead, who had quite shamelessly pressed her to him while dancing, but had hardly spoken a word to her, dared about three o'clock in the morning, to make such audacious advances that she blushed deeply and could make no response.

The blond young man asked her quite frankly if he might not see her again. She denied his request. Still, for several days following the ball, she entertained the hope that she might somehow meet him on the street. And when, a few weeks later, some mention of him was made by the Greitlers at table, she became aware that, at thought of him, her consciousness was oppressed by a sort of disillusionment, not so much on account of this neglected tryst of which he had known nothing, as because of the many other painful and inexplicable deflections which her hopes had suffered in the past few years.

As the Greitler family were invariably a few days late in paying her her salary, Theresa hardly noticed that a full month had passed since she had last been paid. But when, on the first day of the next month, nothing was forthcoming and she stood in need of money, she felt compelled to speak to Frau Greitler. She was asked to be patient for a few days; and, as a matter of fact, she soon received the greater part of her pay. This would have satisfied her, had not the maid, on the same day, asked her how much they still owed her. It was by no means her habit to allow herself to discuss her employers with the hired help. This time, however, she could not resist the temptation; and she soon learned that the Greitler family was in debt on all sides; that, for example, the caterer's bill from the last dance was still unpaid. Theresa could not and would not credit this. Everything in the household continued without change. The family were still served well. They still ate the very best. They still received guests. Their carriage still stood before the house. The ladies ordered their summer dresses from a first-class dressmaker, just as before. Even the mood of Herr Greitler showed no modification. He still retained the same aloofness toward his wife and children, and never displayed a sign of haste or impatience. At dinner, they would discuss the question of selecting a summer resort, and not a single sign or word suggested that any considerable change in their circumstances was imminent.

One day, however, Herr Greitler left on a trip, as he frequently was in the habit of doing, bade his family a pleasant farewell, as usual, and promised to return within ten days. Even during his absence, not the slightest unusual event troubled the household, until, early one morning, voices and movements in the hall awakened Theresa. She sat up in her bed and listened. Two hours later, the maid informed her that Frau Greitler had unexpectedly been called away. At dinner, the eldest son told them of the sudden illness of a distant relative. But before evening, Frau Greitler returned, deathly pale and looking as though she had been weeping profusely. They could not longer conceal what had happened. The evening papers published the news. The bank had failed, and Herr Greitler had been arrested that morning while on a train, two hours distant from Vienna. Frau Greitler told Theresa that she was at liberty to leave the house at once. But she asked for permission to remain until she had found another position.

It was remarkable to her how quickly the members of the family adapted themselves to their changed circumstances, although at first hardly any change could be detected. They ate as well as before; the children continued to go to school; Margaret remained as stubborn as usual; Siegfried continued to make his droll remarks; the teachers appeared at the usual hours; and there was no lack of company, although among them were many who had not been there before.

When Theresa left the house Frau Greitler, who in these difficult days had exhibited an altogether unsurmised spirit of calm and strength, wished her the best of luck. The remaining salary, of course, was not paid.

LIII

Theresa was compelled to take the first reasonably good position offered to her. In her new place of employment, she had to take care of three entirely untrained children, between six and ten years of age, who gave her nothing but trouble. The father was an insurance agent, who did not come home until evening, and then was invariably in a bad temper. The mother, a dull, stupid, and apparently phlegmatic individual, would scream two or three times a day at the children, and quarrel with each child as it approached her. She soon began to treat Theresa as a common servant. Frequently too, she would sink into a sort of lethargy, from which neither household duties nor the clamours of the children could arouse her, so that the whole responsibility of the household would devolve upon Theresa's shoulders. She tolerated this existence for two months; then she gave notice, and left for Ensbach.

It was not merely the reaction, the weariness of feeling, which Theresa experienced after the excitement of the last few months; it was also a sudden desire, not entirely untroubled by qualms of conscience, that drove her now to her Franz. She had concerned herself too little about him in the last three years; she had hardly taken any interest in his growth and education. She tried to justify herself by telling herself that she had lacked the time; that on her free days, she was too exhausted physically and spiritually, to make the journey to Ensbach. Although this might be true, to a certain degree, she felt nevertheless that generally her desire to see her boy had not been too keen. Indeed, at times, when the weeks of separation lengthened, she had sometimes felt the small payments which she made to Frau Leutner as an unwelcome burden.

She would excuse herself on the supposition that Franz's love for his foster-mother was greater than his affection for herself; that he was gradually becoming a peasant child; and that, at certain times, he recalled, in a disturbing way, the hated features of his father. But of late a certain consciousness of guilt repeatedly attached itself to these ideas, and she felt as if she were under an obligation to expiate a wrong done to her boy. She felt as if the weakness and irresolution of her maternal instincts would be avenged upon her and upon the boy. It was with such thoughts that she approached the Leutner's farm, with a trepidation such as she had not experienced for a long time.

She felt a sudden fear of finding her boy ill. For, in fact, she had received no news of him in almost three weeks. Perhaps he did not care to know her any more; perhaps he would say to her:

"Why do you come back, again and again? I do not need you any more!"

She burst into tears, when she saw him run joyfully out to meet her. How gladly she pressed him to her heart, as though now she had won him back for ever! Even Frau Leutner seemed to her more friendly than usual. Frau Leutner was much disturbed by Theresa's worn appearance, and advised her most earnestly to remain in the country, at least until autumn. Theresa felt herself physically and spiritually so fatigued that she acquiesced in this proposal at once. Within a few days, her improvement was marked.

She derived more joy from her boy than she had had in a long time. This time, all his strangeness seemed somehow to have disappeared. He voluntarily joined her on her short walks, a thing which he had never done before, and for the first time, she noticed that his face was frank and open.

A few months before, he had begun to attend school; and his teacher, to whom she once spoke, termed him a bright and active child. Frau Leutner had had to provide various necessities for him. Theresa was behind in her payments and could not defer them any longer. For the first time, she felt compelled to ask her mother for assistance. The money did not come for some time, and as the days passed, the behaviour and disposition of Frau Leutner, and particularly that of Herr Leutner, toward Theresa gradually became less cordial. After a second call for help, she received from her mother a sum so meagre that it did not enable her to fulfill all of her obligations. Theresa paid a portion of her debt. The attitude of the Leutners thereupon became more and more disagreeable, and Theresa realized that she could not remain any longer in Ensbach. So on a frightfully hot August day, hardly ten days after her arrival, she departed again for Vienna, determined to accept the very first position which might present itself.

LIV

THE two girls, of four and six years, who were entrusted to Theresa's care gave her much worry, particularly as the mother was employed during the day in an office, and did not come home until late in the evening. The father was ostensibly on a business trip, but as no letters ever came from him, Theresa soon quite clearly perceived that he had deserted his wife, who was a bluff, uncharming creature. The youngest girl was sickly. She was perpetually restless at night, which, however, did not seem to disturb her mother, who slept in an adjoining room. When Theresa once spoke of the child's condition, and suggested that it might be advisable to consult a physician, she assured Theresa with some curtness that she knew her duty perfectly well. One word led to another, and Theresa gave notice that she would be leaving her position. She had not realized before that she might be grieved at parting with the small, sickly little girl, but such proved to be the case. For some time to come, she would be thinking of the pale, pathetic face of the little creature and of her smile when, at night, she would throw her small arms about Theresa's neck and cry, and Theresa would comfort her.

She did not want to go back to Ensbach until she was in a position to pay off her small indebtedness, and as she did not at once find another position, she decided to stay at a small hotel. She had never lived in a more miserable, forsaken place. She slept without undressing. Unfortunately, too, it rained constantly during these days when she was running up and down a hundred stairs in her fruitless efforts to find a new position.

She did not wish to be too hasty in her decision, this time. She preferred to take her time, and get on meanwhile as best she could, rather than again enter a house where she could not be certain of remaining. It happened that in many homes, where she herself made a good impression and where she would have gladly stayed, she noticed that she was refused because of her shabby clothing. What should she do? Should she turn again to her mother, and be made to receive grudging charity? Should she call upon her brother, with whom she had had no connection of any kind for years? Should she beg for assistance from some of the ladies for whom she had previously worked? All these ideas were repulsive to her. And furthermore, she did not know whence she might reasonably expect really adequate assistance.

That night, as she lay, fully dressed, on the wretched bed, she conceived the idea, which she had once thought of years ago, in a similar situation, of selling herself. She thought of it as of something indifferent to her personally, yet difficult to achieve. Was she still a woman? Did she feel even the slightest desire to lie in the arms of a man? The miserable existence which she led, as a creature who did not belong to herself, who had no home, who was a mother, but, instead of caring for her own child, was compelled to protect and train the children of strangers; a creature who did not know where she would repose tomorrow night, who went about for a day amid the experiences, the affairs, and the secrets of strange people, as a chance confidante, or as one purposely initiated, only to be thrown out on the sidewalk as an inconsiderable intruder the very next day—what right had such a creature as she to the love of a man, to womanly happiness?

She was alone, and fated to a solitary existence. Was there still any creature to whom she might cling? Her child? Her mother's heart was numbed, as was her whole soul, her body, and everything in it. Even her beauty— she had never been really beautiful—her appearance then, and her youth, were gone. She felt how her lips were drawn into a tired smile. She was twenty-seven years old. But was it not too soon to relinquish all hope? She remembered the Greitlers' ball, which had occurred only a short time ago, where she had made so many conquests in a single evening.

In the quiet and darkness of her room, while the raindrops pattered ceaselessly against the window pane, she became suddenly conscious, beneath her shabby coat and miserable clothing, of her body, of her skin, and of her throbbing arteries. She became more conscious of them than she had ever been before, even in a luke-warm bath or in the arms of a lover; this was a long-forgotten sensation.

On the following morning, she awoke from a pleasant dream, the details of which she could not recollect. In this mood, with a sudden access of courage, she dared to visit a ladies' tailor whom she knew. She was approached with great friendliness. She apologized for her somewhat shabby appearance, by saying that she had lost her trunk. At her request, they made her, within twenty-four hours, a plain, well-fitting costume, without insisting upon immediate payment. She started out on her search anew. God, how often, how often, had she done that already! But this time, she went with renewed courage.

LV

THE next day, she found a desirable position, in the home of a professor's widow, where it was her duty to supervise the education of two quiet, flaxen-haired girls of ten and twelve years, who were not attending a public school this year, on account of their health. The good treatment which Theresa received in this house, the pleasant and agreeable conversation which prevailed there, the simple and obedient natures of the young girls, and the friendliness of the mother, who was still mourning her late husband's death—all these pleasant circumstances at first delighted her. Even the teaching proved an interesting occupation, since it was entirely confided to her hands. She began again, as she had done while at the Eppichs', to prepare herself for her lessons, thereby refreshing her knowledge of many things, and recovering many interests which she had thought were lost to her. She was readily permitted a vacation at Christmas time, and at once went to Ensbach, where she enjoyed the company of her boy as she had never done before. Yet, she could not explain, even to herself, what it was that drove her back to the city during the early afternoon of her second holiday.

As she sat at the simple dinner that evening with the

widow and her two children, silent, as usual, while the
others thought with melancholy of the deceased head of
the family, a sudden, disturbing sense of monotony overcame her. She began to feel a dull hatred against these people, into whose sorrow she, a stranger, was thus irresistibly
drawn.

She had, of course, learned often enough that no one
took the slightest cognizance of her spiritual condition;
that people would weep or laugh with equal indifference
to her presence. But she had never felt such rebelliousness
against this as in this house, where she really had nothing
to complain of, and where, indeed, everybody desired to
please her. Moreover, she had not been expected to dinner that evening and in consequence, she arose from her
meal, rather more hungry than usual. Theresa determined
that night to leave the house as soon as possible; but it
was not until spring that she was able to put her decision
into execution.

LVI

A‌FTER an almost painful leavetaking, when for the first time she left a home with a feeling of guilt toward its occupants, she accepted a position in the household of a hat manufacturer.

She was to act as the teacher of their only child, a badly disciplined and exceptionally handsome seven-year-old boy. What chiefly attracted Theresa's interest was the constant good cheer which reigned in this home. There were guests at dinner almost every night—an uncle, a cousin, a business acquaintance, or a couple of relatives from the country. They ate and drank well, told anecdotes, gossiped, laughed continually, and were plainly delighted and even flattered, when Theresa joined in the laughter.

They treated her as an old acquaintance, and questioned her about her parents and her youth. It was the first time that she could talk freely about her father, the dead officer; her mother, the beloved novelist of Salzburg; and of all the men and women whom she had learned to know in the process of time. It was the first time that she could talk without seeming forward. In such a household she soon felt at her ease.

But the boy, however much trouble his spoiled nature

created for her, positively charmed her. She soon discovered that his parents knew well how to humour him, but did not quite understand how to appreciate him. She found that he was not only brighter than his age warranted, but was possessed of a unique, almost superhuman beauty, which reminded her of the costume picture of some prince, she knew not whom, which she had once seen in a gallery. And soon she realized that she loved this child, as much, even more than her own. When he became sick of a fever, it was she who spent three anxious nights at his bed, while his mother, who was also ill at the time, was satisfied merely to obtain reports of the condition of the boy.

Soon after his recovery, suggestions were made for the disposition of the summer holidays. They took the neighbourhood of Salzburg into consideration, and welcomed Theresa's counsel.

Then, one bright Sunday morning, the lady of the house called Theresa to her room and explained to her, in her usual friendly way, that the former governess, who had merely received a half-year's leave of absence to visit a relative in England, was expected to return within a few days. Theresa could hardly grasp the situation. When she could no longer doubt the fact that she must leave, she burst into tears. The lady comforted her, and even teased her, in a good-natured and thoughtless way, about her childishness.

Neither the mistress of the house nor the husband seemed to entertain the slightest suspicion that they had wronged Theresa or caused her pain. The attitude toward her in the house altered so little after this notice that Theresa continued to hope that she might be permitted to remain. Indeed, the family still discussed with her, as before, the various details of the approaching vacation, and the boy spoke enthusiastically of the trips, canoe rides, and mountain climbs which he would take with her. She had to fight back the tears, again and again, at table. One night, half in a dream, she pondered all kinds of romantic plans: to kidnap the boy, to fight against the return of the other governess. Even darker plans, concerning herself and the child, flashed through her mind. Of course, by morning, all these fantasies had vanished.

At last, the day of parting came. The master and mistress had arranged to have the youngster away on a visit to his grandparents. They gave Theresa an inexpensive box of candy and wished her good-luck, without, by even a single word, indicating that they would like to see her occasionally. As, tense and tearless she walked downstairs, she knew that she would never enter this house again. It was not the first time that she had made such a decision. But this really signified very little, for even in those few instances when she had departed from a house without making such a resolve, when she had left a house in amity and friendship, she had never returned.

She rode to Ensbach, in the hope of recovering her peace of spirit amid natural surroundings and the healing pulsation of intimacy there. She had, too, the additional hopeless desire of loving her child more than she had done before.

None of these hopes were fulfilled; indeed, everything seemed more gloomy than ever. She had never inhabited such a totally strange world. It seemed to her as though everything were antagonistic to her, and, try as she would, she could not succeed in stirring herself to any maternal tenderness toward her child.

It was worse when Agnes, who had meanwhile become a children's nurse in Vienna, came home for a few days. She hated the tenderness which the sixteen-year-old girl showed toward the boy, and she could not bear to see the young girl usurp what should have been her own maternal functions. Sometimes, however, she felt that the attitude of Agnes did not wholly arise from tenderness. It seemed rather as if Agnes only wanted to arouse her anger, to hurt her, to make her jealous. When Theresa accused her of this, she replied contemptuously and insultingly. Frau Leutner took sides with her daughter. A quarrel ensued, in which Theresa lost all control of herself. She was angry with the others, unsatisfied with herself, and she realized that everything would only become worse if she remained longer. And so it came about, for the first time, that she left Ensbach without a real farewell: she left like one escaping.

LVII

On a hot day in August, Theresa began work in her new position. She found that the agency had misinformed her concerning many matters with regard to her latest incumbency. In the first place, there was no elegant villa, as she had been assured. True enough, there was a rather large house, situated in the country; but four families were spending their summer vacation there. And these four families were constantly at loggerheads with one another. They even went so far as to quarrel for the benches, chairs, and tables in the garden, and were always backbiting. All of which set the example for the crew of squalling children, of whom the worst were Theresa's three charges—not two, as the agency had said, but three boys, between the ages of nine and twelve.

The mother was still a young woman, though she had already grown corpulent. Early in the morning, she was already bedecked and powdered, and could be seen walking about in a none-too-tidy negligée, though evening always found her smartly dressed. All the members of the family habitually conversed in that terrible Jewish jargon, which Theresa disliked, even as she rather vaguely disliked Jewish people as a whole, although the treatment accorded her by

212

the Jews with whom she had thus far come in contact had not been worse than that of any other class.

The Eppichs, too, although baptised, had belonged to this race, against which she was frankly prejudiced. It was only shortly before her departure that she learned this fact. The father of her new charges was a small, repressed man, with mild, melancholy eyes, who was hardly ever present except on holidays, when he arrived about noon and at once plunged into a quarrel with his wife. In the afternoons, as Theresa discovered from his wife's contemptuous remarks, he betook himself to a coffee-house, where he played cards until late at night, and gambled away, so his wife asserted, the whole of her dowry.

Theresa wondered why she should complain about being neglected, when she actually had not a moment of the day to spare. All afternoon, she lay on the divan; and all evening, she was "out for a walk," coming home long after the hour when she was expected. Toward Theresa, she behaved quite amiably. Sometimes, she even curried favour with her; at other times, she was violent and impatient, while at all times, her behaviour was characterized by a shamelessness that Theresa often endured with pain.

Theresa intended to give up this position, as soon as the family left their summer home. She therefore took as little pains as possible with the three little Jew-boys, as she called them, and allowed them to play and behave very much as they pleased. And, as time lay heavy on her hands, she would now and then pick up an abandoned novel and, opening it casually, read a chapter here and there.

She once took up one of her mother's books, with no more interest than she felt toward any other novel, for the fragments which she had read of her mother's previous efforts had struck her as being not only dull, but, which was even worse, as being positively ridiculous. Now, she sat in the garden, one afternoon, and read, while some one played the piano. She read apathetically, until suddenly she was deeply moved, she knew not why. It was, after all, a story no different from what might be found in a hundred other cheap novels, so hackneyed, in fact, that she seemed to have read it many times before.

Then Theresa realized why she was so deeply touched. She had been reading the letters of a deceived lover. No wonder they struck her as being so true to life! They were none other, except for some necessary changes due to the plot of the novel, than the letters from Alfred which she had once almost caught her mother pilfering from her drawer.

At first, Theresa felt only that tender sorrow that always overcame her when anything reminded her of Alfred. But then she was seized by a violent feeling of anger against her mother. This mood soon turned to hearty amusement at the thought of how she was, in a sense, a collaborator in her mother's novels. That very evening, she wrote as much to her mother, telling her how flattered she was to have helped a great novelist, even in a modest way.

A few days later, she received from her mother a rather business-like, but quite jovial letter, demanding to know what her daughter expected in payment of her services. And this was followed, two days later, unasked, by the gift of some linen and a white batiste blouse, instead of money. Theresa at first thought of sending them straight back, but reconsidered and kept the things, for it was undeniable that she needed them badly.

LVIII

A FEW days before the contemplated departure for Vienna, Theresa received a letter, asking for a rendezvous.

The signature was that of an officer whose name was totally unknown to her, but in whom she thought she recognized a certain lean, dark-moustached Lieutenant whom she had often noticed in the Kurpark. He was in the habit of measuring her with a peculiarly appraising expression on his face. The officer confessed, unashamed, his deep love, his passion, and his desire, in words that at first aroused her to indignation, but ultimately stirred her deeply.

The whole day, she fought down her own impulses. But that evening, after she had put the children to bed, she could no longer resist, and hurried to meet the Lieutenant in the Kurpark. He was expecting her. As soon as he saw her, he seized her hand in a strong grip and drew her with him along a dark, deserted path. Theresa scarcely knew how it all came about, but she soon found herself answering the passion of his kisses.

He wished to lead her to an even more deserted and remote portion of the garden, but she tore herself free and went home. Only now was she aware of the fact that she had scarcely spoken ten words to the officer during their passionate meeting. She was ashamed of herself. He was to meet her again the next day, but she made up her mind that she would not be there.

She passed an almost sleepless night, during which her desire for the officer mounted to actual bodily pain. At noon, she received a letter from an anonymous "well-wishing friend," warning her to be careful with whom she consorted, for at least one particular officer was here to be cured of a venereal disease, and his cure was still in the early stages. The "well-wishing friend" hoped that this warning had not come too late.

Theresa was panic stricken. She would not leave the house. She was well aware that even last night's kisses might have terrific consequences. She hoped, madly, that God would not punish her with so horrible a fate. She promised that she would never go back to this dangerous man again. In fact, she managed to keep to the house during the next few days, and finally, a violent quarrel with the mother of her charges gave her an excuse for leaving before the expiration of her period of notice. On the way to the station, she saw the Lieutenant in the distance, but managed to slip away before he had noticed her.

Her next employer was a rich manufacturer, in whose house she was not so much governess as nurse to a nine-year-old girl, who was incurably lame and in a gradual decline. Theresa herself was unable to understand why she was so deeply touched with sympathy, not only for the poor child, but for the parents who had been the inconsolable

witnesses of this painful tragedy for nine long years, and
had been forced to keep up their courage in the face of the
realization that there was nothing that they could do. At
first, Theresa was prepared to sacrifice herself, along with
the parents, in this abyss of sorrow; but she soon realized
that she lacked both the physical and the spiritual strength
to long endure the strain, and she was forced to leave.

A friendly letter from her mother determined her upon
a visit to Salzburg, where she was graciously received. Conditions in the small town had changed very favourably for
Frau Fabiani. Society women visited her, and among others,
the wife of a Major, who had been recently stationed there,
and the wife of an editor, all of whom held the novelist in
great esteem.

Theresa felt both more comfortable and, at the same time,
more estranged in her mother's house, as if she were not
with her mother at all, but with some elderly woman whom
she had met somewhere, say during a voyage, and to whom
she was now paying a friendly visit.

When Theresa, in the course of their conversations, spoke
of her many experiences of the past few years, her mother
would listen with great interest, and was not ashamed to
take notes, sometimes word for word. She even suggested
that her daughter send her similar "true experiences," for
which she would be glad to pay.

Even in Salzburg, things had happened. Count Benkheim,
who had once wooed Theresa, and who had finally married
the actress he had been courting, had died, leaving his

widow a tidy fortune. Frau Fabiani also spoke of Karl who, as vice president of a German nationalistic fraternity, was now playing a more and more important rôle in the student life in Vienna and always cut a figure in political circles, when he visited Salzburg. Frau Fabiani was so proud of her son that she did not seem to consider the fact that he not only did not trouble himself about his sister, but did not even care much for his mother.

LIX

WHEN, during the last days of October, Theresa
went back to Vienna, she felt somewhat recovered in health,
but spiritually more impoverished than ever. She had
parted with Frau Fabiani with a perfect understanding, and
now realized more deeply than ever before that she had no
mother. Of her three weeks' stay in Salzburg, she remembered with pleasure only her lonely walks and the solitary
hours which she had spent in the church, where, it is true,
she never prayed, but where she yet felt sheltered and at
peace.

Theresa now took a position in the house of a judge in
the Supreme Court, who, with his wife, his children, and another person, lived in a small suburban villa. The judge
was a silent and melancholy, but withal courteous gentleman; the mother, a kindly, though suppressed creature; and
the two daughters, aged ten and twelve years respectively,
though not in the least talented, were well-behaved and
willing children. Though it was a meagre ménage, nothing
absolutely necessary was lacking. Even where human sympathy was concerned, Theresa had her share in the correct
measure, so that she need not feel spoiled on the one hand,
or quite neglected on the other.

In the same dwelling lived a roomer, a young bank official, who had nothing whatever to do with the family. Theresa saw him only for rare, brief moments on the staircase or in the hall. Occasionally, they exchanged comments upon the weather. Nevertheless, she was not in the least surprised—on the contrary, she was rather expecting it—when, one evening, as they met at a very late hour in the hall, he suddenly took her violently in his arms and kissed her. That same night—she scarcely knew whether she had asked or had been asked by him—she spent the night with him. Thereafter, she was with him every night, though sometimes only for fifteen minutes, for she slept in the same room with the two maids and was afraid of arousing suspicions.

With the exception of these moments, she hardly ever thought of him. And when she met him, she scarcely realized that he was her lover. Nevertheless, she now regretted her wasted years, as she phrased it; for, since the deflection of Kasimir Tobisch, she had had no lover.

When she began to notice that he was falling in love with her and began to question her jealously concerning her past, she knew that it was time to break with him. She caused him to believe that the judge's family was becoming aware of their affair; and she acted as if she were deeply afraid of possible consequences, as, indeed, she sometimes was.

One day, she began looking about for a new place, and left suddenly, while he was away at work, without leaving him her address.

LX

THERESA'S next position was with the family of a money-changer of the business section. Here, she had a great deal of time to herself, for the mother of her seven-year-old charge was an unhappy person, who loved nothing better than to spend hours alone in the company of her boy. Thus, Theresa had not only hours, but frequently whole days, in which to go to Ensbach and see her Franz. But more often she chose to walk about the streets of the city, without any set destination in her mind. She excused herself for not going to her child by fancying that the peasant couple, and especially Agnes, with her forward, yet secretive ways, had become absolutely unbearable to her.

It so happened that, one evening, she encountered the handsome, curlyheaded fellow whom she had met, two years before, at the Greitler ball. He declared that fate had brought her to him. So weak-willed was she that, on their next meeting, she was prepared to give him anything he asked for.

He was a law student, impudent and merry, and Theresa fell deeply in love with him, often sacrificing to him the days which she really intended to devote to her child. She often wished that she might talk with him seriously, to tell him more of herself. But he was always so patently bored when she began that she desisted for fear of annoying him with her personal affairs.

Toward the end of the summer, she received a gay farewell letter from him. He said that she had been a grand girl, and that he would always remember her. He hoped that she would likewise remember him. Theresa cried through two whole nights. Then she journeyed to Ensbach, to her child, whom she had not seen for at least a month. She loved him now more than ever.

Before the image of the Virgin Mary on the oak tree, she made a solemn vow never more to neglect Franz. Since Agnes was not at home, she got on very well with the Leutners; and when evening came, she returned to Vienna, feeling much relieved. She was again at peace with herself. It was as if she had been plagued by a great thirst; and now, her thirst allayed, she could once more calmly resume her tasks. But when she began to pay some attention to her pupil, the mother became distrustful; and one day, she even accused Theresa of seeking to steal the child's love away from its mother. This, together with the fact that her husband had recently acquired a mistress, aroused the woman to fits of jealousy that approached an actually diseased condition. Theresa was simply forced to depart. There was nothing else to do.

LXI

Now she found a place in a quiet and very comfortable house, where she hoped she might remain a long time. The owner was a busy manufacturer, whose very activity kept him happy. His wife was a kind-hearted, pleasant woman; and his two girls, just growing out of childhood, were well-bred, tractable, and musically talented children.

Theresa was by this time accustomed to her rapidly changing environment, and knew how to strike the right note between reserve and familiarity. She was careful not to let her heart go out to her charges. She cultivated an attitude of cool motherliness, which she was capable of raising or lowering by several degrees at will. This was the foundation of her relationship to her employers' children. Thus, spiritually, she was free as soon as she closed the door behind her; and when she came back, she was again at once at home.

She now visited her boy regularly, though in the intervals between these visits she was never troubled by any longing for him.

Once, at the approach of winter, when she was going to Ensbach, she found the train crowded, and was forced to take a first-class carriage. An elegant, middle-aged gentleman was the only other occupant. He engaged Theresa in conversation, and informed her that he was going to Germany; and that, having been on a country estate, he was compelled to take this local train for the first part of his journey.

He spoke with great affectation, and constantly stroked his scrubby English moustache with his index finger. She allowed him to believe that she was a married woman; and after all, he had no reason to doubt her word, nor her information that she was on a visit to a friend of hers, the wife of a doctor, who, with her four children, lived all the year round in the country.

By the time she reached Ensbach, she had acceded to the gentleman's plea that she allow him to see her when, in two weeks, he returned from Munich. He kissed her hand in parting.

As she walked over the snow-covered walk toward her familiar destination, she was aware of her lightened step and her heightened self-consciousness. Toward her child, she felt a curious estrangement. At about this time she became more conscious than ever of his speech, which, if it was not actually dialect, at any rate had a peasant accent. She wondered if it were not high time for her to move the lad to the city. Clearly, it was her duty to do so. But how was she to manage it?

She recalled the elegant gentleman in the railway carriage, with his fine fur coat and his yellow gloves. And as she walked into the snow-covered world, she herself seemed almost a married lady, just as she had told him she was. Then, she saw herself in the small, stuffy room, drinking coffee by the light of an oil-lamp, while Frau Leutner gossiped; while Agnes, in her Sunday dress, sat by the stove and sewed, and little Franz painfully spelled out words from his picture book.

Suppose her fine gentleman suspected that she had not gone to visit a country friend, but instead, to see her illegitimate child, the son of Kasimir Tobisch, the swindler? She trembled and, calling her boy, kissed him and mothered him, as if she were thus making restitution to him for her evil thoughts.

The next two weeks passed with a painful, snail-like pace. It seemed as if her sole object in life was to see this strange man again. When the moment of their rendezvous approached, she was frightened lest he fail to keep the appointment.

He was there; in fact, he had been waiting for some time. His appearance somewhat undeceived her. In the railway compartment, she had not observed that his stature was shorter than her own, nor that he was almost bald. But his words, the very intonation of his voice, again affected her.

She claimed that she had only half an hour to spare; that she was invited to a tea where her husband would meet her, after which they would visit the theatre. He did not insist. He did not wish to be indiscreet, but expressed himself as satisfied that she had come. He apologized for not having sooner introduced himself. He was Dr. Bing, a department head in the Ministry.

"I do not insist, Madame, that you give me your name."

He instantly added:

"I hope you will soon be convinced that you can completely trust me. Then you may give me your name, if you wish."

He then discussed his journey. It had not been a pleasure, but an official trip of political importance. All the same, he had managed, while in Berlin, to see a number of operas. The opera was really his only amusement. Was Madame musically inclined?

"A little," Theresa confessed; but added that she had very little time to go to operas and concerts.

"Of course," Dr. Bing added. He could understand this, what with her domestic duties, family matters, and the like. Theresa shook her head. No, she had no children. She had had one, but it had died. She did not know why she lied, why she sinned and deceived. Dr. Bing apologized for having touched a sore spot in her heart. Theresa appreciated his delicacy as much as if she had actually told the truth.

At a certain corner, she suddenly asked him to leave her and permit her to go on alone. He took his leave of her very politely, and she departed, feeling annoyed with herself for having made a free evening, and then thrown away her chance to do something with it. It pained her; but there was nothing else to be done but to go home.

At their next meeting, one cold winter evening, Dr. Bing invited her to have tea with him in his apartment. She did not hold out any longer than was necessary. And it really did not require the effect of an excellent meal in his comfortable rooms, with the turned-down lights, to bring the adventure to its foreseen and desired culmination.

He asked no questions, and seemed prepared to believe anything that she cared to tell him. Yet, on their next visit, perhaps through fear of once standing revealed before him as a prevaricator, she deemed it expedient to tell him at least a part of the truth.

She was married, she said, but had been separated from her husband for the past two years. After the death of her child, her husband had left her, and despite legal notice, refused to support her. She had therefore determined to earn her living as a governess. The department head kissed her hand, and was more respectful than ever.

They met regularly, once every fortnight; and Theresa was each time happy to go to his well-appointed apartment, with its beautifully shaded lamps, to enjoy the invariably excellently prepared meal which he offered her. The very change in her life which this day brought meant more to her than her lover himself. His voice was still as agreeable as ever; his manner of speech affected her just as delightfully as on the first day; but she could not simulate much interest in the things he told her.

She was most attracted to him when he spoke of his mother, who had obviously been a noble and kind-hearted woman. Concerning the opera, he always spoke in phrases that, it seemed to her, she had previously read in the newspapers. Frequently, too, he spoke of political matters, in a dry, matter-of-fact way, as though he were speaking to a professional colleague of the ministry. He sometimes did this at moments that were certainly incongruous. In his exceedingly discreet manner, which was not, however, quite free from self-gratification, he had declared himself anxious to augment her material situation with a small monthly allowance. At first, she emphatically declined; but, after a decent interval, she accepted.

On the whole, this was a very calm period in Theresa's career, and it might have been a very happy one, had she not been more than ever aware of the aimless, meaningless character of her life. Sometimes, she felt impelled to reveal all the torments of her heart to her lover. But some inner barrier always restrained her. There were moments when she felt that this resistance came from his side, for she had noticed that he avoided moments of confidences, as if to avoid the annoyance, or perhaps the greater responsibility, that such confidences might entail.

Thus, she was well aware that this affair would soon come to an end, just as she was conscious that, no matter how friendly her relationship to her employers and their children might become, she could never find a home among them.

So she realized the unstable pattern of her life. Even in the presence of her child, she could not feel any sense of security. No, she could not even deny the self-evident fact that Franz was closer to Frau Leutner and to the rapidly maturing Agnes, than he was to his own mother.

Sometimes her soul yearned for some one to whom she could speak of her inner emptiness and her desires. And now and then, when Theresa was in the company of some other governess who confided all her troubles to her, then she, Theresa, likewise wished to be able to speak out concerning the secrets of her own heart. But she never did. Perhaps it were best so. Her acquaintances considered her a secretive and haughty person. The best of them thought to excuse her by saying that, coming as she did from an impoverished family of the nobility, she thought that she merited a better position than she held in life.

In May, after a number of days of worry, interspersed with periods of deceitful composure and hope, she was no longer able to conceal the truth from herself. She was pregnant again! Naturally, her first impulse was to inform her lover. But at their next meeting, an indescribable shyness overcame her as she was on the point of revealing her condition, whereupon she decided not to tell him anything at all, but instead, to rid herself of the child in all haste. Rather death, she said to herself, than another child!

She did not hesitate long, but betook herself to a place where, for a sum of money which she had originally laid aside for a new dress, she was quickly relieved of the source of her agitation. The manufacturer's family were somewhat annoyed that it was necessary for her to stay in bed a few days. Suspicion awakened in their minds, and their attitude became so unfriendly that Theresa felt she could no longer endure their censure, which they no longer took the trouble to conceal.

Without revealing the original cause of her misfortune, Theresa one day communicated the story of her misery to her lover. The latter received her tale unmoved, hardly taking the pains to conceal the coldness behind his conventional and affected responses. She noted this with bitterness; and suddenly, offended beyond endurance, she overwhelmed him with all the unspoken reproaches which had been gathering within her heart during the last few months. Words came to her lips of which, a moment later, she was heartily ashamed.

When her lover, however, acted as if it were his part to forgive her, her indignation burst forth again; and this time, she did not spare him a full recital of the cause of all her calamities. She flung it in his face, and reproached him with having treated her as one hardly better than a street-walker. He was touched by her emotion, and sought, in his crude fashion, to appease her. But all that Theresa could feel in his tender words was his exultation at having got off so cheaply. She flung this at him, too, and tried to leave him; but he restrained her. He kissed her hands, and begged her to forgive him. So they were reconciled, but Theresa realized that this revival of their passion would be of short duration.

A few days passed, and the manufacturer's family, having decided to leave for the country, took this opportunity of discharging Theresa. She breathed freely, once more. It was a day of exceptional beauty, of such beauty that it seemed to her a portent of reconciling grace, when she betook herself along the familiar path to the Leutners' place.

Theresa had brought presents, not only for her boy, but also for Herr and Frau Leutner, and even for Agnes, although she liked the girl less and less. This summer, she proposed to consider more seriously her child's education; although it frequently occurred to her that such plans were to little avail, since she could be with him so infrequently, to offset the peasant and rural influences which surrounded him at all times.

Theresa was repeatedly shocked and astounded to observe in her Franz singular gestures and crude mannerisms, which sometimes amusingly reminded her of Herr Leutner himself. She did what she could to eradicate the worst of his boorish locutions and actions. She tried, too, to assist him in his studies. Naturally, he was still in the elementary stages of reading, writing, and arithmetic; but he learned quickly, although he showed no particular interest in his work.

It would have pleased Theresa if her son had shared her love of the beauties of Nature, but he could not appreciate, as she did, the lyrical splendour of the scenery, the odour of the fields, the flight of butterflies. Always surrounded by these things, he took them for granted; and perhaps after all, it was asking too much of him to expect

him to exhibit joy at the sight of what had constituted the
intimate atmosphere of his life from the day of his birth.
Still, she felt that he lacked sensibility.

She became increasingly aware of the narrow circles
in which the Leutners, and the other families of the neighbourhood, moved. To be sure, the people of the community
saw each other frequently enough, meeting as they did
in the fields, at the inn, and in the church. But there existed
no real social life; there was no true communication from
person to person, or from family to family. Their conversations were always the same. It frequently happened
that Theresa was told the same story of some unimportant
event by a dozen different people, over and over again,
and usually in the same words and with the same gestures.
She herself had long since ceased to be of particular interest to the inhabitants of Ensbach. It was commonly
known that she was Franz's mother, and that she held a
position in Vienna. She was on friendly terms with every
one, and conversed with all the people she met; so much,
indeed, that she herself soon fell into the habit of telling
the same inane stories over and over again, with the same
words and gestures.

In an effort to mitigate her carefully concealed boredom, during the two months she remained in the country,
Theresa wrote a great many letters. She entered into correspondence with some of the other governesses with whom
she had become acquainted, and, from time to time, she
sent cards of greeting to some of her former charges. Her

mother, however, was the recipient of her most detailed letters.

Theresa had never told Frau Fabiani of the existence of her child. She merely explained to her that she had gone to the country, in company with a girl friend, in order to enjoy a rest. She was quite certain, however, that her mother suspected the truth, if she were not, indeed, acquainted with all the facts. She did not really care to conceal them from anybody, except her brother. The bond between them had been resumed, to a limited degree, since one day when he had chanced to meet her, and had subsequently paid her a visit when she was employed in the manufacturer's household.

Theresa received several replies to her letters to Doctor Bing. These consisted of short, formal sentences, which were in strange contrast to his glowing perorations and exordiums. They rather disgusted Theresa. Once, she delayed answering him, waiting to see if he would pursue the correspondence of his own accord. But she did not hear from him. And, in her heart, she was glad of it.

LXII

In September, Theresa accepted a position as governess to a seventeen-year-old girl—a pale, homely, somewhat simple-minded child, the only daughter of a retired wholesale merchant, whose two sons, the one a lawyer and the other an engineer, shared the house with him. They lived in the first floor of an old, suburban house, a rather dreary, but well-preserved building, in which some modern conveniences—notably, electric lights—had not been introduced. The wholesale merchant, who had been blind for many years, was still a handsome, well built man, and he wore a neat, gray beard. He personally selected Theresa from among the various applicants, because, as he said, her voice sounded like that of a loyal person, and had moved him deeply and agreeably.

Since Berta, the daughter, lacked all ability to supervise the household, this duty fell upon Theresa; and she was pleased to discover in herself a positive talent in this direction. The house was more frequented and much gayer than Theresa had anticipated. The young men regularly received visits from their colleagues; the daughter, Berta, was visited by friends and relatives: and thus the house was constantly filled with a young, lively, often noisy company in whose presence the old man took obvious enjoyment.

Theresa was invited to participate in the social life of these happy people. She was made to feel as one of the family. One of the cousins—a vivacious, arrogant girl—even made Theresa the confidante of her first passion. She claimed that she was in love with the elder of her uncles, the lawyer. But, to Theresa's eyes, it seemed that the girl was equally in love with the other brother, or even with a certain blond soldier, who was a frequent guest at the house.

Theresa was sensible of a certain envy at these confidences, although she would not confess it to herself, since she had vowed that she would never again enter into any relationship which could lead her nowhere. She was weary of being pushed about here and there in the world. She longed for peace, for a home which she might call her own. How many among her acquaintances, with no particular distinction of person or position, had contrived, without much effort, to find themselves husbands! And if they could do it, why shouldn't she?

Only recently, a governess of Theresa's acquaintance, a meagre, rather faded creature, had married a well-situated bookkeeper. Another governess, and this one a person of none too excellent reputation, had married a rich widower in whose house she had been employed. There was no really good reason why she, Theresa, should not be similarly successful!

Her child would not, must not prevent her. After all, was her condition any different from that of one who had been divorced or widowed? Herr Truebner was no longer young; and, moreover, he lacked his eyesight. But he was a stately, yes, a really handsome man, and she had no difficulty in observing that he enjoyed her presence.

He particularly liked to have her read to him, especially from philosophical writings. At first, these bored her immeasurably, until he began to interrupt her with friendly questions, the answers to which he himself provided, in such a fashion that he almost delivered connected lectures to her. Soon, she not only understood, but became thoroughly interested in an otherwise, to her, strange realm of thought.

Occasionally, he questioned her closely regarding her past. With a fair amount of truth, she related to him the history of her youth, of her parents, of her life in Salzberg, and of her many experiences as a governess. She glossed over her affairs of the heart, leaving him to suspect that she had suffered a great deal, and that once, years ago, she had been "as good as married."

Herr Truebner did not probe further, but, one evening, between two chapters of a philosophical treatise, he asked Theresa, in a serious but gentle voice, how her child was getting along. She blushed and hesitated. He went on to explain that he had long ago deduced, from the tone of her voice, that she was a mother. Theresa did not answer, and Herr Truebner took her hand and held it for a long time in silence. He did not seek to make her reveal any more.

Some time afterwards, when she came home from some errand and was just mounting the steps, she met the blond soldier on the dimly lighted staircase. As if in jest, he refused to allow her to pass. She smiled and, in the next moment, he had her in his arms, and refused to release her until the sound of an opening door interrupted them. She dashed up the steps without looking back; but she knew all the while that he had already won her.

She felt that it would be useless to protract a meaningless resistance, so, at their next meeting, she gave him an assignation, asking him to promise her only one thing—that he would never reveal their secret to any one.

He promised, and he kept his word. For Theresa, there was a particular charm in sitting across from him in the Truebner house; and in seeing him there, with his eyes still heavy with love and passion, and hearing him address her in the most formal manner. His attitude toward the other girls did not change in the slightest degree. To them, he was still the gallant soldier, bringing them flowers and candy, and, on festive occasions, playing the piano while the young people danced.

No one suspected their relationship . . . that is, no one, except the blind clairvoyant merchant, who one day took it upon himself to warn Theresa, in his gentle way, of the dangers and deceptions to which young people in her position are exposed. Although Theresa suspected that the old man was not interested in preserving her virtue for her own sake alone, she nevertheless took his warning to heart; and her demeanour toward Ferdinand altered at once. She was no longer the thoughtless, gay creature whom he had formerly held in his arms. She began to bethink herself of duties which previously she had never allowed to stand as hindrances to their appointments. And after another talk with Herr Truebner, in which he spoke, in guarded words, of the frivolity of youth and of the duty of single women to society, Theresa, as if under a spell, felt herself compelled to write a farewell letter to Ferdinand. Three days later, to be sure, they were together again; but both of them realized that the end of their adventure was fast approaching.

One day, early in the spring, as she was shopping in the city, Theresa met Alfred. She had not seen him since that day when she had been in the carriage, with her new-born baby and Frau Nebling, on her way to the station. He stood still, no less pleased than she; and both of them at once began to converse in such an exceedingly friendly fashion that, after a few minutes, neither was able to credit the fact that eight years had passed since their last meeting.

Alfred had hardly changed at all. That little shyness which so specially characterized him was still noticeable, although now it no longer made him appear awkward, so much as reserved. Theresa related to him as much as she wished to of her many experiences, and was silent regarding many things which his eyes seemed to ask her, though his lips spoke nothing. No doubt, he suspected that her affair with Max had not been her last. After all, he himself had grown into a man.

She again experienced that strange conviction that sometimes overcame her, that Alfred was the father of her child. She smiled mysteriously. Alfred's eyes returned a questioning look. He began to tell her of his life. His two sisters were married. His mother was ill. He himself was to receive his doctorate this summer. Rather tardily, he admitted, but he was not as industrious as many of his other comrades—as Karl, for instance, who was already an interne, and was surely at the beginning of a great career. If not as a doctor, at any rate, as a politician, he added, smiling.

Did Theresa know that her brother was no longer a Fabiani, but a Faber? Yes, indeed! For one of his strong, pan-Germanic sentiments a name with an Italian sound might one day prove a stumbling-block to his progress and a weapon in the hands of his opponents.

Theresa looked away.

"I hardly ever see him," she said, casually.

Then she begged Alfred to write to her, as soon as he had become a doctor.

"Not before?" he asked.

She smiled, and extended her hand to him. She smiled all the way home.

Herr Truebner departed somewhat from the type of books

which he had formerly preferred. Theresa had to read him some lighter works. Therein, they frequently encountered passages that bore so strong a resemblance to her own life that her voice broke as she read. Once, as she was reading a chapter in a translation of some French memoirs, she was obliged to stop, not only because she was ashamed, but because, due to her emotion, her voice failed her.

Herr Truebner seized her hand and drew it to his lips. Theresa, both frightened and unnerved, made no resistance; whereupon, he became bolder, until Theresa finally had to beg him to leave her alone. She remained at his side in silence for a while; then, she excused herself and left the room.

On the following day, her employer, in his most gentle voice, begged her to forgive him. She was deeply moved. But when he renewed his advances, after an interval of two days, she tore herself loose and shortly thereafter, gave her notice, saying that she had been called to the side of her sick mother.

LXIII

B<small>Y</small> virtue of the excellent recommendations which she received from the Truebners, Theresa was able to exercise a certain choice in her next position. She decided to enter the house of a certain Rottmann family, where the two daughters, aged ten and thirteen, had captivated her by their frank and animated ways. The mother, who was a pianist, and frequently absent for long periods on extended concert tours, became at once almost too friendly with Theresa, and the woman's nervous, capricious manner annoyed her.

As to the father—a serious, somewhat melancholy man of exceedingly youthful appearance—Theresa simply could not understand him. During the first few days, he appeared to be merely a much respected guest, and not really the master of the household. But the whole atmosphere of the house abruptly changed, when Frau Rottmann departed on her tour.

The whole tone of the house was pitched to a gayer note. The daughters acted as if a weight had been lifted from them. The father's melancholy disappeared. The servants obeyed the new governess much more readily than they had ever obeyed their mistress. No one ever mentioned the absent member of the family. No letters ever came from her—only occasional picture post-cards from the German cities where she was performing.

Theresa was happier than she had ever been before. The management of the household and the teaching of her clever pupils kept her both busy and satisfied.

Six weeks later, Frau Rottmann returned, and at once everything lapsed into its former state. Even worse, as far as Theresa could judge from the meagre progress made by her pupils, as compared with the rapid strides which they had made during the absence of their mother. Herr Rottmann again relapsed into his former melancholy.

During August, the family moved to a nearby, very unpretentious resort. Seemingly out of sheer boredom, Frau Rottmann took Theresa into her confidence, and related to her all the various experiences and adventures which she had encountered on her numerous journeys. Theresa would have preferred not to listen but her quite apparent reserve mattered very little to Frau Rottmann. She, as Theresa quickly noticed, was interested only in breaking the monotony of their sojourn in the country; and it mattered little who her audience was, as long as she had an audience.

No sooner had the family returned to the city, than Frau Rottmann ceased her confidences. In the autumn, she went to London, ostensibly to extend her studies with a famous pianist resident in that metropolis. At once, the house breathed freely again. And Theresa felt so perfectly at home in the company of the daughters and their father that she often asked herself if she were not indeed better fitted to be the mother of this household than the wandering pianist.

Herr Rottmann pleased her immensely. She made this much plain to him, and their proximity, together with their constant association in their daily life, did the rest. She became his mistress. Both observed the strictest secrecy, and were careful not to conduct themselves, when in the presence of others, in any way that might betray their relationship.

At Christmas time when Frau Rottmann returned, although Theresa realized the necessity of caution, the manner in which Herr Rottmann seemed to have completely forgotten her existence, angered her beyond endurance. She suffered much on account of his exaggerated wariness; and when his wife left again, after a few weeks, she obstinately refused to permit a resumption of their former intimacy.

But he managed to explain to her the necessity of his actions, and secured his pardon from her, with the result that their old life was resumed, after all. Sometimes, Theresa caught herself wishing that some anonymous letter would come to inform Herr Rottmann of the manner in which his wife demeaned herself while on her tours. Once, she even dared, in a half jocular manner, to suggest to him the possible dangers that threatened beautiful women, especially artists, on their sojourns in foreign countries. Herr Rottmann, however, appeared not to understand that any reference was being made to his wife.

Frau Rottmann returned a few days earlier than she was expected, and at once exhibited a changed attitude toward Theresa. She shut herself up with her husband and, when she reappeared, summoned the governess, while Herr Rottmann escaped from the house, and abruptly declared that she knew everything. Then she berated Theresa violently, and without sparing her language in the least.

Theresa did not know how to reply. She was mad with humiliation that the man to whom she had given herself could have been such a coward as to leave her alone. Apparently, he had given his wife full authority to act as she saw fit. Frau Rottmann had so managed the scene that her daughters were not at home, and she insisted that Theresa should leave the house forthwith, before they returned.

Theresa went to her room and packed her belongings, overcome with the stupidity of her behaviour. Suddenly, she decided not to leave the house until she had flung into the face of this man and his wife all that she knew of them and that they deserved to hear. But Frau Rottmann had already departed. The servant grinned as she informed Theresa that the couple had gone to the Theatre. Did the Fraulein wish her to fetch a cab and take her things down? No, Theresa replied; she still had something to say to Herr and Frau Rottmann, and would await their return.

She was dressed and ready to leave. Her trunk and her bag were packed, but she waited with compressed lips, while a terrible rage filled her heart. Then the two girls came home, and, finding Theresa prepared to go away, assailed her with questions. Theresa wept, and at first was unable to answer. Then she declared that she had received a telegram saying that her mother was very ill, and that she must return to Salzburg at once.

She arose, kissed the two girls as gently as if they were her very own, begged them not to make her departure difficult, and went below to await the arrival of the servant girl with a cab.

LXIV

LATE that night, she arrived at Ensbach—a discharged, expelled, shamed, unhappy creature, with whom the world was disgusted, and she herself more than any one else. Her boy was fast asleep. In the dark, she could see only the pale glow of his beloved, childish face. She was grieved to reflect that it was two months since she had last seen him. She had belonged to other people, and had been obliged to obey others. Once again, the injustice of her fate oppressed her. She swore that she would never again sacrifice herself to the children of strangers; that she would see to it that her own child no longer had to live with strange people.

For a long time, sleep would not pity her. It was incredible that she had spent the previous night at the Rottmanns'; in fact, in Herr Rottmann's own bed! She buried herself deep in the covers and pillows, as though she could hide her shameful experience from herself. What had come over her in this last year?

In the morning, however, she awoke feeling gay and more refreshed than she had been for a long time. It was like a miracle! A single night away from the city, away from the Rottmanns', had, so it seemed, restored her to health. Was not life an easy matter, so long as such miracles were possible?

Never before had the radiance of the sunlight, the calm of the country-side, made her so happy. If only she might remain here forever! Well, in any case, there were many goodly days of peace before her to enjoy, and now she was not sorry that she had not been too stubborn in her refusal to accept the occasional gifts of money which Herr Rottmann had pressed upon her. These sums would enable her to remain somewhat longer at Ensbach.

Everything about her boy delighted her. Even a certain way that he had of holding his head, which used formerly to remind her, painfully and with uncanny intimacy, of Kasimir Tobisch, no longer disturbed her. She took long walks with him, or she would play with him in the fields. She was young again, almost a child once more; and her son Franz was a child, too, more than he had ever been.

About a week after her arrival, Agnes returned from the city, to pay a visit to her family. Franz received her with wild exclamations of joy; and all during the day, he scarcely bothered at all about his mother, who was made to feel almost like a stranger by his neglect. When Agnes departed, leaving Franz actually miserable and in despair, Theresa felt unreasonably angered against him, as though he were a grown man and answerable to her for a great misdeed. Toward Agnes, whom she had always disliked as an impudent and secretive person, Theresa now felt a veritable hatred.

Her whole attitude was suddenly reversed. She had temporarily rejected the idea of taking her son with her, on account of the present impracticality of the plan. Now she dismissed the idea completely. After all, what could she do, except to make her living educating other people's children, while she left her own child in the country?

One thing, however, she solemnly swore to herself. Never again would she commit a stupidity such as that which had upset the comfortable scheme of her life. Of late, as she well knew, she had become particularly attractive. No matter how economically and how simply she was clothed she knew that she presented a striking appearance. And, despite her modest and even reserved demeanour, there was some gesture or look that she gave unconsciously, that promised things which she had no idea of giving.

She determined henceforth to make better use of the gifts that Nature had bestowed upon her. After her recent experience in the Rottmann family, she felt prepared and fortified to hold herself calculating and cold toward all men, except when it might be definitely to her advantage to be otherwise. She was in communication with several agencies, and now and again she answered advertisements; but nothing seemed to come of it in the field which she especially desired—employment with a widow with children.

Among the letters which she received, there was one from Alfred. It was the belated printed invitation to his graduation, which had already taken place. The same day, she received a letter from her mother, asking her if she could not shorten her stay with her "girl-friend"—the word was set between quotation-marks—and come to Salzburg for a few days.

To Theresa, this invitation, arriving as it did at that particular moment, seemed like the beckoning finger of fate; for she suspected that Alfred, after his graduation, would have gone to spend some time with his parents. It was the hope of seeing him that caused her to leave Ensbach on the following morning.

LXV

Nor was she mistaken. On the very first day of her stay in Salzburg, she met him in front of the Cathedral. They took a walk along the same streets which they had traversed years before, to the same park, and indeed, to the very bench where the two officers had once passed, the dark eyed one holding his cap in his hand.

This time, she told Alfred many things concerning her life. She felt that Alfred would understand these confidences. She felt certain that if she had revealed even more, he would have understood. She did not conceal the fact that she had a son nine years old, and Alfred told her that he had known it long since. When he had seen her, that time, riding past in an open coach, he had not failed to observe the old woman with a child in her lap, and he had never doubted that the child was Theresa's. He did not agree with her that it was necessary to maintain such a strict secrecy concerning the child. Of late, people were much more liberal in that respect, and there were many families where her past would surely not be held against her.

They met several times again in the following days, accidentally, and yet they had both been certain that they would encounter one another. Alfred spoke of his interneship in the General Hospital, which he was to assume upon his return in the fall. They exchanged no promises, but when he took leave of her on the day of his departure, they both knew that they would soon see each other in Vienna.

Three days later, Theresa also left for the capital. Her mother accompanied her to the train. She had never been so amiable to her daughter as in the last few days, and yet Theresa felt in her presence some inexplicable resistance which prevented her from disclosing her most intimate self.

When the train was already in motion and Theresa stood at the window of her carriage, her mother suddenly called to her:

"Kiss your little boy for me!"

Theresa blushed, and then nodded to her mother, as if to a newly acquired friend.

LXVI

HER next position was not with a widow, but with a couple who had one child—a boy about the age of Franz. The father, an editor, was a rather young but grayhaired, slender man, who was friendly, abstracted, and generally rather excited. He was in the habit of rising at noon, and did not come home from work until about three in the morning. His wife, petite and graceful like her husband, was the manager of a gown shop, and left the house very early in the morning. Thus, the Herr and Frau Knauer took their meals separately, and at all hours. Yet Theresa had never encountered such a smoothly run household, or such a well-mated couple.

She followed Alfred's advice, and demanded two successive free days each month, so as to be able to spend them with her child at Ensbach. Frau Knauer offered no objections. In fact, her attitude was exactly as Alfred had thought it would be, and she seemed even to take an especial liking to Theresa on this account. Each time Theresa returned from Ensbach, Frau Knauer never failed to ask concerning the child, and she rather liked to talk about it.

Her own child, Robert, was a blond, curly-headed, beautifully built boy—so perfect a child that Theresa could not

253

understand how his parents had begotten him. From the very first moment she saw him, Theresa took the child to her heart and grew to feel for him a greater affection than she had ever felt for any of her charges.

Robert did not go to school, so Theresa had complete charge of his education. She devoted herself to this difficult task with all her soul—so much so, that sometimes she felt abashed at her neglect of her own child; and on such occasions she was especially gentle with him, and rejoiced that her son was, after all, the stronger and more rosy-cheeked of the two, even if he were not actually prettier than Robert.

Nor was he less apt than Robert, though his speech was full of peasant locutions. Nevertheless, in her heart, Robert continually surpassed her Franz; and Theresa suffered thereby, for she realized that this was not the first sin of which she was guilty in her relationship to her child.

One day, when she was out walking with Robert, she met Alfred, whom she had not seen since they were in Salzburg together; and she seized the opportunity to tell him that she wished to speak to him at greater length, as soon as a suitable meeting could be arranged. Very soon thereafter, on one of her free evenings, she met him by appointment, at a place not far from the hospital, and acquainted him with the details of her relationship to her own child and the other one who was superseding him in her heart.

Alfred quieted her conscience, and explained to her that it was quite natural that she could not have the same feeling

toward her child as she might have in happier circumstances, for even so fundamental an emotion as mother love
required constant renewal by the presence of the living object.

He concluded by expressing a desire to see the child; and
so, on their next evening walk, they made an appointment,
and he accompanied her to Ensbach on her first Christmas
holiday. He sat with the child and together they went
through the picture book which he had brought with him.
Alfred was friendly, but inquisitive; reserved, yet amiable;
and Theresa could not but admire his ability to sound the
right note, not only with her son, but also with Frau Leutner and her dull, unsociable husband. In consequence, their
visit to the country passed quickly and pleasantly.

On the train, en route for Vienna, Alfred did not conceal
from Theresa his conviction that her child was neither
in the proper environment nor with the right people. She
ought to find some place nearer the city—in some suburb,
perhaps—where she could see him more often and supervise his further education.

Before they left the train at Vienna, Alfred kissed her. It
was their first kiss since that evening in Salzburg, when they
had parted, without suspecting how long it was to be before
they should see one another again.

Shortly thereafter, it so happened that Frau Knauer asked
Theresa if she would not forego her coming two days off,
and instead, invite her son to pass the day in Vienna with

them. Theresa was at first reluctant to accept this suggestion. She was somewhat afraid to see the two children side
by side.

In her indecision, she turned again to Alfred, who
quieted her fears. So, one day, she had Frau Leutner bring
Franz to the house. The day passed more pleasantly than
Theresa had anticipated. The two boys struck up a friendship at once, and chatted and played together all day long.
In the evening, when Frau Leutner came to get Franz, Robert insisted that his new friend should soon return. Frau
Knauer nodded her assent, and her friendly comments concerning Franz made Theresa very proud.

It was settled, now, that Frau Leutner was to bring Franz
to Vienna, two or three times each month. Robert always
received him with great joy, and Frau Knauer took a genuine liking to him. Even Herr Knauer, who sometimes
passed half an hour in the children's room, seemed to take
to the lad. This was not particularly significant, however,
for Herr Knauer was always happy and always quite abstracted. He was always in complete agreement with everybody and everything, and presented everywhere the same
superficial amiability.

This gray-haired, unkempt journalist aroused in Theresa
a growing sense of strangeness and impenetrability. Sometimes, it seemed to her as if his constant jocularity were a
mask behind which he concealed his real self.

Theresa fell into the habit of going over her experiences
and opinions with Alfred, and the latter always smiled

at her propensity for discovering strange and exceptional characteristics in everything. The two grew more and more intimate. Their meetings were now much more frequent than before, but usually they were very brief, although sometimes they went to the theatre together, and afterwards had supper in some small, inexpensive coffee-house.

Theresa's attitude toward Alfred was now similar to what it had been many years ago. She wished that he were more bold, that he were gifted with a great initiative. But no sooner did he betray any such impulses, than she at once became frightened; as if she feared that, in becoming more beautiful, their happy moments were but fated to end the more quickly.

LXVII

At length, one evening in the early spring, she gave herself to him, in his bare but exceedingly neatly-kept room in the Alser suburb. In thus becoming his at last, she had a sentiment that she was fulfilling a long-neglected obligation, rather than that she was acceding to any suppressed longing of her own. That night was the first time that she had ever been unable to speak freely to Alfred of the emotions which filled her heart. The thought came to her with an almost physical pain.

Gradually, however, she came to feel more happy when she was in his arms than she had ever in her life been before. Alfred was veritably the first man whom she had ever known, the only man whom she could trust. To all the other men whom, from time to time, she had permitted to enter her life, she had remained relatively a stranger, or at least, a person of ambiguous status, if not merely an easily possessed and quickly forgotten victim. But Alfred belonged to her.

The only thing about his attitude which occasionally offended her was his all too apparent unwillingness to be seen in public with her; a precaution for which he endeavoured to find excuse in the embarrassment which he would feel if he were to encounter Karl while in her company. He sullenly refused to go with her again to Ensbach. She no longer importuned him, since she observed that her requests irritated him.

One of the most pleasant days which Theresa ever experienced occurred the first time Frau Knauer gave her permission to take Robert with her to Ensbach. The sight of "her two children"—as she called them in secret, to herself and, on this occasion, to Frau Leutner—playing together in the fields, made her heart throb with pleasure. Sensing anew of how much she deprived herself by her continued separation from her son, she resolutely determined to take Franz away in the autumn, and thenceforth to keep him near her.

She was able to carry out this plan even earlier than she had thought possible, for she had no difficulty in finding a place for Franz in the family of a tailor, who lived in Hernals. Now, Theresa had more frequent opportunities of visiting her son than she had ever enjoyed before; but she spent all her Sunday afternoons with Alfred, and so saw less of the boy than when he had been far away.

Early the next spring, it became necessary for Theresa to remove her child from the tailor's household, chiefly because of an inveterate ill-feeling existing between Franz and the tailor's eldest boy. This episode involved Theresa in a violent quarrel with the tailor's wife, in the course of which the latter delivered herself of certain vague insinuations regarding various evil traits which Franz had exhibited. Theresa was inclined to dismiss these allusions as mere spite.

She soon found her child a better place in a cleaner house, with the elderly childless widow of a teacher; so that she really had no reason to complain of the failure of her first venture. Franz made fair progress at school. He was always welcome at the Knauers' and no one there seemed to find him wild or unruly. The widow, to be sure, soon made complaints, but not so violently as had the tailor's wife.

These considerations did not touch Theresa as deeply as they should have, and she could no longer deny the fact that the central point of her emotional life was neither Franz nor Alfred at all, but Robert. Her love for this child gradually took on the aspect of a malady. She took care not to show his parents the greatness of her passion, lest they should therein find cause for dismissing her.

Theresa was aware that, although they loved their child, he did not mean more to them than a living and precious toy. It was certain that they did not appreciate him as fully as she did. As for the little fellow, he made hardly any discrimination between his parents and his governess. Like all spoiled children, he took all their love and idolization as a matter of course.

During the winter months, Frau Knauer became ill of pneumonia, and for a few days, her fate hung in the balance. Theresa assuredly wished her to recover, but there were times when vague, unutterable hopes came to her

heart. Although Herr Knauer had never given her the
faintest sign which she could interpret as an indication
that he might desire her as a wife; although he had remained strange and, in fact, as unlikeable as ever, she
knew that, if his wife should die and if he should offer his
hand, she would not hesitate a moment to become Robert's
step-mother. For the hope of that alone, she would have
broken with Alfred—all the more so because, while nothing suggested that their relationship was soon to end, she
realized that it had no real permanence.

Frau Knauer recovered slowly and, as a convalescent,
made a most attractive picture. She and Theresa had several
small quarrels, to which Theresa attached no importance.
One day, Theresa was requested to make a certain purchase. She, feeling unwell, passed on the request to the
chambermaid. Frau Knauer refused to allow this, and
Theresa was led to answer her mistress somewhat harshly.
Frau Knauer thereupon suggested that Theresa might leave
her employment, whenever it might be convenient for her
to do so.

Theresa did not take Frau Knauer seriously. She had
become almost indispensable in this house, and how could
any one think of separating Robert from her, or her from
Robert? Moreover, from that time forward, neither Herr
nor Frau Knauer, in their conduct toward her, gave the
slightest indication that any change, any estrangement, or
any hostility had occurred.

Theresa was on the point of dismissing the episode completely from her mind when, one day, Frau Knauer spoke to her of her impending departure as if it were a foregone conclusion, concerning which there could not possibly be any more discussion. With the most friendly concern, she inquired if Theresa had already found herself another position. She mentioned that she intended to go to the country during the summer, and would try to get on without the assistance of a governess.

Theresa felt certain that the Knauers would want her back in the fall, but she was too proud to say anything about the possibility; and so the days passed without her having taken advantage of the opportunities which they offered her of determining her real status in the household. She was unable to believe that they would deal so cruelly with her as actually to separate her from little Robert. At the last moment, she was sure, they would make some effort to retain her.

She therefore neglected to make any preparations for her departure, feeling certain that, on the morning of the last day, Frau Knauer would retract her words. But the latter only asked her, in a friendly way, if she would not linger long enough to lunch with them. Theresa, on the point of tears, her throat choked with sobs, could only nod. Frau Knauer was doubtless embarrassed at her emotion, for she left the room; then, at once, Theresa burst into tears, falling on her knees before Robert, who was sitting at his own little white table, drinking his breakfast cocoa.

He had been informed, in a vague way, that his Fräulein was going away for a time. He could not, however, understand her violent weeping, nor the cause of the many kisses which she showered upon his hand; but he took it all without astonishment and, feeling impelled to do something in return, bent down and kissed her forehead. When Theresa looked up and saw his cool eyes, she realized how completely selfish he was. She ruffled his hair playfully, wiped away her tears, and began to help him dress, as if nothing had happened.

Then she took him to his mother's room and stood by, with an expression of fixed amiability on her face, while he kissed his mother good-bye before taking his customary morning walk. Theresa chatted with the child, just as usual, and she did not even forget to take a roll along to feed to the swans.

Robert met a few playmates, and Theresa spoke condescendingly to a nursemaid with whom she had struck up a slight acquaintance. She asked herself what it was that made her feel superior to her fellow nurses and governesses. Was she really any better than they? Was she not just as homeless a creature? Were not all of them tossed round the world, from one house to another, even though they gave to their charges the motherly love and attention which the real mothers could not or would not give? And did they ever acquire any rights, even when they loved the child they cared for more than they did their own?

She worked herself into a mood of angry rebellion. Robert was playing about the lake in the comfort-conserving way which was all his own, allowing himself to be caught by his playmates before he was actually tired. Theresa called to him suddenly, with unusual severity. It had become late, and it was high time that they were going home. Robert obeyed at once, indifferently, and the two proceeded homeward.

After the noon meal, Theresa begged Frau Knauer to be allowed to pass the night in her house. Frau Knauer assented at once, but it was noticeable that she considered herself somewhat gracious in doing so. Theresa promised, as though she were in duty bound to do so, to leave the house very early in the morning, without seeing Robert again. Herr Knauer thanked her for her excellent service and hoped that she would come and see them sometimes. She and her boy would always be welcome.

She hastened to meet Alfred in the afternoon, and did not conceal from him the extent of her desperation. She declared that her present condition was simply intolerable, and that she must get into some more stable profession. Alfred patiently explained to her that she would have plenty of time to think things over. At any rate, she ought to devote this summer to recovering her health. She ought to spend a few weeks in Salzburg, and a few weeks with Franz, preferably at Ensbach, where the Leutners would doubtless be glad to welcome her.

Through the veil of her tears, Theresa was conscious of

Alfred's indifferent, even bored eyes, that looked past her, just as Herr Knauer's and Frau Knauer's and little Robert's had done. Her astonished glance, revealing her inner torture, did not escape him. He was embarrassed, and tried to be especially tender to her. She accepted his love because she thirsted for it, but she felt that, no matter how long she remained with Alfred, she would always recognize this moment as the beginning of their parting, even though they should continue together until the end of their lives.

Alfred had frequently asked to be allowed to assist her financially. Now, when he renewed his offer, against the exigencies of the next few months, she felt obliged to accept it.

LXVIII

THE following morning, she left the house of the Knauers. She went at once to Salzburg, where her mother received her most cordially. It seemed to Theresa as if her mother had rid herself of all the sickly, confused, and unclean parts of her being, those things which had so often pained Theresa, by putting them into her novels. Now, she had become a charming and reasonable old lady, with whom she could get on delightfully, and whom it was even possible to love.

Her mother expressed the desire of settling in Vienna, as soon as possible. Salzburg failed to provide her with sufficient excitement and an adequate outlet for her energies. Moreover, Karl was now engaged, and she dreamed of passing her old age, surrounded by her grandchildren. She made Theresa tell her about the various families in which she had been employed, and she did not attempt to dissemble her curiosity concerning her daughter's most intimate experiences. She confessed that every year it became more difficult for her to find the right words by which to describe the indispensable love scenes in her novels. Would not Theresa help her in her next novel, by supplying the passionate interludes? In any case, she insisted that Theresa should consider the matter, and examine her manuscript.

Theresa complied, but later declared that it would be impossible for her to gratify her mother's request. Frau Fabiani at first took this as pure rudeness; but, soon thereafter, dropped the matter, without cherishing any malice over her disappointment.

A week later, Theresa went to fetch her child from Vienna, in order to go with him for a time to Ensbach. She was determined to love him; and in this she succeeded, because she could not now think of Robert without bitterness, since her heart was so filled with impossible longing for him.

Alfred met her later, and the two set out on a little journey through the lesser Alps of Styria. Theresa enjoyed the excursion immensely. Alfred had to go back to his hospital in Vienna, so Theresa returned alone to Ensbach.

This time, Frau Leutner insisted that she could keep silent no longer about Franz's misdeeds. His stay in Vienna had not, apparently, done him much good. He had become quite intractable and impudent; he had torn up the flowers from the beds at one of the villas and, worst of all, he had perpetrated all sorts of petty thefts. Franz denied everything. It was true that he had plucked a few flowers. And, yes, he had once pocketed a few kreutzers that Frau Leutner had left on the table—but that was only for a joke!

Theresa was unwilling to take these matters too seri-

ously. She promised Frau Leutner that Franz would change
for the better, and she brought him to the point where
he was willing to ask the kind-hearted old woman to forgive him. She herself redoubled her love and tenderness
toward him. She occupied herself with him the whole day,
instructing him and going on long walks with him; and
it seemed that, within a few days, his whole nature had
improved.

One day Agnes came home on a visit, dressed in her
most attractive Sunday clothes, and looking four or five
years older than her actual eighteen years. Again, Franz
received her with delight. She kissed him as if she were
his mother, and yet indifferently, and she winked saucily
at Theresa as she did so.

At table, she related all manner of gossip about the
noble family for whom she worked as a second chambermaid. She treated Theresa as an equal, asked her where
she was now "in service," and dropped hints concerning
the things which a young and beautiful girl had to put up
with at the hands of young, and particularly old, gentlemen.
Without doubt, Theresa could tell a great deal about that!

Theresa, incensed, forbade her to make any further remarks. Agnes became sarcastic, and Frau Leutner had to
interfere, in order to prevent a quarrel.

"Come, Franz!" Agnes said; and the two of them ran
away.

Theresa wept bitterly. Frau Leutner consoled her.

Later, visitors came. Then Agnes and Franz returned,

and the latter, just before her early departure, came up to Theresa and extended her hand.

"Don't be angry," she said. "I didn't mean anything!" And thus peace was reëstablished.

Meanwhile, the time was fast approaching when it would be necessary for Theresa to look about for another situation. She made an attempt to secure an appointment in a school, but was unsuccessful, due to the fact that she had not taken the necessary examinations. She once more determined not to neglect this matter. Meanwhile, she did what she had so often done before—read the advertisements in the newspapers and wrote letters of application to the most promising addresses.

Now, more than ever, this struck her as wretched and pointless. It often occurred to her that Alfred might be of greater assistance than he actually was. The least he could do was to watch for chance advertisements which might interest her. But in all these matters pertaining to her work, he took no interest at all. Nor did he return to Ensbach to seek her.

LXIX

At length, Theresa secured a position in the house of a bank director, who had two daughters, aged eight and ten. She had firmly resolved never again to allow her heart and soul to become engaged by her charges. Hereafter, she would always bear in mind the fact that she was a stranger, and she would always make it her business to remain one.

Nevertheless, only a few days had passed when she began to take an interest in the younger girl, who was of an affectionate and pliable nature. To offset this, she resolutely hardened her heart against the elder one.

The bank director was a man of fifty or more, still what one might term handsome, and not without a certain inclination to dandyism. He was in the habit of choosing his words very carefully, and he had a peculiar way of looking at one—almost coquettishly. He had a way, too, of brushing against Theresa whenever he passed her and of blowing his breath down her neck.

Theresa was certain she could have him, if she liked, for his wife was an ailing, rather elderly person, who was not too scrupulous about her appearance. It made Theresa bitter to reflect that this woman could go to bed and rest whenever she pleased, whereas she, Theresa, who after all was a woman, too, had no such privileges and was given consideration by no one.

She remembered an occasion years ago, when she had really been very ill, yet had been forced to go out in terrible weather and fetch the children home from school. After that, she had come near to being very ill indeed. Formerly, she had taken such conditions as the unavoidable accompaniment of her profession; now, she felt quite differently about it, although she could make no open manifestation of her sentiments.

When she spoke of these things to Alfred, he would point out her unjustness and her occasional exaggeration, and would seek by her words to inspire her to a greater kindliness and attention. Then she would accuse him of being the son of a good bourgeois family, and say that, never having known any worries, he had a greater feeling of kinship with a Jewish banker than he had with her. She would declare that he was heartless and egotistical, and sometimes she would even go so far as to accuse him of being the cause of all her misfortunes, because he had abandoned her when she was still a young and innocent girl. Alfred would receive these recriminations with a shrug of his shoulders—a gesture which would make her simply furious. Thus, their meetings became less and less frequent, and were more and more characterized by quarrels and ill-temper.

She found a place for her son in a nearby suburban

district called Liebhartstal, where she had arranged with another tailor's family to take care of him. Theresa no longer thought of having her son go to high school, so she took fate as it came, and had Franz apprenticed to the tailor while he was still attending the lower grades.

It seemed to her that he was developing a more agreeable disposition than he had exhibited in the last year. His master was a kind-hearted man, although somewhat addicted to drink; and neither he nor his wife had anything to say against Franz's character or actions. He got on well, too, with the somewhat older son of his new guardians.

One day, Alfred surprised Theresa with the information that he was about to depart for a small university town in Germany, there to study under a famous psychiatrist. He himself seemed to think that their separation would not be for long; but she, although she betrayed her conviction by no sign, realized that the end for them had come. Nevertheless, she now treated Alfred with a tenderness and a confidence which she had not shown toward him in many months.

In his first letters, Alfred exhibited more candour and joyousness than he had been able to summon at their last meeting, but there was not a hint of love in even the most familiar passages. Theresa, half unconsciously, half purposely, tempered the style of her own letters accordingly.

When summer came, she went with the banker's wife and children to a comfortable villa near Vienna, where she was just beginning to recover her good spirits, under the influence of the friendliness of her employers and the gaiety of the children, when a short letter from the tailor's wife informed her that they could no longer keep Franz in their house.

"Shall I ever have any peace?" Theresa thought. She at once asked for a short leave of absence, made the trip to Vienna and, at Liebhartstal, was hardly astonished at being informed that Franz was "altogether rotten," and that he had led the tailor's son into "all kinds of mischief."

She was told that Franz's teacher wished to speak with her. Theresa went to him and found a clever, friendly little man, who counseled her to take her son back to the country, where he would be in healthier surroundings. Although she was determined not to take anything which her child might do too much to heart, this advice shocked her deeply, and she was unable to rid herself of a feeling of bitter regret that she had not had the courage, while there had yet been time, to seek out the accommodating woman who might have spared her all the cares and vexations which she had since suffered. And a dull anger arose within her, such as she had not suspected herself capable of, against the long forgotten, ridiculous, and almost non-existent Kasimir Tobisch. She was fully capable, she felt, of doing him physical harm if he should ever again offend her sight.

She conceived the idea of having her son adopted by some childless couple—Alfred had sometimes casually suggested this but each time she had indignantly rejected the idea—and thus be entirely relieved of her trouble. But she had no sooner begun to consider this plan than her mood changed. She was overwhelmed with a motherly sympathy for this poor lad, who was, after all, not to blame for his nature and his fate, and who, in other circumstances, might have developed into a fine and capable young man. She was more conscious of the enormity of her sin than she had ever been before.

She had so often failed her child! She had so often preferred strange children to him—children who surpassed him in nothing, save in the good fortune of having been brought up in better homes, and of being better cared for and more healthfully influenced than her own child.

One hot summer day, as the dust of the city blew through the poor suburb out toward the hills, Theresa sat with her boy on a bench by the side of the street and talked very plainly to him. She thought she saw the light of resolution—yes, regret—in his eyes, and she was suddenly filled with renewed hope. He moved closer to her, and she began to feel that the stubbornness in his heart was beginning to yield.

She ceased to despair and, with sudden inspiration, asked him if he would like, in the future, to live with his mother.

Tears came to her eyes when she heard him exclaim, with genuine joy, that he loved no one but her, and that he could not endure it to be alone with other people. And he would gladly learn more, but his teachers did not like him, and treated him so that he had no desire to please them. It was a lie that he had stolen a piece of cloth from the tailor's wife. Frau Leutner, in Ensbach, had lied, too. His mother should hear what she and Agnes had told Herr Leutner about her. There were lots of things that he could tell.

And as for his master's wife, she was a bitch! Theresa was astounded at her son's language, and forbade him ever to use such a word again. But Franz, not heeding her, went on to tell her of a teamster who often came to the house and what went on then; and Theresa was forced to listen to words and expressions which she had never heard before. She continually interrupted him, to make him alter his speech; and finally, she was constrained to change the subject altogether.

Her heart was oppressed by a dreary sadness, as she retraced her steps along the dusty street. She still held his hand in hers, but gradually her fingers relaxed and slipped from his grasp, and she was all alone. She took Franz back to the tailor's home for this last night, and herself went to a local inn, after a fruitless search for a place to lodge her son. Before going to bed, she wrote a detailed letter to Alfred, speaking to him openly as to a friend.

The next day, she felt more calm. She was fortunate in discovering a small, neat room for Franz, in the home of a childless couple. She felt then that she had fulfilled her duty to him, and returned to the country. A few weeks of comparative leisure gave her an opportunity of recov-

ering herself. The banker had gone on a long journey.
The girls gave her very little trouble. She was scarcely
ever disturbed by the banker's wife or his children, and
so she passed whole days, reading and sleeping in the
shady garden, whose walls shut in the house and its inhabitants and protected them from the harsh world outside.

LXX

In the autumn, Frau Fabiani moved to Vienna, where she at first found accommodations in a boarding house. Her son had meanwhile married the daughter of his landlord in a small Austrian city, where he had served for a short time as an assistant doctor. Now he had established himself as a general practitioner in Vienna. Politics, however, still remained his principal interest.

Since he had been relieved of his material cares, Karl had become more genial and approachable, as Theresa was able to note when she once chanced to meet him in her mother's rooms. His young wife, who was also present, proved to be a pretty creature, and sympathetic, if limited and somewhat provincial in her ways. She went up to Theresa at once and, with ingenuous kindliness, invited her to visit her new home.

Thus Theresa, who, a few weeks before, had not the slightest expectation of such an eventuality, had the pleasure of dining in the house of Dr. Faber, as her brother was now legally known. The evening passed perfunctorily and without embarrassment, but Theresa felt little of the spirit of family relationship. After all, she was a stranger everywhere, and this meal *en famille* left her with an unpleasant after-taste.

She did not see her son more often than she had before.

The pensioned official, Mauerhold, who, with his wife, had undertaken the care of Franz, had not done so for any pecuniary gain, but because they had lost their only child a few years before, and longed, in their approaching old age, for the presence of a young person in the house.

It seemed as if their constant thoughtfulness and care exercised a beneficial influence upon Franz's character. Theresa heard nothing ill concerning him, either from the Mauerholds or from his teachers. It did not greatly disturb her that Alfred's letters were constantly becoming more reserved. She had the feeling of satisfaction which arises from duty well accomplished, and from the circumstance that her presence in the banker's house was becoming more and more indispensable by reason of the failing health of his wife.

Sometimes she indulged a momentary thought of the possibility of marrying one of the men who visited the house: the doctor, for instance—an old bachelor; or the widowed brother of the banker, both of whom casually courted her. She knew she might take advantage of these situations, if she were to make some consistent effort to do so. But, in matters of love, she abhorred the idea of employing skill and guile; and so she permitted these opportunities to pass, without once accusing herself for her laxness.

Once, she answered an advertisement for a housekeeper to a well-to-do widower, forty-odd years of age. The answer which she received was so disgusting that she took care never to lay herself open to such an experience again.

LXXI

ONE spring day, as she was walking with her two girls in the Stadtpark, she met Sylvia, whom she had not seen in several years. She was sitting in the sun with her charge, an eight-year-old boy. Sylvia seemed delighted at meeting Theresa again, and told her how she had passed several years in Rumania, and had only recently had a position on an estate in Hungary. She did not appear changed in the least. She looked just a little faded, but, on the whole, more charming than when Theresa had first known her.

On their next meeting, Sylvia unexpectedly proposed that they should spend their next Sunday together. She had an appointment for that day with a close friend of hers, a student-officer, who wished to bring along a comrade. Theresa glanced at Sylvia with a surprised and almost indignant expression, but Sylvia only smiled.

It was a beautiful spring day. The two governesses sat on a bench near the lake, while the children entrusted to their care fed the swans. Sylvia at once began telling of her affair. She had met her soldier friend the last winter, at a masked ball—yes, she went to masked balls!—and he was a handsome, blond, rather short, and very happy-go-lucky fellow. He would doubtless remain in the service, and not return to his student life, for he preferred the Army to the University. When she had mentioned to him her recent meeting of an old friend, he had at once suggested a little foursome. They would take a row-boat up one of the branches of the Danube. Then they would go somewhere to eat—either on Mount Constantine, or else in their favourite coffee house. Well, there was no point in laying out a programme, for everything would take care of itself. Theresa declined. Sylvia insisted, until finally they agreed to let the weather decide for them.

When Theresa awoke, on the morning of the following Sunday, and saw the sky covered with dark clouds, she was somewhat disappointed. In the afternoon, however, the weather cleared up, and Sylvia came at an early hour to fetch Theresa. The two proceeded to the Prater Circle, where the two gentlemen awaited them smoking cigarettes, near the monument of Admiral Tegethof.

They greeted the ladies with consummate courtesy, and really looked quite elegant in their uniforms. Practiced gallants, thought Theresa; and, at first glance, the short, blond fellow who was Sylvia's lover, pleased her rather more than the other. The second man reminded her of Kasimir Tobisch, by his spare figure and his long, sallow face. He wore a dark moustache and a small beard, such as the Austrian student-officers and officers in general were certainly not in the habit of affecting. His slender, almost too thin fingers held a peculiar, inexplicable fascination for Theresa.

Both gentlemen thanked her for having come. Sylvia at once led the conversation, in her lively and joyous way. Every one spoke French. The blond fellow was very fluent. The other spoke with difficulty, but his accent was meticulously correct.

They walked down the main road, but the crowd was so great—its odour none too good, as this man added—that they soon turned into a by-path which led beneath tall trees with delicate green foliage to a quieter section of the park. The blond officer recounted some experiences which he had had while shooting in Hungary, on the estate of a nobleman, whose guest he had been the year before. Sylvia mentioned the name of an aristocrat whose acquaintance she had made during her stay in Hungary. Her friend ventured a bold insinuation, which she received with bursts of laughter, replying in kind.

Theresa and her escort remained somewhat in the rear. He spoke to her of more serious matters, in a low voice, which at times struck her as being intentionally mysterious. He had allowed his monocle to fall out of his eye, and looked ahead with an indifferent air from under his reddened eyelids.

He found it difficult to believe that Theresa was a Viennese. She looked so much more like an Italian—yes, a chestnut-brown Italian, from Lombardy. Theresa nodded, not without pride. Yes, her father was really of an old Italian family, and her mother had come from the Croatian nobility. Richard expressed surprise that she should be a governess. Surely, there were professions better suited to one of her birth and capabilities. With her brilliant eyes and dark complexion, she would have gone far on the stage. In any case, he was at a loss to comprehend how any one could choose such a servitude of her own free will, since certainly she had not been forced to undertake it.

Theresa was again strongly reminded of Kasimir Tobisch, who, years ago, had employed the very same words. She looked away, and Richard went on, in still more emphatic fashion:

"To have only a few hours of liberty, every holiday! It is positively incomprehensible how any one can endure such an existence!"

Theresa felt the passion beneath his speech, although he had not shown any emotion on his face.

They had coffee and cookies on Mount Constantine. The two men made several sarcastic remarks at the expense of the "low" people at the other tables. Theresa did not see anything particularly wrong with the crowd about her. It occurred to her that their escorts forgot that the two poor creatures with whom they were sitting must likewise be considered among the lower multitude.

They descended the hill and rented a row-boat at the lake which lay at the foot of the hill. Theresa could feel that the gentlemen considered it rather sport to mingle thus with the lower classes; a kind of patronizing condescension on their part, to be willing to row their boat along among the many other boats in which were the inferior creatures. Gradually, they pushed their boat into one of the narrow branches of the river which serpentined along through the meadows between the green shores.

Sylvia smoked a cigarette, and Theresa, who had not tried one since her evenings in Salzburg among the officers and actresses, made another attempt, but liked it no better than she had before. Her escort, observing her distaste, took the cigarette from her fingers and smoked it himself. He ceased rowing, leaving the job to his blond comrade. It would do the boy good, he remarked, what with his tendency to lay on flesh.

On the shores, beneath the lofty and ancient trees, lay amorous couples and family groups. Presently, they came to a lonelier and more quiet stretch. Finally, they went ashore, securing their boat to one of the posts provided for the purpose along the shore. Then they walked on further through the bushes, which became thicker and thicker, toward the meadows. They went two by two, clinging to one another. They crossed one broad road, and then at once found themselves in a path that brought them with surprising rapidity into what seemed the far-removed heart of a deep forest. It was magical!

Sylvia went on with her blond friend. They were holding each other closely. Richard suddenly stopped and kissed

Theresa passionately on the mouth. She made no resistance whatever. He began at once to talk very seriously, as though what had just happened had no particular meaning. At a casual question from Theresa, he began to tell about himself.

He was studying law, and was going to be a lawyer. Theresa expressed surprise. She had thought that he wished to become a professional officer, like his friend. He shook his head, almost contemptuously. He was not even considering that idea. Besides, a military career necessitated a great deal of money, and he was really quite a poor devil. That was not to be taken too literally, to be sure; but, in comparison with his blond comrade, he was a beggar. Far ahead, the loud laughter of that fortunate gentleman was audible.

"Always jolly," Richard observed, "and for all that, he has a fixed idea that he is melancholy!"

A young couple went past them. The girl, a well-dressed, pretty blond, stared at Richard with such evident pleasure that Theresa felt flattered.

A cool, moist, sweet-odoured breeze was wafted to them from the near-by stream. The path grew fainter and fainter, until it disappeared. They had to push the branches out of their way. Sylvia gaily called back to Theresa:

"A la fin je voudrais savoir, où ces deux scélérats nous mènent," she cried.

But Theresa had lost all sense of direction. Now and then, they could see the river, glistening through the bull-rushes; and then, at a turn, they had lost sight of it again. From somewhere came the long, drawn-out whistle of a locomotive. Close by, an invisible train rattled over a bridge. Theresa had the feeling that she had lived through all this once before, she could not remember where or when.

Sylvia and her escort had quite disappeared, though one could still hear occasional laughter, giggling, and low cries of simulated resistance. Theresa could almost feel the frightened expression of her face. Richard was looking at her, smiling. He threw down his cigarette and stepped on it. Then he took Theresa in his arms and kissed her. He held her tightly, while he penetrated further into the bull-rushes and finally drew her down with himself.

To her surprise, Sylvia's laughter now sounded quite close. With terror in her eyes, she looked up at Richard and shook her head vigorously. His face was dark and strange.

"No one can see us," he said.

She heard Sylvia's voice again, asking her a bold, shameless question. How dare she! Theresa thought. But, suddenly encircled by Richard's arms, she heard herself answering. She heard her own voice uttering words almost as loose and impudent as those which Sylvia had spoken. What has happened to me? she wondered.

Richard brushed back the hair from her moist brow and whispered delicate and passionate phrases into her ear. Far away in the distance, a wagon rattled over the cobblestones. She could not see the river, but the dark, blue sky overhead appeared to her as some strange reflection of the Danube.

Later, when they had emerged from the thicket and again found the small path, she nestled close to her companion, whom she had not known three hours ago, and who was now her lover. He spoke of unimportant matters.

"The races are over, I suppose. They are the first that I have ever missed!"

When she looked up to him, as if hurt, he stroked her head and kissed her gently on the brow.

"Are you sorry?" he asked. Then he added: "Silly girl!"

They left the meadows and approached the broad avenue where carriages and cabs went by, veiled in dust. They reached the river, found their boat, and rowed back to the place from which they had started. Theresa was at first afraid, lest she should discover some indelicate or frivolous reflection in Sylvia's eyes; but, to her pleasant surprise, Sylvia was unusually serious and calm.

Her friend began to talk bravely of a voyage which the four of them might easily take during the coming summer. All of them realized, of course, how idle his chatter was. Richard even did not hesitate to condemn travel in general. He could not endure the unpleasantness invariably connected with any change of location; and, worst of all, there was the spectacle of strange faces. His comrade returned that he had no particular affection for acquaintances, as it was. Richard made no reply.

Sylvia insisted that there were, nevertheless, moments in one's life that were worth the trouble. Richard shrugged his shoulders. That did not alter matters. Fundamentally, everything was sad. Beauty, more than everything else; and for that reason, love was the saddest thing of all. The truth of his observation struck Theresa deeply. She shivered slightly, and tears came to her eyes. Richard put his small, cool hands on her forehead. It was growing quite dark when they reached their starting-point, landed, and found themselves among crowds along the avenue. The broad street was still jammed with carriages. The music of a dozen orchestras on every side of them mingled together. All the inns were crowded. The two couples walked on into a quieter section, and presently reached the same modest restaurant where, years ago, as a princess or a lady of the court, Theresa had sat with a ghost—or was it a fool?

She recognized the waiter at once. He looked absolutely unchanged as he rushed from one table to another, just as she remembered him, almost as if he were the only person in the world who had not felt the passage of years. Am I only dreaming this? Theresa wondered again; and she glanced quickly at her escort, in order to assure herself that it was not Kasimir Tobisch with whom she stood. And she looked again at the waiter, who, with his napkin dangling from his arm, was running from table to table. How many Sundays since that one! Theresa thought. How many couples have been here since then; how many so-called blissful hours; how much actual misery; how many children, legitimate and illegitimate! And again the whole stupidity of her fate, the total incomprehensibility of life in general, oppressed her. And the young man who was beside her was, strangely enough, the first person who had at once instinctively understood her, although they had spoken not at all of the indecisions of her heart. And she felt nearer and less a stranger to this man, to whom she had given herself in the very first hour of their acquaintance and who did not despise her for her weakness—she was certain of this—than she had ever felt toward Alfred, or any other man.

They stopped at one of the more quiet inns for their evening meal. Theresa drank more than she was accustomed to, and soon became so weary that she could hardly keep her eyes open, and the conversation of the others became only a murmurous drone in her ears. She was anxious to tell her friend of the things which had come into her mind a short time before, but no opportunity presented itself as they walked homeward.

The separation took place abruptly. The gentlemen remarked that they were due at manoeuvers at four o'clock in the morning, so, at the very next cab stand, they put the ladies in an open carriage. Richard paid their fare in advance. Another appointment was rapidly agreed upon for the Sunday following the next. Richard politely kissed Theresa's hand and said "Au revoir"; and as he did so, she noted, with wide, frightened eyes, his cool and distant glance.

On the ride homeward through the deserted streets, she let Sylvia speak. The latter was suddenly overflowing with undesired confessions. Theresa scarcely listened. A bitter after-taste remained with her. She thought, with curious compassion, of her lover; and it seemed to her as if they had parted for ever, as if he were already far away.

LXXII

A FEW days later, a letter from Herr Mauerhold begged her to pay him and his wife a visit, at her very earliest convenience. Theresa had not seen her Franz for three weeks, and she fell at once into a state of violent excitement. Herr Mauerhold received her in a most cordial fashion, but it was plain that he was embarrassed. He declared, after some hesitation, that, in view of the fact that he and his wife intended to leave Vienna and settle in some small town of lower Austria, he was obliged to ask Theresa to take her child away.

Theresa drew a sigh of relief. She expressed the idea that it might be better for Franz to be out of the big city and in some small country town, and she declared her willingness to have the boy remain with them even after their removal. Her son seemed to be getting on with them so well!

The couple's embarrassment was now very plain, and Theresa had to urge them not to conceal the truth from her, before they would inform her that Franz had recently perpetrated a small theft. Thereupon, Frau Mauerhold, who had thus far kept silent, burst out into a long complaint. Franz's thefts were not the worst thing. The boy had all manner of bad habits and disagreeable ways, of which she would rather not say anything. There were complaints from the school, too. He went about with the very worst boys of the neighbourhood, stayed out until all hours of the night, and there was no surmising what the eleven-year-old boy would eventually come to, if he showed such reprehensible traits so early.

Theresa sat with bowed head, as though she herself were the accused. Well, yes, she realized that her proposal to have them keep the lad was impossible. She would wait until he had returned from school, and take him with her immediately. Herr Mauerhold, first glancing at his wife, expressed the opinion that there was really no necessity for such haste. They would not mind keeping the child for a few days more, while Theresa looked about for a new home. Theresa was surprised to see tears in the good man's eyes. It was his turn now to console Theresa. He had known many children who had been worthless rascals at this critical age, but had eventually developed into quite respectable people.

The hour at which Franz should have returned had long since passed. Theresa had asked for only a short leave, and could wait no longer. She thanked the Mauerholds, and promised to look round at once for a new place for Franz. On the way home, she became more calm, and decided to consult some one on her predicament. But whom? Ought she take her mother into her confidence? Should she write to Alfred? What could they do for her? No, she had to decide everything for herself. She alone could solve her own problems.

The next day, however, she chanced to meet Sylvia in the Stadtpark; and, though she was the last person whom Theresa would have chosen under other circumstances to take into her confidence, in her present anxiety she was glad to find a compassionate soul. She poured out her heart to her friend. She told Sylvia more than she had ever told anyone.

Fortunately, Sylvia proved to be a kind, resourceful, and helpful person in this emergency. She urged Theresa to give up her present position, and not to undertake similar work any more. Instead, she was to take a small furnished apartment and give private lessons. Sylvia pledged herself to find her a few pupils very shortly, and in the meanwhile, she put herself and her means completely at Theresa's disposal. She always had "a little something" put away, she declared, with a roguish smile which Theresa did not much like to see. Nevertheless, she thanked Sylvia for her advice and for her offer.

And so, with new industry and energy, she at once set to work to put the new plan into operation. The banker's family received her notice with great surprise. The two girls were both sorry to see her leave, and the eldest especially, wept disconsolately. Theresa's heart was touched to see how, without having suspected it, she had aroused so great a love in the young girl.

LXIII

ON a sultry day in August, Theresa and Franz moved to the two furnished rooms and kitchen which they had rented. The rather new and modest, but neatly-kept house where they began their life in common was situated in an easily accessible, but quite suburban street.

Before making this move, Theresa resorted to every possible device to secure a few pupils, and in this she had been successful, by dint of answering advertisements, by approaching all the families where she had formerly held a position, and largely through Sylvia's aid. At the worst, these pupils assured her against starvation. The banker's wife had given her a small sum of money as a parting gift, and this came in most handily in her emergency.

It really meant a great deal to Theresa to find herself, for the first time in her life, in the possession of a home. It seemed to her that all her son lacked for his proper development was a life in common with his mother. The school which he now attended was so far distant from his former one that the possibility of his meeting old acquaintances was slight.

As usual, he did not behave badly during the first few weeks at his new residence. To her, it seemed almost as if she were just beginning to learn to know her child. Certain of his childish traits, which had disappeared too early in his life, now gradually reappeared. And was it not delightful to sit down to a noon-hour meal with him, a meal which she herself had prepared; and how marvelous to come home in the evening, after her lessons, and to be greeted by his wild embraces! Her heart swelled with pride when he asked her assistance with some difficult passage in his home-work.

She felt satisfied, almost happy. She began to write to Alfred again, urged by some inner need for some one to confide in. She told him in detail of her new life; and he replied, announcing his approaching return to Vienna, where he was to be an assistant doctor in a psychiatric clinic.

LXXIV

ONE day, Theresa was surprised at receiving an invitation to dine with her brother. It had been a year since she had heard from him. She found two guests there—a young doctor, and a professor in a gymnasium—both, as the conversation indicated, political friends of Dr. Karl Faber.

Karl led the conversation. The other two, even the professor, who was at least ten years older than he, listened respectfully. Theresa felt that her brother somewhat hoped to impress her with his importance in his party.

Her sister-in-law, who had become a mother a few months before, left the table at the conclusion of the meal, while Theresa remained in the company of the gentlemen. The conversation became more friendly and intimate, and soon passed to the subject of Theresa's profession and her experiences as a governess and teacher. The professor did not conceal his regret that Theresa had been obliged to serve in a subordinate capacity, almost as a servant, in the houses of strangers; and he declared that the law ought to prevent such situations, once and for all time. The professor spoke clearly and precisely, in contrast to the young doctor, who continually lapsed into stuttering. Theresa's brother, however, though he now and then nodded with approval, often glanced sarcastically in the professor's direction. Theresa long remembered the crafty, malicious expression in his eyes.

She had not heard from Richard in weeks—months, in fact—and she was almost happy to be able to forget him, when she received a letter from Sylvia, inviting her to go out "avec nos jeunes amis de l'autre jour." Her first impulse was to decline. She was accustomed now to spending all her evenings at home with her son. But Sylvia came to her in person to repeat the invitation, and Theresa allowed herself to be persuaded.

The evening began calmly enough but became more and more wild as it proceeded, and ended in the most flagrant manner. When Theresa came home, early in the morning, she found her son sleeping peacefully in his bed; and this she took as an unexpected and unmerited stroke of luck. Neither she nor Richard had anything but good feeling for each other, yet she determined never to see him again.

The invitation to her brother's house was repeated, now and then, and there Theresa often encountered the professor, who now adopted a clumsily gallant attitude toward her, and would not be denied the privilege of accompanying her all the long distance to her home.

A few days after one of these meetings, her brother acquainted her with the fact that the professor was very much interested in her, and would very probably declare his intentions with due formality on the next appropriate occasion. His brotherly advice was not to reject him with too much finality, even if she found herself bound elsewhere at the moment.

"I am not engaged," Theresa replied, curtly and severely.

Karl did not seem to notice her tone, and went on to explain that the professor was well liked by his superiors, and would doubtless soon be appointed director of a gymnasium in some fairly large city in the provinces.

"And," he added, "so as to consider everything while we are at it, I may remark that the difficulty which you are thinking of would not stand in your way."

Theresa felt the blood mounting to her cheeks.

"You never bothered about my thoughts before. Why should they interest you now?"

He did not seem to heed her anger. Undisturbed, he pursued his argument.

"The matter could be explained thus: you were once married, but it developed that the marriage was illegal. Such cases actually do happen. You are, so to speak, absolutely innocent."

He blinked past her.

Theresa objected.

"I will be responsible for what I have done, and I will never deny my child. I would never have denied him to you, either. But did you ask me?"

"You needn't become excited. It is exactly for the reason that you need not deny your child that I thought of the illegal marriage. You ought to thank me!"

Before she could reply, he went on, vehemently.

"Your mother would certainly be glad to know that your circumstances were more assured!"

Theresa reflected quickly. Why not? The man proposed by her brother she regarded with indifference, but she by no means despised him. Did she not owe it to her son not to allow such an opportunity to pass? Her brother began to set forth the advantages of such a marriage. The position of her husband would enable her all the better to pursue her own profession. She need not give it up. On the contrary, a professor was exactly the right man for her.

Her sister-in-law entered at this moment, carrying her child in her arms. Theresa took it, and recalled the first weeks of her own son's life—those piteous, scanty hours when she had been able to press him against her breast. And she thought that, in her new, real marriage, she might have another child and enjoy to the full the happiness which had been denied to her when Franz had been born.

Then it occurred to her that her thoughts were unjust and disloyal to her son. All the other injustices that she had been guilty of in her actions toward her son rose in her mind. Tears came to her eyes, even as she still held her brother's baby. She felt incapable of pursuing the conversation, and left the house in a painfully disturbed condition.

A few days later, she accidentally met Richard. In his civilian clothes, he appeared very elegant, and yet as though he had come down in the world somewhat. His overcoat fitted him perfectly, but the velvet collar was a little worn, and his well-made shoes were cracked. His monocle was fixed immovably in his eye. He kissed her hand and asked her, almost without any preliminaries, if she would not spend the evening with him. She declined. He did not urge her, but on the chance, gave her the address of his parents, with whom he lived. She wrote to him the very next day.

It was a strange meeting. She did not really understand why he had insisted upon dining in a private room of an exclusive restaurant, for he acted very reserved and scarcely even touched her hand. She liked him all the better for that. He spoke a great deal about himself. His understanding with his parents was not of the best. His father, a well-known attorney, was generally dissatisfied with him. He was quite right, too. He had never gotten on with his mother. He casually termed her a silly goose, which rather frightened Theresa. He was soon to undergo a third state examination, and he asked himself what it was all about. He never intended to be a lawyer or a judge.

He had no serious ambitions at all. That was because he really had no particular talent, and nothing in the world amused him very much. Theresa observed that his remarks did not correspond with his nature. If he was so indifferent to the whole world, how could he attach as much importance as he obviously did to the selection of his necktie?

He looked at her with a certain pity, which wounded her; and she experienced a burning desire to convince him of the fact that she was quite capable of understanding such seemingly conflicting characteristics. But she could not find the right words.

After the meal, he took her home in an open carriage. They had not been together for more than an hour. He kissed her hand very politely, and she was sure that she would never see him again.

Nevertheless, she received a letter from him within a few days. She was more delighted than she had thought she would be to receive an invitation from him. This time, he was an entirely different person. He was gay almost to boisterousness and, for the first time, he exhibited a little interest in her personal life.

He made her tell him of her youth, of her parents, of her seducer, and of her other lovers. She also revealed to him the existence of her child, and confessed that she frequently neglected her duty toward her boy. He shrugged his shoulders almost angrily. There were no duties, he declared. No one owed anything to any one else. Children owed nothing to their parents, and parents nothing to their children.

The whole business was a fraud. All people were egoists; only, they would not confess it to themselves. Besides, what he chiefly wanted to tell her was that he had won at the races what to him was quite a sum of money. That ought to interest her more than anything else.

What he proposed to do, after this stroke of good fortune, was to follow up his luck at Monte Carlo the coming winter. He had thought up a system of breaking the bank. After all, money was the only thing worth having. Money gave one power over people. When you possess it, you can put people in their places. And she was to come with him—to Monte Carlo. She would get along there; she could be sure of that, though not as a teacher, of course!

She spoke against his plans, but could not prevent the charm of the adventure from wholly enthralling her. And she was very happy that evening.

A letter from Alfred, which arrived the next morning, completely destroyed her mood. The world appeared dull again, and the future dismal. She had told him of the probable proposal of marriage from the professor, and Alfred urged her to consider the matter carefully; but from the way he worded his letter, it was plain that he would not be sorry to see her married and himself freed from any responsibility which he might have incurred in consequence of his affair with her. Theresa replied to him in a cold, almost sarcastic letter.

LXXV

S<small>HE</small> continued to be tolerably contented with Franz.
Whenever she came home, she invariably found him seated
and pondering over his books and notes. Of his early un-
ruliness, but little remained. If he occasionally showed a
tendency to cast politeness aside, or forget himself, a warning on her part generally sufficed to convince him of his
error. She was accordingly most disagreeably surprised
when, at the end of the school term, he brought home his
report card which, in addition to having very low marks,
showed that he had missed no small number of hours at
school. There, to her dismay, she learned that, during the
past several months, he had attended classes only sporadi-
cally. The class instructor brought forth written excuses
bearing her signature.

Theresa was careful not to admit them to be forgeries.
She, on the contrary, maintained that her boy had been
ill this year; she took it on herself to see that he caught
up with his studies. All she asked on their part was patience.

At home, she took him to task. He was at first stubborn;
then, he proved impudent; finally, he simply fled from the
room and house. It was late at night when he returned

and immediately flung himself on the couch in the living room that served in place of a regular bed. His mother sat nearby, entreating him to reveal to her where he had been during his absence. He refused to answer, sullenly staring at the wall. Only now and then she intercepted a sinister flash from his eyes, a look in which Theresa this time recognized not only stubbornness, not only a lack of understanding and a poverty of love, but bitterness, derision, and even a hidden reproach, which he might not wish, out of a last vestige of respect for her, to utter.

And from this sombre glance, a memory, far-off and blurred, returned to her. She strove to dispel it, but ever it loomed nearer, growing more living. Now, for the first time in a long while, she bethought herself of the night when she had given birth to him—that night when she had first supposed her new-born babe dead, had wished him dead. Wished—had she only wished? Her heart froze with terror, lest the boy, who had turned away and pulled the covers up over his head, might again penetrate her with his knowing, hating, deadly glance.

So she rose, stood trembling for a short space, her breath held tight; then tiptoed into her room. Now she was certain that this child, this twelve-year-old boy, not only lived as a stranger, but as an enemy beside her. And never before had she at one and the same time realized how unhappily she loved him, and yet how forlorn was any expectation on her part of her boy returning that love. Still, she could not yet abandon him as lost. All that she had neglected to do, her every act of thoughtlessness, her wrong and guilt—these things she must rectify, must atone for. She must be prepared for sacrifices far more difficult than any that she had yet made. And if she could find the opportunity to provide him with better surroundings than he had yet known, the possibility of entrusting him to fatherly supervision, she had no right to hesitate. The sacrifice—was it, after all, so tremendous? Might not such a marriage bring salvation to herself, as well?

So that, when Professor Wilnus, purposely left alone with her after lunch, on the occasion of their next meeting at the house of her brother, asked Theresa if she would marry him, she first hesitated an instant, then, steadily regarding him, asked:

"Do you know me well enough? Do you know who it is that you propose to marry?"

With an embarrassed nod, he awkwardly reached for her hand. She withdrew it, and asked:

"Do you know that I have a child, a rather difficult boy of almost thirteen? Whatever gossip you may have heard, the truth is that I was never married."

The professor frowned; he blushed, as if some one had related a bawdy joke. But he quickly recovered his poise:

"Your brother told me something," he said. "But he gave no details. Yet, I can say that I expected something like this."

He paced up and down the room, his hands behind his back. Then he stopped before her. With well chosen words, as if in walking he had studied a little speech, he made her a definite proposal. Under no circumstances must the fact of a child interfere with their future.

"What do you mean by that?"

He explained. There existed childless couples who desired nothing better than to adopt some child. And if they carefully . . .

She interrupted abruptly:

"I shall never part with my child!" she exclaimed, her eyes flashing.

The professor, silent, reflected. After several seconds, he remarked, in a clear, noble voice, that he would first like to meet the boy. They might then discuss matters again.

Her first instinct was peremptorily to refuse, and not accept him under any conditions. But her recent resolution soon reverted to her mind; and she declared her willingness to receive the professor the following evening at her home.

Franz she succeeded in detaining; he was on the point of leaving the house, unobserved, as he usually contrived to do at this hour. The professor made his appearance, only faintly concealing his embarrassment under a gay and forcibly worldly manner. Franz contemplated the visitor with obvious distrust. And when he suddenly and surprisingly declared his wish to examine Franz's school report, it was no easy matter to overcome the lad's resistance. That which the eyes of Professor Wilnus beheld was not too favourable. But he was gracious enough to

express his displeasure through words of humorous understanding. He next tried to ascertain the extent of the boy's
knowledge; he asked all manner of questions, supplying the
answers, too, by practically putting them in his mouth;
and, in general, comporting himself like a teacher who,
for reasons of his own, is anxious not to fail a sorry pupil
during the examination.

What he most strongly objected to was Franz's pro-
nunciation, which he characterized as a mixture of suburban dialect and peasant speech. When he casually hinted
at his connection, and ventured the possibility of placing
the lad in a monastery school in upper Austria, Franz
bolted from the room.

His mother knew that he would not soon return. She
excused him to the professor. It was his habit, she explained, to spend his evenings in the open with his comrades. The professor appeared to be relieved to be alone
with Theresa. She wished to hear no more of the school;
and, at last, definitely answering the cautious hint of the
professor that it might be possible to find adoptive parents for the boy, she resolutely declared that under no circumstances would she consent to part with her son.

The professor seemed inclined toward leniency. His eyes
began to shine. Moving closer to Theresa, he ventured on
boldness. Each moment, he became more ridiculous and
obnoxious to Theresa. She was wondering whether or not
to show him the door, once for all, when there was a
knock. To Theresa's surprise, Sylvia, who for weeks had

failed to put in an appearance, entered. Following the casual introduction, the professor expressed the hope of seeing Theresa the following Sunday at the house of her brother, and left.

Sylvia was pale and excited. She hurriedly asked Theresa if she had read any of the papers that day?

"What has happened?" Theresa asked.

"Richard has committed suicide!" Sylvia replied.

"For God's sake!" Theresa exclaimed, helplessly letting her hands fall on Sylvia's shoulders.

She had not seen Richard for so long! And with eyes downcast, Sylvia confessed that she had seen him quite frequently. Theresa felt no twinges of jealousy, no real pain. Suddenly, she felt a certain superiority! It was she who must console her friend! She stroked her head and caressed her cheeks. Never had she felt so sisterly, so close to another person.

And Sylvia went on to tell her story. The thing had happened in the early hours of the morning. He had spent the night with her. He had been in particularly high spirits, had escorted her to her door in a carriage, waved to her from the window of the vehicle, and then, while being driven to the Prater, had in that self-same carriage shot himself. She had been expecting this a long time.

"Debts?" Theresa inquired.

No. He had recently been a steady winner at the races. But life disgusted him. People, rather. Almost all people.

"He liked you, Theresa, very much," Sylvia said. "Much,

much more than he did me. Do you know why he did not wish to see you any more?"

In great excitement, Theresa took Sylvia's hand and looked questioningly into her eyes.

" 'She is too good for me!' Those were his words. 'Trop bonne!' "

Then they both wept.

They entered the church two days later for the consecration. After the ceremony, the funeral procession passed Theresa, who was seated on a bench, far in the rear. Richard's mother, a thin, pale woman in whose reserved, proud features, Theresa thought she recognized something of Richard's expression, passed her so closely that Theresa involuntarily recoiled. At the same time, she felt a deep pain. Sylvia firmly grasped her arm. The funeral procession passed.

She beheld familiar faces there: the bank manager, in whose house she had had her last position, and who stared at her without recognizing her in the half gloom of the church; and a young man who had once been her sweetheart.

As if weeping, she hid her face in her handkerchief. She stared at the coffin as it was borne out of the church door into the open, where a dark, blue, summer light welcomed it. That evening on the banks of the Danube returned to her mind; a few days more, and it would be just three years ago. Too good for him! She wondered. As if she were either too good or bad for any one! She heard, outside, the funeral carriage getting under way. The door closed slowly, and the incense enveloped her.

Sylvia was resting her head on the praying bar, sobbing under her breath. Theresa rose silently and left the place alone. A mild summer day received her. She had to hurry home quickly, for at five o'clock she was expecting pupils.

LXXVI

For a time, she devoted herself exclusively to her
profession, in which she was steadily advancing, by dint
of constant labour and through the utilizing of all her spare
hours to perfect herself, to the position of a capable and
sought-after teacher. She taught and prepared young girls
exclusively for their examinations. Two youths who had
applied she dismissed, since it was quite apparent that
their aims were other than the passion of mastering English and French. A letter from Professor Wilnus, asking
permission to visit her again, she had answered with a
definite refusal. This she did not for an instant regret,
although she occasionally felt that she had some reason
to be grateful to him. Since his visit, a temporary change
for the better was apparent in Franz's behaviour. He seemed
to be attending school regularly, as a casual inquiry of
Theresa's revealed. How and with whom he spent his many
hours outside the house, she dared not attempt to discover.

She heard nothing from her brother, and was convinced
that he resented her refusal of Professor Wilnus. Her
mother, too, kept away from her. But for Sylvia's occasional visits at night, she would have been quite alone.

Richard was dropped from their conversation within

310

a surprisingly short time. But they related all kinds of other occurrences of past days, Theresa resorting to hints, Sylvia sometimes expanding her narratives in more than lively descriptions. The men whom the two women had met in the course of their lives did not escape unscathed. Both warmed their hearts on the memories of by-gone days. Sylvia intended to return to her home in southern France as soon as possible. She had not visited it in almost twenty years. What she wished to do there, how she intended to maintain herself—naturally, she had been unable to save anything—she did not know. But her nostalgia for her home had almost assumed the character of a sickness. Tears streamed down the cheeks of this still gay creature whenever she spoke of the place of her birth. At such moments, Theresa noticed how withered and old Sylvia's features had become. It shocked her. But she consoled herself with the conviction that she herself was seven or eight years younger than her companion.

During this epoch of her life, the church again came to stand for an often visited and ever consoling haven. She prayed, or at least fervently wished, that she might continue to remain satisfied with her lot; that Franz might not cause her too much worry; and especially, that passion might never again disturb the quiet current of her life and torment her innermost being.

It happened that, during this summer, she was to prepare a ten-year-old pupil, the youngest girl child of a celebrated actor, for her entrance examinations. To this end, the parents invited Theresa to a summer cottage in the Salzkammergut. Her activities were practically limited to instructing the little girl for several hours each day, most of the time sitting in the garden. An older daughter, not yet eighteen years of age, was in love with a young man, who frequently called. A cousin courted the still attractive lady of the house; and the husband devoted his attention to a sixteen-year-old girl friend of the daughter, a spoiled creature whom he practically pursued.

For Theresa, it was strange to observe how father, mother, and daughter each followed his or her own bent, utterly indifferent to everything else, and mistaking for harmless whims the profound emotions that were causing the others such untold suffering. Her eyes sharpened by so much experience, Theresa viewed this play of passions without herself being touched. She was affected less than a spectator at a theatre, and felt particularly glad that she was done with all such matters of the heart, both outwardly and inwardly.

Indeed, everything seemed to be running smoothly with her. But ultimately, a victim had to fall. The daughter of the house attempted suicide. Now, it was as if they were all rudely shaken from a dangerous dream. Without any painful discussions, these relationships, interwoven as by the play of summer winds, dissolved into an airy nothingness. They left the cottage earlier than they had planned. The entire family went south, Theresa returning to Vienna long before she had anticipated.

She had entrusted her son to the care of a neighbour, the widow of a government employee—a somewhat stupid creature, who was herself the mother of an eight-year-old boy. Although this woman was careful not to speak unfavourably of Franz, she felt obliged to inform Theresa that occasionally he had not come home for several days at a stretch.

Theresa talked to him. He lied so stupidly that Theresa was unable to believe even the most likely things. Upon reproving him, he became more than usually aggressive. But what shocked Theresa most deeply was not his words so much as his gestures and glances. There were no traces of the countenance of a boy remaining; instead, a precocious, spoiled, evil youth insolently stared at her. When Theresa began to talk of school, Franz brazenly declared he could not think of continuing. He had other, more clever plans.

He then discussed his former teachers, in the ugliest terms. A particularly offensive word hurt Theresa so much that she could not restrain herself from slapping his face. His face grew distorted with rage. He lifted his arm to strike her. Theresa could not parry the blow. Franz's fist crashed against her lips, which immediately began to bleed. Paying no heed to her, he rushed out, banging the door after him.

Filled with cruel despair, Theresa remained behind. But she did not weep.

That evening, for the first time in a long while, she

again wrote to Alfred. The answer arrived in two days. Alfred counselled sending the boy somewhere to the provinces, as an apprentice, or a clerk, or anything. Her obligations were more than fulfilled. He did not wish her to worry. The most important thing was that she might finally be liberated of her worries and fears. Fears? The word at first seemed strange. But immediately afterwards, she felt that it was the correct one. Alfred, in another paragraph, mentioned that he was now engaged to the daughter of a professor in the University of Tübingen. He would probably return to Vienna with his bride between Christmas and the New Year. But never would he forget what she, Theresa, had meant to him, and what he owed her. She could count on him under all circumstances. The taste of bitterness was in her mouth. But even now, she did not weep.

She had been invited to dinner the coming Sunday at her brother's. Since she need not fear meeting her rejected suitor, she accepted. Karl welcomed her with obvious friendliness. She soon realized that he now favoured her refusal of the professor, who had proven thoroughly unreliable, he having left the Nationalistic party, for opportunistic reasons, to join the Christian-Socialists. He was now a promising candidate for the Board of Aldermen.

Karl next spoke of their mother, who, he claimed, gave him cause for grave concern. What, he asked, does the old lady do with her money, and what does she intend to do with it in the future? It was obvious that she must by now have saved a quite tidy sum. The children, and himself in particular, as the father of a family, had undoubtedly the right to investigate this matter. He wondered if Theresa, who as a single daughter could most gracefully do so, would mind talking over this delicate matter with her mother, and point out that he, Karl, was prepared to take their mother into his home, where she could certainly live more economically than at a boarding house. Although Karl's method of discussing the subject was distinctly offensive to Theresa, she promised to talk to her mother. But she had no intentions of acting on her promise, at least for the time being.

One evening, she encountered Agnes in the middle of the city. Theresa did not at once recognize her. She looked vulgar, almost disreputable. It was unpleasant for Theresa to stop in the street to talk with her. Agnes informed her that she had some time since given up housework, and had secured a position as a saleslady at a perfumery shop. Theresa inquired after the old people. Agnes replied that she but seldom visited Ensbach now. Her father, moreover, had died last summer. Then she asked to be remembered to Franz, and took her leave.

A few days later, uninvited, she called on Theresa. Franz, with whom Theresa had hardly spoken a word since he had lifted his hand against her, and who now only came to the house for meals, and then late, happened, surprisingly enough, to be home. He greeted Agnes, not without embarrassment. But this he quickly lost in the face of her

unconstraint. Soon the pair were hardly paying any attention at all to Theresa, but were conversing in some sort
of familiar street dialect, which she could barely follow.
They exchanged memories of Ensbach, with secret hints
which they felt fairly certain that Theresa would not understand.

Sometimes, however, Agnes, with her daring, crooked
glance, grinned at Theresa. In her look, one could clearly
read the taunting boast: Do you think he belongs to you?
Well, he's mine!

Finally, and in a coarsely friendly fashion, she shook
Theresa's hand and departed. Without saying a word to
his mother, Franz rejoined her. How he looked in his cheap,
not at all boyish suit, with the checkered trousers, the too
short jacket, and his red, seamed handkerchief! How pale,
how vile . . . and yet, his face was not bad looking. A
boy? No! That he decidedly no longer was. He seemed
to be sixteen or seventeen years old. A young man? That
word hardly fitted him, either. Another term forced itself
on her mind, but she resolutely banished it. Her breast
shook heavily with repressed tears.

LXXVII

Several days later, Franz became sick, and exhibited dangerous symptoms. The doctor diagnosed it as meningitis. On the occasion of his third visit, he seemed prepared to abandon all hope. Theresa wrote an imploring letter to her brother. The latter came, thoughtfully shook his head, and prescribed internal and external remedies which, after a few hours, actually seemed to break the power of the malady. He came again on the following day.

Franz was soon out of danger. And now, for Theresa, it was a surprising and marvelous experience to observe how Franz seemed to alter during his convalescence. When she sat by his bedside, he liked to hold her hand. Then she felt the pressure of his fingers, like a prayer for forgiveness, like a promise. She would occasionally read to him. With grateful, even child-like attention, he would listen. To her, it seemed as if he were manifesting distinct signs of interest in certain subjects, particularly stories of animals, travel, and discoveries. She resolved to talk seriously to him about his future, at the first opportunity. She even dreamed of having him continue his studies, so that he might become a teacher or a doctor. Still, she dared not yet talk to him of such plans.

But the deception could not long continue. She soon knew that she had merely been fancying a change in her boy. The more definitely Franz's recovery was marked, the more quickly he reverted to his former state. The childish and grateful look in his eyes disappeared. His speech regained that intonation, that timbre that she remembered all too well from the days preceding his illness. At first, he still kept himself in control. He still answered his mother. But his answers became ever more impatient, rude, and coarse. The instant he was permitted to leave his bed, he could not be kept at home. And a night came—it was not to be the last—when Franz failed to come home till morning.

She no longer asked questions but let things slide. She was weary. There were hours when, feeling no pain, she felt that her life was ended though she was hardly thirty-three years old. But upon gazing into the mirror, particularly in the early hours of morning after rising, she felt that she looked older by years.

As long as her overpowering fatigue endured, she quietly accepted her fate. But when spring returned, and she felt her strength once more renewed, she fought against she knew not what. Her lessons began to be painfully tiresome. She showed impatience, even rudeness, toward her pupils; a thing which had never before happened. She felt lonely. But it was worse when Franz was at home. In this, she immediately felt that she wronged him. How she would have loved to pour her heart out to Sylvia! But that friend, having changed her position, was with a family in the country, and therefore could not be reached. For this reason, and to free herself of the occasionally quite unbearable feeling of desolation and desertion, she more frequently visited the home of her brother. She observed that he received her visits not without surprise, and certainly without enthusiasm.

Her sister-in-law, on her part, was doubly amiable at that time when she was awaiting her second child. Theresa, once or twice, opened her heart to her, confessing a number of things which she had formerly kept hidden. It touched her to find understanding and compassion where she had least expected it. It was as if the period of pregnancy had not only softened the woman, but had seemingly made her more intelligent than she really was.

As soon as the child was born, the woman relapsed into her former indifference and narrowness, apparently remembering not a single fragment of the various secrets entrusted to her by Theresa. Theresa was glad that it should be thus.

LXXVIII

At the beginning of the winter, Theresa chanced to meet Alfred in the city. She had not received an answer to her last letter which he claimed never to have received. At first somewhat cool and embarrassed toward her, he soon was as cordial as ever. The manner in which he spoke of his young bride did not permit the supposition of a particularly passionate affection on his part. Theresa immediately imagined her as a poor, pale, German provincial creature, at whose side he would certainly be assailed by renewed desire for her, Theresa. She liked him more than ever. Even his appearance had improved, and he seemed better groomed than ever before. They made no appointment when they parted; but now he was again in the city, and it was possible for her to see him whenever she so desired. She dreamed of a new affection on his part, and was happy in the thought. She began to look fresher and younger again.

A young man, almost a boy, who occasionally called for his sister after her lessons with Theresa, fell in love with her, although she had not paid any special attention to him. Once he came early in the morning, to bring her a message from his sister. His embarrassment amused her, and she herself ventured some advances. He remained as embarrassed as ever, probably not even understanding her smile and her glances—and when he had left again, she was ashamed of herself, and resolved to be cold to him from then on.

One day, Theresa was again requested to visit the school. She was not particularly surprised to learn that, for many weeks, Franz had not attended his classes. When she talked to him about it, at home, he told her of his resolution to become a sailor. Theresa remembered that he had expressed similar desires before, and had referred casually to the subject during his talk with Agnes. Now, however, it seemed to be his earnest ambition. Theresa had nothing to say against it; they talked the plan over quite thoroughly and, after a time, they were conversing with each other decently and in an almost friendly manner, and not like enemies forced to live together under the same roof. But during the next few days, the plan was not mentioned again. Theresa did not dare to bring it up, as if she feared to be blamed some day for having driven her son out into the world.

A sallow, lanky youth, who claimed to be a clerk in a grocery store, had called at her house a few times, and frequently took Franz to the theatre, for which, as he said, he always received free tickets. After the theatre, Franz usually stayed the night with his friend; that, at least, was what he told his mother. Once it happened that he did not appear during the entire day following. In a sudden access of fear, which she thought she had long since stifled, Theresa sought out the parents of the friend, and learned that he, too, had not been home. That evening, Theresa was summoned by the police. It developed that Franz, together with a few other half-grown boys and girls, had been arrested as a member of a band of youthful thieves.

Franz, as the only one who had not reached his sixteenth year, was delivered over to his mother for punishment. The police commissioner had him brought into the room, talked to him seriously and, in a cold monologue that sounded as if he had learned it by heart, expressed the hope that this might be a lesson for Franz, and that he would hereafter conduct himself as a decent member of society.

Theresa walked home with her son in silence. Finally, she resolved to question him. At first, he answered in a peculiar, constrained manner, his words sounding like a defense prepared for the courtroom. To listen to him, one would imagine the whole thing to have been merely a joke. In fact, nothing had been stolen at all. When Theresa tried to appeal to his conscience, he did not seem to be as stubborn as before; in fact, it seemed as if the confession forced out of him in the presence of his mother had made it easier for him to talk—something which he had not heretofore found the courage to do.

He spoke of the boy and girl friends with whom he used to foregather every night; and, for a while, it actually seemed as if he were talking only of youthful mischief. He mentioned names which could not possibly be genuine; they were, as he confessed, surnames of a peculiar nature, and full of double meaning. Gradually, he seemed to forget that it was his mother whom he was addressing. He told of nights spent in the Prater during the past summer, when they all, boys and girls alike, had slept in the open. Only when he caught a terrified look in her eyes, did he laugh impudently and become silent. And she knew that this sudden burst of confidence had more definitely and hopelessly alienated her from her son than anything that had passed between them before.

LXXIX

THENCEFORTH, she asked nothing. Without remonstrance, she let him leave the house nightly, knowing that he would not return until the next morning. Once, however, when morning came and he had not returned, an anxious, inexplicable presentiment overcame her. She did not doubt that once more he had been caught in some vileness, and that, this time, it would not end so happily for him. And when he finally stood before her, her excitement, probably ascribable to the fact that her fears had proved without foundation, expressed itself in particularly harsh words.

He let her talk on, hardly replying. He even laughed at her, as if he enjoyed her wrath. Still more excited by this attitude of indifference, she talked herself into a state bordering on hysteria. Then, quite suddenly, he flung at her a word which at first she could not believe that she had heard correctly. With wide, almost crazed eyes, she stared at him. But he repeated the insult, and continued:

"And one like you would tell me what to do! What the hell do you think you are?"

His tongue was now unleashed. He kept on talking, heaping curses, sneers, and threats upon his mother. She lis-

324

tened helplessly, rooted to the spot. It was the first time that he had thrown the blame of his birth at her. But he did not talk to her as to an unfortunate girl, deserted by her sweetheart. No; he talked as if she were a hussy, who had had bad luck and did not even know who was the father of her child. Nor were these the accusations uttered by a child who feels himself handicapped, endangered, and disgraced through being born in bastardy. These were the common, foul curses which gamins shout after harlots.

Theresa consoled herself with the thought that, in spite of his baseness, he hardly understood what he was saying. He was simply expressing himself in the manner of the circle in which he moved. She neither took offence nor felt hurt. It was simply the horror of a tremendous loneliness, such as she had never felt before. And from an immense distance came to her the voice of an inexplicably strange person—a human being to whom she had herself given birth.

That same night, she wrote a special delivery letter to Alfred, telling him that she must see him. Several days passed before he asked her to call on him. He proved amiable, but a little distant. His searching glance made her feel as if he wanted to ascertain first that nothing in her appearance was amiss. While she talked of the reason for her visit, speaking in a somewhat forced, hardly coherent way of the last experiences she had had with Franz, she tried vainly to catch a glimpse of her own reflection in the mirror on the opposite wall. When she had finished, Alfred remained silent for a moment before stating his opinion. Then he made some sort of speech on the case, from which Theresa learned hardly anything that she had not known before. Nor was this the first time that she heard the words "moral insanity" issuing from his lips. And he finished his remarks by stating anew his conviction that he could not give her better advice than he had done some time before—to give the boy away; if possible, to send him to another city, before something that could not be otherwise averted should happen.

Theresa, rocking forward and backward in her chair, had finally caught a glimpse of herself in the mirror, and was shocked. To be sure, the lighting of the room was not of the best; but that the mirror could transmute the beautiful into the ugly and the young into the old, could not possibly be credited. And she saw, she seemed to discover irrevocably in this strange, unfamiliar mirror, that at her thirty-four years, she was becoming withered, elderly, and sallow, like a woman of more than forty. Well, she had lost weight, especially in the last few weeks; besides, she was not dressed to advantage, and her hat particularly did not suit her face. But even taking these things into consideration, the face staring out at her from the mirror brought her a painful surprise. When Alfred stopped talking, she was aware that she had hardly listened to him. Now he stepped up in front of her. Feeling obliged to add a few softening words, he remarked that it was possible that, to a certain extent, the age of puberty might be responsible for Franz's ugly attitude. Before everything else, he warned Theresa against those self-accusations in which, as he thought, she was likely to indulge in her predicament, and for which no foundation whatever existed.

She protested vehemently. What, had she no reasons for self-accusations? Who, if not she? She had never been a real mother to Franz! For a few days, or a few weeks at a time—only occasionally, so to speak—she had behaved like a mother toward him. Most of the time, she had been exclusively occupied with her own affairs, with her profession, with her own problems, and—yes, why should she deny it?—with her love affairs. And how often had she thought of the boy as a burden; yes, just that: as a misfortune—even a long time ago, before she had ever thought of any such thing as moral insanity, or found the slightest traces of it. Even at the time when he was a tiny, innocent baby, even before he had been born, she had not wanted to have anything to do with him. And on the night of his birth, she had hoped and prayed that he might not live!

She had wanted to say still other, truer things; but at the last moment she held them back, in the fear that still more detailed confession might definitely lose this friend to her, and that she might put herself too completely into his power. So she was silent. Even if he did put his hand affectionately and kindly on her shoulder, she could not help seeing that, with the other hand, Alfred took his watch from his pocket; and when Theresa thereupon rose with a certain haste, he remarked, in excuse, that he had to be at the hos-

pital before six. But he did not want Theresa to do anything
before she had talked to him again. And—probably it had
had not been his intention to go quite so far, at first—he
proposed that she should bring Franz with her the next
time she came; or, better still, that he himself should call
on her some day, perhaps on Sunday, at noon. He would
talk to Franz once more, and endeavour to get a clear, personal impression of the boy's character.

Theresa herself did not understand why this very natural
offer of her onetime lover, her friend and physician, should
now impress her as if a way to salvation had suddenly
opened. Out of a full heart she thanked him.

LXXX

THE proposed visit of Alfred was not destined to take place, for the next morning Franz had disappeared from the house of his mother, without leaving a word of explanation. Theresa's first impulse was to notify the police; but she finally decided not to do so, lest the officials should regard his disappearance as flight, and be set in pursuit of him through her. She telephoned Alfred, who at first seemed displeased at being called during his working hours. He assured her that he could see nothing wrong in this new turn of events. It might be most wise for her to take no new steps, but instead, to let the affair run its course.

His indifference pained Theresa. She could not but realize that it hurt her more than Franz's disappearance. Soon, though, on her son's account alone she was experiencing interminable hours of pain and despair. Through a sleepless night, she felt an unbearable longing for her missing boy. She even thought of inserting an advertisement in the papers, such as she often read: "Return, and all will be forgiven!"

But by morning, she realized the stupidity of her plan. She did nothing and, after several weeks had passed, she was obliged to admit that her life, if it was not actually happier, was at least quieter than when her son had occupied her home.

She told the neighbours that Franz had found a position in a small town in the Austrian provinces. It mattered not whether they believed or disbelieved her. Nobody was particularly concerned with the family life of Fräulein Fabiani.

Her professional duties, which she had long followed mechanically and listlessly, once more began to afford her a certain satisfaction. Not only did she give individual instruction, but she also succeeded in grouping in classes a number of young girls of the same age.

Beyond this, she once more relapsed into the lethargy of a lonely life. Neither mother, nor brother, nor sister-in-law showed any interest in her. Nor did she hear from Alfred. She left the house as little as possible, and arranged matters so that she need but rarely teach beyond the confines of her own four walls.

Rarely did she manifest any interest whatever in her pupils, beyond the limits of her lessons. Sometimes, bitterly and ruefully, she thought of the days when, as a governess, she had given her heart to and felt a motherly interest in pupils to whom, certainly, she had then been nearer through the very fact of sharing their domiciles.

But once, several months after Franz had run away from home, it chanced that one of the girls attending her classes remained away a number of days. This absence of the sixteen-year-old girl stirred her more deeply than any-thing of the kind had ever done before. When a letter from the girl's father explained the absence of his daughter as being due to a sore throat and fever, Theresa developed a restlessness which she herself hardly understood. Thilda appeared again after a week's absence. Theresa felt her face redden with joy, and knew that her eyes were shining. This she would hardly have realized herself, but for the fact that, like an answer, a smile, strange, indulgent, and yet superior, played round the girl's mouth. Then Theresa knew that she loved this child, and that her love presaged unhappiness. She also knew that this sixteen-year-old girl belonged to a species of mortals different from herself; that she belonged among the cold, the resourceful, the self-satisfied: among those who never suffer from anything really difficult or important, understanding as they do how to preserve themselves and, from every one coming within their sphere, taking what they can—precisely as much or as little as they need or as may seem agreeable to their caprice.

Now, when Thilda entered the room, after a week's ab-sence, several minutes late as usual, with a graceful ges-ture; when she instantly moved her chair to the table to join the five other members of the class, a barely per-ceptible, well-bred movement of her hand prevented The-resa from interrupting the class one instant for her sake. And that moment was one of those when a ray of light

suddenly pierced the slumbering soul of the teacher, revealing the sentimental relationship between herself and
this pupil, once and for all time, definitely and vividly.

The lesson over, it seemed most natural that Thilda
should remain alone with her teacher. A conversation followed, beginning with the girl's illness. Thilda confessed
that it had first appeared dangerous. Her parents had even
engaged a nurse.

"What, a nurse?"

"Why, yes! Mother, you know, does not live in Vienna."

Did Fräulein Fabiani not know that? Her parents were
divorced. The mother had been sojourning in Italy these
many years, the climate of Vienna not being propitious
for her. Thilda had spent all the preceeding summer, until late in the autumn, with her mother at one of the Italian
bathing resorts on the Mediterranean. She did not divulge
the name, for she loved to be casual. And Theresa felt
it would be tactless, that it would sound too inquisitive,
to ask the name of the resort. The nurse had proved to
be a pleasant enough person. They were able to dismiss
her, fortunately, on the fourth day. It had seemed a relief to be alone and undisturbed in her bed, at last able
to read an interesting book. Though Theresa was tempted
to ask what the book was, she dared not.

"So you live alone with your daddy?" she inquired.

Thilda smiled. Her answer spoke of a father, not a
daddy. While talking of him, she grew a little more warm

than was customary with her. It was quite simple living with him. After the mother had "departed," Thilda had a governess for a while. It had soon become evident that she could manage as well, in fact better, without one. She had attended a girl's school until last year. Now she studied at home, taking piano lessons, even harmony,— and here a shadow of envy passed across Theresa's features—and twice weekly, she attended lectures on the history of art, in the company of several friends. Almost instantly, she corrected herself: a few acquaintances, for she had no friends. She made short trips each Sunday with her father, who also took her to concerts, for her sake alone, since he himself cared but little for music.

Then she bent her head forward. Theresa did not at once understand that this signified good-bye. A slight handshake followed, and Thilda had left.

Theresa, strangely numb, remained where she sat. Something new had entered her life. She felt both older and younger—older in a motherly way; younger as a sister.

She was careful not to let the other girls, or Thilda herself, for that matter, perceive how peculiarly she felt toward the latter. She sensed Thilda's gratitude for this. Her reward soon came. One day after class was over, Thilda invited her, in behalf of her father, to dine with them the coming Sunday. Theresa blushed with joy; but Thilda was kind enough not to notice it. She spent a little time arranging her books; then, taking her coat, talked of a Bulwer novel recommended to her by Theresa, and which had somewhat disappointed her. Finally, with a happy face, she again turned to Theresa:

"Tomorrow, then, at one!"

And she was gone.

LXXXI

THE old, well-preserved, and from all appearances but recently renovated house in one of the side streets of the Mariahilf suburbs had belonged to the Wohlschein family for nearly a century. In the rear stood a small manufacturing plant where leather-goods were made. The ground floor was occupied by a store. A larger, more fashionable store had been established elsewhere in the city, but the old customers preferred to make their purchases here. The living quarters were one flight up. The drawing room into which Theresa was ushered was comfortable, though somewhat old-fashioned, with heavy, dark green plush curtains and overstuffed furniture in the same colour. The dining room, the door to which stood ajar, was bright and modern.

Thilda came running up gaily to greet her guest.

"Father is home, too," she said. "We can begin to eat immediately."

She was wearing a blue dress, with a white silk collar. Her brown hair hung free down her back. Theresa had only seen her before with her hair braided. She looked younger and more childish now.

It was a dull, wintry day. The massive bronze lamp standing on the table was already lit.

"Where do you think father and I spent the day?" Thilda asked. "In the Dornbach Park and on the Hameau! We started at half past eight."

"Wasn't it rather foggy?"

"Not so terribly! Toward noon, the weather cleared up beautifully. We enjoyed a good view of the Danube."

Herr Sigmund Wohlschein entered from the adjoining room. He was somewhat heavy. Despite the bald spot on his head and his grayish hair, he was still youthful in appearance. He had a roundish face, a dark, heavy moustache, and light-coloured, medium-sized, friendly eyes.

"I am glad to have you here, Fräulein Fabiani. Thilda has told me a great deal about you. Forgive me, please, for presenting myself in sports clothes."

He spoke in a remarkably deep voice, using a dialect faintly Viennese. He wore quite handsome sports clothes, with dark stockings and patent leather house shoes.

An elderly servant served the soup, while Herr Wohlschein himself filled the dishes at every course. It proved to be a homely, well-prepared Sunday dinner, accompanied with a light Bordeaux wine. The talk led from the Wienerwald, lauded by Herr Wohlschein for its autumnal charms, to other hilly, mountainous sections through which, as an enthusiastic climber, he had wandered. In answer to friendly questions, Theresa described her childhood, Salzburg, her dead father the colonel, and her mother the writer whose name seemed to be entirely unknown in this household. She also casually mentioned her brother, though she did not tell them that he carried another name. Her son, naturally, she did not discuss, though she took it for granted that he was known to Thilda, as he was to her other pupils, who might have observed him while he was living at home. Never before had his existence, his relationship to her, seemed so ambiguous and remote as now. Herr Wohlschein retired shortly after the meal. Thilda led Theresa into her own airy room, which contained a small, well-chosen library. Together, they pored over the illustrations of an historical work. While she looked at a view of the Barberini palace, Thilda asked Theresa if she knew the original of the print, which was hanging in the Art Museum? Theresa was obliged to admit that, since an early visit there with one of her pupils, she had never revisited the place.

"We must make up for that," Thilda said.

A little later, Herr Wohlschein, now in street clothes, wearing a rather too high collar and a fur coat, again appeared, kissed his daughter on the forehead, and said he was going to his game of tarock at a nearby café, and would return for supper at eight o'clock.

"You may stay longer," she replied, glancing at him with an understanding smile. "I have letters to write."

Letters, Theresa thought—probably to her mother, who is abroad. Herr Wohlschein certainly thought so, too, for he remained silent a moment. His kindly brow wrinkled.

Then he took an amiable leave of Theresa, but without
expressing any desire to see her again. Theresa shortly
thereafter thought that it was time for her, too, to go.
Thilda did not detain her.

Thus was her introduction to this house effected. At
intervals of two or three weeks came further invitations
for Sunday meals, at which other guests occasionally participated. There was the widowed sister of the head of the
house, who, despite her gay temperament, loved sadly
to shake her head and discuss the serious maladies of her
acquaintances; the reserved and uncommunicative manager of the Wohlschein firm; an older girl friend of Thilda's,
an art student, who talked, amusingly and sarcastically
enough, of the professors and girl students at her school.
They all made but vague impressions on Theresa, who
forgot practically all of them before she had left the
house. It seemed that, as compared with Thilda, although
she hardly participated in the conversation, the others had
no light of their own.

Theresa could not help feeling the girl's sustained intelligence, her superior qualities, and, at the same time, her
aloofness.

This aloofness persisted. Always, not only during the
classes, but afterwards during their talks, in Thilda's
own room as at the Museum, which she visited with Thilda
for the first time one Christmas day, Theresa was conscious of this sometimes embarrassing detachment. She occasionally felt jealous of the blond wife of Palma Vecchio,

of Rubens' Maximilian, since Thilda seemed, in their presence, to be more free and intimate and tender than when she was with Theresa, perhaps with any living human being.

LXXXII

ONE night, while she was preparing for bed, the door bell rang. Franz was standing outside, covered with snow, without a winter overcoat, but wearing what appeared to be a somewhat gaudy new suit of clothes. His red, seamed handkerchief protruded as before from his breast pocket. This was a person entirely different from the one he had been half a year ago. No longer could he be justly called a boy; he was rather a young man, although not one of the best quality. His face was pale; his greased hair was parted in the middle; there was the promise of a moustache under his pug nose. His shifting, piercing eyes gave him a suspicious air.

"Good evening, Mother," he said, with a stupid, insolent laugh.

She gazed at him steadily, unshocked. He beat the snow from off his clothes and shoes. With a somewhat gawky politeness, as if entering a strange house, he followed his mother. The remains of the supper were still on the table. His hungry glance rested on the plates of butter and cheese. Theresa cut him a slice of bread and pointed to the food.

"Please!" she said.

340

"Yes, the cold weather makes one hungry!" he said, spreading butter on his bread and eating.

"So, you are back again?" Theresa said, after a short silence.

She felt that she had turned pale.

"Not for ever!"

Franz, his mouth full, replied quickly, as if to reassure her.

"You know, Mother, I got sick on the way."

"On the way to America!"

Theresa, completely apathetic, finished the sentence for him.

Franz continued, paying no heed to her:

"After all, it was only a hurt foot. But the money didn't last, either. The friend who was with me left me in the lurch. Then somebody told me that you need papers of some sort for the ship. I'll be sure to get them, somehow. But for the time being, I thought it best to come home."

"How long are you back?" she asked, slowly.

"Not for such a long time, you may be sure!" he replied evasively, with a defiant laugh.

He told her he had worked as an extra waiter at a restaurant on Sundays and holidays. He claimed that he had a chance to find steady work there. He would have secured it long before, he said, but for the fact that he needed all manner of small things. Shirts, for example. His shoes were in bad shape, too. He showed his mother the pair he was wearing—thin, patent leather shoes, practically without soles.

Theresa nodded her head. She would not let herself be conscious of whether the emotion she felt was pity, or fear lest her boy should become a drag on her again.

"Where do you live?" she asked.

"Oh, there's no need for you to worry on that score. Thank heaven, I'm not without a roof over my head! I've got friends enough for that."

"Why don't you stay here, Franz?" she asked.

Hardly had she uttered the words, when she regretted them. He shook his head.

"I don't belong here," he said, dryly. "But if you will let me sleep here tonight, I won't refuse. It's a long way. And in this weather, with these shoes . . ."

Theresa rose, but again hesitated. She had intended taking one of the few banknotes she possessed from the linen chest where she kept them concealed. She realized that this would be worse than careless. Instead, she said:

"I'll make you a bed on the couch. Perhaps I can raise a few gulden for you, so you can buy a new pair of shoes."

Franz wrinkled his forehead, without as much as saying "Thank you!"

"You'll get it back, Mother, I promise, not later than three weeks from now."

"I don't want it back," she said.

Franz lit a cigarette and stared into space.

"You haven't got a bottle of beer, Mother, have you?"

She shook her head.

"Well, then, perhaps a glass of rum?"

"I'll make you some tea."

"No, thanks, no tea. Only rum makes a fellow warm. I know where you keep it."

He rose and went to the kitchen.

Theresa spread the sheet on the couch. She heard Franz fumbling about outside. My son? she asked herself, shuddering. While Franz was still outside, she took a five-gulden bill from the chest. While she was locking it, Franz tiptoed in again, the rum bottle in his hand. He acted as if he had noticed nothing.

She kept the bill in the palm of her hand, holding it so until the bed was made. He poured the rum into a water tumbler, filling the glass almost to the brim, and raised it to his lips.

"Franz!" Theresa cried.

He drank it, shrugging his shoulders.

"When a man's cold!" he said.

He threw off his coat, vest, and collar. He wore only a torn undervest, and was without a shirt. Then he stretched himself on the couch and covered himself with the blanket.

"Good-night, Mother," he said.

She stood motionless and silent, while he turned his face to the wall and instantly fell asleep. She took a second five-gulden bill from the chest and placed it with the first one on the table. Then she sat down for a while, reflecting, her head on her hands. Finally, she put out the

light and went into her bedroom. She did not completely
undress, but lay down, trying without success to fall asleep.

Shortly after midnight, she again rose and tiptoed into
the room. Franz was breathing quietly. She thought of
the way she had formerly watched over him in his sleep,
when he was still a child. Tonight, too, he was lying in
the same way, the covers piled up to his chin. As the room
was dark, she saw not his face as it looked now, but another face of past years. Yes, he too had once had a child's
face; he too had once been a child. Today, even—oh, this
much was certain—his face would be different today, had
she not murdered him once.

Involuntarily, as from profound depths, this word had
entered her consciousness. Yet, it was something else that
she had meant.

"Had I only been able to devote more attention to him"—
that was what she had wished to think—"he might be
different now. Had I been a different mother, my son would
have become a different man!"

She trembled. Carefully, almost without touching him,
she stroked his smooth, oiled hair.

Under her breath, she said:

"I will keep him with me. Tomorrow morning, I shall
talk to him again."

She returned to her bed. This time, she fell asleep. Awakening at seven the next morning, she entered the adjacent
room. The blanket lay crumpled on the floor. The bottle
was three-fourths empty. Franz had vanished.

LXXXIII

SHE told nobody of this visit. Sooner than she had thought possible, it became a dim memory. Even the fact that, a week later, an elderly, plain-featured woman, with a kerchief round her head, brought a letter from Franz which read: "Help me again, Mother, I need twenty gulden urgently!" hardly touched her. Without an accompanying line, she sent him half the sum which he requested. Even that entailed no small sacrifice.

Shortly afterwards, and most unexpectedly, her sister-in-law paid her a visit. She seemed friendly, though embarrassed. She would have come long before, she explained, but for the difficulty of leaving her household and her two children. And the reason she came today . . . Here she hesitated, and handed Theresa a letter, several lines in length, from Franz, written in a childish, clumsy scrawl and badly spelled:

My dear Mrs. Faber,
    Permit me, in my temporary embarrassment, to address you. Would you be kind enough to help me, because just now my mother can't, and get me a pair of shoes? Also, lend me eleven gulden."
                                    Very respectfully,
                                        Franz Fabiani.

"I hope you sent him nothing," Theresa said.

"Even had I wished to, I could not. I must account for
every penny. I only wanted to ask you to tell him, for
God's sake, never to write me another such letter. If my
husband intercepted one like this! It's for your sake, too,
Theresa!"

Theresa frowned.

"Franz has not lived with me for a long time. I know
nothing about him. What I could do, I have done. Only
a few days ago, I sent him some more money. What can
I do? You don't suppose I prompted him to write that?
I don't even know where he lives!"

She suddenly burst into tears. Her sister-in-law sighed.
"Every one must bear his cross!"

Now, as if she had been waiting for her chance to unburden her heart, she talked on. Not everything was smooth
running with her, either. But for the children—a third
one was now expected! Another worry, but perhaps better luck. She needed it!

"You can imagine that it's not so easy, living with Karl.
He thinks only of his societies and his meetings. He hardly
spends an evening home. Naturally, his professional work
suffers too."

She bitterly complained of his surliness, his harshness,
and his fits of temper. There were still tears in her eyes
when she left, her departure precipitated by the arrival
of two pupils. One of these was Thilda.

Her glance rested questioningly and not without compassion on Theresa, who felt obliged to offer an explanation.

"That was my brother's wife," she remarked.

"My brother's wife," Thilda repeated, transposing the German into English. She unpacked her notebooks. Her interest in Theresa's family affairs was exhausted.

LXXXIV

During the following week, they planned no walks or visits to the galleries in each other's company. Nor did Thilda remain with her teacher after the lessons as was her custom. But one day, and most unexpectedly—it was almost spring—she again invited Theresa for Sunday dinner.

Theresa breathed more freely. She feared that she might have fallen into disfavour with the Wohlscheins, for she knew not what reason. Moreover, only yesterday, she had been agitated by a renewed demand from her son for money, the demand transmitted again by that ugly old woman. She had sent him five gulden, and had availed herself of the opportunity to warn him never again to approach her brother's wife.

"Why don't you find a position, somewhere outside of Vienna," she wrote, "if you can't find one here? I am not in a position to help you any more."

Hardly had she dispatched the letter than she regretted it, feeling that it might be dangerous to excite Franz. Now, with Thilda again kind to her, she felt stronger, as if steeled against further impending mishaps.

Thilda was alone when Theresa arrived. She greeted

her teacher with special warmth, and expressed her joy to find her looking so much better than usual. As if answering Theresa's questioning look, she spoke, almost in an aside, and with a knowing air:

"It's always so! No good ever comes of family visits, particularly when they are unexpected."

"Well," Theresa replied, "I fortunately receive them but rarely, whether expected or unexpected."

She spoke of her retired, almost reclusive mode of life. Now that her son had finally found a position "abroad"— she blushed, and Thilda busied herself with the books on the racks—she hardly saw any of the members of her family. Her mother was completely immersed in her scribbling; her brother had his professional duties, and was moreover interested in politics; and her sister-in-law was completely absorbed by her home and children.

Thilda quite unexpectedly remarked:

"Do you know, Fräulein Fabiani, what Father said, the other day? But you won't feel offended?"

"Offended!" Theresa repeated, in surprise.

Thilda added quickly:

"Father thinks—how shall I phrase it?—that you don't quite know how to make the most of your opportunities."

At Theresa's blank stare, she explained.

"He thinks that such an excellent teacher should be entitled, in fact obliged, to demand higher fees."

"I'm afraid, Thilda," Theresa protested, "that even what I get is too much. I am only a private teacher. I have never passed a single examination, and never held a public position."

She told how she had early been forced to earn her own living, and had never had a chance to make up her deficiencies—all that she had missed, perhaps through the fault of no one but herself. But, as always happened, it was now too late appreciably to better her condition.

"Heavens, it is never too late!" Thilda replied.

Again, she most unexpectedly asked Theresa if she might take the liberty of asking her a favour. She was not quite sure when Theresa's name-day occurred.

"I have none, you know," she explained.

That was why she now begged her to accept a belated present. Before Theresa could answer, Thilda had disappeared into the adjoining room. Returning with an English tailor-made coat, she asked Fräulein Fabiani to rise and helped her into it. The coat fitted as if it had been made to her order. If any alterations were needed, Thilda explained, the tailor would make them at any time.

"Why, you look extremely trim!" Theresa told herself, as she stood before the huge mirror in Thilda's room. It was indeed a tasteful, correctly fitted coat. It made her appear as a fairly youngish young lady of good family.

"Oh, yes, before I forget!" Thilda proceeded, handing Theresa a small package, wrapped in thin paper. "This goes with it."

It contained three pairs of white, dark-grey, and brown gloves, of the best quality suede.

"Six and three-quarters—isn't that the size?"

While Theresa was trying on one of the gloves, Herr Wohlschein entered.

"Congratulations, Fräulein Fabiani!" he said.

"Why, Herr Wohlschein?"

"This is your birthday, Thilda tells me."

"Why, no! It is neither my birthday nor my name-day! I really don't know! . . ."

"Well, we are celebrating it today!" Thilda declared. "And that is that!"

The dinner progressed, with every one in the best of spirits. They drank white Burgundy. Theresa was toasted. She began to be persuaded that it was really her birthday. A sister of Herr Wohlschein joined them for coffee. Later, a business friend came, a Herr Verkade, of Holland—a man past the flush of youth, smoothly shaven, with dark hair, gray temples, and light blue eyes beneath black eyebrows.

They discussed Java, where Herr Verkade had lived for many years, sea journeys, luxurious steamers, balls at sea, improvements in trade and commerce throughout the world, and the deficiencies of Austria.

Herr Wohlschein's sister defended her country. Herr Verkade did not care to presume with a judgment of local conditions, and so adroitly diverted the talk into other channels, speaking of operas, famous singers, concerts, and the like. In the course of his conversation, he several times addressed Theresa with particular politeness.

She had often participated in such conversations, but never before on equal terms. Today, she several times found herself eager to speak, but afraid to venture an opinion. At a convenient opportunity—nobody but Theresa noticed the strategy of the manœuvre—Thilda made her talk. Gradually—the wine may have been in part responsible—Theresa's embarrassment disappeared. She spoke with a freedom and vivacity that had almost become foreign to her nature. She occasionally noticed the somewhat surprised, but certainly not displeased glance of the master of the house.

LXXXV

THE following Sunday finally brought about what had frequently been planned, but never carried out—a long walk with Thilda, her father, and a young married couple, whom they had encountered in the street car.

It proved to be a beautiful spring day. They lunched at an inn in the forest. Theresa knew it as the very one where she had, many years ago, spent several hours in Kasimir's company. Was she not sitting at the identical table, on the very chair, perhaps? Were not these perhaps the same children scampering about the tiny plot of grass yonder, just as that was the self-same sky above her, the same landscape, the same confused hum of voices? Were not the people at the adjoining table the very people with whom her companion, much to her displeasure, had begun a conversation?

Only a second later did she realize that the man with whom her thoughts were preoccupied was the father of her child. Something else occurred to her which, strangely enough, she had not thought of until this moment—that only last night, Franz had reminded her of his existence, in a most disagreeable fashion. He had sent her a letter requesting two hundred gulden. He was in trouble. This would save him. Moreover, with that sum, he could begin anew.

"Mother, don't fail me, I beseech you," he had written. It was not the old woman with the kerchief who had brought the letter, but instead, a lanky, dilapidated youth, who had roughly pushed open the door, closed it behind him, and silently handed her the letter, with an impudent expression on his face. It was as if it were Franz's intention to frighten his mother by his messenger's appearance. She had sent him thirty gulden, which had been difficult enough for her. How was this affair to end? Oh, if he had only gone to America; if only she had money enough to pay for his passage! But what guarantee had she that he would actually board the vessel and depart?

Suddenly, as if in a picture, she beheld him aboard a freighter, in a frayed suit, with torn shoes, no overcoat, and with the collar of his coat turned up about his neck, freezing in rain and storm. And simultaneously there returned that sense of guilt which again and again came back to her, though but for a few fleeting moments only, and which, disappearing, left her suspended in space— floating, as it were, as if everything which she experienced were unreal and dream-like.

"Your soup will be cold," Thilda said.

Theresa glanced up, and recovered her self-possession. The others had not noticed her absent-mindedness. They ate, talked and laughed. Even Theresa breathed freely again. She relished the soup and enjoyed the air, the landscape, the people, the season, and the Sunday spirit which surrounded her.

The married couple, wishing to climb a nearby hill, took leave. The others started homeward. In a beautiful open spot in the forest, overlooking the wide expanse of the Danube, they rested. Herr Wohlschein fell asleep. Theresa sat at some little distance and began to talk at length. She recollected much of by-gone days; people she had not thought of for a long time; others whom she had completely forgotten; families with whom she had lived; fathers and mothers; children she had educated, or at least tutored. It was as if she had opened an album of photographs, passing over some, superficially regarding others, and pondering on still others with deep emotion.

It was sad, yet consoling, to think that of all the children to whom she had been practically a mother, there was hardly one who would still remember her; certainly, there were none who knew anything of her present existence.

Attentively, her hands linked round her knees, occasionally with a child's wondering eyes, or deeply touched, Thilda listened; and as she listened, those pictures of the past assumed a more definite reality to Theresa than they had had at the time of their occurrence. She was grateful to Thilda because, through her, her poor life had become rich for the space of one brief spring hour.

Herr Wohlschein awoke, looked up, rose, and asked if they had discussed many interesting things. Theresa and

Thilda also rose, and shook the grass and dust from their clothes. The three made their way down the hill. Thilda linked her arm confidentially into Theresa's. Occasionally they ran ahead, while Herr Wohlschein, his coat slung over his arm, followed. It was the same path that Theresa had taken, so many years ago, with Kasimir Tobisch . . . in those far-off days, when she had carried his child within her.

Long before dusk, Herr Wohlschein and Thilda took leave of Theresa at her door. She felt doubly lonely, that evening, in her house into which the warmth of the burgeoning spring had not yet found its way.

Soon her life, which had been rich for a moment, was as barren as before.

LXXXVI

A WEEK or more passed, during which Thilda's behaviour was hardly more intimate than that of any of Theresa's other pupils. The girl seemed, in fact, anxious to leave the instant the classes were dismissed. Then, quite unexpectedly again, she brought an invitation, in behalf of her father, to attend the opera with them.

For Theresa, it was marvelous, after these many years, to be enjoying a performance of "Lohengrin" in this spacious and beautiful theatre, particularly with Thilda at her side. She felt almost like an older sister, and hardly required the excellent perfection of the performance to make her happy. Herr Verkade, too, had been invited to join the box party.

Afterwards, they supped in the elegant restaurant of a hotel. There Theresa, in her poor dress, no longer felt like Thilda's older sister, particularly since the Dutchman talked almost exclusively to Thilda, while the generally talkative father seemed engrossed in his own thoughts. Theresa ascribed his abstraction to possible business difficulties, but was not particularly affected by the contingency. She continued to ruminate, picturing the old factory in bankruptcy, Wohlschein's fortune lost, and Thilda, no longer a rich young lady, but a poor girl forced to earn her own living, and consequently that much the closer to her.

But the real cause of Herr Wohlschein's ill humour, or what Theresa had mistaken as such, became apparent several days later, when Thilda surprised her in her light matter-of-fact way with the intelligence of her betrothal to Herr Verkade. The wedding would occur late in autumn. The future home of the married couple would presumably be Amsterdam, for which destination Herr Verkade had, incidentally, departed yesterday for a prolonged stay. As Thilda spoke, a frozen smile was fixed on Theresa's features, which might be construed as an expression of the congratulations she could not formulate into words.

She could not understand Herr Wohlschein for giving permission to this betrothal, and thought him weak or devoid of feeling. She even thought of baser motives for his action. Perhaps his firm was in financial straits, and Herr Wohlschein had actually contrived the engagement to save himself and his factory. She refused to believe that a mere child actually loved this man, who was twenty or more years her senior, and neither particularly interesting nor even handsome. She was inclined to consider this pretty young thing as an innocent victim, hardly conscious of her sacrifice. She even planned to talk to Herr Wohlschein. But she immediately realized the futility of such an expedient. Indeed, she knew that Thilda was not the type of girl who could be persuaded or bullied into any act that did not meet with her full approval.

The thought of the impending separation so engrossed her that she hardly felt the many other minor and major cares of the day. Having lost a number of pupils, she was forced to live on a still more meagre scale than ever. She was barely conscious of the actual privations which she endured. Even the fact that Franz, one night, had suddenly reappeared with a small satchel, and accepted as his right her bed and food, without a word of thanks or explanation, was merely one added unpleasantness, though one no more grievous than the others. At first, he seldom disturbed her. Ordinarily, he rested on the couch until noon, disappearing after his meal and reappearing late at night, or even in the small hours of morning. He never came in contact with her pupils—a thing which she was most anxious to avoid.

Sometimes Franz, who was behaving more quietly and politely than before, would be called for by friends after the meal. One of them was a tall, rather handsome lad, who looked as if he might be a student of the poorer middle-class. In another person, however, she recognized the evil-looking individual whom Franz had sent to her house for money. He seemed specially garbed to awaken the suspicions of every policeman, with his loud-patterned, gray trousers, short brown jacket, gray cap, and the small ring hanging from the lobe of his left ear. His voice was hoarse; his glance, evasive and threatening.

Theresa was ashamed to have such a creature received at her house, and afraid lest the neighbours might see him emerge from the door of her flat. She could not help speaking of this to Franz. He suddenly stepped in front of her and roughly forbade her to offend his friend.

"He comes of a better family than I do," he shouted. "He, at least, has a father!"

Theresa shrugged her shoulders and left the room. Even that scarcely touched her spirit, which was now freighted with more painful things.

LXXXVII

Thilda continued to attend classes regularly. She never discussed her intended husband, nor even the approaching marriage; so that Theresa occasionally was convinced that the engagement was broken. But, at another Sunday dinner at the Wohlschein home, attended as well by the sister of the master, only the topic of the marriage was discussed and things relevant thereto: Dutch lessons which Thilda had begun to take, and of which Theresa now for the first time learned; her trousseau; the Verkade villa on the Zandvord shore; the farm in Java, belonging to one of the intended husband's brothers. And Herr Wohlschein was today neither sullen nor meditative, but quite gay, as if the marriage absolutely met with his approval and it were the most natural thing in the world to dismiss one's own daughter, a child to whom he was sincerely attached, into the world and to lose her for ever.

The wedding occurred earlier than originally planned, during the first days of July, in the City Hall. Theresa heard of it the next day when a printed announcement came by mail. The card in her hand, she now admitted that she had known all along that this would happen. She felt that Thilda, after the last lesson, had pressed her hand

more significantly than ever before. She also remembered
a parting look at the door, in which she seemed to detect
at once an expression of regret and a trace of mockery,
like that of a child who had perpetrated some prank as
yet undiscovered by its victim.

Theresa, all the same, hoped to receive a personal note
during the honeymoon. Nothing of the sort happened,
nor was to happen for a long time. Neither letter, nor card,
nor greeting of any kind, arrived.

One fine summer evening, toward the end of the week,
Theresa walked toward Mariahilf with the hardly sincere
resolve of congratulating Herr Wohlschein on his daughter's wedding. But once before the house, she saw the shut-
tered windows and remembered that Herr Wohlschein had,
weeks before, expressed the intention of starting on his
vacation immediately after the wedding. She slowly started
back to her home, through the half-deserted, summer-baked
streets. Even Franz had gone. Theresa, the day before, had
thrown him out when he came home late at night, in the
company of a friend and a girl. She had seen none of
them; but their laughter and whisperings had awakened
her from sleep. At first, Franz had tried to lie, claiming
that no woman had been present. Then, with a defiant
shrug of his shoulders, he finally admitted it, packed his
belongings, and left the house without saying good-bye.

As July advanced and the last pupils left for their va-
cations, the loneliness which enveloped Theresa was complete. As was her habit, she rose early each morning and

was at a loss how to dispose of her day. Her housework was finished in no time at all. Walks during the morning hours through the hot streets wearied her. She tried to read during the afternoons, for the most part novels that either bored or else superfluously excited her by describing exotic environments and delicate love scenes.

Walks over the Ring or through the parks at dusk left her profoundly sad. It still happened that, during these hours, men in quest of adventure would follow her; but she was too abashed to let them talk to her, or even accompany her. She knew that her appearance was still sufficiently youthful. But in her heart, she carried the picture that the mirror used to reveal to her each morning when she arose: a pale, finely chiselled face, prematurely withered, with two heavy, gray streaks in her otherwise still full dark blond hair. When her loneliness, patiently borne all day, pressed at night like a heavy burden on her shoulders, she would think for the briefest of moments of calling on her brother. But she always abandoned the idea, uncertain how he would welcome her, or, if he would receive her at all. And to call on her mother, after having avoided her for a whole year, seemed too difficult.

And yet, one fine summer morning, she resolved to go thither, as if her decision were born of a dream. It was not longing. Nor was it the instinct of fulfilling a long-forgotten duty which suddenly drove her there, but simply the circumstance that she did not know any one else who might lend her the money to spend a few quiet weeks in the country. For the desire to leave town for at least a few days, to flee to the country, had grown overwhelmingly compelling within her, as if her health and her happiness rested upon that, and that alone. And these terms—country, rest, renascence—she had lately come to identify with the picture of a certain grassy spot in Ensbach where, many, many years ago, she had played with a little boy who had then been her child.

Theresa's mother was living in an ugly four-story tenement house on the Hernalser Hauptstrasse, occupying a dingy hall-room with a window. Theresa did not know whether the money which her mother had earned so abundantly these many years had been lost in speculating, whether it had been given away foolishly, or whether it was merely parsimony which caused her mother to lead the miserable existence she did. Small as was the hope of securing a loan from that source, it was perhaps the impetuousness of her desire, perhaps her mother's quite genuine joy at her unexpected visit, or perhaps merely the definiteness with which Theresa expressed her wish, which caused her mother, without hesitation to declare herself ready to put 150 gulden at Theresa's disposal—against a note, to be sure, which obligated her to repay the money not later than November first, with interest at two per cent monthly, in case this date was not kept. Beyond these stipulations, she hardly asked her daughter for what purpose she needed the money; in fact, she asked her nothing at all concerning herself. She merely chattered, in a strange, uninhibited way, of her daily tasks, gossiped about her uninteresting neighbours, abruptly showed her the manuscript of her new novel—hundreds of pages, closely covered with script, which she kept in a drawer in the kitchen—vaguely answered the questions which Theresa asked about her brother's family, greeted a woman across the street through the open window when she watered her flowers, and finally permitted her daughter to depart, without attempting to detain her and without asking her to call again.

LXXXVIII

Theresa left for Ensbach the very next day. It was six years since she had last been there. Shortly after the death of her husband, the widow Leutner had remarried and moved to an adjacent village. Theresa had first planned to engage a room in a farmhouse, but, fearing the possibility of contact with her former acquaintances, she decided to live at the inexpensive village inn.

On her first short stroll through the familiar countryside, over the grassy fields to the nearby woods, she met occasional villagers whom she remembered. Nobody seemed to recognize her. She was as isolated as she had wished she might be. But the sense of comfort which she had hoped to derive from this solitude, did not come to her. She was weary when she returned to the inn. The innkeeper recognized her while she ate supper, and even asked after Franz. With an impassiveness that caused her to shudder, she replied that he had a good position in Vienna.

During the whole of the afternoon, she remained in her room. Outside, the warm, summer air trembled. Through the shutters, the sun checkered the walls with blinding, small, white stripes. Half asleep, she lay on the uncomfortable, hard bed. Flies buzzed; voices, far and near,

366

arose and died; all manner of noises from the street and from the fields blended into her dreams. Not until dusk did she rise and go out again. She passed the house where Franz had been a child, and which had now changed its owner. It seemed remote, as if it had never held any significance for her. In front of the house, on the grass, she noticed a low, light mist, as if autumn were sending advance couriers to announce its impending arrival. Unchanged, untouched, surrounded by withered leaves as before, and still with the crack in the glass, the image of the Virgin Mary gazed down at her from its maple tree. From the hill, she descended to the main road, bordered by unpretentious cottages.

Here and there, on porches, under hanging lamps, the summer boarders, couples, and children sat. Nothing had changed. Other children, other parents—and yet ever the same children, for this solitary walker, as their unfamiliar faces disappeared in the twilight. Over on the railway embankment, the express train rushed by, its rumble receding with incredible swiftness. And now the gloom, ever more oppressive, weighed on Theresa as she walked in the darkness.

Later on, she sat in the restaurant, eating her supper. Since she did not fancy the idea of going at once to her dingy, little, stifling room, she remained downstairs a long time. She read the "Farmer's Journal of Lower Austria," the "Leipzig Illustrated News," the "Huntsmen's and Foresters' Journal," until she was tired. Then she slept, heavily and dreamlessly, having, contrary to her habit, drunk two glasses of beer.

After a few days, however, she was able to enjoy the summer air, the tranquillity of the region, the scent of the hay, with the same zest that she had formerly experienced. She would rest on the fringe of the forest, thinking sometimes of the Franz who had been, as of some child long dead. She would feel a gentle longing for Thilda. This desire, she realized, was the sweetest that she had known in her life, and bore her to heights where she was a stranger. An old wish again awoke in her—the desire to spend her remaining days quietly somewhere in the country, surrounded by green, growing things, and as far removed from people as possible. The evening of life! she mused. The thought suddenly struck her with bold emphasis. And since she was attentively considering it, she smiled wanly. The evening of life? Had she really come so far?

Her fatigue gradually fell from her, and her cheeks grew ruddy. By the evidence of her mirror, she was decidedly rejuvenated, as compared with what she had been a few weeks ago. Vague hopes arose within her. She thought of reminding Alfred once more of her existence. Then she thought that Herr Wohlschein was probably returned from his vacation, and that she might inquire after Thilda, who had still not deigned to write to her.

The thought of her profession, too, returned. With it came a half longing for some regular work to do. The last days of her vacation were passed in mounting impatience, almost restlessness. Rainy weather suddenly decided her to cut short her stay. She was back in town long before the date which she had set for her return.

LXXXIX

GRADUALLY, the number of Theresa's pupils increased. Another class was formed. Rested and refreshed, she fulfilled her duties without too much effort. As was her practice, she met her pupils with the same rather distant amiability, even though some one or other of them might have been quite sympathetic to her. There was no Thilda among them.

One afternoon, in the city, she met a well-dressed, elderly gentleman, who wore a stiff, dark hat at a rather rakish angle. She recognized Herr Wohlschein only when she had come directly in front of him. Her face beamed as if some unexpected happiness had befallen her. He, on his part, was obviously glad to see her as he shook her hand.

"Why doesn't one see you ever, my dear Fräulein Fabiani? I would have written, but, unfortunately, I had no address."

Well, well, Theresa thought, that could easily have been found! But she suppressed the observation, and inquired after Thilda.

More than a fortnight often passed, she learned, without any word coming from Thilda. That was, however,

370

hardly surprising, since the honeymoon had been transformed into a sort of vagrant trip round the world. He
was surprised that Theresa should not know of it. They
were now probably somewhere on the high seas. He did
not expect them back before spring.

"And you, Fräulein Fabiani, are really still without news
from Thilda?"

She shook her head, almost bashfully. He shrugged his
shoulders.

"That's just how she is. And yet, you can take my word
for it, Fräulein Fabiani, she has a very warm feeling for
you."

He continued to talk—of his dreary, empty, big house,
of his dull whist parties at the club, and of the sad fate
of finding himself as a bachelor or widower one day, after
having for years lived with a wife and child. It was as
if ten years of happy, and several other years of unhappy
married life, as if that whole existence with his wife and
child, had become merely a dream.

She was surprised at hearing him expressing himself
with such freedom and friendliness. She said nothing, for
she understood his relief at this opportunity to unburden
himself. Then, suddenly, he sighed, consulted his watch,
and remarked that he was that night going to the theatre
with several acquaintances—to an operetta, if he must confess it; not to a legitimate play. He felt in need of distraction. Did Fräulein Fabiani ever visit the theatre? She
shook her head. She had not, since that night at the opera,

had another such opportunity. And no time, either. Did she still give as many and—he hesitated a moment—as ill-paid lessons?

She smiled and shrugged her shoulders, realizing that he had other questions which, for the moment, he did not care or dare to ask. He took leave of her abruptly, but with a hearty "Till we meet again!"

As she continued on her way, she had the feeling that he had stopped to look after her.

The following Sunday, the mail brought her, by special delivery, an envelope containing a theatre ticket and a business card:

SIGMUND WOHLSCHEIN
LEATHER GOODS
ESTABLISHED 1804

She had expected something of the kind. And, though the form of the invitation displeased her, she accepted it.

The house was already dark when Herr Wohlschein appeared, sat down beside her, and pressed a box of candy into her hand. She nodded and smiled her thanks, but did not allow the incident to distract her. The caressing dance rhythms pleased her and she was amused by the droll libretto. She felt her cheeks redden and knew that her features softened from scene to scene. To herself, she became younger and prettier. During the intermission, Herr Wohlschein was quite gallant to her, although not utterly at ease. When the play ended and they stood in the foyer beside the cloak room, he remained at her side, but not in the manner of an escort; rather, like a person who has made a casual encounter at the theatre.

It was a beautiful, clear autumn evening. She wished to walk home, and he took her the whole way. Only now he began to talk of Thilda, of whom he had not yet received intelligence. His invitation to supper she declined. He did not insist and, when they had arrived before her house, said a polite good-bye.

The week was not yet done when Herr Wohlschein again invited Theresa to the theatre—this time, to a modern society play at the People's Theatre. Afterwards, over a bottle of wine, in a comfortable corner of a restaurant, they chatted more freely and easily than the last time. He hinted of the last few difficult years of his marital life. She spoke of various sad experiences of her own, without permitting any of them to appear more than in vague outlines. When they parted, both felt that this night had drawn them closer together.

The next day, he sent, with a bunch of roses, an invitation—"in memory of Thilda"—to accompany him on a hike through the Wienerwald. And so she walked with him, in the first mild snowfall of the winter, along the same road that they had taken that spring day, half a year ago, with Thilda. Wohlschein had brought along three picture postcards from Thilda, all of which had arrived the day before. One carried a postscript: "And

will you not occasionally look up Fräulein Fabiani? Her
address is Wagnergasse 74, two flights up. Remember me
to her. I'll write her a long letter, soon."

It was on this walk that she told Wohlschein for the first
time of her boy, who had emigrated to America a year
ago, and from whom she had not since heard.

After several evenings together, at the theatre or in restaurants, Herr Wohlschein knew not a little of her, despite
the veil of generalities and wilful variations in which she
had enshrouded her anecdotes, and which he tactfully accepted. He himself continued to talk a great deal of his
wife; and he did this, to Theresa's great surprise, always in
tones of the highest esteem, even of adoration, as if he were
speaking of an extraordinary creature, not to be measured
by the standards of ordinary mortals. Theresa began to realize that he loved Thilda really as the daughter of this lost
woman, with whom she seemed to have many traits in common. And she knew that she, Theresa, had offered Thilda
a more genuine, enduring, true love than had her own father.

The ensuing weeks in their relationship were not marked
by any exceptional occurrences. They visited the theatre and
restaurants together. He sent her flowers and candy. Then
came a basket filled with preserves, exotic fruit and wine.
She protested, but not too strenuously. When two holidays
fell close to one another, early in December, he invited her
to accompany him on a trip to a little village at the foot of
the Semmering Mountains. She was convinced that, despite

his former reserve, he at length hoped for certain definite results. She resolved not to forget herself.

During the journey, he grew intimate, in a rather clumsy fashion. She accepted his approaches with coldness. The fact that their hotel rooms did not adjoin at once reassured and disappointed her. Nevertheless, she failed to lock the door to her room that night. Next morning, she awoke as solitary as when she had retired. She thought this reticence most respectful of him.

But while dressing before the mirror, she suddenly thought she discovered a more pertinent reason for his backwardness. She simply was no longer sufficiently beautiful to tempt any man. Even though her body had retained its youthful contours, her features were old and lined with care. How could it be otherwise? She had undergone too much. She was a mother; the unmarried mother of a quite grown-up boy. It had been a long time since any man had desired her. And had she herself ever felt any stirrings of desire for this elderly, commonplace man? He was the father of one of her pupils, who, for his daughter's sake, had met her to spend two days in the fresh winter air.

Only her fevered imagination, she assured herself, could have fancied the possibility of an adventure which she herself did not crave.

Dressed in her sport dress, she again appeared fresher and younger to herself; almost graceful, in fact.

After breakfasting together in the pine-seated restaurant, in a corner of which crackled a huge oven, they drove in a sleigh through the firs and pines of a narrow valley, and at noon sat in the open, in the centre of a snow entrenched glade, warmed by a sun so strong that Theresa removed her jacket and her companion his short fur overcoat and jacket. In his shirt-sleeves, his huntsman's hat with its chamois flap, and with his turned-up moist moustache, his appearance was slightly comical.

On the return trip, it turned cold rapidly. They were happy to be back in the comfortable hotel. They dined in Theresa's room, which was more cozy than the restaurant.

They returned the next day to Vienna, like a pair of lovers who had finally found one another.

XC

I T was as if, from the obscure distance where he dwelt, Franz had sensed the change in the manner of her life. Just when Theresa had received another basket of edibles, he unexpectedly reappeared. At first, in his winter overcoat, he looked fairly decent; in fact, he almost inspired confidence, despite his worn and frayed velvet collar. But when he opened his coat and showed his grease-spotted tuxedo and his maculate shirt-front, the original favorable impression vanished.

"To what do I owe this pleasure?" his mother coldly inquired.

He was again without a position and homeless. The hall room which he had for a few weeks occupied, had been rented to some one else. He had been back in Vienna for some weeks.

"After all," he said pointedly, "even if one has no home, one has a home town."

He thought it most considerate on his part not to have molested her for so long. Would his mother not give him shelter and food for two or three days, as a recompense?

Theresa firmly declined. From the basket which her pupils had given her for Christmas, he might take what he needed. She would also give him ten gulden. But she kept no public house. That was final. He pocketed a few preserves, took a bottle of wine under his arm, and turned to go.

The heels of his shoes were worn. His neck was scrawny, his ears protruded, and his back was strangely bent.

"Well, you needn't be in such a hurry," Theresa said, suddenly moved. "Sit down a while and tell me about yourself."

He turned round with a laugh.

"After such a reception, I wouldn't think of it!"

He opened the door and banged it so rudely that the house shook.

She told Wohlschein of the visit. When he called for her a week later and found her pale and excited, her eyes still red with weeping, she could not help confess that, for the second time within a week, Franz had come to demand money of her. She had lacked the courage to deny him. Now she confessed that Franz had never gone to America at all, but had led a fugitive life here in Vienna, of which she knew nothing and cared to know less.

Her tongue once loosened, she more frankly related, and at greater length, what suffering he had caused her. She first thought that Wohlschein was quite disagreeably affected. The more he listened, the more pity he felt. Finally, he declared that he simply could not watch her paltry and tormented life any longer. He felt ashamed to be carelessly rolling in wealth, while she—oh, he had noticed it—sometimes lacked the very necessities.

She protested. Under no circumstances would she listen to his proffer of a small monthly allowance to better her condition. She made a decent living, she said. It was her pride—her sole remaining pride, perhaps—that all her life she had been able to maintain herself, and for a long time, her son as well, on her earnings.

But when, on another occasion, he insisted on being allowed to replenish some of her worn wardrobe, she no longer protested. When a severe cold confined her for some weeks to her bed, she was obliged to permit him to pay for the doctor and prescriptions, and the necessary improved quality of food; eventually, too, to indemnify her for the money lost through having had to give up her lessons. He also insisted, thenceforward, that she should take better care of herself. Nothing remained for her but to accept his aid with gratitude.

XCI

ONE day in January, they were given a wonderful surprise. Thilda arrived suddenly, though her father did not even know that the young couple had returned to Europe. Theresa learned the news from Wohlschein, who telephoned her. She owed the telephone, by the way, to his generosity. He excused himself from meeting her that evening, as they had planned, Thilda's coming having disrupted the even current of his present life. He excused himself so hurriedly, so embarrassedly, and with such an obvious sense of guilt, that Theresa had no opportunity to ask a question. As she hung up the receiver, she felt no joy; she only felt dismay and a heavy oppression.

She felt wronged, betrayed. And doubly so by Thilda, who had never written to her; never even included a message for her in the meagre news sent to her father. And by Wohlschein, to whom—how keenly she felt it!—she was again an unimportant, even disturbing interloper, now that Thilda was back.

All the following day—how correctly she had guessed how matters stood!—he did not communicate with her. Toward noon of the third day, he appeared. Certainly he had chosen an untoward hour, for she was not prepared to receive him. After her recent illness, from which she was not yet fully recovered, and in a grey flannel house-dress, with her hair in disorder, she did not look as well as she would have wished. But he seemed to notice nothing; he was inattentive and in high spirits.

The first thing he said was that Thilda had immediately asked after her and would particularly like to see her for dinner next Sunday. Theresa, however, felt no gladness at this. Suddenly and painfully, she realized her position. She was the mother of an illegitimate child, and had yielded herself too often to unworthy men. And she had become the maintained mistress of Thilda's father. Though she said nothing, Wohlschein realized what her thoughts must be. He tried to console her with caresses. She at first remained rigid and cold. But she gradually became conscious of the happiness she felt in Thilda's return, in the sure knowledge that she would again see her on the morrow. When she asked him to remember her to the beloved creature, she had sufficiently recovered a certain composure to remark good-naturedly:

"You need not tell her that you called on me. We might have met on the street."

He was prepared to go, his fur overcoat already donned, and holding his stick and hat in his hand. He replied, with pompous seriousness:

"I have, of course, informed her that we have been seeing a great deal of one another, and that we are—very good friends."

Thilda greeted Theresa as nonchalantly as if they had bid each other farewell the preceding day. This fact was stressed by her girlish, unaltered, still delicate appearance. She seemed, however, slightly more pallid than before. On her side, Thilda found that Theresa had changed for the better, that she seemed, in fact, rejuvenated. She inquired after several of her fellow students of the past year, without waiting for the replies, and presented greetings from her husband.

"He did not accompany you?" Theresa innocently asked, as if compelled not to appear informed.

"Certainly not," Thilda replied. "That would have been improper."

She blushed slightly and continued:

"One must be quite the young girl when returning home."

She spoke as if she were quoting.

"You are here only for a few days?"

"Naturally, my visit will be a short one. Herr Verkade" —thus she termed her husband, and it did not affect Theresa disagreeably—"did not want to let me come at all. Well, I presented him with a *fait accompli*, I bought my ticket from a traveller's bureau, packed my trunks, and, next day, told him: 'Tonight at eight-thirty my train leaves.'"

"And were you quite homesick?"

Thilda shook her head.

"In such a case, I might not have come at all."

And, answering Theresa's somewhat astonished glance

with a smile which seemed to comprehend it, she explained:

"I would, in that event, have tried to suppress my longing. Where would one be, if one yielded to every longing? No, I was not particularly homesick. But now I am really glad to be back. Besides, lest I forget . . ."

She presented Theresa with a little package, which had been laying on the couch. As Theresa opened it, discovering a big box of Dutch chocolates and a half dozen of the finest silk handkerchiefs, Herr Wohlschein, accompanied by his sister, entered the room. While the aunt embraced Thilda, Wohlschein and Theresa could, without embarrassment, exchange cordial glances.

They were the only guests invited. Dinner passed pleasantly, as in the past, in quiet contentment. Had Thilda not related sundry details of her trip and of her new home, one might have believed—Wohlschein did not hesitate to say as much—that she had not been away at all. But she talked more of the hours when, alone between heaven and the sea, she lay on her deck-chair, than of landscapes and cities seen, or of the house with the immense glass windows and numerous flowerbeds in which she now lived. And though, in her fashion, Thilda praised the glorious boredom of these days, Theresa sensed that these hours of solitude, of distance, had been the truest and deepest adventures of this journey—more important than the visit to a South American *hacienda* which she described; or than the view from the heights overlooking Rio de Janeiro on the bay glowing with myriads of lights; or more impressive even than the dance with the young French astronomer, who had utilized that same ship to observe a solar eclipse in South America.

Shortly after the meal, Theresa took leave, secretly hoping that Thilda would ask her to remain. But she did not. She even neglected to make any definite appointment for the next few days, and only uttered a sincere, though noncommital:

"I hope to see you again, before I leave."

"I, too," Theresa replied, though timidly. Then she added:

"Please remember me to Herr Verkade."

The package of chocolates and the handkerchiefs in her hand, she said good-bye and slowly descended the stairs— a former teacher, to whom a married pupil had considerately brought a small keepsake.

That evening at home was unspeakably dreary. Two sad days followed, during which news was forthcoming neither from Wohlschein nor from Thilda.

Dolorous thoughts arose within her.

XCII

At an early hour on the morning of the third day, Herr Wohlschein appeared in person. He had returned directly from the station, whence he had escorted Thilda, who, upon receiving an urgent telegram from her husband, had departed earlier than she had anticipated. She had probably acted with more independence and superiority than she really possessed in returning home. How hastily, how excitedly she had torn open the telegram; how she had frowned, and then laughed lightly, blushing a deep scarlet! But it was difficult to say whether she coloured from wrath or pleasure. One thing was certain, and that was that she was already in the express train that would carry her to Holland and to the arms of an impatient husband. She had deeply regretted not having the chance to see Fräulein Fabiani a second time, and asked to be remembered to her.

But now, there was something else, something pleasant to tell, something wonderfully agreeable. Could she guess? He took her by the chin, as he might a small girl, and kissed the tip of her nose, as he liked to do—much to Theresa's displeasure—when he was in good spirits.

Theresa unfortunately could not guess that pleasant thing. An invitation, perhaps, to Holland for Whitsuntide? One to spend the summer at Zandvord in a cottage? No, not that. No such invitation could be expected, for this year, at least. What, then? She was not clever at solving riddles. He must be good enough to tell her what it was that would make her so happy.

Yesterday, at table, Thilda had made a remark that was most characteristic of her, and that yet had come as a thunderbolt.

"Well, Father," she had said, "why don't you marry her?"

"Marry whom?" Herr Wohlschein had asked.

Did Thilda take him for a Don Juan, who could at will ask any number of ladies to become his wife? No. Thilda's question had obviously meant Fräulein Fabiani, and none other.

"Why don't you marry her?"

She could not understand why he, Herr Wohlschein, did not take Theresa for his wife. The clever little rascal had at once realized how matters stood between them, even from the way he wrote Theresa's name in his letters to his daughter.

Yes, she was a graphologist. She had added:

"You could probably do nothing better. You have my blessings!"

And what did Fräulein Theresa think of the possibility?

Though she smiled, her smiled lacked gaiety. And Herr Wohlschein wondered why no answer other than this forced smile rewarded him. Theresa was even more surprised. What she felt was not joy, and certainly not happiness;

only unrest, if not actually fear—fear of the great change that such an occurrence would bring into her life, and to which a woman of her age, accustomed as she was to independence, would find it difficult to adjust herself. Or was it perhaps the horror of being irrevocably bound to this man, whom she liked a little, but whose love seemed unimportant, even at times distasteful, to her, and most often slightly comical. Did she perhaps vaguely fear the disagreeable incidents which might threaten her in connection with her son, and for which Wohlschein, unable to avoid them, might in the long run hold her accountable?

"Why don't you speak?" he finally asked.

Theresa then took his hand. Somewhat hurriedly, with features that lit up too quickly, and in a tone at first dubious, then bantering, she asked:

"Do you think I would be the right wife for you?"

Reassured, he seized her in his awkward, bearish fashion, which she usually detested, but which she now tolerated so as not to endanger the spirit, and with it perhaps more than the mere spirit.

He wished her to cut down the number of her lessons, beginning the following day. At first, she would not listen, even insisting that, after her marriage, she must have some occupation from which she would derive satisfaction and occasional joy. Notwithstanding this, she refused to accept a new pupil, who applied shortly afterwards. She cut down the number of her weekly lessons from six to three. This Wohlschein accepted as a special favour.

XCIII

A LETTER soon arrived from Franz, with a curt demand for money. He also mentioned a forwarding address, to which the sum of 100 gulden should be sent without delay. Theresa would not and could not withhold this incident from her betrothed, especially since this amount would have been missing when her rent fell due. Wohlschein gave her the sum without much ado, but took the occasion, for which he had apparently been waiting, to mention a plan of his own—he was ready to pay Franz's transportation to America, or rather—you could not afford to neglect anything with such a man—to send him to Hamburg in company with one of his trusted employees, who would buy the ticket for him and see him installed on the steamer. But instead of gratefully accepting Wohlschein's proposal as a welcome solution of her problem, Theresa interposed fears and obections; and the more insistent Wohlschein became, citing innumerable excellent reasons for his attitude, the more obstinately she insisted that she could not bear the thought of being separated by the width of the Atlantic from her son; and that, especially now that her own circumstances had taken such a decided turn for the better such an action would appear to her heartlessly selfish, and even as a sin

388

which would sometime return to accuse her. Wohlschein contradicted her; and, as frequently happens in such cases, each one placed too high a value upon his own opinion, with the result that the quarrel grew more and more violent. Wohlschein strode up and down the room, his face distorted, while Theresa finally burst into tears. Then they both realized that they had gone too far. Theresa perceived at the same moment that her attitude toward her future husband certainly lacked prudence; but their relationship was still sufficiently young for the dispute to end in caresses.

But when Wohlschein, a few days later, departed on a short trip concerning which he had mentioned nothing in advance, Theresa was not so sure that this temporary parting was not intended to prepare the way for a definite break; and the unusually large sum which he left for her as a gift almost confirmed her fears. She felt, however, that this temporary separation was good for her spirit, and she imagined that she could bear the thought of a final parting without great agitation.

He returned sooner than she had expected and met her with such a strange reserve that at first she was again troubled. He did not keep her long in suspense, but said that he had interested himself in the affairs of her son on his own responsibility, and had learned that Franz at that moment was serving a prison sentence of several months— not his first one, as she probably knew. No, she knew nothing. Well, what did Theresa think now? Did she wish—

did they both wish—to spend the remainder of their lives under such a strain? Could one foresee where this fellow might end, what he might do, into what painful situations he might yet bring them, in case he remained within the city or in the country? He, Wohlschein, personally and with the aid of a reliable private detective who had aided him before in other investigations, desired to arrange everything, once and for all. Perhaps they could manage to start Franz on his journey to Hamburg and to America directly he had left the prison walls.

Theresa listened quietly, without protest; but from moment to moment, she felt an increasingly corroding and terrible torment in her heart, which nobody, above all not Wohlschein, could have understood; indeed she hardly understood it herself.

"When will he be free again?" she asked. She said nothing else.

"He has another six weeks to serve, I think."

She remained silent, but resolved to visit Franz in jail, and embrace him one last time before she took leave of him for ever.

And yet, she postponed that visit again and again. For although the thought of never seeing Franz again was most painful to her, she did not really feel any longing for him; on the contrary, she was almost unwilling to face him. Nothing further was said between her and Wohlschein of the whole affair; nor was the question of the wedding date discussed. Nevertheless, the character of her relationship became somewhat more formal. While, thus far, he had frequented ordinary restaurants when in her company, they now occasionally ate at the best places in town. Sometimes, too, he spent the entire night with her, and finally, he invited her for Sunday lunch at his own house. But the courtship was lacking in spirit and gaiety. And that Wohlschein, in spite of the fact that they were as good as betrothed, continued to address her with formal reserve when in the presence of the servants, and did not admit the truth when later his sister arrived, apparently without having been invited, appeared just a little too cautious and almost in bad taste.

XCIV

As far as the evening's entertainment went, he no
longer repressed his rather cheap tastes. One night they
visited a vaudeville house in one of the suburbs—a tenth-
rate music hall, where the entertainment was poor enough
to be mistaken for parody. A singer, about fifty years old,
appeared, ridiculously painted, in a short gauze frock.
With a broken voice, she sang an arch comic song about
a Lieutenant, saluting in military fashion at the end of
each stanza. A clown produced sleight-of-hand tricks, such
as could be found in any of the magic sets purchasable at
children's toy shops. An elderly man in a silk hat exhibited two trained poodles. A Tyrolese quartette, consisting of a heavily bearded man, a grotesquely thin dotard
with piercing eyes, and two fat, colourless peasant girls
in Greek laced shoes, sang songs and yodeled. A troupe of
acrobats, "The Three Windsors," turned out to be a fat
man in dirty tricot lifting two children of about ten and
having them juggle; the children, after some listless applause, stepping forward and blowing kisses to the audience.

While Theresa grew melancholy, her escort seemed to
be in his element. Theresa was surprised to find that this
house could support a small orchestra, consisting of an

upright piano, violin, 'cello, and clarinet. On top of the piano stood a glass of beer for the piano player. One of the other musicians reached for it now and then, and took a sip. Finally, a ridiculous paper curtain was lowered with a crackling sound. On it was painted a Muse in a blue tricot, with a purple belt, carrying a lyre in her arm; she was accompanied by a shepherd lad, wearing sandals and red tights.

Theresa's eyes automatically followed the beer glass, which at that moment again disappeared from the piano.

She observed the hand that had taken the glass—an emaciated, hairy hand, protruding from a cuffless, green and white striped shirt-sleeve. It belonged to the 'cello player, who had left the others for a moment to play alone. He raised the glass to his lips and drank. Some of the foam remained on his grey moustache. He raised himself slightly from his chair to restore the glass on the piano. While taking his bow, he bent over to the clarinet player to whisper something in his ear. Without paying any attention to him, the clarinetist kept on blowing. The other person, however, quite stupidly wagged his head from side to side, and licked the foam off his moustache.

His forehead was unnaturally high. His dark, greyish, short-cropped hair stood up like bristles. He half closed one eye when he joined the others again in playing. He had a poor instrument and, besides, played so obviously out of tune that he deserved the glare the pianist directed at him.

The curtain was raised again. A negro in greasy swallow-tail coat and grey top-hat entered and was greeted by the audience with loud shouts of derision. The 'cellist raised his bow, saluting the coloured man on the stage, though nobody but Theresa—not even the negro—observed it.

There was no doubt about it: it was Kasimir Tobisch who was playing the 'cello in this dingy place. She was sitting far in front. Wohlschein filled her wine glass. She raised it to her lips, staring fixedly at Kasimir until she had forced him to answer her glance. He regarded her, then her companion, then the audience round about, let his eyes return to her and withdrew his glance. He had obviously not recognized her.

The performance proceeded. A dirty-looking Pierrot, a tubercular Pierrette, and a drunken Harlequin offered, almost with desperation, a pantomime. Theresa in fact forgot, for a brief time, that Kasimir Tobisch was playing the 'cello there; forgot that her son was a jailed thief and pimp; forgot even the man beside her, comfortably smoking his cigar through a white holder. With him, she laughed when Harlequin, in attempting to embrace Pierrette, fell prone on the floor.

Several hours later, however, in bed beside her snoring lover, she lay sleepless, weeping silently, her heart in pain.

XCV

AT an early morning hour, while Theresa was still giving her lessons, Karl appeared, to her great surprise. The expression on his face, the very manner of his entrance, augured ill. When she asked him to wait for a quarter of an hour, until the class was finished, he brusquely asked her to dismiss "her young ladies." The last three words he pronounced with contempt. What he had to say brooked no delay. Theresa could not but fulfill his wish.

He turned his face away while the young girls passed him, not caring to greet them. Alone with his sister, he began:

"Your son, the scoundrel, has had the impudence to send me this letter from jail."

He handed it to Theresa, who read as follows:

My dear Uncle:
   Since I am about to leave jail after serving a term, although I am innocent, and as I intend to begin a new life far from home, I respectfully ask you, in view of our close relationship, to contribute toward my expenses. I want 200 gulden of Austrian denomination. They are to be held in readiness, beginning tomorrow.
   With the expression of my highest esteem, I am, dear Uncle,
                    Your nephew,
                                        Franz.

Theresa lowered the letter and shrugged her shoulders.

"Well!" Karl shouted. "Be good enough to say something!"

Theresa, quite unmoved, replied:

"I have nothing to do with this letter, and I don't know what you want of me."

"That's really excellent. Your son, in jail, writes me a blackmail letter—yes, it's blackmail!"

He tore the letter from her hand and pointed to the line: "in view of our close relationship . . . to be held in readiness, beginning tomorrow."

"The scoundrel knows that I hold public office. He will go to other people, beg, tell them that he is my nephew, the nephew of Representative Faber . . ."

"I can find no such intention in the letter. You are, in fact, his uncle."

This detached, mocking attitude completely infuriated him.

"And you dare to defend the rascal! Do you think I don't know that he has sent us letters before, asking for money? My wife, good-natured, but as stupid as ever, tried to hide them from me. Do you think you can hide anything from me? You think I don't know the kind of life you live under cover of your so-called profession? Yes, look at me with those big cow eyes! Some day you will lie on a manure pile, like your fine son. Do you think me blind? No! You are content with things. When you are shown a way out and get a donkey foolish enough to want to marry you—no, you prefer your freedom and change your lovers like shirts. It's more comfortable; it's more fun. And with those girls here . . . what are you doing with them? Lessons, I suppose! Ha, ha! You are probably making them ready for Jewish libertines."

"Get out!" Theresa ordered.

She did not raise her arm, did not stretch out her hand. Almost inaudibly, she said:

"Get out!"

But Karl would not be interrupted. He continued to pour forth a flood of abuse. Theresa, he shouted, had behaved just so in her youth. And she continued to do so, at an age when other women slowly came to their senses, if for no other reason than because they feared to make themselves ridiculous. Did she really imagine that she could ever have deceived him? As a young girl, she had flirted with his friends and colleagues. And that episode with the accursed Lieutenant! And whose child that fine son of hers was who held the fate of the whole family in his hand, she herself probably did not know. And what she had later done as a governess, as the guardian of little girls—he had had vague reports of that, too. And now, he knew that, as well, she was keeping company with an elderly rich man, whom she probably tried to hold by using her pupils to . . ."

Wohlschein entered. He had apparently not heard or understood the last words. He nevertheless continued to stare in surprise from Theresa to Karl, and back to Theresa again. Karl thought it an opportune time to depart.

"I don't wish to disturb you any longer," he said, and with a brief, almost mocking bow to Wohlschein, he turned to leave the room.

"Just a moment, Karl!" Theresa said.

Utterly calm, she made the introduction.

"Dr. Karl Faber, my brother; Herr Wohlschein, my intended husband."

Karl distorted his mouth.

"I am honoured!" he said. "So much the more reason why I should not disturb."

"I beg your pardon," the other man said. "I am inclined to believe that I was the disturber."

"Not at all!" Theresa replied.

"Certainly not," Karl added. "Some small differences of opinion cannot be avoided in families. Please excuse me, and accept my congratulations. Good afternoon, Herr Wohlschein."

Hardly had he left the door when Theresa turned to Wohlschein.

"Please forgive me," she said, "but I was forced to say it."

"What do you mean?"

"I mean that I obligated you to nothing when I introduced you as my future husband. You are still quite free in your decision."

"I see what you mean. But I don't at all wish to be free, as you put it."

With clumsy tenderness, he pressed her to his breast.

"And now, I would like to know what your brother wanted."

She was glad that he had heard nothing of the conversation. She told him as much as she deemed proper. When he left, it was definitely arranged that the wedding would be held on Whitsuntide, and that Franz's departure for America would occur before that date.

XCVI

WHITSUNTIDE was almost three months away. Wohl-schein's postponement of the wedding to the distant date was due to two imperative business trips: one to Poland and another to the Tyrol; also, to certain changes which he desired to make in the house. Beyond this, various matters had to be discussed with his attorney, since it was expedient to insert a number of clauses in his will before the wedding. "We are all mortal," he said. Theresa had nothing to urge against the delay, cherishing the idea of not being forced completely to discontinue her teaching, particularly since she now found herself attracted to her duties in the same degree that they had ceased to be imperative.

It was as pure recreation that she considered those periods of Wohlschein's absence—one week in February and another in March—when she need expect no morning visits from him. Nevertheless now and then she felt something akin to longing for him. During the past few weeks, she had gradually grown accustomed to a sort of married life which—she could not gainsay it—had in every respect exercised a good influence on her. And from numerous signs, external and internal, she realized that her life as a woman was by no means ended. It added to her good spirits that now she could dress better than ever before.

She looked forward eagerly to the promise he had made, to go shopping with her for the purchase of her further necessaries.

Shortly after Wohlschein's return, she spent the Easter holidays with him in a comfortable little hotel near Vienna. As yet, the days were quite cool. But the trees were already in bud, and the bushes had blossomed. There were evenings when, in her charming room, they felt like true young lovers, so that after her return, during many lonely hours in her own house, she became conscious of the fact that she would be very comfortable as Frau Wohlschein, sharing their home together. More precious, however, than everything else was a card from Thilda, which Wohlschein had shown her: "With a thousand Easter greetings for you and Theresa." Yes, that is what it said—plain "Theresa"!

As yet, she had not been able to bring herself to visit the jail. Too strong was her horror of this meeting, which at the same time was supposed to be a final parting. During the few weeks, Wohlschein had not once mentioned Franz; and Theresa thought that he meant to speak only after everything had been arranged. In point of fact, soon after returning from their Easter vacation, he told her that he had sent his attorney to the jail, but that Franz, for the time being, would hear nothing of the American plans. He was not sentenced to deportation, he had declared. Nevertheless, Wohlschein felt confident that the promise of a larger sum of money, to be paid to him upon his arrival in America, would substantially alter his point of view.

XCVII

A FEW days later, Theresa was expecting Wohlschein, who was to call for her at ten in the morning with a carriage, to go shopping, as they had done a few times before. It was a warm spring day. The windows were open, and the near-by woods scattered their fragrance. Wohlschein was habitually punctual. A half hour after the appointed time, she began to wonder. Already dressed for the streets, she stood waiting at the window. Another half hour passed. She grew restless, and decided to telephone. There was no answer. After a time, she telephoned again.

"Who is this?" a strange voice demanded.

"I only wished to ask if Herr Wohlschein has already left the house."

"Who is this speaking?" the unknown voice insisted.

"Theresa Fabiani."

"Oh, Fräulein Fabiani, it is too dreadful!"—now she recognized the voice of the old bookkeeper—"Herr Wohlschein, yes, Herr Wohlschein suddenly died!"

"What?"

"They found him this morning, dead, in bed!"

"For God's sake!" She rushed downstairs.

She did not think of using the street car or of taking

a carriage. Mechanically, as if in a drugged dream—not exactly shocked, and at first, hardly in haste, although later almost running—she made her way toward the Ziegler-gasse.

There was the house, seemingly unchanged. A carriage was standing before the door, as happened frequently enough. She ran up the stairs. The door was locked. Theresa had to ring the bell. The maid opened.

"Good morning, Fräulein Fabiani!"

For a moment, Theresa thought that it was not true; that she had misunderstood, or that some one had played an impudent jest at her expense. And she asked, with a strange feeling that her question might still alter the situation: "Is Herr Wohlschein . . ."

But she did not finish.

"Why, don't you know?"

Now she nodded quickly, made a meaningless, protesting gesture with her hand, and, without further question, opened the door to the living room. Grouped round the table, she saw the bookkeeper and two gentlemen whom she did not know. One of them was on the point of leaving. Two ladies were sitting near the fireplace; one of them, the sister of the deceased. Theresa went over to her.

"Is it really true?"

The sister nodded and took her hand. Theresa stopped helplessly. The door to the adjoining room stood ajar. Theresa walked over, and felt them all watching her. The dining room was empty. At the window of the next room, the small smoking-room, two men were standing, conversing earnestly but softly. The next door, too, stood open. Here was Wohlschein's bed.

The outline of a human figure, covered with a white sheet, was recognizable. There, then, he lay dead, as alone as only dead men can be. Theresa felt no pain—nothing except embarrassment and strangeness. She would have liked to kneel down, but something restrained her. Why did they leave her alone? The sister might have followed her. Had the last will already been read? Was she thinking of that now? Of course, it was not without importance—this much she knew even at this moment. But everything else was more important than that. He was dead—the lover, the future husband, the good man to whom she owed so much!

Thilda's father! Ah, now Thilda would have to come, too! Had they wired her already? Certainly! Under this sheet was his face! Why were the candles not burning? Yesterday, at this hour, she had been at Herrenhuter's with him, to order bed linen. What were they whispering in the next room? The stranger with the black moustache was probably the attorney. Did the people at all surmise who she was? Well, the sister certainly knew. She might have been a little more sympathetic to the sweetheart of her dead brother. If she were his wife, they would all behave differently, that was sure!

I want to go in to his sister again, she thought. We are the two real mourners, we and Thilda. Before she left the

room, she made the sign of the cross. Should she not have
looked upon the face of the deceased? But she did not want
to see his face again. She was afraid of it, that rather fat,
shiny face. Yes, he had been a little fat—that was perhaps
why . . . But he had been no more than fifty . . . And
now she was his widow, without ever having been married
to him.

On the table in the living room she saw cakes, wine and
glasses.

"Don't you want to take something, Fräulein Fabiani?"
the sister asked.

"Thank you, no," Theresa replied.

She took nothing, but sat down beside the ladies. The
sister introduced her. Theresa did not understand the name
of the lady. And she heard her own: "Fräulein Fabiani,
for many years Thilda's teacher."

The lady extended her hand.

"The poor child!" the lady said.

The sister nodded.

"By now, she probably has the telegram."

"Does she live in Amsterdam, or at the Hague?" the
stranger asked.

"In Amsterdam," the sister replied.

"Were you ever in Holland?"

"No, never. This summer I wanted to go there, with
my poor brother."

A brief silence.

"After all, he never was ailing," the strange lady said.

"Sometimes pains in the heart," the sister replied. And then, to Theresa:

"Don't you really want to take something, Fräulein Fabiani? A sip of wine?"

Theresa accepted a glass of wine. An elderly man in a gray summer suit came in. With a sorrowful expression on his face, his round, sad eyes wandering round the room, he approached the sister and shook her hand, twice, three times.

"This is terrible! So unexpected!"

The sister sighed.

Then he gave Theresa his hand, and only when he had done so became aware that he did not know her. The sister introduced him. Theresa could not understand the name of the man. Then, again:

"Fräulein Fabiani, for years the teacher of my niece, Thilda!"

"The poor child," the gentleman remarked.

Theresa said good-bye. Nobody detained her.

XCVIII

WOHLSCHEIN in his last will had stipulated for a simple burial. His entire estate had been bequeathed to Thilda. Legacies were given to several benevolent societies, and ample provision was made for his divorced wife. The old employees of the factory were not forgotten, and the servants, too, received their share; the piano teachers, two former governesses, and Fräulein Fabiani, under a codicil made the previous summer, received one thousand gulden each. Through a special provision, the deceased had arranged that the heirs should be notified immediately after the reading of the will, and should receive their respective shares directly after the testator's decease.

Theresa was asked to call on the attorney, to receive her share in person. She recognized in him one of the men whom she had seen at the home of the deceased. He seemed to know everything, and volubly regretted the premature death of Herr Wohlschein, who, shortly before his death, had declared his intention of making radical changes in his last will, but had—unfortunately, although characteristically enough,—postponed the matter until it was too late.

Theresa was hardly disappointed. Only now did she realize that she had never really expected to become Frau

Wohlschein; that she had never believed a quiet, untroubled existence might fall to her lot, or that she might ever become Thilda Verkade's stepmother.

The next morning, she stood at Wohlschein's grave with the other relatives and friends. She too let fall some earth upon the coffin. Thilda was there. The two women exchanged a glance across the grave. Thilda's eyes held so much warmth and understanding that a dim hope, an expectation of happiness, furtively arose in Theresa's heart. Garbed in black, leaning on the arm of her tall husband— closer than any human contact that Theresa could have imagined Thilda as capable of suffering—thus Theresa saw her, after the ceremony, walk through the gate of the cemetery and disappear.

It was arranged that Theresa should call on her, the following afternoon, at the house in the Zieglergasse. But she could not muster sufficient courage for the ordeal. The morning afterward, when she really wished to call, the daughter of the dead man had already departed with her husband.

XCIX

And now she was alone—completely alone, as she had never been before. She had never been in love with Wohlschein. And yet, how painful it was, evening after evening, never to see the door open again, never to hear the bell outside announce his coming.

And then, once, the bell rang, late in the evening. Her knowledge of the irrevocable annihilation of Wohlschein had not as yet become an integral part of her existence; and so, for the fraction of a second, she thought: He! What does he want so late at night? Of course, before she had arisen, she had realized that it might be any one in the world save only him.

It was Franz who stood before her door. Was he already free? In the dimly lighted hall, his cap pulled down over his forehead, a cigarette end between his lips, emaciated and pale, his glance uncertain and dejected, he seemed rather more pitiable than dangerous. But Theresa felt nothing: neither pity nor dread. Perhaps she felt a certain satisfaction that, after all, at least some one had come who, for a moment, would relieve her of the heavy pressure of loneliness which weighed upon her.

"Good evening, Franz!" she said, calmly.

He looked up, as if surprised at the mild, almost loving tone of her welcome.

"Good evening, Mother!"

She gave him her hand, and even kept holding his in hers as she led him in. She turned on the light.

"Sit down."

He remained standing.

"So you are already free?"

She said it quiet casually, as if she had said: "Are you back from your trip?"

"Yes," he answered, "since yesterday. They gave me a week for good behaviour. What do you think of that, Mother? So you don't need to be afraid. I have even found myself lodgings. But I have nothing else."

He laughed shortly.

Without answering, Theresa laid the table for him, gave him what she had in the house, and poured out a glass of wine.

He ate ravenously. When she put a piece of smoked salmon before him, he said:

"You seem to be well-off, Mother!"

And suddenly there was a threat, a demand in his voice.

"Not quite as well-off as you may think!" she replied.

He laughed.

"I won't take anything away from you, Mother!"

"You would not find much, any more."

"Well, thank goodness, new supplies will come soon."

"I don't know from where."

Franz glanced at her menacingly.

"I wasn't in for burglary, you know! If somebody forgets his pocketbook, I can't help it. My lawyer claimed, too, that they could sentence me only because I had kept something I had found."

She protested.

"I didn't ask you for an explanation!" she exclaimed.

He kept on eating. Then suddenly he said:

"But I don't want to hear about America! I can get along here just as well. The day after tomorrow, I start work. Yes! Thank God, a fellow still has friends who won't leave him in the lurch when he has a stroke of bad luck!"

Theresa shrugged her shoulders.

"Why should a healthy young man not be able to find a position? I only wish it may last, this time."

"As far as I was concerned, the others would have lasted, too. But people think you've got to stand for everything! And I'm too good for that. I won't stand for anything from anybody. Do you understand that, Mother? And if I wanted to go to America, I'd go by myself. I won't be packed off! Tell that to your—your man!"

Theresa remained absolutely calm.

"He meant well," she said. "You may believe me."

"What was meant well?" he answered, rudely.

"This trip to America. But you can rest in peace. It won't happen again. The man—my intended husband—died three weeks ago."

He looked at her incredulously, as if suspecting that by falsehood she wished to safeguard herself against fresh demands on his part. But on her pale face, in her sorrowful features, even he could read that this was not an evasion, not a lie. He kept on eating, saying nothing, and lit a cigarette. And only then—and as cold as it sounded, as coldly as it was probably thought, for the first time Theresa detected in his voice something like a warm undertone:

"You have no luck either, Mother!"

Then he declared that he was too tired to make the journey to his distant lodgings, and stretched out as he was on the couch. Soon he fell asleep. The next morning he was gone before Theresa had arisen.

But at noon he was back again, this time carrying a dirty cardboard satchel, and saying that he wanted to stay with her for three days, until he could start on his new job—to which he never referred again. Theresa at least persuaded him to remain away during her hours of instruction. But she could not do anything against the fact that a friend and a girl—there might even have been three or four people, of whom she never caught sight—spent half the night drinking, whispering, and laughing with him. Whatever she had left from the table she gave him for his nocturnal gatherings. The fourth morning he waited in for her awakening. She gave him all that she had in the house; the larger portion of her money she had carefully put into the savings bank. And it was fortunate that she had done so, for before he left, Franz was brazen enough to rummage through all the drawers of the furniture. Then, for the next four weeks, he disappeared.

C

THE days passed and Whitsuntide came—the day that had been set for the wedding. Theresa marked the occasion by a visit to Wohlschein's grave, upon which, among the withered wreaths without names and inscriptions, she found her bunch of violets, too. For a long while, she stood there under the clear, blue, summer sky—without praying, almost without thinking, and in fact, without any sensation of sadness. That word of her son's in which she had heard his heart speak, after its fashion, was still within her: "You have no luck either, Mother!" But in her memory, it did not refer exactly—and certainly not exclusively—to the death of her intended husband, but rather to her entire existence. Of a truth, she had not come into this world to be happy. And as Frau Wohlschein, she probably would not have been more happy than in any other condition. The fact that somebody dies is not in itself significant—it is one of the hundreds of ways in which a person disappears or sneaks away. So many were dead for her, of both the living and the dead! Dead, for example, was her father, who had been non-existent these many years. Dead, Richard, who, of all the men she had loved, had been the one nearest to her heart; and dead also her mother, whom she had told of the impending marriage only a few days before Wohlschein's demise, and who had hardly taken any notice of her words, continuing her talk about her literary estate, which she intended to bequeath to the City of Vienna. Dead was her brother, too, who had not communicated with her again after his last unwelcome visit; and dead, Alfred, who had been her lover and friend; dead, too her lost son, the pimp and thief; and Thilda, dreaming in Holland behind high, bright window-panes, who never thought of her teacher; and dead the many children, both boys and girls, for whom she had been a preceptor and sometimes almost a mother. Dead, all of the many men to whom she had belonged. And it was almost as if this Herr Wohlschein were proud that he slept so irrevocably beneath this mound, as if he took an unction to himself for being more definitely dead than the others.

Oh no, she had no special tears for him. The tears which she was shedding now flowed for so many others, and before every one else, she probably shed them for herself. And perhaps these were not tears of pain at all, but rather tears of weariness. For she was weary as she had never been weary before. At times, she was aware of nothing else but her weariness. Every evening, she sank into her bed so fatigued that she thought she would never be able to sleep enough and feel refreshed again.

But it was not destined to be so easy for her. She lived and worried on. Twice again, she was obliged to assist

Franz. The first time, he came himself, in broad daylight, with a small satchel, while her pupils were in the house. He intended to stay at her house again. She sent him away, refusing even to let him in the door. But, in order to prevent worse, she could not help but give him all the ready cash she had in the house. The second time, it was not he who came, but two of his friends. They looked just like his kind, talked absurdly in stilted phrases, claimed their comrade's life and honour were at stake, and refused to leave until Theresa had again yielded up almost everything that she possessed.

Now, summer was at hand. Theresa's lessons had stopped entirely. The last few gulden she had saved had been eaten up, and she sold her insignificent trinkets—a small golden bracelet and a ring set with a semi-precious stone, which Wohlschein had given her. The small sum which she received for these was sufficient to help her over the summer until autumn, and she was even reckless enough to go to the country for a few days in August, to the same spot where she had spent the Christmas holiday with Wohlschein —although this time she stopped at a less pretentious hotel.

It was during these days that, for a short time, she was aroused from her lethargy and determined to bring security and reason into her existence, as far as this might still be possible. Before everything else, she definitely resolved to oppose, once and for all, any further attempts on Franz's part to blackmail her; yes, even if she were forced to seek protection against him from the police. What did it matter, anyway? Everybody knew that she had a bad son, who had served time in prison, and nobody in the world would hold it against her if she were finally to resign him to his fate. Furthermore, she determined to communicate with her former pupils, some of whom were already grown and married, in order to ask them for recommendations. She had made her own living thus far and she was quite able to continue doing so. Even these few days in the country, the fresh air, the rest, the freedom from painful and disagreeable excitements—how favourably it all reacted upon her spirits. She was not so utterly exhausted, after all, as she was made aware by many a man's intercepted glance. Indeed, if she had encouraged that young tourist in the slightest degree—the one who each night, sat in the hotel restaurant, smoking his pipe, after returning from his mountain tours, and who kept his friendly eyes fixed on her—she might even have had her little "adventure" again. But it sufficed her to know that this was still possible. It would have seemed to her unworthy, almost insolent, like a challenge to fate, to have tempted the young man by coquetry to her side, and thus to give him hopes which she did not propose to gratify.

One morning, from her window, she saw him drive away in a motor car. His knapsack was at his feet and, as if he had felt her looking after him, he suddenly turned round and, with a broad gesture, lifted his head with its chamois beard, and she waved back a farewell. He, however, shrugged his shoulders regretfully, as if he wished to say to her: "But now, unfortunately, it is too late!" Then he drove on. For a moment, she felt sad. Was that happiness, perhaps her last happiness, driving away? Nonsense! she answered herself, and was a little ashamed of such sentimental reflections.

The next evening as she had planned, she returned to Vienna.

CI

PRIMARILY because she feared Franz, she had left no forwarding address. Thus, she found the printed announcement of the death of her mother only now, almost a week after the event had occurred. The names of her brother and her sister-in-law on the announcement were coupled with her own. She was more shocked than grieved. The next morning, at an hour when she knew Karl would not be at home, she went to his house. She was received somewhat coldly by her sister-in-law. Frau Faber held it against her that she could not be reached; a reproach which seemed merited for once as during her last few days the mother had repeatedly asked for Theresa.

It had unfortunately been necessary to complete all the arrangements without her consent. The last will, which Theresa might read at her convenience, was deposited with the notary. It contained hardly anything else except instructions for disposing of the literary estate of the deceased, which was surprisingly rich, but with which the City of Vienna, as the real heir, did not know what to do, and which had not as yet been called for. There had been very little cash; and against that little, a few creditors, small business people of the neighbourhood, had put in claims. In order to pay the more pressing debts, the few possessions of the deceased were to be auctioned off, within a few days. In the somewhat unlikely case of a surplus, Theresa would be notified through the notary.

It could not escape Theresa that her sister-in-law again and again glanced anxiously toward the door. She understood that the woman expected the appearance of her husband with evil forebodings, and she said:

"It might be better if I were to go now."

Her sister-in-law breathed more freely.

"I'll visit you as soon as I can," she said, "but it is really better that you should not meet Karl just now. You know him. He did not even attend the funeral, for fear that he might meet you."

"Then why is my name printed on the announcements?"

"That announcement—just imagine it—was prepared by your mother herself before her death. I'll tell you all about that in detail some time."

And she almost forced Theresa out of the door.

On her way home, Theresa, for the first time in a long while, once more paused at a church. She felt herself compelled to do that much, in memory of her mother, although her mother herself had had little enough to do with religious observances. And again it happened, as it had happened so often during the past year, that in the gloom of this place, filled with the fragrance of incense, a wonderful peace came over her—another and a deeper peace than that which had so often come upon her in the stillness of the forest, on a grassy plot in the mountains, or in any other solitude. And while she sat in the chair, with her hands unconsciously folded as if in prayer, she saw in her mind not only the picture of her mother as she had seen her the last time, but other departed ones who had meant something in her life; they appeared now, not as dead people, but rather as people risen from the grave; who had gained eternal bliss. Wohlschein, too, was among them; and for the first time, he appeared to her not as one suddenly taken away from her, as a decaying corpse, but rather as one who looked down upon her from heaven, smiling and understanding. And far away, impure and almost damned, appeared those who were yet alive. Not only men who had brought her sorrow, like her brother, her son, and the contemptible Kasimir Tobisch—those whom one could well imagine as being damned even while they were alive—but men, too, who had never done her wrong; even such a creature as Thilda seemed to her more remote than the dead, more ambiguous, more to be pitied, yes, more truly damned.

CII

WITH autumn, Theresa's school work was resumed. Only a few pupils from last year reappeared, but Theresa succeeded in finding an afternoon position, which she accepted as a particularly fortunate opportunity. It was a position as governess to the two daughters of the owner of a department store in the suburbs, and it was her duty to teach and take the children walking. The father, himself only half educated and in rather mean circumstances, was the more anxious to have a governess for his daughters, since the mother was actively occupied in his store. The two girls were pleasing enough, but somewhat stupid; and occasionally, when Theresa would take them for a walk in the rather poor park nearby and vainly begin a conversation with them, more from habit and a sense of duty than for any other reason, she was oppressed by that same weariness which had so tormented her in her earlier days, but which weighed so terribly, so heavily upon her now that sometimes it resembled a dull despair. The agreeable result of her sojourn in the country disappeared with disturbing rapidity.

Thus when, one night, Franz appeared, not as rude and impudent as he usually was, but rather timid and quiet, she did not have the courage to refuse him lodging, as she had determined to do. During the first few days, he did not, in fact, appreciably disturb her. He spent his time outside the house, received no visitors, and continued so depressed and silent that Theresa was almost brought to the point of asking what it was that troubled him. On the third night, he came in after she had gone to bed. He was in haste. He claimed to have found a furnished room at last, to which he proposed to move immediately, for which purpose he needed the sum of ten gulden. This sum he wanted her to give him at once. Theresa refused, protesting that she did not have anything left. It was almost the truth. But Franz would not believe her, and at once began to search the entire place. As his attitude became increasingly threatening, Theresa thought it wise to open a drawer and, before his eyes, take out a few gulden which she had hidden among some linen. He doubted that this was all that she had hidden away, but she swore that now she had given him her last coin. She breathed more freely when he suddenly gave up the search and took himself off with extraordinary haste.

The next morning, she understood why Franz had been in such a hurry. A detective awakened her from sleep at six o'clock in the morning. He asked for Franz and inquired if she knew his new address, informing her politely that it was her right to withhold any information which she might possess.

"We will get him soon, anyway," he remarked amiably, and left, with an officially regretful glance.

Now Theresa thought that the last vestige of feeling for her son was dead in her heart; that all that still united them was her fear of his return. The baleful glance which he had given her when she had taken her few gulden from the drawer caused her to fear still worse the next time. And she resolved never again to admit him to the house, under any circumstances, even if she had herself to summon the police.

Serious difficulties pressed her ever more closely. Never before had she been forced to ask anybody for help, and she was obliged to confess to herself that any such appeal in the present circumstances was hardly better than begging. And who was there from whom she might expect help? Alfred, of course, would not have refused her. Thilda, too, would help her, in the event of necessity; but the very thought of writing to either one of these two was painful. The lessons which she gave still brought in enough to keep her from actual hunger. No new purchases, for the time being, were absolutely necessary. She was accustomed to a precarious existence, and so she lived on—in seclusion and poverty, but at least peacefully, since Franz had once more disappeared.

And one morning, during the winter, she actually experienced a moment of joy. A letter from Thilda arrived, smelling preciously of the familiar perfume which she had been accustomed to use ever since she was a young girl.

"My dear Fräulein Theresa Fabiani," she wrote, "I frequently think of you—almost as often as I think of poor Papa. Will you not be good enough, my dear Fräulein Fabiani, to place a few flowers on his grave for me, the next time you go to the church-yard? And I would particularly appreciate it if you were to write and tell me how everything is going with you. Does the "class" still exist? How is little Crete? Has she learned to spell yet? It is very foggy here, these winter days; that is because the sea is so near. There is hardly any snow. My husband wants to be remembered to you. He is frequently away, and then the evenings are lonely and long—but you know that, after all, I am not so unwilling to be alone with myself, and for this reason it doesn't occur to me to complain. I send my most affectionate regards, dear Fräulein Theresa, and I hope to meet you again some time. Your grateful Thilda.

"P.S.—A sum for the flowers is enclosed."

Theresa stared at the letter for a long while. "I hope to meet you again some time"—that did not sound very promising, after all. Perhaps the letter was written solely because of the flowers for her father's grave. As a matter of fact, the "sum" was not enclosed. Thilda had either forgotten to enclose it, or somebody had stolen it from the letter. Well, after all, a few asters would be sufficient, and these she could buy herself, if necessary. "The next time you go to the church-yard"—Theresa had not been there again since Whitsuntide. She would surely go during the

Christmas holidays. To miss a lesson and buy flowers besides, was quite beyond her means. The letter she would answer later. Frau Thilda Verkade had kept *her* waiting long enough.

CIII

A FEW evenings afterward, quite late, the bell rang. Theresa's heart stopped beating. She crept to the door and looked through the keyhole. It was not her son. A still youthful woman stood outside, whom Theresa did not immediately recognize.

"Who is there?" she asked, hesitatingly.

A high, somewhat hoarse voice answered:

"A good old friend. Please open the door, Fräulein Theresa! It's Agnes—Agnes Leutner!"

Agnes? What did she want? What tidings did she bring? Probably some news of Franz! She opened the door.

Agnes entered quite timidly and paused in the hall to shake the snow from her garments.

"Good evening, Fräulein Theresa!"

"Won't you come in?"

Agnes followed Theresa into the living room, and her uncertain glance fastened upon the table littered with books and papers. Theresa looked at her. Oh, one could not doubt for a moment what manner of woman she was! Her face made up, heavily rouged, under the violet felt hat with a cheap ostrich feather; the curls, dyed blond, falling over her eyes; big imitation jewels in her ears; worn-out imitation astrakhan jacket, with a muff to match—thus she stood, impudent and embarrassed at the same time.

"Have a seat, Fräulein Agnes!"

Agnes had noticed Theresa's searching, damning look well enough, and, in a somewhat mocking tone, she said, apologetically:

"Naturally, I would not have disturbed you—but I have a message."

"From Franz?"

"With your permission!"

And she sat down.

"You see, he is at the hospital of the Jesuit Fathers . . ."

"For heaven's sake!" Theresa cried; and she knew suddenly that it was her son who was lying at the hospital—sick perhaps, sick to death.

Agnes reassured her.

"There, there, it's not dangerous, Fräulein Theresa. He will get well again, long before the trial. He is under arrest, you know! But they won't be able to get the goods on him, this time, because he had nothing to do with it. The police always get the wrong ones, anyway!"

"What is the matter with him?"

"Nothing at all—he is just a little sick!" She hummed a popular ditty—"Love, love, that's all it is . . ." And, with a mocking laugh: "Well, it will last a little while. And afterwards, you've got to be careful. For the sake of the others. As if the others were careful! I had it real bad. I had to spend six weeks in the hospital!"

Theresa grew alternately red and pale. Beside this woman, she felt like a little girl. She had only one desire—to get rid of her as quickly as possible. And, moving away from her as far as she could, she said:

"What is the message that you have for me from Franz?"

Agnes, obviously piqued, aped her intonation:

"The message that I have for you from Franz? That ought not to be so difficult to guess! Or do you think, perhaps, that they give the patients enough to eat at the hospital? Unless you have tuberculosis, or something like that, they certainly don't! He needs money, to buy a little something to help out his meals. A mother's got to see to that!"

"Why didn't he write, if he is sick? I would have tried to raise it, somewhere!"

"He probably knows why he didn't write!"

"I always helped him, when I could . . ."

She stopped abruptly. Was it not shameful, after all, to account to such a person for what she had done?

"That's all right. I can imagine that you haven't got anything to blame yourself for. It's always the same story —sometimes one has more, and sometimes less. But you still look good enough. You'll find somebody yet who'll spend something."

Once more the blood rose to Theresa's face. This person! —did she not talk as if Theresa were of her kind? Oh, how Franz must have talked to her and to others about her—the son talking thus of his mother! In what a light he saw her! She tried to find an answer, but could not. At last, helplessly and hesitatingly, she said:

"I am giving lessons!"

"Oh, of course!" Agnes replied. And, with a disparaging look at the books and papers, she added: "I can see that! It's lucky that you had an education. I'd prefer to pick my own man, too!"

Theresa rose.

"Go!" she said. "I will bring Franz what he needs."

Agnes, too, got up, slowly, as if offended. But now she seemed to realize that she had employed the wrong tone, and she did not want to return to Franz with empty hands. So she said:

"Very well. If you want to visit him in the hospital, do so. But that is probably something that he doesn't expect. And you didn't think of it, either!"

"I did not know that he was in the hospital!"

"Nor did I. I found him accidentally. I was calling on an old friend of mine, to take him some food. Yes, the likes of me have got to save a little, too, and we've got to earn it hard enough, Fräulein Theresa—harder than by lessons! Well, you can imagine my surprise when I saw Franz lying there, across from my friend. He was glad to see me, too. Old love doesn't rust! Well, and after one word had followed the other, I asked him if he didn't need anything from outside, and then he said: 'Perhaps you would go to my mother, and see if she can't send me a little money for food.' 'Why not,' I said, 'your mother will probably remember me. And she may prefer to send something by me, rather than come here herself. That's disagreeable for people who aren't accustomed to it!"

Theresa had a few gulden in her purse.

"Here, take this. I am sorry, but I have no more."

She noticed that Agnes glanced at the chest of drawers. So Franz had told her about that, too! And, with trembling lips, she added:

"In there, I have nothing, either! Perhaps for Christmas . . . But then, I shall come myself."

"By Christmas, he may be free again. I'm telling you, Fräulein Theresa, this time they haven't got anything on him! Well, anyhow, I thank you many times, in his name. And we understand each other, don't we? Haven't you got a few cigarettes for me?"

Theresa's first impulse was to answer that she had none, but then she remembered that a half empty box Wohlschein had once left was still somewhere around. She disappeared into the next room, and returned with a handful of cigarettes.

"That will please Franz particularly," Agnes said, and thrust them into her muff. "And I'll smoke one now if I may?"

Theresa did not reply, but offered her hand. She no longer had any ill feeling nor did she feel any superiority over the girl. There was really not such a tremendous difference between her and Agnes. After all, hadn't she sold herself to Wohlschein?

"Give him my regards, Agnes," she said, gently.

It was dark on the stairs. Theresa guided Agnes through the hall. And before the janitor came to open the door, Agnes raised the collar of her astrakhan jacket. Theresa knew that she did so to save her from embarrassment.

That night, she sat awake for a long time. Now she had gone through that, too. Why, after all, did it seem extraordinary? She had a son who was a good-for-nothing, who kept company with strumpets and thieves, and was occasionally wanted by the police, arrested at intervals, and who was now at the hospital with a foul ailment. She might have accepted that, by now. And yet, he was her son! Time and again—she might fight against it as best she could—in her own heart she felt pity, she felt guilt, when he suffered and did evil. Guilt; that was it! Strange, that in moments like this she always thought of her own guilt only, as if she who had borne him were alone responsible for what he did; as if the man who had begotten him and then disappeared into the darkness of his existence had had nothing at all to do with it! Well, yes! For Kasimir Tobisch, the embrace which had begotten her son had been one of many—not happier and not of greater importance than any of the others which he had enjoyed. He did not know that the man for whose existence in this world he was responsible, was a scoundrel; he did not even know that he had a son. And if, by chance, he had learned it—what would he have understood of it all? What had this lost soul at the criminal hospital to do with the aging man who, after twenty dark, stupid years of swindling, was playing the 'cello at a cheap music-hall and drinking the piano player's beer? How was he to feel any relationship, when even she herself could imagine only with great difficulty that from a fleeting moment of lust a man had sprung who was her son? That union of a moment long since forgotten, and this one of today—how was it possible to employ the same word for them? And yet, that which for years had been absolutely unimportant, suddenly took on an incredible importance and meaning for her, as if the moment that Kasimir, too, should know of the existence of their child, her own life would take on a new substance, a new sense, a new form. She felt like one standing beside the bed of a sleeper, uncertain whether merely to stroke his forehead quietly and take leave without disturbing his slumber, or whether to shake him awake to life and responsibility. Then she reflected that Kasimir Tobisch was only a dreamer, who knew nothing of the essence of his own existence. Doubtless there had been other women in his life. Perhaps he had still other children; perhaps he knew of one or two of them, for he might not always have succeeded in sneaking away. But for the one whom he had forgotten completely, suddenly to stand before him, twenty years after he had left her, and say: "Kasimir, you and I have a child!"—that was certainly something which had never happened to him before. And, as in a picture, she saw it all played out before her mind's eye: how she aroused him from his slumber; how she took his hand and led him through innumerable streets symbolic of the many crossways of his life; how she, with him, knocked at a door, the door of the criminal hospital, and how she led him forward to the bed of a sick boy who was his son; how he opened his eyes wide in surprise, beginning to understand, and finally, how he sank on his knees at the bedside and turning round to her, whispered: "Forgive me, Theresa!"

The first Christmas holiday, she went to the cemetery. It was deceptive spring weather. A lukewarm wind was blowing over the graves, and the ground was wet with melted snow. She had brought asters, white ones for Thilda, and violet ones for herself. She did not find Wohlschein's grave as easily as she had expected. The tombstone was not yet erected. Only a number told her where Thilda's father lay buried. Thilda's father, she thought; then she realized that it was her lover who lay here in his eternal slumber. Now we would have been married almost three-quarters of a year, she thought. Today I would be sitting in a warm, nicely furnished room, and, like Thilda, I would be looking through a clean window at the street outside, and would have no difficulties at all. But she hardly felt regret that it had not happened that way; and she thought of the deceased without tenderness. Am I so ungrateful, she asked herself—so cold, so extinguished? But the fancied images of other men arose before her—men to whom she had belonged. And today she knew that it was only memories of these others that had lent a passing joy to the hours which she had spent with Wohlschein.

And suddenly—but she remembered at once that even during his lifetime she had felt similar reactions—she asked herself whether her lover had not surmised this repeated and deep infidelity, and had disintegrated in a moment when the pitiful rôle he played had become painfully apparent in his mind—that he had then, as they termed it, died of heart-failure! Oh, such connections existed; of that she felt certain! Theresa's was a mysterious, deeply hidden guilt, which burned only occasionally, far down in her soul, and was extinguished again almost immediately. She felt as if her responsibility for Wohlschein's end were not the only one smouldering like an uncertain, pale flame in the abyss of her soul. The knowledge of a great, dark guilt was slumbering within her; and after a long, long time, she thought once more of a far-distant night when she had given birth to her son and when she had murdered him. But this dead man, who had been her son, was still playing the ghost in this world. Even now he was lying in a bed at the criminal's hospital, waiting for his mother, the murderess, to come and confess her guilt.

The violet and white asters fell from her hands and, with eyes staring like those of a mad woman, she gazed into space.

And yet it was the same person who sat, that night, with the family of the department store owner before a well-laid table, and who talked of everyday trifles with the husband and wife and with another middle-class couple who had been invited: she chatted about the snowy weather, prices, teaching in grammar, and the high schools, and she no longer took thought of her dead.

During the next few days, Theresa considered the question of writing to Kasimir Tobisch. Perhaps that was not even his name. In any case, it was by no means certain whether he was now using that or some other name. Moreover, it was possible that he would pay no attention to the letter at all, especially if he fully realized who sent it. So it seemed wisest to wait for him, some evening, after the performance. She might act as if she had met him accidentally.

One night, at eleven o'clock she stood beneath the lighted sign of the Universum. At the entrance stood a gigantic porter in a shabby green livery with gold buttons, a long stick with a silver balloon in his hand. The performance was not yet over. Theresa looked for the door through which Kasimir Tobisch would have to leave the hall. It was easily discovered: round the corner, another street; around the next corner, in another dimly lighted lane, over a glass door, she found the inscription: "Stage Entrance." At that moment a woman was leaving it—an emaciated, common looking creature in a poor, much too thin raincoat. She disappeared round the corner. To tell the truth, her own coat was not quite correct for snowy weather, either. She wore the elegant spring coat which Thilda had given her, and underneath it, a heavy woolen sweater. Oh well, after all, she was better dressed than many another woman in her circumstances. Her feet grew wet and cold. She should have taken her heavy shoes which she had last worn in the country when she was with Wohlschein. In spite of her continuous pacing up and down, she felt frozen. Perhaps it would have been more sensible to have bought a cheap seat and waited inside for the end of the performance. And she kept pacing up and down round the building, in the snow-covered streets, keeping her eye on both the main door and the stage entrance. For a moment, her waiting seemed ridiculous and senseless to her. What did she want? Whom did she expect? An old musician playing the 'cello within, or a young man in a soft black hat, whose moustache smelled of perfume? He had nothing to do with her; and yet it was as if just such a young man would come through the glass door in the next moment: a man in a wide coat, with a soft black hat in his hand. And she, upon her part, fancied herself as the pretty miss who is free on a Sunday, and anticipates a tryst with her lover. Of course, it had then been spring, too. But what was she doing here? It was not spring, nor was she the pretty miss any more. Was she not really that very Fräulein Steinbauer, whom she had pitied so much at the time, because she had no lover? She was not that girl and he was not that man; then what did they want of each other? No, truly in all her life she had not done anything quite as

stupid as this. Would it be better to give it up entirely, and
return some other time, when she would be in a better frame
of mind?

She was already on the point of leaving the building,
when she regretted her decision and again turning round,
noticed that the performance had just come to an end. The
porter had taken up his position, with his stick held stiff
and the balloon swaying in the wind. People poured out of
the door; carriages drove up. Quickly, Theresa crossed
the street, ran toward the stage entrance, and took a position on the opposite side, where she could keep her eye
on it.

Kasimir was the first to leave. Tall, swathed in his coat,
with his soft, black hat in his hand and a cigarette between
his lips, he hardly looked different from the man whom she
had known twenty years ago. It was like a miracle. He
looked round on all sides, then gazed up at the sky, and
shook his head, as if surprised and disgusted at seeing the
snow. He put his hat on; then, suddenly, as if realizing
that somebody was waiting for him on the other side of
the street, he crossed, with long strides, directly toward
Theresa, passed her with a superficial glance, and had
gone.

"Kasimir!" she cried.

He did not even turn, and walked quickly away.

"Kasimir Tobisch!" she shouted.

He stopped, turned round, came toward Theresa, and
looked into her face. She smiled, although now he looked

quite different and older than he really was, with many wrinkles on his forehead and still deeper ones between his nose and the corners of his mouth. Now he recognized her.

"What do my eyes see?" he cried. "This is—this is— Her Highness the Princess!"

Her smile remained. It was this that first occurred to him after twenty years—that when he had first met her, he had acted as if he had taken her for an archduchess or a princess! Well, at least, she had changed less than she had feared. She nodded in confirmation. Then her smile became empty, and she said:

"Yes, I am Theresa!"

"This is indeed a surprise!" he said, and shook her hand. She would have recognized him by the hard touch of his long fingers. "And where do you come from?"

"I happened to attend the performance, and recognized you."

She paused.

"And recognized me?"

"Naturally! You have hardly changed."

"Nor you!"

He lifted her chin and, with glassy eyes, stared into her face. His breath reeked of sour beer. "So this is really Theresa! That we two should meet again! How have you been, Theresa?"

She was still conscious of the smile on her lips. She

could not efface it, although it signified nothing whatsoever.

"That is not so easily told."

"Surely, surely!" he assured her. "It's half an eternity, after all, since we met the last time."

She nodded.

"Almost twenty years!"

"Yes, much can happen in twenty years! You are probably married. Children?"

"One."

"Really? I have four!"

"Four?"

"Yes, two boys and two girls. But shouldn't we walk on? It's too cold to stand here!"

She nodded. Suddenly, she realized again that her feet were cold.

"Where is your companion?" he asked, stopping abruptly.

She looked at him without understanding.

"You haven't been alone in such a place as this? You were probably with your husband?"

"No, my husband unfortunately is dead. A long time ago. I was with friends, but they had to leave before the end."

"Not very polite friends, if I may say so. May I take you to the street car?"

They went down the street, Theresa Fabiani and Kasimir

Tobisch, as they had gone down many a street twenty years before. They had little to say to one another.

"This is really a surprise," Kasimir began again. "So you are married, or rather, widowed?"

She noticed that he estimated her spring coat through the corner of his eye. His glance became dull when he looked down and noticed her shoes.

"I didn't know that you played the 'cello, too," she said, quickly.

"You don't mean it!"

"You were a painter, then."

"A painter and a musician. I am still a painter, though now that is more a trade than an art, to tell you the truth. One always needs extra money!"

"I can imagine! With four children, it can't be too easy."

"Two are already grown. My oldest is assistant to a dentist."

"How old is he?"

"Twenty-two."

"How old?"

They now stood at the street car stop.

"Twenty-two? Then you were married when we met?" She laughed.

"My, my!" he replied, and joined in her laughter. "I think I have said too much."

"Never mind," she answered. And his information really, had hardly moved her. She simply thought: So he had a wife and children even then! That's why he used a false name and fled. For now she realized that Kasimir Tobisch had never been his name. What was the name of this man? Who was this man at her side, by whom she had had a son now lying at the criminal hospital, and whom she had intended to introduce to him. Now she might have asked him his real name, and perhaps he would have told her the truth. But it was utterly unimportant what his name was, whether he was painter or musician, whether he had four children or ten. He was a poor, silly devil, and he did not even realize it. In a certain sense, even she was better off than he—or was she worse off?

"There is the street car now," he said, obviously breathing more freely.

"Yes, here it is," she repeated, amused. But now she began to regret that this interlude was at an end, and that Kasimir Tobisch, or whatever his name might be, would again disappear among the other nameless ones—forever. The street car stopped, but she did not board it, although his look politely invited her to do so. And she said:

"I would have liked to talk with you a little longer. Wouldn't you care to call on me, some time?"

He looked at her. Oh, he no longer bothered to act for her benefit. In his look, she read quite clearly: To what end? As a woman, you don't count for me; and as for your spring coat, that does not attract me, either! Still, he seemed caught by the fear in her eyes, and courteously replied:

"Gladly, if I may take that liberty."

She gave him her address.

"You probably remember my name, don't you?" she added, a little sadly. She smiled, and whispered:

"My name is Theresa!"

"Surely," he said, "I remember. But the family name?"

"That you forget?"

"Not at all, but now your name is probably different."

"No, my name is still Theresa Fabiani!"

"Then you aren't married?"

She shook her head.

"But didn't you say that you had a child?"

"Yes, I have a child!"

"Well, well . . ."

Another street car came, Theresa looked Kasimir Tobisch straight into the eyes. Now he might have asked more; now he could have asked, now he should have asked! And something like a question did appear in his eyes; something even like understanding. Surely it was understanding, and for that reason he did not ask.

The street car stopped. Theresa boarded it. From the platform, she said, quickly:

"You might telephone me."

"You have a telephone? You must be well off! I must go next door, to the store, when I want to telephone! There, then, au revoir!"

The street car rolled on. For a while, Kasimir Tobisch stood where he was and waved after Theresa. Suddenly, her smile disappeared. Without responding to his gestures, gravely and coldly, she kept her eyes on him, and saw him turn and walk away. Softly, in dense flakes, the snow fell. The streets were almost deserted. And the man who had for so long a time been Kasimir Tobisch, the father of her child, disappeared, nameless now, among the other nameless ones—disappeared for ever.

CV

THE small sum which Theresa had mailed to Franz after Agnes Leutner had called on her, was returned to her. The addressee had been dismissed from the hospital, and the post office was unable to trace him. So they had set him free again? It was not a comforting thought for Theresa. And—not for the first time—she wondered if it would not be wise for her to change her lodgings. But what would that avail? He would know how to find her out! Unluckily, it was an even more pressing question whether she would be able to keep her present flat. The rent had gradually become too high for her. It was due again in February and she did not know how she would scratch it together again. Her classes had gone to pieces, perhaps because the parents were no longer satisfied with the results which she obtained. Well, what she was able to do—that she had always realized—had never been too much. Only her conscientiousness, her friendly way of dealing with children, had enabled her to compete against better teachers than she. How sadly she had retrogressed during the last few months, she knew only too well.

Shortly before her rent was due, the notary informed her that a small sum was waiting for her from the sale of her mother's furniture. Until autumn then, she could feel secure. That improved her mood, so that she could return to her efforts with renewed perseverance. In March, she found two new, if poorly paying, pupils in the suburbs.

Then, once again, news came from Franz. An old woman brought the letter. He was about to take a position, and his mother should help him now for the last time. He named a definite sum—150 gulden. This demand shocked her. Apparently he knew that she had inherited something. Without a word, she sent him the fifth part of what he had requested, and the next day she took what was left—about 500 gulden—to the savings bank. She breathed more freely, once that was done.

Spring had come again. And with the first caressingly warm days, the familiar weariness and a melancholy of a deeper kind than she had ever known before, overcame her. Everything that, thus far, had made life easier for her, now merely made her the more sad: short walks, and even a theatre performance which she once attended. More depressing than anything else, though, was a letter from Thilda—a belated answer to one of her own, informing her that she had adorned her father's grave with flowers. It contained the news that Thilda was pregnant. Theresa felt only one thing: how empty and hopeless her own life was. And it happened, during these days, after long months of quietude, that—uncertainly, without actual desire, and yet strangely tormenting—her senses reawakened. She had carnal dreams, ugly and beautiful, but always of unknown persons, men without distinguishable faces, in whose arms she dreamed she lay. Only once it happened that she dreamed of walking with Richard along the Danube, where she had been his. This particular dream lacked all animal elements, but she felt enveloped by the tenderness which she had always longed for from him, and which she had never known. A tormentingly unfulfillable tenderness and the apprehension of endless solitude remained.

CVI

Late one evening in May, her door bell rang again. She was startled. For the payment of a bill which was due the next day she happened to have a somewhat large sum of money in the house, which she had just fetched from the bank. And for that very reason, she did not doubt that it was Franz who was standing outside the door. She vowed to herself that he should not get a kreutzer. Besides, she had hidden it so carefully that she was sure he would not be able to find it. The window was open, and if the worst came to the worst, she would shout for help. She tiptoed to the door, but did not even dare to look through the keyhole. He knocked so violently that she feared the neighbours might hear him, and so she opened it.

At first view, Franz appeared to be better dressed than usual, but he looked more sick and pale than she had ever seen him before.

"Good evening, Mother," he said, and attempted to enter. But Theresa restrained him.

"Well, what is the matter?" he asked, looking at her viciously.

"What do you want?" she asked, harshly.

He closed the door behind him.

"No money," he replied, laughing derisively, "but if you would let me stay over night . . ."

She shook her head.

"For one night, Mother! Tomorrow, you'll be rid of me for ever."

"I have heard that before!"

"Oh! Perhaps some one is here already! Perhaps somebody is lying on the couch!"

He shoved her aside, opened the door to the living room, and looked round on all sides.

"You won't sleep in my house again," Theresa said.

"Just this one night, Mother."

"You have some sort of lodging. What do you want from me?"

"They have sent me away for the night. Things like that happen, and I haven't got money enough for a hotel."

"Whatever you want for a hotel, I can give you."

His eyes glistened.

"Well, then, give it to me!"

She took her purse and gave him a few gulden.

"Is that all?"

"With that, you can stay at a hotel for three nights!"

"All right, then, I'll go."

But he did not go. She looked at him questioningly. He proceeded, with a mocking laugh:

"Yes, I'll go, if you will give me my share of the inheritance!"

"What inheritance? Are you crazy?"

"Oh, no! I want my share of my grandmother's money!"

"What are you entitled to?"

He came quite close to her.

"Well, then, listen to me, Mother. You heard me say this before. You are seeing me for the last time tonight. I have a position—not here in town, but somewhere outside. And I'll never come back. How am I to get my inheritance, if you won't give it to me now?"

"What are you talking about? What kind of inheritance do you claim, since I have inherited nothing myself?"

"Do you really think I'm so stupid? Don't you think I know that you have received money from Wohlschein and from your mother? And am I to beg for the few gulden I need so badly? Is that the way a mother treats her son?"

"I have nothing!"

"Well, we'll see whether or not you have anything!"

He went to the chest of drawers.

"How dare you!" she cried, and seized him by the arm with which he was fumbling in the drawers.

"Give me the key!"

She let him go and, running to the window, bent out as if to cry for help. He rushed over to her, pushed her back, and closed the window. She hurried to the door. In an instant he was at her side. He turned the key and put it into his pocket. Then he grasped both of her hands.

"Give it to me voluntarily, Mother!"

"I have nothing!" she whispered through set teeth.

"I know that you have something. I know that you have it! Give me something, Mother!"

She was mad. She was not afraid now. She hated him.

"If I had a thousand gulden, there would not be a kreutzer for one like you!"

For a moment he let go of her, seemingly sobered.

"Mother, I'll tell you something. Give me half of what you have. I need it for my trip. I have no position! I've got to disappear! If they get me this time, they'll give me a year or two."

"So much the better!" she cried.

"So? You think so? All right!"

And again he rushed to the chest of drawers, striking at it with his clenched fist. The drawer still held. He hesitated for a moment. Then he took a jimmy from his pocket, and broke it open. Again Theresa tried to interfere, to hold his hands. He pushed her aside and plunged his arms into the linen, throwing piece after piece on the floor.

Meanwhile, Theresa had opened one of the inner windows, and was about to open the outer one when he tore her back.

"Robbers!" she shouted. "Thieves!"

Franz, with inflamed eyes, stood before her.

"Will you give it to me or not?"

"Robbers!" She shouted again.

Now he grasped her, pressed one of his hands over her

mouth, and dragged her, pushed her into her small bedroom, at the foot of her bed.

"Have you got it in here? In the mattress? In the pillows?"

Again he had to let her go in order to ransack the bed. And again she shouted:

"Robbers! Thieves!"

With one hand he now grasped her wrists, closing her mouth with the other. She kicked at him. He let go her hands, and grasped her by the throat.

"Robbers! Thieves!"

She shouted again and again. Then Franz began to choke her. She sank down to the floor by the side of her bed. He loosened his grip on her throat, and taking a handkerchief, folded it and thrust it into her mouth, then he took a towel hanging near the wash stand and bound her hands.

She panted for breath. Her big, staring eyes shone up at him through the darkness. A ray of light came in from the next room. Like a madman, he searched the bed, tore the cases off the pillows and looked in the wash-basin, in the pitcher, under the chest of drawers, under the carpet.

Suddenly he stopped. The outside bell was ringing. Through the closed doors, he heard voices. No doubt they had heard his mother shout, and perhaps they had also heard the noise which he had made with his fists and with his jimmy. Quickly he unwound the towel from her hands and tore the gag from her mouth. She lay prone on the floor, gasping.

"Nothing has happened, Mother," he cried.

Her eyes were open. She looked; she stared. No, she was not dead. But little could have happened.

Again the bell rang three times, five times, ever more persistently. What was he to do now? Through the window? Three flights! He looked again at his mother. No, there was nothing the matter with her. She looked at him with open eyes, moving her arms. Her lips were trembling. The bell rang incessantly. There was nothing to be done but open the door. Then he might still rush through the people, run down the stairs and reach the street. If only she were not lying there, like one dead! He bent down and tried to lift her. But it seemed that she still fought against him! She even shook her head. No, she was not dead! She had merely swooned. Or had she only pretended to faint, so as to defeat his purposes?

The bell kept on ringing. There were knocks at first, then bangs against the door.

"Open! Open!" they shouted outside.

Franz opened the inner door and rushed into the anteroom. The main door shook under the banging fists. No recourse was left to him; he had to open. Was it possible? Only two women were standing outside, staring at him, horror-stricken. He pushed them aside and dashed down the stairs. He heard them shout behind him: "Stop him!"

A man's voice joined in. It came from above. And before he had reached the house door, somebody had seized him from behind by the shoulders. He could not free himself. He shouted and cursed. Then he became silent. It was over. But his mother was not dead. She had merely swooned. What did they want of him? Nothing had happened to his mother. People thronged around him. A policeman, too, was there.

Meanwhile, the two young women had rushed into the flat and found Fräulein Theresa Fabiani stretched out beside her bed. Directly behind them came others—another woman and another man. They lay Theresa on the disordered bed. She looked around unable to speak. She hardly recognized the people who were gradually filling the room —the neighbours, the police captain, the police doctor. She probably did not understand the questions which they asked her. So they did not insist on confronting her with her son. The physician established the fact that no fatal wound had been inflicted. The flat was sealed by the police, and Theresa was taken to the hospital that same night.

There they found that a cartilage in her neck had been broken—a circumstance which made the outlook for both her and Franz very much worse. Depositions by the neighbours established the fact that the teacher Theresa Fabiani was a sister of Representative Faber. He, too, was informed, in the course of the night, that a crime had been committed against his sister. Early the next morning, he appeared together with his wife at the bedside of his sick sister, who had been placed in a special room. She had a high temperature, which the doctors attributed to the shock rather than to her injuries. Apparently, she had not completely regained consciousness. She did not recognize her visitors who departed shortly after they had come.

CVII

Toward noon, Alfred presented himself at her bedside. He had read of the crime in the papers. Although her temperature was already lower, Theresa was delirious. Restlessly, she tossed her body to and fro. Her eyes alternately opened and closed. She whispered incoherent words. Nor did she at first appear to recognize her latest visitor.

After the physician in charge had informed Professor Doctor Nuellheim of the details of the case he left him alone with the patient. Alfred sat down beside her and felt her pulse which was weak and irregular.

And now, as if the touch of this once beloved hand had an efficacy that other and more casual touches did not possess, the patient's restlessness seemed to subside. When, without any particular purpose, he kept his eyes fastened upon her forehead and her eyes, something still more extraordinary occurred. Those eyes which until now, even while open, had failed to recognize any one, shone as if with mounting consciousness. The withered features grew softer, younger.

When Alfred bent closer to her, she whispered:
"Thank you!"

He protested, took her hands, and uttered the words of consolation that came to his lips. She shook her head, more and more vigorously, not only as if she did not wish to be consoled, but as if she wished to confide something to him. He bent down to hear her.

"Promise me that you will say in court—" she began.

He thought that her delirium was about to begin afresh, and rested a hand on her forehead. She continued, however, to talk, or rather to whisper, not able to speak aloud:

"They will believe you—a doctor. He is innocent. He has only repaid what I did to him. They must not punish him too severely!"

Again Alfred tried to quiet her. But she continued, hurriedly, as if realizing how limited was her time.

What she had begun to do but never finished was described; that which her desire had craved but her will refused, and which she always remembered but had never dared definitely to recall—that hour, perhaps it had been a swift second, when she had murdered her child in her heart. All this she lived again, vividly, as if she were just living through it at that moment. From her lips Alfred was able to read a few words, though without completely understanding their purport. But he interpreted them as an attempt to absolve her son of all guilt. Whether this secret palliation would stand before a heavenly or an earthly tribunal, it did exist for this dying woman—and dying she would be, whether she lived ten years longer or died that very instant. Alfred realized that the confession of her guilt did not oppress her in this hour, but rather liberated her, since it made her end less meaningless.

He did not even attempt to offer her words of encouragement or of solace. They would not have reached her consciousness in this hour. He sensed that she had at last found her son, so long lost to her, at the moment when he had become the instrument of an eternal justice.

Her plea finished, she fell back exhausted. Alfred felt her consciousness gradually receding farther and farther into the darkness until she no longer recognized him.

During the next few hours her condition grew worse. This was as the physicians had expected. Suddenly, unexpectedly she died, before an operation could be performed.

Alfred talked to the attorney who had been appointed to defend Franz. The obliging counsellor tried to introduce Theresa's confession at the trial as a mitigating circumstance. It found little favour with the court. Half mockingly, the district attorney pointed out that the defendant had probably not retained any memory of this first hour of his life, and spoke disparagingly of certain metaphysical tendencies in these days to veil, with the best of intentions, obvious proofs of guilt and thus circumvent justice. The motion to consult an expert was overruled, if for no other reason than that it was impossible to decide whether to call a physician, a priest, or a philosopher for this responsible task.

The court only permitted the defendant's illigitimate

birth and his consequent lack of a proper education to be advanced in his behalf. So Franz was sentenced to twelve years of solitary confinement in prison, with bread and water to be served him on the anniversary of the day the crime had been committed.

Theresa Fabiani, of course, was buried long before the trial began. Beside a cheap, withered evergreen wreath, bearing the inscription, "To my unfortunate sister," there lay a cluster of spring flowers. The beautiful flowers had arrived from Holland—too late.